T0161938

THE SCHOLARSHIP

By the Author

Agnes

The Common Thread

Bouncing

Deadly Medicine

Hooked

The Scholarship

Visit us at www.boldstrokesbooks.com

THE SCHOLARSHIP

by
Jaime Maddox

2017

THE SCHOLARSHIP
© 2017 By Jaime Maddox. All Rights Reserved.

ISBN 13: 978-1-63555-075-7

This Trade Paperback Original Is Published By
Bold Strokes Books, Inc.
P.O. Box 249
Valley Falls, NY 12185

First Edition: August 2017

This is a work of fiction. Names, characters, places, and incidents are the product of the author's imagination or are used fictitiously. Any resemblance to actual persons, living or dead, business establishments, events, or locales is entirely coincidental.

This book, or parts thereof, may not be reproduced in any form without permission.

Credits
Editor: Shelley Thrasher
Production Design: Stacia Seaman
Cover Design by Tammy Seidick

Acknowledgments

The main character in this book is a fund-raiser, and I am fortunate to be related to the Fund-raiser of the Year. Thank you to my sister Carol for sharing her exploits in development with me. It is a more authentic book because of her.

One of the biggest challenges for me in writing is naming my characters. Thanks to my niece, Ella, and my nephew, Townes, for lending me their names.

The great people at Bold Strokes Books work tirelessly to put out such good works every month. Thanks to Rad, Sandy, Ruth, Cindy, and Stacia for all your hard work. I've never worked with anyone except Shelley Thrasher, so I'm not kidding when I say she's the best editor I've ever had. Thanks to her, this book is much better than it would have been without her.

Carolyn, Jamison, and Max are the loves and lights of my life, and I appreciate the time with me they sacrificed while I was working on this manuscript. It's a crazy life sometimes, but you guys make it wonderful.

To my son, Max,
for teaching me the meaning of unconditional love.

May 1993
Darkness

It was dark. Though the earlier rain was no longer falling, the clouds that had given birth to a ferocious downfall now cloaked the heavens in darkness. Even the moon, which would only have given off a small crescent of light, was nowhere to be seen in the night sky.

The darkness matched his mood; the intermittent swipe of the wipers across his windshield mocked his efforts at blotting the flow of tears that seeped from his eyes. What had happened to his life? Why had it fallen apart this way? He was a good kid. Did what he was supposed to, fulfilled his obligations, and avoided trouble. Was it the Bible or the fabled American dream that told him his goodness would be rewarded? If it was the Bible, did he have to wait until the next life for happiness to find him? He couldn't wait that long. He wouldn't. He wanted it—he deserved it now.

She was not going to take it from him. Thinking of her, of the decision she'd so callously made, he felt his face flush as the blood in his veins boiled with anger. He pushed his foot down harder on the gas pedal, then immediately braked as he entered a bend in the country road. It wouldn't do to die now, he told himself as he slowed both the car and his breathing, gaining control of both by the time he reached his destination.

The house was surprisingly well lit, considering her parents were out for the evening. He'd confirmed that fact before coming over. He didn't want any witnesses to his shame. He parked beside the garage, on an extension of the driveway that came in handy when the Gates family threw one of their famous lake-house parties. On those occasions, a dozen cars filled the drive, and dozens more lined the road in front of the house. On this Friday, a week before Memorial Day weekend, his was the only car around.

A week from now, everyone who summered at the lake would be there, rain or shine, to open their houses for the season. Cars would come and go in all directions, and every house would be lit from top to bottom as people aired out the winter and welcomed the spring. Every surface would be scrubbed to a shine, and the smell of backyard barbecues would fill the air. Everyone would be here, and they would all know what she'd done to him.

He had to stop her before she told anyone. He still had time, if he acted quickly.

He turned off the car and stepped out into the light drizzle. Following the winding flagstone sidewalk along the front of the house, he ascended three stairs to the front porch. Or was it the back porch? Or maybe the side. The massive house was oddly angled on the lot, optimizing the views from every window, with covered patio-porches accessed via French doors. Only the garage, which faced the road, lacked a lake or forest vista, and even that wasn't bad. The front yard was landscaped with flower beds, now just blooming, and dotted with dwarf trees.

Anxiously, he pushed the doorbell, and in the quiet night, he heard it ring on the other side of the tall, half-glass door. No answer. Thirty seconds later, he rang again, this time tapping his finger several times against the glowing white button. Again he heard it, but no answering call of a human, no footsteps heralding her arrival at the door. Growing angrier with every second she made him wait, he depressed the button one more time, with the same results.

Fuck! He knew she was home; she'd called him to tell him the awful news. Called from her balcony, overlooking the lake, telling him how peaceful she felt with her decision. Peaceful! Even as she was tearing him apart, throwing his world into chaos, she felt *peaceful.*

That was it! The balcony. He'd climbed the trellis beside her balcony on more than one occasion, and if she was going to hide in the house to avoid him, he'd just have to climb it again. If she wouldn't come to him, he'd go to her. She couldn't hide.

The walkway circled the house, and he followed it to the side, past his car and into complete darkness. He saw no welcoming lights in this part of the house, and the irony of that absence didn't escape him. He certainly wasn't welcome here anymore. He could barely make out the wooden structure, and if the trellis had been painted any color other than white, he wouldn't have been able to see well enough to make the climb. In a minute, though, he swung his leg over the top and stepped onto Steph's balcony.

Obviously, Steph was way ahead of schedule with her summer decorating. Already her balcony was furnished with side-by-side chaise lounges and benches, and a table with four chairs. He shook his head, pushing away the memories of Steph and him enjoying this very space the summer before. They were good times, but they were over.

His eyes had adjusted to the night, but here, light poured out from Steph's bedroom and filled the void. He took a step, still hidden in the darkness, and watched her.

Standing before a full-length mirror, Steph brushed her long brown hair and then shook her head, allowing it to fall where it wanted. She turned left, and then right, studying her reflection, tilting her head up, then down. He shook his head, filled with sadness. Was this what girls did? Break a guy's heart and then worry about how they looked in the mirror?

Steph sat on a big, cushioned bench before a smaller mirror, leaned in, and added a touch of color to her winter-white cheeks. Again, she turned each way to survey the results. Beautiful, he said softly. You look beautiful, Steph. Don't you know that?

Her eyes were next, and suddenly he became concerned. What was she doing? It was after eight o'clock. What was she getting ready for? Was she going out? Or was someone coming over? The thought infuriated him as he watched her dab gloss onto her bottom lip, then rub it across the top one. After smiling at the effect, she turned off the vanity light and stood.

Surveying the room as she'd just studied her reflection, she went to the bed and rearranged the pillows. Next, she repositioned the photos on her dresser and then angled the ottoman before a large chair in the corner. She switched on the lamp behind it and then turned it off.

She was preparing the room for someone! That fucker really did have a date. He couldn't take it anymore. Summoning his courage, he stepped into the light and knocked softly on the sliding-glass door's frame.

A smile spread across her face as she turned toward the door, but a frown quickly replaced it. She knew it was him, he realized, and she wasn't at all happy to see him.

Not surprising, considering the conversation they'd had a few hours earlier. It didn't matter, though. He had to talk to her. He had to make it right, before she humiliated him before the entire world. Before she ruined his life.

Her stride was not the normal, confident one he was accustomed to. She walked slowly, as if measuring each step, gaining time—to gather her courage or her thoughts. It was harder to face someone than deliver bad news over the phone, and it seemed she was just coming to grips with that fact now. She was nervous. Good. Maybe she'd reconsider her ridiculous decision.

She pulled the door back and stepped onto the balcony, rubbing her arms as she did so, reminding him that it was a little cool out. He hadn't noticed. Emotion had driven him and apparently was warming him, too.

"Hi," she said. After stepping through the threshold, she closed the door behind her. "What's up?"

So she'd rather talk to him outside than invite him in. How quickly her manners had eroded. Didn't she say they'd always be friends? Wasn't that what she'd told him as she'd cast him aside hours earlier? Now she'd withstand the cold to avoid inviting him into her room. He took a breath and blew it out, slowly. He had to stay calm, find his reasonable voice.

He held his hand out to her. "I had to talk to you in person. Face-to-face. Talk some sense into you. Why are you doing this to me, Steph?" He realized he sounded pathetic, and it angered him. He'd wanted to sound authoritative. He wanted to tell her to change her mind, not ask her to.

Sighing, she reached across the distance, touched his shoulder. "I'm sorry. Things changed. *I* changed."

"But why?"

She looked out over the lake, barely visible in the darkness, but there, its blackness was another mirror for his despair. Her source of peace. He followed her gaze and felt nothing but angst.

"I wish I could explain it," she said softly as she looked at him with pity. Then she turned back to her beloved lake, and her voice grew stronger. Resolute. "Maybe one day. I just can't talk about it right now." She seemed convinced, and he knew her decision was final.

"You're ruining my life!" He raised his voice, and he hated that. She was growing calmer while he was falling apart.

"I'm not ruining your life! This is such a small thing. In the whole course of our life histories, it won't even really matter."

"Maybe not to you, but to me, it's huge! Don't you have a heart?" What had become of him? Now he was begging, like a bum on the street hoping for a little loose change.

She sniffed back the products of the cool night air. "Of course I have a heart. And I'm following it. I have to do what's best for me."

"And it's just fuck me, then, huh?"

The tone of the conversation had shifted, grown angry, and Steph seemed to sense that. She stepped back, signaling an end to their conversation. "I've made my decision. I'm sorry, but it's done."

Turning, she reached for the door handle.

"Bitch!"

He made no conscious decision, just reacted. Driven by his rage, his frustration, his humiliation, he reached for the statue beside the door. It was perhaps eighteen inches high, carved in white faux marble, and it gleamed in the sliver of bedroom light as he swung it toward her.

The sound as it hit her skull was a sickening thud, and he immediately wished he could take the blow back. She fell into the glass, and he reached for her, catching her before she could fall. "Steph," he called softly as she collapsed against him. "Steph, I'm so sorry. I didn't mean it."

Easing her onto her back, he couldn't help noticing her weight. She was tiny—only five feet tall and a hundred pounds, but she suddenly felt much heavier. As he lowered her to the stone balcony, her head dropped back, her mouth fell open.

So did her eyes. In that cruel light that sought him in the darkness, he saw her eyes, blue and lifeless.

"No! No!" he said, shaking her as tears fell from his face. "Steph, no! Don't die." His pleas were unanswered, and he held her, sobbing. After a minute, he composed himself, then collapsed to the balcony floor. Leaning back, feeling the weight of her on top of him, he began to sob again. He'd just killed one of the most important people in his world. He'd just killed himself, really, for what would become of him now? His life had just gone from bad to incredibly worse.

More tears came, and he again blotted them with his sleeve. And then he took some breaths as his mind raced, realizing he had more wiping to do. This was not the end for him. His life wouldn't end because hers did. Jerking his sweatshirt over his head, he picked up the statue. It was now covered in blood, but he'd only touched the top, where he'd gripped it when he picked it up. He rubbed it with his shirt, from top to bottom, removing the blood and, hopefully, his fingerprints.

What else had he touched? Probably just the top of the balcony and the trellis. How to know which pieces of wood he'd grasped during his climb? Glancing down, he knew he couldn't scrub that clean.

What to do?

Using his shirt, he deliberately wiped every surface of the balcony and then stepped around the lifeless body on the floor. He opened the door and walked through her room, to the jewelry box on the dresser. Again, leaving no prints, he opened it and scooped out a handful of gold. After glancing at her once more, he walked into the hallway and found a similar box on the dresser in her mother's bedroom. He raided that one as well, then quickly descended the grand staircase and raced out the front door, without bothering to close it behind him.

Seconds later he pulled out of the driveway, grateful for the darkness that concealed him.

You were great! he told himself. Way to think on your feet! The police will suspect a burglar, and there's no evidence to implicate you. Steph had only told him her decision a few hours earlier, and he'd asked her if she'd told anyone. She hadn't. At least she'd denied telling anyone else. With no one to give the police reason to suspect him, they'd never think it was him. He was a good kid. An honor student. Without having a motive, they wouldn't look twice in his direction.

Now all he needed was an alibi.

He didn't know where to go, what to do next. The rain that had helped cover his crime had stopped, and it made him nervous. It was a Friday night in May, people were out and about, and the clearing skies meant someone might notice him. He drove faster, distancing himself from Lake Winola and the dead body on the balcony. The farther away he got from the Gateses' house, the less likely he could be tied to the murder. He'd wiped away the evidence; there was nothing to incriminate him.

Moonlight filtered through the window as he stopped at a traffic light in Clarks Summit, and it drew his attention to the passenger seat of his car.

Fuck! He'd been so hasty in fleeing the lake he'd forgotten about the bloody sweatshirt he'd been wearing. Lying beside him on the seat, it not only held Steph's blood, but all of her jewelry as well. What was he going to do with it?

The light turned, and his panic pushed bile up in his throat, until he could taste it. He barely had time to pull to the curb before the vomit rushed from his mouth, covering the street beside his car. He pulled away just as quickly, hoping no one had noticed. If someone thought he was drunk, they might call the police. A traffic stop now would be a disaster.

Mindful of his speed, he drove slowly, and though he wasn't sure where he was going, he wasn't surprised to see where he was when he finally turned off his car. He exited and looked around, happy to see Nay Aug Park so quiet on a Friday night. Grabbing the evidence from his floor, he walked quickly toward the park. He'd spent enough mornings there to know the park maintenance staff would be there first thing to empty the trash. The garment's red color hardly showed the blood, and hopefully, no one would pay any attention to it if they happened to see it in the garbage. If they did notice the stains, hopefully no one would suspect it came from the body of a young woman felled twenty miles away.

He walked a hundred yards into the park and removed the gold from the shirt, placing it in his pocket. The maintenance guys might not care about an old sweatshirt, but gold in the trash would definitely draw attention. Looking around for witnesses and finding none, he rolled the shirt into a ball and shoved it deep into the garbage can, then turned and walked back to his car.

Just as he reached the driver's door, the sound of a voice startled him.

He looked up, surprised to see Cassidy Ryan a few feet away. What the fuck was she doing out at this hour? Cass was the younger sister of one of his classmates, but because she had Down syndrome and often hung out with her sister, he'd gotten to know her pretty well. She lived with her family in the house directly across Arthur Avenue from his car.

"Hey, Cass. What are you doing out so late?" He looked around, wondering who else was out and about, wishing he had a statue he could use to hit her.

"I saw your car from my window. I thought you were coming to visit Reese. She's sleeping."

He edged around the car, back toward the park, and as he hoped, she followed. "Oh. Then I won't come in."

"You can still come and talk to me."

Cass's sister Reese had warned him that Cass had a crush on him. He'd always liked Cass and went out of his way to engage her. It was all very innocent, but he could understand that Cass might take his kindness the wrong way.

"I always like to talk to you. Do you want to sit in my car with me?" If he could get her into the car, he could buy a little time. Formulate a plan.

"My mom says I can't go in a car with strange men."

"Do you think I'm strange?"

She giggled. "I guess not."

The sound of her laughter pierced his heart. What the fuck was he thinking? He'd just murdered one innocent girl; he couldn't kill another one. Especially not one as pure and sweet as Cass. Unlike Steph, she'd never hurt him.

He asked her a question, kept her talking while he tried to come up with a plan. An idea occurred to him. "So, what's up with Reese?" he asked.

"She's sleeping. She has a headache."

"I was going to ask her if I could borrow some money. For gas."

Cass shook her hand excitedly, a habit he adored. He hoped she'd put it in her pocket and bring out some money. Cass never went anywhere without a few dollars.

He watched as she reached in and pulled out a roll of money and offered it to him. "I can lend you some."

"Can it be our secret, Cass? I don't want anyone to know. It's sort of embarrassing."

She shook her head. "I won't tell anyone."

"Not even Reese?" he asked.

Her expression was serious. "No."

"Okay. Do you think you could just pretend I never came over tonight? Because if you tell anyone I came over, you'll have to tell them *why* I came over, and then they'll know that I had to borrow money from a girl."

"It's okay to borrow money from a girl. Girls have lots of money."

"It's not okay if you're a boy. Boys are supposed to pay for girls, not borrow money from them."

"You can have all my money. Here," she said, thrusting her hand toward him again.

He took the cash and counted it. Eight dollars.

"I'm just going to take two. For gas. I'll pay you back soon, okay?"

"When?"

He almost laughed at the change in her attitude but held his tongue. "At graduation."

"Okay, that's good."

"You won't tell anyone I was here, will you?"

She shook her head.

"Promise?"

"I promise."

"Thanks, Cass. You're the best." He pulled her into a hug, and this time, instead of laughing, he wanted to cry.

Pulling away, he kissed her cheek. "I'll see you at graduation," he said.

He watched as she crossed the street, but before she could climb the stairs, he was behind the wheel of his car. A second later, he turned onto the cross street and away from the park and the bloody sweatshirt in the trash can. He hoped he could trust Cass to keep their secret. His life depended on it.

CHAPTER 1: THE INTERVIEW

Present Day

"What makes you think you'd like living in the Poconos, Elizabeth? It's not quite what you're used to."

Ella looked over Mary Ann Bingham's shoulder to the impressive vista of the mountains behind her. The presidency of a large university had its perks, she thought, and a corner office with a view was one of them.

Swallowing her nerves, she thought of an appropriate response. This job would be a promotion for her. It would mean more money, more responsibilities, more rewards. It would mean she'd made it, climbed and battled her way to the top of her field. Really, though, the job in the Poconos was more than that to her. It was a homecoming of sorts.

Turning her attention to the president and her question, she realized the view out her window really was the answer.

Her office windows in a similar university in the suburbs of Philadelphia also showed her a shaded courtyard, filled with ancient trees and a circus of squirrels, but beyond that, the differences were more evident than the similarities. There, nature was an illusion, growing dimmer with each year that developers built another shopping mall or housing development. The cost of the homes they built in Philadelphia was two or three times the cost of comparable dwellings here. She knew; she'd done her homework before applying for the job as vice president of development at Pocono Mountains University.

It would be more difficult to find great Thai food in the Poconos, she was sure, and there were probably not as many single lesbians as in the Delaware Valley. They certainly didn't have the Phillies, and not even their AAA minor-league team, either, since traitorous parties had moved them to Allentown. But the Poconos had other benefits, and over the past few years, Ella had realized the other things mattered most to her.

Meeting Mary Ann's piercing gaze, she nodded. It wasn't what she was used to. Ella was accustomed to the great food, and culture, and sports, and occasionally women, too. Yet in spite of all that, she still found herself in this interview, hoping to find a way of soothing the discontent she couldn't quite explain. That was why she'd responded to the ad she'd read in one of her professional journals. It was why she'd awakened at four o'clock and driven two hours to the mountains. She needed a change, and she couldn't help feeling the corners of her malaise cracking as she thought of her childhood spent not so far from the PMU campus. This was the next leg of her journey, she was sure of it.

"Please, call me Ella," she said as she adjusted in her seat, facing the president head-on. "You're right. It would be a different experience for me, but not one I'm unfamiliar with. I spent the first twelve summers of my life at Lake Winola. Do you know where that is?"

The stern façade softened, and a smile appeared in Mary Ann's eyes as she nodded briefly. "I certainly do. I grew up not far from the lake. You say you lived there as a child?"

"My dad grew up *on* the lake and graduated from Pocono Mountains Prep before going off to explore the world. He sent my sister and me here every summer so we could spend time with our grandparents and have some fun. We swam and rode bikes and climbed trees, caught fireflies and toasted marshmallows at night. My parents would drop us off in June, and we wouldn't hear from them until Labor Day. I think those were the best times of my life."

"How come you stopped coming?"

"My grandparents died. They went within months of each other, and my dad's family sold the lake house. After that we went to camp in the summer. It was definitely not as much fun as here."

"I'm sorry about your grandparents."

Ella acknowledged the condolence with a nod. "They lived a great life, and I have fond memories."

"So, you're saying you wouldn't mind trading all the excitement of the big city for a chance to revisit your perfect childhood?"

Mary Ann's smile reached all the way to her mouth this time, and Ella replied with one of her own. "Not at all."

Sitting taller in her chair, Mary Ann glanced down at the notepad on her desk. "As you probably know, we conducted a national search for candidates for this position. The former VP had health issues and had to leave rather suddenly, but the office is functioning without him. The other development officers are doing some of his promotional work. We've already mailed out Save the Date postcards for next year's scholarship luncheon, for example. We haven't been out on the road, though, staying in touch with our alums and donors. We need to get back to that."

"I can understand why."

"I don't want to hire someone who looks good on paper but doesn't really have an idea what this place is about. We're a good school, and we draw students from all over the country, but we focus on educating local students. That's our mission. And I don't care if you've been a VP at Harvard. Cambridge is not the same as the Pocono Mountains, our alumni are not the same, and our students are not the same. If you spent your childhood here, I believe you understand that difference."

Ella was encouraged by Mary Ann's soliloquy yet felt her nerves firing, felt every beat of her heart, and she fought the urge to bite her lip. Instead, she adjusted her posture once again. While she contemplated an appropriate reply, Mary Ann spoke again.

"If you'd like the position, it's yours."

"Wow," she said, and began to laugh. "I didn't expect that."

"Why? You're qualified, and you know the place. What more could I want?"

"I guess I'm just shocked."

"Get over it," she said as she pushed a red-and-white folder bearing the PMU logo across her desk. "Obviously, I need to hire someone soon. I'd like it to be you. This is the entire package. Review it and get back to me with any rebuttals in the next forty-eight hours."

After placing the folder in her bag, Ella stood and thanked Mary Ann for the opportunity.

"Two days, okay? If I don't hear from you, I'll assume you don't want the position."

"I'll talk to you then," Ella said as she followed Mary Ann through her office and toward the elevator.

After the door closed behind her, Ella pumped her fist before pressing the button for the lobby. She had the job, if she wanted it. If? There was no if. She wanted it. She fought the desire to do a little dance, just in case security cameras were watching. Five floors down, she exited into a glass and tile foyer boasting three stories of student art. Beyond, the July sun beckoned her, and she found a bench in the courtyard and sat, pondering her next move.

Answering the first question was easy. She really wanted this job. The next question was a little more difficult to answer. Could she handle it? Her qualifications spoke for themselves, obviously loudly enough for Mary Ann Bingham to hear. Starting with her alma mater, Villanova, she'd been in development since earning her bachelor's degree. Working at 'Nova had allowed her to pursue her master's, and she'd used that accomplishment to propel her to the next level. Twenty years and three schools later, was she ready to take the next big step? She had no VP experience, and she'd seen enough incompetent people hold the position to know that her qualifications didn't mean she'd do a good job. She thought she would, though. She loved what she did, and as a single lesbian, she really was married to her work.

The rest of her family had no hold over her, either. Her parents were retired in Florida, and her sister was married with children in Chicago. Although they gathered somewhere for their annual Christmas celebration, and again every summer for a vacation, the ties that bound her were not in Philly. When she thought about it, she realized she was all by herself.

Yes, she had plenty of friends, but not much time to enjoy them. Hers really was a demanding field, with many evenings spent wooing donors and at university functions. It had occurred to her on more than one occasion that she could simply rent a hotel room and give up her town house, because she spent so many nights on the road. Good universities spawned successful alums, who spread like seeds in the wind. One week she was in San Diego, the next in Boston, the next in St. Louis. Wherever the money was, she followed, asking the successful businessmen and accountants and physicians to remember the school that gave them the opportunity to fulfill their potential, to live their dreams. Her donors had given everything from $5,000 scholarships to $5,000,000 buildings. In return, she gave her time, and that didn't leave much opportunity for socializing.

Would her friends even know if she moved? Chuckling, she realized they might not. That didn't bother her, though. She was doing exactly what she wanted to. Somehow, though, it had lost some of its charm. It wasn't as exciting to board a plane as it had once been. It wasn't as thrilling to hook a big fish. She'd never tire of slipping on a little black dress and a pair of heels, though. And maybe when she took them off, pulling on a pair of hiking shoes and going for a walk in the woods might feel right. Or swinging a golf club in her backyard. Or cooking a steak on her grill. Rather than coming home to her town house in Philly, returning to a place she actually wanted to be might be just what she needed.

Thinking of the possibilities filled her with an excitement she hadn't felt in ages. Yes, she really did want this job.

Ella glanced around the deserted patch of green and smiled. The shouts and laughter of students would soon shatter the quiet of this early July morning. They'd read in the shade of the trees, toss Frisbees in the open spaces, gather on stairs to discuss classes and gossip. Imagining such scenes nearly brought them to life, and she could feel herself absorbing the energy of the students' collective youth. It would be a wonderful place to work.

During the first interview at PMU, a month earlier, Mary Ann Bingham had given her the campus tour, and it included the spacious corner office the VP would claim. That, too, was appealing. Her current office was small, and too close for comfort to the men's restroom across the hall. This one afforded more privacy and a small anteroom for intimate meetings with donors. Although she would travel a great deal for the university, when she was home, she'd have lovely surroundings to inspire her.

The salary and benefits package had been outlined before the interview, to make sure it met her expectations before anyone's time was wasted. It had. PMU would give her a raise, more PTO, and a car. Since her current model—a BMW convertible—wouldn't do well in the snow, that was a definite plus.

Her personal research into PMU had been promising, as well. The school was small, and private, and didn't offer a ton of majors, but instead it focused doing a few things rather well. Their alums included a host of doctors, Wall Street wizards, computer analysts, and even a United States senator.

As she did the mental math, Ella found the plusses far outweighed the minuses. Standing, she glanced around one last time before heading to her car. It was time to check out the local housing market.

CHAPTER 2: THE DELICATE BALANCE

Holding a syringe in one hand and a bottle of lidocaine in the other, Reese Ryan turned at the sound of her name.

"Medic on the line wants to talk to you," the nurse said.

Reese followed her from the supply room and a few feet to the phone and allowed her to hold it against her ear as she coaxed the clear, colorless liquid from the vial. "Dr. Ryan," she said.

"Hey, Doc, it's Engle here. I thought you'd want to know I'm bringing Mrs. Nathan in. Shortness of breath."

At the sound of Millie Nathan's name—for it could only be Millie Nathan who warranted such a warning—Reese stood a little taller. "CHF?" she asked.

"I think so. I gave her a squirt of Lasix, have her on 100 percent oxygen by face mask, and we'll be there in five."

"How's her pressure?"

"That's the funny thing. It's a little low. And her heart rate's fast, too."

"Has she had any chest pain?"

"No."

"Hmm," Reese said, quickly running through the possibilities in her mind. If Millie Nathan's heart was failing, it was in real trouble, because her vital signs weren't so good. But she had a bad heart, and Reese supposed it was only a matter of time with her. "See you in five."

Pulling away, she looked at the nurse holding the phone in her hand. "The senator's mom is coming in. Put her in the penthouse suite and page me immediately. I'd like to get these stitches in before she arrives. Otherwise, this guy may be waiting another hour."

"You bet," the nurse said, heading toward the resuscitation room.

Reese headed quickly in the other direction, toward the trauma bays, where an elderly patient awaited her. "Mr. Park, your CT scans are all normal. I'm going to put two stitches in your forehead, and then your daughter will pick you up."

"What about my car?" he asked for the fifth time.

Reese had seen the pictures, and Mr. Park was lucky to be alive. His car was barely recognizable. When she'd called his daughter, Reese had initiated a discussion about his ability to safely operate a vehicle at the age of eighty-five, and his daughter had seemed relieved to hear Reese's opinion.

"I think you should rest for a few days, Mr. Park. No driving. And then you need to have a complete physical by your doctor, to make sure you can still safely drive."

"What are you talking about?" he demanded, the scowl on his face telling her exactly how he felt about any such discussion with his doctor.

As Reese prepped his skin and injected the anesthesia, she tuned out Mr. Park's tirade. Every eighty-five-year-old thought they were the safest driver on the road, yet the statistics didn't lie. People his age were involved in more collisions than any other group except teenagers, and much more likely to die from the injuries. It wasn't something he wanted to hear, she knew that. But he needed to, and if she said it, and his daughter repeated it, and his family doctor reinforced it, perhaps they'd collectively help keep Mr. Park alive a while longer.

The skin came together beautifully, and Reese pulled the drape back from over his face to find his flecked-blue eyes squinting at her. "You're not taking my car, Doctor."

Reese bent and placed a playful kiss on his nose. "I have my own car, Mr. Park. And it doesn't have any dents in it."

He wiped away the kiss and brushed her away with his hand, and Reese laughed as she skipped out of the room and headed for the critical-care area. "You can leave as soon as your daughter gets here."

The medics were just pushing a stretcher through the door, and when the crowd cleared she saw the familiar face of Millie Nathan.

Skirting the human traffic, Reese reached the stretcher and grabbed her hand. "What kind of trouble are you up to this time?"

Looking quite comfortable, Millie winked at Reese. "I'm so happy to see you, Christine. You always take such good care of me."

Reese swallowed an unexpected tear. Indeed, she'd been taking care of Millie Nathan since she'd arrived in the ER in Scranton more than a decade earlier, but their relationship went back much further. Four decades. She'd known Mrs. Nathan her entire life.

"Do you realize you're dating yourself by calling me Christine? Ever since Cass could talk, she's called me Reese. No one calls me Christine anymore. Even my mom gave up."

"It's more feminine, so if you don't mind, I'm going against the tide."

Reese didn't comment about her obvious lack of femininity, and she knew Mrs. Nathan wasn't judging her. It was nothing personal, but professionally, she was pleased by their banter. Mrs. Nathan's brain was working just fine, a sure sign that her oxygen level was adequate. "You don't seem short of breath. Is the oxygen helping?" Reese asked, and when Millie nodded, she continued. "Tell me what's going on."

"I don't know. I don't feel right. I'm terribly tired, and weak. And then this morning, I felt like I couldn't catch my breath."

"No chest pain? Pain anywhere?" Reese asked as she glanced at the heart monitor.

"No."

"Here's the EKG," the nurse said as she handed it to Reese. It showed damage, evidence of enlargement Reese knew toxic doses of chemotherapy had caused, but she saw nothing new on the EKG. Nothing to suggest a recent heart attack as the cause of her new symptoms.

"Looks good." She returned the EKG to the nurse and began her exam. All the typical signs of heart failure were missing. She found no distention of the neck veins, no swelling of the legs, no congestion of the liver. And for someone with a bad heart, Millie's oxygen level was pretty damn good. Her heart rate, though, was way too fast and her blood pressure a bit low.

Reese opened the room's laptop computer and pulled up Millie's chart. "Let me refresh my memory, here. Any changes to your medications?" Reese read the list, and Millie indicated that it was correct. "Allergic to penicillin?" she asked.

"Yes, since my bone-marrow transplant." That was a quirky phenomenon, one of the wonders of the body that fascinated Reese. When bone marrow was transplanted, the recipient often developed the donor's allergies, indicating that the allergic response was generated in the bone marrow. She'd first seen it as a student, when one of her patients celebrated her birthday, in the ICU, with a strawberry cake.

She'd immediately developed hives. After investigating, she learned later that the donor was known to have an allergy to strawberries.

Reese gave the nurse some orders and then pulled a nasal canula from the wall basket, replacing the mask covering Millie's face.

"Oh, thank you. That thing isn't very comfortable."

"Well, this is the penthouse suite, Mrs. Nathan. We aim for comfort."

Millie squinted at her. "Are you being sarcastic? I can still call your mother and tattle on you, you know."

"We can't have that."

"How is your mother? And your dad? And Cass?"

Reese smiled. Her parents had just reached retirement age and hadn't wasted a moment enjoying it. Her sister was the happiest person she knew. "They're great. They just got back from whale-watching and hiking glaciers in Alaska. I kept Cass while they were gone."

"Alaska?"

"Yeah," Reese said.

Reese saw Millie's eyes cloud over for a moment, and she couldn't help but feel badly for her. Mr. Nathan was barely forty when he'd fallen over, the victim of clogged coronaries and good health. If he'd ever been to a doctor, his high cholesterol might have been detected in time to save him. He'd never been sick, though, not until the day he died. She'd spent the next years focusing on her own health and her children, and lately her grandchildren, but she'd never remarried. Even though she projected a happy, upbeat image, Reese suspected Millie was lonely.

"How's Josh?" she asked, knowing the topic of her son would cheer her. The light returned to her eyes.

"He's good. Great. He's optimistic about getting the gun-control bill passed. All the grassroots efforts are starting to pay off, and perhaps we'll see an end to all these mass shootings with automatic weapons."

Reese didn't argue with Millie. She'd spent countless hours debating guns and shootings with Millie's son, Senator Josh Nathan, and she knew they'd never completely agree. Josh thought the solution to the problem was completely eliminating guns from society. Reese thought the key was completely eliminating mental illness from society. Since the odds of curing mental illness were slim, she wasn't hopeful. And since no one in America was giving up their guns without a fight, she feared the consequences of Josh's proposal. If it passed, it was likely to spawn the next civil war.

"I'm happy to hear that. He's a good senator, Mrs. Nathan. Now, I'm going to check on some other patients, and I'll see you when the labs and chest X-ray are done." Reese squeezed her hand and went back to work. Thirty minutes had passed when the nurse handed her a white sheet of computer paper showing the results of Millie's blood work.

"Well, that explains it," she said to herself as she headed back to the penthouse suite. En route, she pulled up Millie's chest X-ray and examined it. The heart was markedly enlarged, but the lung fields were clear, giving absolutely no clues to explain her symptoms. That was okay, though. The answer was in Reese's hand.

"Mrs. Nathan, I have to get to know you a little better," Reese said as she walked into the room.

"What do you mean?"

"Your blood count's low. That's why you're tired and weak, and also short of breath. I need to do a rectal to see if you're losing blood."

"I haven't noticed any."

"Most people don't."

"Is it absolutely necessary?" she asked, and at that moment she sounded very much like the mother of one of the most important men in Washington.

"Absolutely," Reese answered, not in the least bit intimidated.

After easing Millie onto her side, Reese procured her sample and smeared it onto a cardboard tester. After adding a few drops of developer, she watched the paper turn blue. Bingo.

"There's blood in your stool," she said simply.

"But why?"

"I'm not sure. I'll leave that to the specialists to figure out. In the meantime, I'm going to order a transfusion for you. We have to give you the blood slowly, so it doesn't overwhelm your heart."

"That's what happened when I had my bone-marrow transplant," she said.

"What happened?"

"The bone-marrow transplant made me short of breath. The doctors said I had too much fluid in my lungs. Didn't you read that in my chart?"

Reese shook her head. Millie's medical chart was about two feet high, not counting the past few years, which had been recorded electronically.

"Yes. I was very sick. Josh saved me, though. He gave me his bone marrow."

Reese nodded. "That, I remember." Josh hadn't been around during one of the darkest times of Reese's life because he'd been in Philly with his mom. They'd talked every day, though, and cried about the loss of one of their classmates, a dear friend to them both.

"When can I go home?"

Now Reese laughed. It was one of the most common questions her patients asked, and the sickest of them most commonly asked it. "I'll call your doctor, and should I let Josh know?"

"I don't want to worry him. He's very busy this week."

"Nothing's more important than you," she said, simply because she knew it was true.

Reese ordered the blood and then pulled her cell phone from the pack she wore around her waist. It took only a second for her to find Josh's number; he was in her favorites. Holding the phone with her shoulder, she began typing, listening for the rich timbre of her old friend's voice. She was quickly rewarded.

"Hello, Doctor," he said.

"Hello, Senator," she replied with a smirk. She'd known Josh Nathan since kindergarten, and it was often hard to reconcile her image of him as a toothless playmate with the suit-clad political leader he'd become.

"Are you calling to beg for a spot in my foursome for the PMU golf tournament? If so, you're too late. I've found some ringers, and this year, you're going down."

Reese laughed. "Maybe I should just withdraw. Save my money."

"No. Don't do that. I relish the thought of beating you, and it would break my heart if it's by forfeit. Besides, it's a good cause. Where would either of us be without PMU?"

"Josh, you could charm the habit off a nun. I suspect you'd have done fine if you got your degree online."

"Aw, shucks. You're so sweet, Reese. I should have married you when I had the chance."

Reese shook her head and chuckled. "You never had a chance, Josh."

"What?" he demanded with mock surprise in his voice. "What about our dance?"

"That was sixth grade!"

"Yeah, but it was special."

"The entire time I was dancing with you, I was making eyes at Emily Baker."

"Emily? I can see that. She was cute. So if you don't want to seduce me, and you don't want to golf with me, what's up?"

Reese didn't even laugh as she suddenly remembered the purpose of her call. This message wasn't an easy one to deliver, and Josh was clearly not prepared for it. He and his mother were as close as could be. He had always been the doting son, since his mother had been diagnosed with breast cancer during their senior year at Pocono Mountains Prep. Josh's father had just died when his mother was diagnosed, and he'd given up a scholarship to Harvard, pushing aside his dreams so he could stay home and take care of her. He'd nursed her through her illness and only left four years later, when she was well and law school beckoned. He came back to the mountains to start his law practice, but politics took him away again. Somewhere in the suburbs of Washington he'd met his wife, and now he spent much less time at home. Even though he'd asked, his mother would never move, not even to be close to her son.

"It's your mom. She's really sick, Josh."

Reese heard him suck in a breath. "How bad? Should I charter a helicopter? I can be there in two hours."

"Not that sick. But she's lost blood and needs a transfusion. There's blood in her stool, so that's likely the cause."

"Why would there be blood in her stool? You know me. I was a history major. I know nothing about medicine."

The lab results indicated a chronic loss of blood, probably from the colon. The most concerning cause in someone her age was cancer. Reese wouldn't tell him that, though. It would only worry him. "Could be lots of things. She's on an anti-inflammatory, which could cause it."

"What else?"

"Infection, polyps, diverticulitis. It could be anything."

"Okay, so what now? Can you just give her some blood or something?"

"Yes, I ordered a transfusion. I have to run the blood slowly, though. All that fluid could throw her into heart failure."

Reese was in the electronic medical record checking on Millie's heart as she spoke. Her last echocardiogram showed the heart wasn't pumping very well. Of course it hadn't been for some time. "Her echocardiogram sucks."

"What's that? The EKG?"

"No. That's the one that tells how her heart is pumping. It's not doing very well."

"Fucking chemo," he said.

"The chemo saved her, Josh. She was thirty-eight, with stage-four breast cancer. If they hadn't given her that experimental stuff, she probably would have died back then."

He was quiet, and Reese suspected she knew his thoughts. As grateful as he was for the doctors and treatment that saved her life, he blamed them for taking it away. Millie's regimen had caused cardiomyopathy, and even though she'd lived, she'd been a slave to oxygen tanks and water pills. Josh's first official act as an attorney had been to sue the hospital that had treated her, as well as all her doctors. He'd won, and the millions of dollars had helped Millie buy a condo with a bedroom on the first floor and all the help she needed to care for herself. At forty-six, she'd had all the money she could ever need, but essentially no life.

Even though he'd made his fortune in medical malpractice, and as a doctor, that might have bothered her, it didn't. The cases he took were good ones, legitimate malpractice claims. And Reese understood his anger. Within the span of a year, and at the fragile age of eighteen, he'd lost one of his best friends, his father, and essentially his mother as well.

A message flashed onto Reese's computer screen.

"Her blood's ready, and I have to get back to work. Take your time, Josh. Get here safely. I'll take good care of her."

Chapter 3: A Room with a View

E lla picked up copies of the *Pocono Record* and the *Scranton Times*, along with a deli sandwich from Abe's, and followed the map to Nay Aug Park. It had been many years since her last visit to the park, but she fondly remembered an elephant and hiking around the gorge with her sister and some friends from Lake Winola.

It had been thirty years since she'd been at the lake, but she still thought of those people. If her grandparents hadn't died, she had no doubt those friendships would have lasted forever. Bucky Draper, who could hit a baseball to the moon but couldn't catch one to save his life. Scoop Timlin, whose family had the biggest boat on the lake. It was housed in an appropriately sized boathouse, with a diving board anchored onto the roof and a slide at the end of the dock. They'd had so much fun there. Vicky and Val, who lived across the street on a farm that provided acres and acres to run and play. Stephanie Gates, Ella's dearest childhood friend.

When she was in high school and began to understand her sexuality, Ella began to appreciate the depth of her feelings for Stephanie. She'd had many friends, but none of them like her. Steph was special, the connection they enjoyed one of the greatest Ella had ever known. They talked and giggled as little girls do, ran and climbed, but sometimes just sat quietly together, or lay side by side in the grass, studying cloud formations by day and stars by night. It was all innocent—they were only children, after all—but Steph was the measure by which she judged all friendships since.

If it were a different time, when kids had cell phones and social-media accounts, they might have all still been friends. They'd known each other in the 1970s, though, when calling long distance cost money and meant she didn't even have most of her friends' numbers. When her grandparents died, her connection to all the people at the lake had ended.

Over the years, she'd wondered what became of her old friends, especially Steph. Google searches showed a gynecologist named Scott Timlin, who could have been Scoop. There was a local attorney named Warren Draper, practicing in the family law firm. She was sure they were her old friends. Ella hadn't been able to locate the girls, though. No doubt they'd all married and taken their husbands' names. The only way to find them would be at the lake, where, perhaps, their families still lived. It was a long shot, but she thought it worth a try. If she was going to live here, what better way to start her new life than by meeting up with old friends?

An abundance of parking spaces at the park seemed to be a good omen, and after changing in the restroom, Ella found a picnic table centered in a copse of trees and opened her sandwich and the newspapers. If she was going to work at PMU, she'd have to live here. Renting her town house in Philly would be easy, and practical. Why sell until she knew she'd like it at PMU? Why sell at all? The stock market scared her, and the property was a good investment. Buying a second place didn't seem like a good idea, though, until she knew the area better and was sure she'd stay in the mountains.

That settled, she focused on the rental section of the paper and quickly found several prospects. Her lifestyle made an apartment a better choice than a house, and she circled the numbers with a pen and began making phone calls. Just as she was finishing her first inquiry, she looked up to the comical sight of a small black dog running in her direction, pulling a young woman. Her face displayed the telltale features of Down syndrome, and she was followed by another woman, this one much older and struggling to keep up.

The pooch didn't stop until he was at Ella's feet, and then he stood on his hind legs and put his front paws on the picnic bench. Huge brown eyes caught her gaze, and he turned his head, studying her. Ella allowed him to sniff her fingers before she began scratching behind his ears.

"Bijou!" the younger woman yelled.

"Cass," the older woman called.

"Hi," the younger woman said as she sat across from Ella. "I'm Cass." Her smile seemed to jump off her face.

"Hi, Cass. I'm Ella. And this guy must be Bijou."

Ella smiled as the dog jumped up to the bench seat and wedged his way onto her lap, provoking a laugh from Cass. He settled in as if he belonged there, and instantly Ella realized how much she missed having a dog. When she'd split with her ex, Cindy had been the logical choice to take custody of their dog, Hudson. Her job didn't require travel, and she worked close enough from home that she could stop by the house at lunch to let him out. A year later, he'd been hit by a car and Cindy had to put him down. The thought still brought a tear to her eye, and Ella focused instead on the little ball of black fur in her lap.

"He likes you," Cass said just as the older woman joined them.

"Hi," she said as she reached for the dog and pulled him from Ella's lap. "Sorry about Bijou. He likes to explore."

"No worries. That's what parks are for, right?"

"Do you live here? I've never seen you before," Cass said. "I live over there, in the blue house," she said as she turned and pointed.

Ella was concerned about the personal details Cass so readily revealed, but she didn't have time to ponder her thoughts.

"Cass, what did I tell you about talking to strangers? You can't tell people where you live."

"She's not a stranger, Mom. She's a lady."

Ella couldn't help smiling. "Why, thank you, Cass. And to answer your question, no. I don't live here. But I just got a new job, and I'll be moving here soon." Pointing to the newspapers, she said, "I'm looking for an apartment."

"Would you mind if I sit?" Cass's mom asked.

Ella shook her head. "No, of course not. Maybe you can give me some tips about the local neighborhoods."

"Thank you. I'm Sharon Ryan, by the way."

"Ella Townes."

"What kind of apartment are you looking for? Something modern in a complex or older and more sophisticated? Something in a converted house perhaps?"

Sitting side by side, Ella couldn't help noticing the similarities between the women. Cass was shorter but had the same brown eyes as her mom, and her black hair, while short, was full and wavy. Sharon's was much the same, although silver had replaced much of the black.

"One that doesn't require me to do anything. Other than that, I'm not particular."

"Where are you looking?"

"Well, that's the thing I'm not sure about. I was just hired at Pocono Mountains University, so I can go more toward the mountains or stay here in Scranton. I'd like to be within a half hour of school if I can."

"Congratulations on the new job. My elder daughter graduated from PMU. It's a great school. There isn't much housing out by the campus. Not that I know of, anyway. You might have to check the listings. If you don't mind Scranton, though, you'll find plenty of places for rent."

"Yes. I can see that from the ads. I guess it won't be a problem. I'd like to check the places out today and make a decision if I can. I'm supposed to start in two weeks."

"Well, you have your work cut out for you, then. Where do you live now?"

"Philadelphia."

"I love Philadelphia," Cass said. "The Phillies are the best baseball team, next to the Yankees."

"Well, if you root for the Yankees, you're usually happy at the end of the season."

"She became a Yankees fan when they took over the AAA franchise," Sharon said.

"I work at the stadium. I'm an usher. Do you want to go to the game tonight? I get free tickets."

Ella nodded. "I love baseball, especially the Phillies, and I'd love to go to a game, but not tonight. After I find an apartment, I have to drive back to Philadelphia and start packing."

"I can help you pack. My sister moves all the time, and I always help her pack."

"Cass, she doesn't move all the time. You make her sound like a vagrant."

Cass furrowed her brows. "She's not a vagrant, mom. She's a doctor."

"My other child is an ER doctor, and she's had quite a few moves for school and residency and all that."

"She doesn't sound like a vagrant at all," Ella said.

Sharon laughed.

"PMU has quite a few doctors on the alumni rolls. The pre-med program is well respected, and every year dozens of our students are admitted to medical school," Ella said as she pushed a lock of hair back behind her ear. The blond strand reached just past her shoulders, not quite long enough for the scrunchie to hold it in place. That was another thing she'd have to worry about after the move. Finding someone to color and cut her hair. The salon in Philly wouldn't be convenient from here.

"Oh, yes," Sharon said. "It's a great school. I know half the doctors and lawyers and accountants in town, just from the parties my daughter used to host."

"That sounds like a big bonus."

"They're all good kids. Most of them went to Pocono Mountains Prep, too, so I know them from way back." Sharon shook her head. "Time flies. They have their twenty-fifth high school reunion in a couple of years."

Ella would also have hers soon. "I must be the same age as your daughter. Mine's coming up as well."

"When you get settled in, I'll introduce you to Reese. She's lived here her entire life and knows everyone."

Ella nodded. "That would be very nice. It's great to have local people to give you the scoop." Bijou stretched his front legs as far as he could toward Ella and began batting them at her from across the picnic table. She reached over and took his paws in her hands, and he continued the game.

Sharon stared at her for a moment. "This dog really likes you. You wouldn't be interested in a different sort of living arrangement, would you?"

Ella studied Sharon for a moment, curious. "What sort of arrangement?"

"Bijou's mom, my neighbor, is going to California for a few months. She wants to study film." Sharon shrugged as if she'd never heard of anything so ridiculous. "Of course, my husband and I will look after the house and the dog while we can, but we've started wintering in Florida, so we'll be leaving right after Christmas. Ideally, Pip would love to find someone to live in the house while she's gone. She's even willing to pay a small stipend."

"Is the house furnished?"

Sharon nodded.

That was an interesting concept. No lease, just a fully furnished house for a few months until she got to know the area well enough to decide on something more permanent. And a small stipend as well! Money wasn't an issue, but free rent would be nice, particularly until she found a tenant for her house in Philly.

"I'm not too handy around the house," Ella said. "I can barely change a lightbulb, and I've never taken care of a lawn in my life."

Sharon waved her hand dismissively. "Pip has Frankie. He takes care of the house and the lawn. She just wants someone to stay so the place isn't abandoned. You know, what if something leaks while she's gone, and no one discovers it for two months?"

"Can't Frankie do that?" Ella asked as she mulled over the prospect of house-sitting.

"I suppose, but it's not the same."

"Yes! Stay at Pip's house," Cass said.

"Do you live alone?" Sharon asked before Ella could reply. "Any pets?"

"I guess that would be the problem. I'm alone, but I travel about half the time, so I wouldn't be the ideal dog sitter."

"He's not a problem. Cass can usually help with him."

"Are you getting a commission on this rental, Sharon?" Ella asked.

Shaking her head, she laughed. "No, but I like you, so I wouldn't mind you as my neighbor. What if she finds some young kid who blasts rock-n-roll all night long?"

"What makes you think I don't blast rock-n-roll all night long?"

Sharon winked. "Something tells me you're a little more refined than that."

Ella swallowed a smile. Coming from Sharon, the compliment almost sounded like an insult. What would she say if she saw the fifty women in her backyard during her annual breast-cancer fund-raiser? Drinking beer, dancing, playing volleyball and horseshoes until the beer ran out? Or caught her sunbathing in almost nothing? No, she didn't tend to play her music loudly, except while housecleaning on Saturday mornings, but she wasn't *that* refined.

"Would you like to see the house?" Sharon asked. "Pip is home. I'm sure she'd be happy to show it to you."

Her hesitation was brief. What did she have to lose? "Sure."

"Yeah!" Cass said, clapping her hands, causing Bijou to start barking.

"See. Everyone thinks it's a good idea," Sharon said.

After gathering the newspapers, Ella stood, and they walked together the short distance to Arthur Avenue, then crossed the street in front of a stone home in the style of a French country manor, with a sloping roof and stone wall surrounding the grounds.

"What a lovely place," Ella commented.

Bijou jumped from Sharon's arms as they approached an arched gateway, immediately running in circles and then squatting to do his business.

"He has an entire park at his disposal, and he comes home to do that."

Ella looked up to see a woman reclining on a chaise positioned to get her a face full of sunshine, if a large-brimmed hat and glasses hadn't hidden her features.

"There's no place like home," Sharon said.

"Who's your friend?"

"Pip, this young lady is Ella Townes. She's starting a new job at PMU, and we found her in the park studying the newspaper. She needs an apartment. I thought I'd introduce you. Perhaps you can help each other out."

Ella walked forward and offered her hand. Pip responded with her own and shook it gently. "Ella Townes."

"Penny Perkins. Everyone calls me Pip."

"It's a pleasure to meet you."

"So where do you come from, Ella?" she asked.

Ella told her she'd traveled as a child, because of her father's job, but that she'd spent her summers at Lake Winola.

"Wait a minute. Are you related to Carl and Elizabeth Townes? They lived at the lake when I was young, about a mile from my parents' place. Their daughter, Nance, was my sitter."

Ella laughed. "You're kidding me! Their son, Ron, is my father. I stayed with them every summer until they passed away."

Pip shook her head. "That was awful, Ella. One fall we said good-bye to them, thinking we'd see them the next spring, and the next thing we knew, the house was for sale."

"Listen, we'll leave you two in peace," Sharon said, handing Ella a piece of paper. "This is my phone number. If I can do anything else for you, call. And even if you don't need anything, call anyway, so I can hook you up with Reese. I enjoyed talking to you. Good luck with the apartment hunting."

"Hey, what about my dollar for walking Bijou?" Cass chimed in.

Pip reached into her pocket and pulled out a folded bill, then handed it to Cass. Cass proceeded to unfold it and studied it, as if making sure Pip hadn't tried to pass her counterfeit money.

"How much money do you have now?" Pip asked.

"Forty-two dollars."

Pip looked at Ella. "Tell Ella what you're saving for."

Ella looked at Cass, who looked from Pip to Sharon and finally to Ella.

"Go ahead," Sharon said. "You can tell her."

Ella turned her full attention to Cass, who began flapping her hands excitedly. "When I have enough money, I'm going on a cooking cruise with Chef Vito."

"That sounds wonderful," Ella said.

"If you stay here, you'll meet Vito. He walks his dog in the park."

"Best soup in town, and wonderful sandwiches."

"And he runs a cruise?"

"Yes. It's very popular," Sharon said.

"I'm an excellent chef," Cass added.

"Well, I hope you have fun on your cruise, then."

"We should get going so you can talk."

Ella felt so comfortable with Sharon that she opened her arms. "It was so nice to meet you." Sharon stepped in, gave her a gentle hug, and when she stepped back, Cass attacked, clasping her ferociously. "I hope you move here with Pip."

"Nice people," Ella said when they'd disappeared through the gate.

"I've known them my whole life, it seems. I grew up in this house, but of course, we summered at the lake. The Ryans bought the house next door when I was a teenager, and they've lived there ever since."

"Are your parents still living?"

Pip shook her head. "No. My mom died years ago, and my dad just recently. It's just me now. And Bijou, of course."

"Of course. So, Sharon tells me you're looking for a house sitter for a little while. That could possibly work for me. It would give me a little time to acclimate to the mountains before I decide where I'd like to live. I'm not sure about Bijou, though. My schedule is a little odd, and I travel often."

"Oh? What do you do?"

"I'm in development. I meet with donors all over the country. I'm often gone for a week or ten days at a time."

"Don't worry about the dog. The Ryans are wonderful with him. Cass loves him. If you're here, it gives them a little break. It could work. I assume you have references I could check? Your Aunt Nance, for instance."

Ella laughed. "Don't believe a thing she says about me! But of course, it sounds great for me if it works for you. Would you mind showing me around?"

Beginning with the ample grounds, Pip showed her the converted carriage house, which now had space for four cars. Only one, an SUV, was parked inside. Flower beds and stone pathways dominated the back of the house, and a covered porch looked over it all. Pip led her up a step and into a foyer and gave her the tour. The house was surprisingly small but very efficiently designed, and more than ample for Ella's needs. Pip, or perhaps her father, had modernized all the important things—kitchen, baths, electrical. Since the master suite was on the first floor, Pip offered Ella exclusive rights to the second floor and use of the common areas as well.

After the tour, Pip poured them both glasses of ice water, and they settled in on the covered porch. "It's so amazing that I should have met you, Pip. I can't believe the way this day has gone," Ella said, shaking her head.

"Sometimes the fates work that way."

"It's funny. I was just thinking about my old friends from the lake, hoping I'll have a chance to get together with some of them once I'm settled, and I meet you, and you also have a connection to the lake. It's like my old friends are calling me."

"Do you keep in touch?"

Ella shook her head. "My last summer at the lake, I was only twelve years old. I never even had phone numbers for them. It was a different time, you know?"

"Well, with the internet, I'm sure you'll be able to track them down."

"I hope so."

"Who are you looking for? Even though my dad sold our lake house, I still know some of those people."

"There are a few people I'd like to catch up with, but the one I'd most like to see is Stephanie Gates. Do you know her?"

Pip took a sip of her water and tilted her head. She'd removed the hat and glasses when they went into the house, but her expression was still unreadable. "Stephanie? Sophie's daughter?"

"Yes. She lived in the house next to my grandparents. She was my very best childhood friend. Do you know her? Is she still in the area?"

Pip nodded and rested her glass on her knee. "You didn't hear,

I guess. No. How would you?" She seemed to be talking to herself, staring into the distance before she met Ella's gaze. "Stephanie died quite a few years ago."

Ella felt the words like a slap to the face. She was only forty-two; Steph was the same age. How could she be dead? "What?"

"She died."

How could this information, after no news for more than thirty years, hit her so hard? Thoughts of Steph suddenly filled her—riding her bike, long before the days of helmets, a mane of brown hair blowing behind her, a hundred-watt smile on her face. Sitting together in their tree house, built high up in the tree closest to the lake. From there they'd watch the fireworks on the Fourth of July and spy on boaters and partiers. They'd caught neighbors skinny-dipping and teenagers making out in their parents' boats, even had ringside seats for a few drunken brawls. It had been great fun, and it would have been nice to travel back to those days with Steph and find out what kind of person she'd become. Perhaps, they'd even make new memories. The sadness, she supposed, wasn't just because of the friendship they'd shared back then, but the one Ella had hoped to rekindle now.

"What happened to her? Was it an accident?" What felled the young other than accidents? Drowning? Steph had been a strong swimmer, but she knew from her time at the lake that anyone could drown.

Pip shook her head and stared again, her eyes unfocused. "No, not an accident. Stephanie was murdered."

CHAPTER 4: GHOSTS

Even though Ella should have pointed her convertible toward Philadelphia, when she got behind the wheel she didn't hesitate to drive in the opposite direction. She'd talked with Pip a while longer, already decided that she would house-sit while Pip was away, but she could no longer focus on the details or the conversation. All she could think of was Stephanie Gates, her cherished childhood friend, and the fact that she was dead. Not just dead, though. Murdered. Somehow, that made the reality much worse. Murder seemed even more senseless than cancer and accidental deaths.

Even though it had been so long, Ella felt compelled to talk to Steph's mom, Sophie. Pip had also mentioned the passing of Steph's dad, and although Pip didn't spend much time at the lake anymore, she'd heard rumors that Sophie still lived there, in the same big Mediterranean-style villa Ella recalled from childhood. Ella would go there and talk to Sophie, and offer her belated condolences.

It seemed right that Ella should stop in to say hello. She'd known Steph well, and she'd planned to look her up, so why not her mother? Of course, it was entirely possible that Mrs. Gates wouldn't remember her or wouldn't want to talk with her because of the memories a conversation with her would inevitably bring to life. Perhaps she was demented and wouldn't even remember her daughter.

None of the scenarios she envisioned could stop her from doing what she thought was the right thing. She knew Mrs. Gates and liked her. Because Steph was an only child, she often took friends along on trips, and Ella had been privileged to enjoy Hershey Park with the Gates family, as well as Niagara Falls, Nantucket, and Cape May. Not to mention the hundreds of sleepovers and thousands of hot dogs she'd consumed on the Gateses' patio.

Mrs. Gates, she immediately realized, was a big part of her childhood, too.

It was a gorgeous day to take the top down, and the ride was peaceful. It had been more than thirty years since she'd visited the lake, and she'd never driven there, so Ella relied on her GPS to guide her from Scranton. Once the car rounded that last bend and the lake came into view, her instincts took over. She'd navigated that stretch of road hundreds of times, on her bike and on foot, and she knew exactly how to get to Sophie Gates's place.

Slowing the car in front of her grandparents' former house, she marveled at the changes. Someone had put love and money into restoring the old Craftsman cottage, and it gleamed with fresh paint. Flowers poured from baskets hanging from the porch eaves, and children's toys dotted the yard.

Her father had often talked about his childhood at Lake Winola, and Ella and her sister had treasured memories as well. It was good that another generation of kids had the same opportunity to enjoy it as they had.

Pulling the car ahead a hundred yards, Ella caught sight of the Gates place. The house was much as she remembered it, the classic Mediterranean style making it difficult to tell if the house was five years old or fifty. Ella parked on the macadam driveway before the garage doors and looked around. Lush green landscaping dominated the front property, with intermittent splashes of color provided by thick beds of flowers. Was Sophie a gardener, or did she hire one? Ella's memory failed her on that point, but clearly someone was taking good care of the landscaping.

Hesitating just a moment, she exited the convertible and rang the bell. It took a minute, but Ella could hear footsteps approaching and was filled with a strange sense of dread. All of a sudden, this visit seemed like a stupid idea. What was she doing here?

Before she could further debate the question or change her mind and leave, the lace curtain on the glass-paneled door was pushed aside, and a familiar face peeked through. It had been a long time since she'd seen her, but Sophie looked the same. Older—brown hair had been replaced by white, and she had more wrinkles—but Ella would have recognized her anywhere. Another emotion replaced her dissolving anxiety—sadness, perhaps? Ella didn't have time to examine it before Sophie unlocked the heavy door and pulled it back, assessing her.

"Hi, Mrs. Gates. I'm Ella Townes." Pointing across her body to the left, she said, "I used to live over there. Carl and Liz's granddaughter."

"Say it again," she said.

"Ella. Townes."

The light of recognition flushed her face, and she smiled. "Ella! Look at you, all grown up. Come in, come in!"

Ella followed and wasn't surprised to see that Sophie's house hadn't changed much over the years. Her job took her through the front doors of many homes, and it wasn't unusual for someone Sophie's age to lose appreciation for the latest fads and keep things as they were.

Heading toward the kitchen, Sophie paused a few times to look at Ella. "I can't believe you're here. I still miss your grandmother. She was one of my favorite people."

"It was a shock when they both died so suddenly," Ella said through tears that suddenly filled her throat. Being back at the lake and remembering her grandparents brought back memories she hadn't expected. The tears, she realized, were not all happy ones. They'd died, and she'd never had a chance to come back to say good-bye to her lake friends. She'd spent ten of her summers there, and if her dad's parents had lived, she would probably have spent another dozen.

As if understanding her earlier thoughts, Sophie nodded. "The house changed hands a few times, and a few years back I finally bought it. The family I rent to is really sweet. The wife looks out for me, and the kids remind me of you guys when you were small. They're everywhere, little bundles of energy on the move from dawn 'til dusk."

"That's good." She wasn't sure why, but she hated the thought of weekenders living in the house, using it for parties but not really loving it the way her family had. For a moment, she cursed her dad and his sister for selling it after their parents' death, but she knew in her heart it was the right move. They were too busy for a lake house in a remote corner of Northeastern Pennsylvania, and too poor to pay someone else to care for it in their absence.

After instructing Ella to sit in the sunroom beside the kitchen, Sophie procured two glasses and filled them with home-brewed tea, then pulled cookies from a plastic container and plated them. When she was done, she sat across from Ella and studied her.

"Your hair's lighter. You must color it." She didn't wait for a reply. "And you don't wear a ring, so you must not be married. Other than that, I don't know a thing about you. What's become of you? What are you doing here?"

"You're right about the hair and the marital status. To answer the last question, I just got a job at Pocono Mountains University, and when I thought of moving back, the first person I wanted to reconnect with was Stephanie." Ella swallowed. "I'm so sorry to hear about her, Mrs. Gates. I had to come over and say hello to you and tell you how much I treasured her friendship. Even though we were only kids, I've thought about her my entire life."

If Sophie felt any emotions at the mention of her dead daughter, she hid them well. "How sweet of you! I do so love to see Steph's friends as they grow. It helps me think of what she'd be like now. Keeps her fresh in my mind, you see."

"I think it could be painful for some people. I'm glad it's not for you."

"Oh, it's painful, Ella. How could it not be? But when you say something so kind, like you think of her, it lightens my heart. I know a little piece of her is still alive in you."

Mrs. Gates might not have teared up, but Ella did, and she used one of the napkins Mrs. Gates had provided to dry her eyes. Mrs. Gates patted her hand. "Steph was a wonderful girl, Mrs. Gates. She was kind. So kind to everyone. And fun. We had so many adventures as kids—treasure hunts and obstacle courses and bike races. Remember when we held the 'Tour de Winola'? There must have been a hundred people out on their bikes that day."

Sophie nodded. "I think she charged a quarter to enter the race and donated twenty dollars to the animal shelter."

Ella nodded. "I remember!" Together, they had designed a poster, and her father had printed copies at his office. All the neighborhood kids had hung them around the lake, and they carefully mapped the course. It had been a huge event, followed by drinks and cookies at Bucky's house.

"They still have it. The race. Every year on the Fourth of July weekend. Hundreds of people of all ages. Most people don't remember that two eight-year-old girls started it. Some of the old gang still ride in it."

"Do you see her friends often?" Ella asked. The lake was a small community, so it wouldn't have surprised her.

"From time to time. Valerie still lives here, and she runs me to the doctor and takes me for groceries. Bucky treats me to lunch every week. I think he and Steph were secretly dating. He still seems to be in love with her, all these years later."

"I suppose he had a crush on her even when we were eight years old," Ella said. Long after the other kids went home, Bucky had hung around, typically agreeing to do whatever Steph wanted. If he'd been invited, Ella had no doubt he would have come to their sleepovers, too.

"I still see some of her high school friends, too. I don't think you'd know them. Most of them were from town, not from the lake."

Ella bit into a jelly-filled cookie and looked out the window toward the lake. Steph's tree house was gone, but she could imagine just where it was, could still see the panoramic view of the lake from up there. Even from here, the sight was magnificent, with an expanse of water just beyond the boat dock, cottages and homes in the distance around the shore, and a cloudless blue sky framing distant mountains.

Noticing her stare, Mrs. Gates turned and shared the vision. "It's why I stay here," she said. "The view. There's nothing like it."

"It is something. I've remembered it my whole life. I'm sorry I didn't drive up here years ago."

Mrs. Gates patted her hand.

"Do you still own the print shop?" Ella asked, feeling a change of subject was in order.

"No. We sold it a few years ago. It just got to be too much, driving back and forth to Scranton, holding meetings, disciplining employees. Who needs the aggravation?"

Ella chuckled. "It must have changed over the years, with everyone owning personal computers and printers."

"That didn't impact our business very much. We did more commercial stuff. But we went into business at a good time, when there was some profit to be made, and we sold it at a good time, too. How about you? What do you do at the university?" she asked.

"I'm the new vice president of development," she said, and explained a little about her job.

"Is it hard? To ask people for money, I mean?"

Ella shook her head. "Surprisingly, no. Many people want to give, and I help them figure out how to do it. I help them create their legacies, and that makes most people very happy. Long after they're gone, they'll live on in a young doctor or artist whose education they helped provide. And of course, they get their names on a big plaque, too." Ella winked.

"I see," she said as she nibbled a cookie, seeming to digest the thought as well.

"I'm surprised you haven't asked about Steph," she said a moment later.

Ella knew just what Sophie meant. But she hadn't wanted to come in and seem like a gossip, eager for juicy details about her friend's murder. She'd come to honor Steph and, in a sense, pay her respects. Even if she'd died years ago, she'd been alive to Ella. To her, Steph had only died an hour earlier when Pip told her the news. "I didn't think it was polite."

"It's not hard to talk about her. Remember, that's what keeps her alive."

"Even speaking about her death?"

"It's therapeutic. And I keep hoping that someday, someone will come forward and give us some piece of information to help solve the crime. And as long as I keep it simmering, instead of letting it rest, that might happen."

Ella hesitated just a moment, unsure if she really wanted to know. Not only had Steph been murdered, but her killer hadn't been caught. How awful for Steph. How awful for her mother. Would discussing it really be okay? After a moment, she decided to take the chance. Telling her seemed to be important to Sophie. "What happened to her?"

"An intruder murdered her. He's never been caught. There had been a few break-ins around the mountains, and the police think she surprised a burglar. Steve and I were out at a party, and she was home alone. In her room, studying. Even though the lights were on, there were no cars in the drive, and he must have thought the house was empty. She startled him, and he hit her over the head. The coroner said she died instantly."

How dreadful, Ella thought. Steph had always been petite and would probably have had little chance of her fending off an intruder. Just like her, though, to go down trying, instead of hiding in her closet hoping he'd go away. "It's so awful. I can't believe that happened to her. It's hard to imagine someone you know being murdered. How old was she?"

"Seventeen. It happened just a few weeks before she would have graduated from high school."

Shaking her head, Ella closed her eyes. It was just so sad. Steph hadn't even had a chance to live her life. "What were her plans, Mrs. Gates? Did she still want to be a vet?"

Mrs. Gates nodded enthusiastically. "She sure did! She was at the top of her class, on her way to college on a full scholarship. After that, vet school."

Remembering, Ella nodded. "It was what she always wanted."

"She was a determined young woman. Had it all planned, even picked out office space next to the print shop, so she could have lunch with her father every day."

"Sounds like she had it all worked out," Ella said softly, sorry for the dreams that had died with Steph. The animal kingdom had lost a friend, too.

"I've no doubt all her dreams would have come true, if someone hadn't stolen her from us."

"From what I remember, I think you're right. And they never found him? The burglar?" It seemed strange to say the murderer.

"There was really no evidence. It was raining, so no one was out and about to see anything. If he left footprints, they were washed away. She didn't put up a fight, so they didn't find any of the killer's blood or skin under her nails. Not much to go on."

"That must be frustrating."

"Yes. But I keep hoping. Someone may know something. Someone *must* know something. Jewelry was stolen—that's never turned up. The killer most likely had her blood on him."

Ella didn't want to point out the obvious, that an eye witness coming forward at this point was unlikely. But if Sophie needed to hold on to her hope, Ella wouldn't try to change her mind. She was surprised by what Sophie said next.

"They're going to reopen the investigation."

"Really?"

"The sitting DA is retiring at the end of his term. Bucky is running for the position, and one of his campaign promises is to try to solve cold cases. Steph's is one of them."

"Well, good for Bucky! I hope he wins. And I hope he finds some answers for you."

In spite of her claim that talking about Steph was a good thing, the conversation seemed to tire Sophie. "I should get going," Ella said a moment later.

Sophie didn't argue with her. "I'm happy you stopped by today, Ella. Will you come again?"

After exchanging numbers, and hugs, and promising to see each other again, Ella headed out the door.

CHAPTER 5: TAKE ME OUT

To Ella. Now that you're moving away, we'll probably see you more than we do now! Good luck!"

Ella laughed at her friend Gary's toast and raised her champagne glass, circling it in the direction of the dozen or so friends who'd gathered to wish her well.

"I'm going to miss you guys!" she said, suddenly regretting what an awful friend she was. She'd known most of the people on Gary's patio for twenty years, yet she saw them only on occasions like this—when someone was transferred because of work or moving because of a breakup. Fortunately, they hadn't gathered to bid any permanent good-byes yet, but Ella couldn't deny that inevitability. Plenty of people died in their forties—one of them was bound to be someone she knew. Hell, Steph Gates had died in her teens. She'd tried to wrap her mind around that thought as she'd packed for the move and concluded that she just couldn't do it. Even after talking with Steph's mom, the edges of reality were too sharp to settle into her mind.

"If the Phils ever make the playoffs again, you'll come back, won't you?" her friend Joanne asked.

Ella hung her arm over Joanne's shoulder. "If that should ever happen, because miracles do happen, I will be here, babe."

"It's so strange to think of you leaving. A month ago, we were in Rehoboth and you didn't mention a thing. Now…"

Ella offered a hint of a smile as she answered. "I didn't think I was unhappy. I'm not. Unhappy. I'm just…missing something, I guess. And when this job opportunity came across my desk, I thought of my grandparents and the great times I had up there as a kid, and I had to check it out. And, well, the rest was easy."

"So you think you'll find this missing something there? In the middle of nowhere? What are you looking for, a wild animal?"

Ella laughed. "I think it's more of a professional something. A chance to prove myself and move up the ladder a little higher."

"How much higher can you go? You're already super important and successful."

"This is about it, unless I move to a much bigger school."

"Is that on the agenda?"

Ella thought about it for a moment, sipping her champagne and savoring the little explosion in her mouth before swallowing. All of her thoughts of PMU had felt so comfortable to her that she honestly believed like it was a destination for her, not a stop on the road. That wasn't the case with her current job, where she constantly found herself reading the professional journals "just to see" what positions were available. Her new job could turn out to be a disaster, and if it was, she'd do the best she could for as long as she could until she found something else suitable, and she'd move on. After meeting with the president, though, and meeting the Ryans, and driving around the mountains, she sensed everything would work out just fine.

"I don't think so. I think this is my dream job."

Her friend looked at her with love and admiration in her eyes. "Then good luck," she said, and gave her shoulder a squeeze.

"That's one big moving van," her friend Leah said as she placed a kiss on Ella's cheek.

Ella's jaw dropped. "I know, right? I thought I'd be able to pack everything in the convertible, but was I ever mistaken. I couldn't even fit my fall wardrobe in the car. That left three other seasons, plus pictures and books and artwork…I'm basically a hoarder."

"I guess it's good that you're moving, then. It gives you a chance to start over."

"I'm leaving all the furniture, and the tenant is very appreciative."

"Who'd you rent to? This happened so quickly!"

Ella had been delighted when someone had answered her post on the university's e-bulletin board within hours. A newly minted associate professor had rented her place based solely on the photos she'd placed online and was in the process of moving in at that very moment. They'd exchanged money and keys in the driveway before Ella drove off to Gary's for her farewell party. It was hard to believe that she'd been able to orchestrate a move in only two weeks, but she had. She'd packed everything in her home and her office, transferred her clients to other development officers, transferred the utilities to her tenant, and was ready to go. It was tremendously helpful that she had no responsibilities with the house in Scranton. All she'd had to do was transfer a few bills—things like credit cards and car insurance—and she was set.

"A new prof. He's a bachelor, so I'm hoping he'll stay for a few years and help me pay off the mortgage."

"You could get lucky there. He probably won't want to buy anything until he gets tenure. How long does that take?"

"A few years, I'd imagine."

"It does sound perfect."

"Yes, and Gary has agreed to do the maintenance, just like he does now."

"It's a good situation in Scranton, too. You're a lucky lady, Ella."

Ella smiled and sipped her champagne. She felt lucky. After confirming the job with Mary Ann Bingham, she'd received a huge fruit basket from her new colleagues in development, as well as a small bouquet from the president herself. They'd sent her a check for moving expenses and told her to provide them a receipt if she needed additional funds, so she was way ahead there. The moving van would cost only a few hundred dollars, and even after she bought Gary and his partner dinner, she'd still have hundreds of dollars to spare. She was surrounded by lovely people who obviously cared about her, even if she was a rotten friend. And she was about to begin an exciting new job. She was very lucky indeed.

Glancing at the group of gathered friends, some single and some coupled, she wondered if a romance was in her future. It wasn't something she craved, but she wasn't opposed to dating, either. It had just become difficult, because of her strange hours and the travel demands of her job. Most normal nine-to-fivers couldn't handle a relationship with someone who was never around. Unless she was in a relationship with someone she didn't want to spend time with, having a girlfriend was difficult. And if she hadn't found one in Philly, how could she ever hope to in the mountains? Yes, she knew lesbians lived there, but statistically speaking, there had to be less of them.

Finding Mrs. Right wouldn't be easy after the move. She was sure of it. And she was okay with that knowledge, too. No matter if she had a woman to share her success with or enjoyed the company of friends or colleagues, Ella was content. Leah was right. Ella was lucky.

❖

Sunday afternoons were always family days for Reese. Even though she had a perfectly functional washer and dryer at her house, she'd carry a basket with her and wash, dry, and fold during the few hours she spent with her parents and sister. If she worked the day shift, they'd have a late dinner and watch sports on TV. If she worked the evening shift, they'd have an early dinner and watch sports on TV.

Today had been a little different, since the RailRiders were in town, and Reese had volunteered to transport Cass to and from the game. She picked her friend Karen up first, then drove by for Cass. She was waiting on the front step when Reese pulled up in her Jeep.

"Hi, sis," Reese said.

"Karen!" Cass shouted, completely ignoring Reese as she gave Karen a big hug and then climbed in back. It was a beautiful sunny day, the top was down, and Reese didn't let her sister bother her.

"Buckle up, so I don't dump you on the corner."

"Reese is a bad driver," Cass said.

Karen nodded. "I know."

Reese shot a look at Karen before turning her eyes back to the road. "I'd be happy to turn the keys over to you. Then I can sit back and enjoy a few beers at the game."

"No deal. But thanks for the invite."

Cass usually gave her free tickets for being an usher to Reese and her parents, who went as a couple. Reese had a few friends who enjoyed baseball and accompanied her on game days.

"Cass, thanks for the tickets."

"You're welcome."

"You could say thanks for the ride," Reese teased her.

"Thanks."

Reese dropped Cass off at the curb and then found a parking space not too far from the stadium's main entrance. After presenting their tickets, she and Karen checked to make sure Cass had made it to her post and then headed to the outfield. They grabbed two beers and sat on the grass to watch batting practice.

"So, how's life?" Karen asked as she rested on an elbow. The knoll beyond the centerfield wall was perfect for reclining, and Reese mimicked her posture.

"It's good. How about with you?"

"I hate my job, but other than that, I can't complain."

Karen was one of the young prosecutors in the DA's office, and the cases she was assigned usually lacked glamour and excitement. Her dedication to putting away the bad guys was genuine, though, and Reese thought she'd be a lifer.

"You love it and you know it."

"I'm not so sure anymore."

Reese sensed she was serious and leaned forward, letting Karen know she had her attention. "Why?"

"Oh, I don't know. Constant chaos. Daily doses of death and destruction. No thanks for a job well done, but plenty of criticism for whatever goes wrong. Too much to do and not enough hands to do it."

"Wait. That sounds like the ER!"

"I guess you can understand, then. Any suggestions from my older, wiser friend?"

"Have another beer."

They laughed, and Reese offered her bottle in toast. "If beer made it better, we'd be fine."

"Guess who's getting the Stephanie Gates murder?"

Reese brought her bottle to her lips and took a long pull to settle her stomach before answering. The topic of Stephanie Gates always unnerved her. "So it's true? I heard a rumor, but..." Shrugging, she looked off toward the baseball field.

"There's more than three months until the election, but the DA thinks reopening the investigation now will give Bucky some momentum."

"What do you think? Are there any new leads?" Doing her best to appear polite rather than interested, Reese rested back on her elbows as she waited for Karen to reply.

"You remember the case, don't you? You were her classmate. They didn't have any leads then and won't find any now."

Reese blew out a sigh of frustration. How could a stranger break into someone's house and murder them without leaving a single clue? That was the rumor back then, and apparently, it was true. Reese never knew for sure, had never talked to anyone about the case. She'd had her reasons for keeping her distance back then, and they still held true. Getting involved was not a good move for her, but she would still like to know what was happening with the investigation. "Steph was a good friend of mine, but I never really knew anything about the case. All I know is her killer was never caught."

"I'm afraid that's about all there is. No physical evidence at all. No witnesses. No motive. Nothing, *nada, nicht.*"

Reese laughed and drank her beer. "If anyone can do it, you can." Reese hoped Karen could find something other investigators had missed, but she didn't hold out hope. After almost twenty-five years, the killer would probably never be caught.

"I'll keep you posted."

"I'd appreciate that. And if you need anything from me...I'd be happy to help."

Karen nodded, and they were silent as a young girl surely destined for greatness performed the national anthem. She had a voice that left the crowd of five thousand fans screaming. When the excitement died down, the RailRiders took the field, and Karen turned to look at Reese.

"How's your love life? Are you seeing anyone?"

Reese had known Karen for more than a decade, since meeting at a party when Karen first arrived back in town after law school at Villanova. They'd always been friends, nothing more, but Karen loved meddling in Reese's love life. "Not at the moment."

"This has been a long moment."

Reese smiled around her beer bottle. "I hadn't noticed."

"Well, let me see if I can refresh your memory. Memorial Day party—no date. New Year's Eve party—no date. Halloween party—no date."

"I see your memory hasn't suffered from the stresses of your job. What about you? Who are you seeing?"

"Ah, deflection. We'll come back to you. Who am I not seeing?"

"Okay, then. Let me see if I can think of anyone." Reese knew Karen had suffered a devastating loss when her first lover had been killed in a car accident. That pain, and the strength and humor with which she endured it, were big reasons why she liked Karen so much. In the years since her lover's death, Karen had never gotten serious again. She hadn't missed out on dating, though, bringing a different woman to each of the events she'd mentioned. Reese knew Karen was protecting herself. She understood.

"Do you have anything going on with Portia?"

Karen shook her head solemnly. "I don't want to piss Ellen off."

"I think that's wise. Besides, there are so many other fish in the sea."

Karen's eyes flew open wide. "Yeah, aren't there? Did you see the new helicopter babe?"

Reese knew just the woman Karen was speaking of. A seasoned flight medic had left the field to work in administration, and his replacement was a beautiful brunette with curves that filled a flight suit like Reese had never seen before. On their first few encounters, Reese had been very impressed by the woman's professionalism. Now she seemed to be flirting with Reese, and for some reason, it was a big letdown.

"She's a hottie."

"I saw her first," Karen said.

"Where?"

"At Suzie's party on the Fourth. You should get out more."

"Oh. I had to work. The ER never closes, and someone has to reattach the fingertips that the fireworks blow off. Good party?" Had it really been that long since she'd talked to Karen? Maybe she did need to get out more.

"Well, her name is Deb, and I want her. Bad."

Thinking of her less-than-professional comments in the ER, Reese frowned. "I think she's a bigger player than you are."

"Oh, I can play big. I've got game."

Reese laughed and touched her bottle to Karen's once again. "I have no doubt."

They were quiet for a moment. "You can have her, if you want."

Reese looked at Karen and saw genuine concern in her friend's eyes.

"No, no. I'm not looking. Really. Sometimes it's nice to be single." In truth, Reese had spent most of her life unattached. She dated, but only for fun and sex. She let her eyes wander along the bleachers to where she saw her sister, watching the game instead of the crowd, and she knew she could never get serious. Her sister was her responsibility, and no way would she ever find a woman willing to take on both Ryan women. A woman like that didn't exist. So Reese kept it casual, and so far, it had worked out great.

Their easy banter continued, and it wasn't until the middle of the game that they made their way to their assigned seats in Cass's section. Reese bought a bottle of water from the vendor and handed it to Cass, who gave Reese a hug. "This is my sister," Cass proudly announced to the crowd. They all cheered for Reese, and she tipped her cap and waved to the fans in Cass's section. Most of them were season-ticket holders, and they saw Cass at every game. Every season, in fact. They were like family to her.

Reese settled into her seat and enjoyed the sunshine, and the baseball, and the easy conversation with Karen. When the RailRiders rallied to win in the bottom of the ninth, she cheered wildly, along with the other five thousand fans in attendance. It was a beautiful day, and they'd all stayed for the exciting finish. When they arrived back at her parents' house to drop off Cass, Reese was momentarily surprised to see a moving van in the driveway. Then she remembered that Pip was going to California and someone from PMU was going to live in her house for a few months.

Then the someone stepped through the threshold, and Reese was mesmerized. She looked toward the van, a smile peeking through the corners of her mouth, then turned and tossed a long mane of blond hair over her shoulder. The spell was broken when she reached to the man behind her, a tall, well-built guy in a Phillies cap, and kissed him.

"Is that the new neighbor?" Karen asked.

Reese swallowed her disappointment. The kiss—the blatant display of heterosexuality—had come so quickly she didn't even have a moment to enjoy the jolt she'd gotten from the sight of such a lovely woman.

"Must be," she said as she pulled around the corner and into her parents' driveway, out of sight of the kissing couple in front of the house.

CHAPTER 6: COLD SWEAT

He disconnected his phone and threw it at his couch, where it bounced off the back and landed harmlessly on the seat. He would have screamed, but odds were good someone would have heard him, and the last thing he wanted—or needed—was attention.

What had been an innocent, friendly phone call to schedule a golf outing had turned his day into a disaster when his childhood friend had shared the current gossip. The investigation into Stephanie Gates's murder was being reopened. Why? What hope could they have after all these years? It was the damned television, he thought. All those cold cases, decades old, solved in an hour of prime-time TV. Their improbable success inspired cops and prosecutors and parents to look into their own freezers, hoping for answers.

He wished he could give them the answers, tell them it had just been an accident, but of course, he couldn't do that. They'd never believe him. They'd never understand how Steph's death had ruined his life, too. How he thought about her every day. How now, sitting in his office, thinking of her, he was drenched by a wave of guilt that all the years hadn't been able to assuage.

Not a day went by without a thought of Stephanie somehow woven into it. If it was a sunny summer day, he thought of her at the lake, sunbathing or swimming, or racing her boat across the choppy surface to the little cove where they all parked, out of sight of parents and other adults. In the fall, he thought of her at school, the serious student who tried so hard—and succeeded—at all her academic pursuits. Top of the class. Student council president. She would have been homecoming queen if she hadn't denounced the event. She could have done anything.

He thought of her in the pool, working to improve her times, and in the gym, lifting weights to gain the strength that would help her swim faster. There were parties on snow days and ski trips where they gathered by the big fireplace in Elk Mountain's lodge or, better yet, the overnight trips to Vermont where they had so much fun. He remembered the first night they spent together there, awakening to find her sleeping beside him. It had been one of the happiest moments of his life.

Spring was the hardest for him, when the world was coming back to life after the cold, northeast winter. The world was coming back to life, and Steph had died. She'd died because of him, and spring would never be the same.

Burying his face in his hands, he shook off the image of her vacant eyes staring at him. He wiped the sweat from his forehead with the hem of his shirt and sighed. He'd never meant to hurt her. He had no reason to feel guilty. Besides, she'd provoked him. It wasn't her fault, and he knew she didn't mean to hurt him, but she had. And he'd reacted badly, in anger. He hadn't gone to her house that night intending to hurt her; he'd only wanted to talk, to convince her to change her decision. Her mind had been made up, though, and he couldn't change it. It had been over before he got there, only he didn't know it.

He could hardly even remember reaching for the statue. One minute Steph was turning her back on him, and the next, she was lying on the ground, dead.

No one could really blame him, could they, if they knew how it had happened? No. No one was to blame. It was an accident.

He still felt badly, though. Stephanie had been a bright, beautiful, young girl, with so much potential. He had no doubt that, if she'd lived, she would have done wonderful things, made the world a better place, as he had.

He'd often reflected on the accident and realized he carried an added burden after her death. Not only did he feel responsible to make his own way in the world, but he felt the need to do extra well, to contribute the things Steph couldn't. It pushed him, made him work harder to be the best he could be. He was kind and generous. He gave back to the world that had not always been so kind to him.

It wasn't the world's fault, though, either. Sometimes, things just happened. Like Steph's accident.

He poured himself a neat glass of bourbon and threw back his head. The golden fire ignited his throat and his resolve. He refused to let Stephanie Gates do any more harm than she already had. For twenty-five years, she had haunted him, taunted him, dictated his decisions. He hadn't done anything without carrying her weight with him. It was exhausting, and it had to end. She'd ruined his past, and he refused to let her ruin the rest of his life, too. He'd do whatever he had to in order to make sure of that.

CHAPTER 7: THE NEIGHBORS' DAUGHTER

I really appreciate you taking me to the airport," Pip said.

Ella nodded. "It's no trouble. Fortunately, I didn't have any university functions tonight."

It was the third week of August, and Ella had been at her job for three weeks. Three crazy weeks composed of sixteen-hour work days and seven-day work weeks. She'd hardly seen Pip at all since arriving, and now she was leaving for California. She'd tried to make time, but with a several-month backlog of work, it wasn't easy.

It was going well, though. The people in her department were solid and seemed to work comfortably together. She'd spent the first days in meetings, getting to know her colleagues and then the workings of the department, and she was just now ready to dig in to the business of fund-raising.

Her personal items fit easily into the second floor of Pip's place, and she'd set up an office in one of the spare bedrooms, for the times she needed to work at night. Although she hardly saw her, Pip seemed like a great roommate, and Ella wouldn't have minded if she stayed in Scranton, but her classes were starting in California, and she was excited to go.

"Okay, let's go over things one more time. You know where the dog food is. Don't change brands. His tummy is very sensitive. The notebook in the kitchen drawer has the number for the vet and all the important numbers you'll need. Alarm-company phone number and account number. Utilities. Lawn care. The neighbor's numbers. They're all there. Cass will probably knock on the door five times a day. You can let her in if you'd like. She likes to look at the old record albums, and sometimes she even plays them. And she'll play in the yard with Bijou for hours if you let her."

"You don't let her take him out of the yard, do you?"

Pip shook her head. "No. She's afraid to leave the yard by herself. But if her mom is with her, or her sister, she'll walk him six times a day."

"Sounds easy enough."

"Just let Sharon know if you need help. She usually knows what to do. She helped my dad for years before he died."

"Don't worry, Pip. Everything's going to be fine."

"I'm happy you're settling in. I hope you'll decide to stay. Rides to the airport are sometimes hard to come by."

"Fortunately, the university pays for my parking at the airport. When I was in Philly, I just took the train."

"They're talking about rail service to New York from Scranton. Maybe we should suggest an airport line."

They were approaching the terminal. "From the look of the parking lot, it might not be a bad idea."

Ella pulled into the drop-off area, where a dozen cars had queued ahead of them. When they reached the front, Ella helped Pip with her bags and then hugged her. "I'll call you every day. Twice."

Ella nodded. "Forewarned. Be safe."

Ella watched her walk away toward her new adventure, feeling quite excited about her own. Pip was off to California to study film and would stay with a movie star from Scranton, a man named Miles Jones, a man whose family had been in business with Pip's since the turn of the last century. Ella, on the other hand, was on her own, with a notebook of contacts and perhaps a few childhood friends she could call upon.

It didn't matter. She was where she wanted to be.

Since Gerrity's was on the way home, Ella stopped for a few grocery items. This was her first night alone, and it was Friday. A steak on the grill sounded perfect, and she'd already found her way to the liquor store in the plaza next to the market. Thirty minutes later, as she was in her driveway unloading her packages, she heard a familiar voice behind her.

"Do you need any help?"

"As a matter of fact, I do. Can you help me carry my groceries?"

Cass nodded. "Did you buy any snacks for Bijou?" she asked as they made their way from the carriage house toward the back door.

"No. I plan to make him some snacks. Would you like to help?"

"How do you make them?"

"With peanut butter and flour. They're delicious. At least, my old dog Hudson thought so."

"Where's Hudson now?"

"Doggie heaven."

"My gram's in human heaven."

"I bet it's a nice place, with dogs and grandmothers."

"I'm not sure. It sounds pretty boring to me."

Ella laughed. She often thought the same thing herself.

"What are you doing tonight?" Ella asked as she slipped the key into the lock and then disarmed the alarm. Before it stopped ringing, Bijou was jumping at her feet, and then when he noticed Cass, he turned his attention on her.

"Hi, Bijou. Ella didn't buy you any snacks at the store, but she's going to make you peanut butter and flour."

While Cass played on the floor with the dog, Ella put her groceries away. It was approaching five o'clock. She had just enough time to whip up a batch of dog treats before dinner.

"Do you like to bake?" Ella asked as she pulled out Pip's mixer and the necessary ingredients for Bijou's snacks.

"I don't know how. I only cook."

"Well, it's time you learned. Come on," she said, motioning with her head. "First, we'll make something for Bijou, and if he likes it, we might try something for us."

After they both washed their hands, Ella gave Cass the recipe and showed her how to measure the ingredients. It was a simple recipe, with just water, peanut butter, and flour, but it took all of Cass's concentration to fill the cups and transfer them without spilling. She loved the mixer, and when the dough was formed, Ella demonstrated how to roll it out between sheets of parchment paper. Her favorite part was using the cookie cutter to make dog-bone-shaped treats. When they'd created nearly four dozen, filling two trays, Ella helped Cass transfer them to the oven and set the timer.

"What now?" Cass asked.

"The no-fun part. We clean up. But do you need to check in with your mom? She knows you're here, right?" Wow, Ella thought. What a screw-up she was. She probably should have asked that question earlier.

"I should go home now. My mom told me not to stay too long. But can I come back later and take Bijou for a walk?"

"Absolutely. And do you really have to go home, or you just avoiding the cleanup?"

Cass looked down, guilt written all over her face, and Ella laughed before pointing a finger at the door. "Go! But next time, you're doing all the dishes."

With the radio playing classic rock at a respectable volume, Ella popped the cork on her wine and allowed it to breathe while she prepped vegetables for the grill. An hour later, as she sat on the porch, digesting a steak grilled to perfection and taking in the lovely view of the stone wall and flower garden, Cass reappeared.

"Can I walk Bijou now?" she asked. As he heard his name, Bijou launched himself from the porch and began weaving through Cass's legs, stopping periodically to leap at her.

"Only if I can join you," Ella said. An after-dinner stroll was just what she needed, and by the look of the sky, the day was almost over. It was now or never for a walk in the park.

"I have to ask Reese. She's Cass-sitting tonight."

"Well, go ask. I'll get Bijou's leash."

Her sneakers tied, Reese stood and pulled a sweatshirt over her head. In an hour, it would be dark, and who knew how long Cass would linger on her walk with Bijou? They were safe from strangers in the park, Reese was confident, but the cold would surely assault them as the sun began its descent.

"Can Ella come, too?" Cass asked, bursting through the door. "She's very nice and beautiful."

Finally, Reese thought, she'd have a chance to meet Ella, whom Cass and her mother talked about constantly. To hear them, Ella was a cross between Christie Brinkley, with stunning good looks, Ellen DeGeneres, with a great sense of humor, and Mother Teresa, with a kind heart. She'd lived in the house next door for only a few weeks, but she'd really captivated the Ryan women. Reese was more than a little curious about her.

"Absolutely. I love nice and beautiful women. Can you grab the flashlight?"

"Why? It's light outside."

"Yes, it is now. But on our way back, it may be starting to get dark."

Cass looked at Reese as if she'd just said something earth-shattering and nodded. "All right."

"And a sweatshirt, Cass. It might get cold."

Color-matching was not one of her sister's strengths, and she came back with a yellow and purple Minions sweatshirt to wear with the light-blue flowered capri pants she wore.

"You don't match," Reese said.

Cass looked down. "Yes, I do. See," she said, pointing to her chest. "The Minion is holding a flower, and there are flowers on my pants. It's a perfect match."

How could Reese argue with that logic? "Okay, then. Let's go."

Although her sister was sometimes exasperating, Reese treasured these times with her. She'd loved Cass since the moment she was born, three years after her own birth. Her little sister was her own personal doll, one she dressed and fed and bathed, and it wasn't until Cass grew to be a little older that Reese understood she'd never have the kind of sister other kids had. It didn't matter, though. They still enjoyed many of the things other sisters did. They watched television together, worked on puzzles, shopped, played ball, rode roller coasters. Mostly, being with Cass was a joy.

And besides, her parents needed a break. For a few hours every week, Reese took charge and forced them to go shopping, or out for dinner, or to a movie. They recharged, and whether they admitted it or not, they were approaching seventy and needed to rest occasionally.

With expert precision, Cass reached over the wooden gate separating her parents' property from Pip's and popped the lock. Reese followed her, careful to relock the gate so Bijou couldn't escape later. Lingering on the footpath, she watched Cass bound up the porch steps and pound on the back door. A moment later, Bijou appeared, and Reese watched as he sprang through the door, stretching his lead, pulling the woman behind him.

Judgment on her personality would have to wait, but Cass had sure been right about Ella's looks. With her blond hair pulled up in a ponytail and a dusting of freckles across her cheeks, Ella was a knockout. She seemed to pull it all together with just a hint of makeup, something with a little sparkle above her big brown eyes and shiny and clear on her full lips. She looked even better than she had on the day of her move, Reese realized.

As she drew closer, Reese could see that the eyes themselves sparkled as well, round and large like a doe's, with perfectly matched dark lashes. She had to wonder if the blond was authentic, but it didn't matter if Ella was born that way or acquired her hair color—the result was remarkable. She was stunning.

"Hi, I'm Reese," she said, holding out her hand in time to cover the fact that she'd been ogling.

Ella's smile seemed genuine, and Reese was relieved she hadn't noticed her staring. "Ella. It's nice to meet you."

"And you as well. You're all Cass talks about these days."

"I'm very fond of her as well." Ella looked into Reese's eyes to show her how serious she was, that she cared about Cass, that Cass was safe with her. Sharon had told her that Reese tended to be somewhat overprotective, and Ella was anxious to prove herself. What had been an innocent gesture quickly turned to something else, though, as she seemed swallowed by Reese's gaze. The two of them were roughly the same size—Reese was perhaps an inch taller—though Reese somehow seemed bigger and stronger, and incredibly sexy.

Ella swallowed the unexpected curiosity, the desire to keep gazing into the warm pools of blue that swallowed her like the sea.

"Can I take Bijou?" Cass interrupted her, and with the spell broken, Ella handed over the reins.

Reese and Ella fell in step behind her, following the pathway along the side of the house, through the arched stone gate, and to the street in front.

"Watch for cars!" Reese yelled, and Ella looked up, horrified, as Cass ran out between two parked cars and into the street.

Cass looked back, a concerned expression on her face, until they caught up to her and Reese patted her shoulder. "Okay, you can go."

Even as she watched Cass reach the safety of the park, the angst on Reese's face remained. Ella longed to tell Reese it was okay, to recover the tranquility she'd seen a minute earlier. Then she realized it wasn't her place, that she really had no idea what it was like to be responsible for Cass for more than a few minutes at a time. Before she could filter her thoughts, they found their way to her mouth and she spoke. "I would imagine that a lot of worry comes with Cass."

A tired smile appeared on Reese's face, and Ella fought the urge to touch her. Over the weeks she'd lived beside the Ryans, she'd come to adore Cass, but she could also appreciate the stress she caused. As the neighbor, she could see the frustration in Sharon's expression when Cass exasperated her, the worry in her tone when Cass made a poor choice. And she only witnessed a tiny part of their life, only a fraction of their troubles. That Reese shared her parents' angst was obvious, and Ella wished she could do something to ease that burden, both for Sharon and for Reese.

"She knows right from wrong, and she's cautious, but sometimes she gets excited and forgets. She's just flitting around now, talking about you constantly, and I think her mind is too full of other things to think about the basics."

"I'm sorry if I've caused a problem," Ella said, suddenly feeling terrible. On the dozen occasions they'd walked together, she'd never thought of telling Cass to watch for cars. But, as she recalled, Cass had walked beside her, rather than running ahead like she did this time.

Reese shrugged. "It'll pass. I'm sure."

Awaiting them at the entrance to the park, Cass smiled, which indicated she'd already forgotten the incident. "Which way should we go? Have you been to the gorge yet, Ella?" she asked, the excitement in her voice making Ella want to see nothing else.

Reese quickly put that idea to rest. "I think it's too late for the gorge, Cass. It's going to be dark soon. Just stick to the path."

Exasperated, Cass sighed and turned onto a paved path, and Ella couldn't help smiling, but she reserved comment. They fell into an easy rhythm, matching each other stride for stride as Cass jogged with Bijou.

"There's certainly a family resemblance. You and Cass could be twins," Ella said. Reese's dark hair was much shorter, but her face was the same as her sister's—angular, with chiseled cheekbones and a pouting lower lip. While Cass had her mom's dark eyes, Reese's were blue.

"Except for the eyes," Reese said.

"I was just thinking that."

"The mailman had blue eyes, so that explains it."

Ella laughed. "And…you're much taller than Cass."

Reese chuckled as she tucked her chin and gazed at her sister. "It's a Down syndrome thing. Most people notice the intellectual disabilities of people with DS, but every chromosome—every cell in the body—is affected. Being short comes with the territory."

"I didn't realize that."

"It was interesting for me as a physician to learn about Cass. My whole life, I just accepted her issues as Cass-being-Cass, but when I started learning about chromosomes and how they affect the body in med school, she started to make sense to me."

Ella processed Reese's words for a moment. "It seems she has a lot of abilities."

Reese nodded. "She sure does." Then, thinking a change of topic was in order, she turned the conversation toward Ella. "My mom tells me you're just started at PMU. What do you do?"

Reese could envision Ella weaving her way through a lab filled with students, dark-framed glasses resting on the tip of her nose, instructing them on the intricacies of circuit boards, or pacing the front of a lecture hall, pontificating about a certain verse of a poem.

"I'm in development."

"Oh," Reese said, trying hard to hide her disappointment as her Ella-fantasy was shattered. She found nothing sexy about the people who called on the phone, nagging her for donations. She couldn't picture Ella doing that, but still…it sounded like an awful job. Hopefully, Ella wouldn't ask her for money. It wasn't that she didn't appreciate the education she'd gotten; she just had other priorities.

PMU was a wealthy school, with thousands of successful alums to help them maintain the status quo. She, on the other hand, had other obligations. Her parents weren't rich, and when they were gone from this earth they'd leave behind two children, one of them severely handicapped. Reese needed to save all her money to help take care of Cass. Her parents never asked it of her, but how could she do anything else? Cass was her sister, she loved her, and everything she had was hers. The people at PMU didn't get that, though, and they still sent their letters. Reese threw them into the trash with all the other junk mail. Would Ella understand that? Probably not. It was best to just keep quiet about her feelings. Surely two mature women walking a dog in a park on a lovely summer evening could find something other than work to talk about, right?

"That's nice," Reese said after a moment. "How's it going for you?"

"It's been busy, mostly with meetings so I can get to know people at the school and become up to date on the current fund-raising campaigns. Your mom mentioned that you're an alum."

"Yes. Class of '97."

"Oh, so this will be your twentieth reunion. Did you get your postcard in the mail?"

"I did note the date."

"It's very exciting," Ella said.

"Is it?"

"Well, of course. It's a chance to catch up with old friends, people you haven't seen in ages, find out how everyone's doing, see pictures of their kids."

"It sounds dreadful."

"What? Don't you have any friends?"

Reese tried not to smile at the playful jab. "A few. But I don't need a reunion to get together with them. I just buy some steaks and a few bottles of wine and send out a group text. They come like mice following the Pied Piper."

"Maybe so, but there's all that cooking and cleanup. At a reunion, you just have fun, and someone else does all the work."

"All for only a thousand bucks, right?"

Ella squinted at her. "For you, five hundred."

"Hmm. I may have to look into that, considering the cost of trash bags these days." Reese did think it might be time for a party, though. Maybe for Cass's fortieth birthday. Her group of friends consisted mostly of the kids from her high school student council, who'd traveled together to conferences and studied together at each other's houses. For one reason or another, they'd all gone to a local college, and their friendships grew even stronger during those days. It might be months between phone calls, but she knew that at any time, they'd pick up the phone to chat or help her with whatever she needed. More than their allegiance to her, though, was their love for Cass. Even though it was just the two of them, Cass had half a dozen pseudo-siblings.

"Your mom tells me you're a doctor," Ella said after a minute of comfortable silence.

"She tells everyone that."

Ella turned to look at Reese, unsure what to make of her. She was attractive, in a very understated way, with no makeup and her shoulder-length hair pushed carelessly behind her ears. Her lashes were long, accenting the blue eyes that seemed a bit guarded now. She was friendly enough, but there was something edgy about her, as if she didn't want anyone to get too close. She might have all the friends she talked about, but Ella sensed they'd had a hard time breaking into her inner sanctum. "Is it true? Or is she just fantasizing?"

"It's true."

"Well, then she has a right to brag."

"It used to be better, back in the days when drug companies gave out freebies. I'd get pens, notepads, bags, clocks—you name it. I'd give it all to my mom. Federal regulations changed, though, and now they can't market the way they used to. My mother has to spend her hard-earned cash at Staples."

"I'm sure Congress didn't consider that before they enacted such harsh laws."

"I have a friend who's a senator. She's spoken to him about it."

Ella nodded. "Is that Senator Nathan?"

"Yes. Do you know him?"

"No, but he's all the buzz around campus. He'll be honored next year. At *your* twentieth class reunion."

Reese ignored the barb. "That's not surprising, considering how much he's accomplished."

"You wouldn't be interested in serving on the awards committee, would you?"

Cass had stopped to let Bijou water a shrub, and Ella turned to face Reese. She looked up an inch or so into Reese's eyes and saw them cloud over. "Definitely. Not."

"Oh. Okay. No problem." Ella wasn't surprised. Most people were too busy with their careers and families to get involved. At least they thought they were. With Reese, though, the rebuff was disappointing. It shouldn't bother her, but it did nonetheless. "We'll work it out."

"I'm sure you will." She paused. "Maybe you should ask Jeremy, the senator's brother. He was a year behind us at PMU, but I'm sure he'd like to be involved. He's always been Josh's biggest supporter."

Ella appreciated the suggestion. They had less than a year to prepare for the ceremony, where Josh Nathan would be given the Pollham Award for his accomplishments. In the interim, between her predecessor's retirement and her hiring, little had been done. Most of the people she talked to thought it would be an easy feat, but Ella had her doubts.

Bijou took off and they followed again in silence, this one not quite as comfortable as the last. After a few minutes, Ella tried again to find a common ground with Reese.

"So, Reese is an unusual name."

"It's short for Christine. When Cass was small she couldn't say Chris. It sounded more like Reese, and it stuck. From the time I was about five, everyone's called me Reese."

"I like it. It's different."

"How about you? Is Ella all there is, or have you hacked off a *nore* or something?"

Ella moved to the side as two boys on bikes came barreling

down the pathway. "Elanore? No, nothing so predictable. It's sort of abbreviated, or perhaps a nickname is a better descriptor. My given name is Elizabeth, after my grandmother, but I've always been Ella, since the day I was born."

A smile curled at the edges of Reese's mouth. "Elizabeth. Ella. I like that. It's clever. Creative."

"I wish I could take credit." They walked on, keeping Cass in sight, every once in a while giving way to bikers and pedestrians, many with dogs of their own. Cass handled Bijou beautifully, reining in his lead when others approached, giving it back when the path was clear.

It was a circuitous route, laid out with little creativity around the park's perimeter, and not very scenic. Ella had walked it a dozen times since she'd arrived in Scranton, and it seemed she already knew the park by heart. The slight tension in the air since she'd asked Reese to join the Pollham committee didn't make the stroll any more pleasant. But she was a people person, made her living by breaking through the tough outer shells of her donors to find the soft heart within. She kept trying.

"Where'd you go to med school?"

"Philly. Philadelphia Osteopathic."

Finally, common ground. Literally. "Oh, I know that area well. I lived in Manayunk for a while."

The tension between them eased as they talked about the neighborhoods where they'd lived, the museums they patronized, the restaurants they loved. And their sports.

"It was my only hesitation in leaving the city. I'll miss my teams."

"How often did you go to games? Because you can see everything on TV here. Phillies, Eagles, Flyers, and Sixers. And someone is always sponsoring a bus trip to the games, if you want to go for the day. And if you must drive yourself, well…it's only two hours."

"It doesn't seem so bad when you put it that way." Reese didn't seem so bad either, once she relaxed.

They stopped walking and found a bench as Cass hopped onto an empty swing and pushed off, Bijou running back and forth chasing her feet.

"She really loves that dog."

"Yes. My dad won't get another one—the last one got hit by a car when she let him out the door. She thought it was funny, to see everyone running around trying to catch him."

"That's awful. Did they ever think of a fence?"

"We have one. She deliberately left the gate open. It wasn't malicious. I really don't think she understood what would happen. But no more dogs for them."

"Fortunately, she has Bijou."

"Yes, but we obviously have to watch her very closely with him."

Ella felt the need to fill the silence after that sad story. "I don't have a dog, either. I have to travel a lot for my job, so it doesn't work out. Having Bijou makes me miss it, though."

"You used to have one?"

"Yes. Ironically, he got hit as well. He escaped from my ex when she opened the garage door."

"Oh, that's rough."

"Yes, she was devastated."

"She?" Reese asked suddenly, turning only her head, the question as probing as her eyes when Ella turned and met her gaze. After she'd spotted Ella kissing the man on her stoop the day of her move, Reese had assumed Ella was straight. Suddenly, the new neighbor became much more interesting.

The confession hadn't been intentional, but Ella wasn't hiding anything, either. She wondered if she'd just brought her friendship with Cass and family to a bitter end.

"Yes, she," Ella said at last, trying to remain cool, hoping it didn't matter. Reese was her age, with no ring on her finger and no mention of a man in her life. Maybe Reese played on her team. Maybe not. But the Ryans were nice people, and she'd already come to adore Cass. Hopefully, her sexuality wasn't an issue.

Then Reese smiled, and Ella felt the weight of the world lift from her shoulders.

"Good to know."

CHAPTER 8: FUN IN THE SUN

"Faster, Reese!" Cass demanded, and Reese deliberately slowed the boat to a crawl.

"No, silly. That's slower."

"I don't want you to throw up."

"I never throw up!"

Reese looked to Sophie Gates sitting on the bench seat at the rear of the boat, facing Cass. It was her boat, and she was certainly accustomed to bouncing around in the back of it, but Reese still worried about her. She was pushing eighty, and no matter how low her blood pressure or how active she was, she seemed fragile. Reese saw her at least once a week, and for many years she'd seemed timeless. That was changing. Sophie was a little slower, mentally and physically. She moved more tentatively, repeated herself more often, and forgot little details she'd once easily recalled. Reese knew she wouldn't live forever, but the idea of losing her was hard. Since Steph had died, Sophie had become like a grandmother to her.

"You heard her," Sophie said. "Let's make some wake."

Reese shook her head and opened up the throttle. The boat responded beautifully, and in seconds they were bouncing across the surface of Lake Winola toward Sophie's house. Her hair flew behind her, and she tucked her chin to prevent it from lifting the baseball cap from her head. It wouldn't have been the first of her hats to drown in the lake, but it would still piss her off.

After almost a mile, Reese saw Sophie's place approaching, and she slowed the craft. Years of practice had paid off, and she floated the boat inside its house. When the prow had cleared the opening, Reese killed the engine and hopped off, then guided it the rest of the way in.

After securing it, she climbed aboard again to help Sophie and Cass alight.

"That was fun," Sophie said as she led the way back toward her house. The stone path had been worn by a million footsteps, many of them Reese's.

"I'm hungry," Cass said.

"It's a good thing I brought food," Reese said. "Do you want to eat on the porch, Mrs. Gates? Or would you like to get out of the heat?"

"The porch is fine."

When they reached the porch, Reese retrieved paper plates and cups, and a pitcher of lemonade from the kitchen she knew as well as her own. She'd stopped at Sophie's favorite sandwich shop and procured sandwiches, salads, chips, and huge dill pickles. Since Sophie had sold her business, she had no excuse to visit the shop, so Reese made a habit of picking up her favorite treats to bring with her when she visited. After placing everything on the table, they all dug in.

"Mmm. I'll never tire of this pasta salad," Sophie said.

"Or the roast beef," Reese added.

"Or the chips," Cass said. "They're really good."

Reese sat back and watched her sister. Cass had more than her share of limitations, but her knack of saying just what everyone else thought was definitely in the plus column. Shoveling chips into her mouth while avoiding the sandwich, Cass eyed the bag. Reese knew what would come next.

"I ran out of chips," she said.

"That's because you ate them all."

"You didn't give me enough."

"I'll make a deal with you. One chip for every bite of sandwich."

Cass eyed the sandwich suspiciously and then looked at Sophie for support.

"Don't look at me, Cass. I'm not sharing my chips."

"Fine," she said as she picked up her sandwich and took a bite.

Sophie smiled at Reese. "Well done," she said.

"I like my hamburgers well done," Cass said.

"I do, too," Sophie said. "How's your turkey?"

"Not as good as my chips," she said as she bit into one, causing Reese to nearly choke on her lemonade.

"So, what's new?" Sophie asked as she handed Reese a spare napkin.

"We have a new neighbor. Her name is Ella, and she's very nice. She's watching Bijou when Pip is at college."

"I actually know Ella. Her grandparents used to live right over there," she said as she nodded toward the cottage next door. "But I didn't realize Pip is going to college."

Reese shrugged. Pip was always doing something unusual. Film school was just the latest. "She's in California, learning to make movies."

"How exciting!"

"Do you remember Miles Jones? She's staying with him."

"Of course I know who he is, but I don't really know him."

"I guess his parents and Pip's parents had some business interests together, so they know each other rather well. She'll be gone for a few months and recruited Ella to watch the house and the dog while she's away."

"I hope it works out for her."

"Me, too. Ella seems really nice, so I'm sure it will be fine." Reese had enjoyed their stroll through the park, even if she was disappointed in Ella's chosen profession. And she was curious about her, too, even more than before they'd met. Reese made it a habit to study people, much like a detective, and she'd picked up a good deal of information during the forty-minute circuit at Nay Aug. Ella was beautiful, and she worked to stay that way. Her nails were manicured, her hair highlighted, her body toned. Even on the uphill portions of the walk, she seemed at ease. She was a seasoned professional, not allowing Reese to fluster her, even when Reese had been less than kind in her remarks. And she was unmarried. There was no ring, and though on numerous occasions during their conversation Ella might have referred to a significant other, she hadn't.

She'd referred to her ex-girlfriend, of course, so Reese knew if there was an S.O., it would have been a she. Not that that mattered to her, of course. Dating, especially someone who lived in the house beside her parents', was not a high priority for her. If she did decide she wanted some female company, though, Ella wouldn't be the worst choice in a date she'd ever made. That was a big if, though.

It wasn't that she had no interest in women. She still appreciated a beautiful face and curvy figure, but she didn't seem to lust anymore. It made her feel like a total jerk, but she realized that hormones had totally driven most of her dating. Her head had never been filled with fantasies of coupling up and settling down, just having some fun and moving on. Much of that fun, she realized, was of a sexual nature. And for whatever reason, that had lost its appeal.

Just past forty and all washed up. Smiling at the thought, she glanced up and saw Sophie studying her.

"You look like you were off to someplace magnificent, my dear."

"Not so magnificent. I was thinking about how old I am."

"Can I kayak?" Cass asked.

"Sure," Sophie said. "If it's all right with Reese. She'll have to rescue you."

Abandoning the food for later, they walked back down toward the lake together, and Sophie headed up the stairs to the top of the boathouse, while Reese helped Cass. "Stay close to the dock, where I can see you, okay?" Reese asked as she walked into the water with Cass and made sure her life jacket was properly secured. When Cass was settled in her favorite blue kayak, Reese pushed her off and joined Sophie. "Remember, if you can't see me, I can't see you."

After securing an umbrella for shade, Reese sat beside Sophie and looked out at the view of the water. She'd first started coming to the lake the summer she met Steph, when she was just fourteen. Even after she died, she'd still visited Steph's parents, at first to just make sure they were okay, and then as they got older, with upkeep on the house and the dock. They really had no one else, and Reese worried about them.

"Other than my daughter, I've never seen anyone who loved to float around in a boat the way your sister does," Sophie said.

Many years of conversations with Sophie told Reese that this was the prelude, the opening she sought to bring Steph into the conversation. Not that Reese minded. Who else did she have to talk to about her forgotten daughter?

"I remember the first time I came out here. She had a sleepover, with about fifteen girls from Prep. She went around to all the neighbors and borrowed all their kayaks and canoes so we could have a regatta. Then we baked cookies and cupcakes as payment for the boat rentals."

"I remember that. Bucky's grandfather called me and warned me that I needed a permit to hold such a large event on the lake."

Reese laughed. "The apple didn't fall far from the tree, huh? Bucky is no fun at all."

"He'll make a good DA. By the book and inscrutable."

"I have a picture of him drunk and nearly naked."

Sophie's mouth dropped. "Where on earth did you get that?"

"A college party. I think it's the only time in his life he let loose. He'd just taken the law-school admission test, which coincided with medical-school admission tests, and all the Prep kids went out to celebrate. He had a good time."

"Sounds like it."

They were quiet for a moment, and Reese watched Cass trying to turn the kayak. Holding her breath, she held her tongue. If she told Cass what to do, it would probably just frustrate her, so she watched, helplessly, as her sister struggled. After a mighty tussle with the paddle, she finally managed to swing the craft around and make her way back toward the boathouse.

"He wants to reopen the investigation into her death."

Reese stiffened and turned toward Sophie. The topic still made her nervous. What if the investigators turned something up? Would it implicate her? "I heard that. But why, just to get elected? Is there new evidence or something?" Reese reached for her water, needing it for her suddenly dry mouth.

Sophie shrugged. It wasn't the reaction Reese would have expected, but then again, what was her own reaction? Mixed. Even though she had her concerns, she wanted Steph's murderer apprehended. But after all these years, did she dare get her hopes up? Clearly Sophie felt the same way, or maybe other factors were dampening her enthusiasm.

"He's relatively unknown, so perhaps something like this would generate enough publicity to help his cause."

"How do you feel about opening those old wounds?"

Sophie looked at Reese and smiled sadly. "Those wounds have never healed, my dear."

Reese swallowed the retort she would love to have shared, but how could she tell Sophie she'd loved Steph, too? What good would that do? It would only lead to questions and possibly warm the cold case and cast suspicion in her direction. The investigators had considered a boyfriend from the first, and Reese remembered being questioned about who Steph was dating. Everyone was questioned, and everyone provided the same answer: Steph dated casually but hadn't had a serious boyfriend her entire senior year. Everyone assumed she was focusing on school, getting ready for college.

No one ever considered the possibility that Steph had a girlfriend, and Reese thought it best to keep it that way.

"Between you and me, Reese, the robbery motive has always troubled me."

Reese swallowed. "Really?" She sipped her drink and cleared her throat. "Why is that?"

"If you were going to rob a house and murder the occupant, wouldn't you have taken something of value?"

"I thought he did," Reese responded, confused. The news had reported that jewelry was stolen on the night of the murder.

"Well, the newspaper reported that he'd robbed us, so I could understand why you'd think that. But look at this place." She nodded toward the house, and Reese immediately understood the implication of her statement. The house was massive, and its grandeur suggested the occupants were wealthy. Extremely wealthy.

Reese nodded, intrigued despite the danger.

"He took my college ring and few chains from a box on my dresser. You remember the thin strands of gold that were popular back then? Hardly worth more than a few hundred dollars. And Steph wasn't really into anything fancy. She had similar stuff in her jewelry box. But he completely neglected the chest in my closet. It was loaded with gold and diamonds. An emerald necklace, a ruby ring. Lots of treasures. And what about the rest of the house? Everything was intact. It doesn't appear he searched a single drawer for money. Steve had six rifles in an unlocked gun cabinet in the den. None of them were touched."

Reese listened to the words and tried to put them all together in a meaningful way. The house was robbed, but not much was taken. What did that indicate? She voiced her thoughts. "Maybe he was just spooked by Steph and ran away after the murder but before he could finish the robbery job."

"I understand what you're saying, Reese. And I've tried hard to believe it so that I could sleep for the past twenty-five years. But it's never made sense to me. A burglar walked through my front door. They found no signs of forced entry, and I know the door was locked, because I checked it before leaving. My daughter must have left him in. Then he followed her up the stairs, where she tried to escape from her balcony. He killed her and then stole some worthless jewelry."

Reese wasn't a police officer, but it seemed to make sense to her. "Why is that so difficult to believe?"

"I'm glad you asked! I've ranted to the police since the shock wore off and I was able to think things through. First, a burglar would have checked out the house. And if he watched for any amount of time, he would have known Steph was home. Every light was on in the house, and her stereo was on, too. Why break in if someone's home? Second, if you're going to bother to break in and murder someone, shouldn't you at least steal something valuable? And think about this—Steph would never have opened the front door for a stranger. Never. If she was still upstairs—that's where we left her—when she heard the doorbell, she would have gone out onto the terrace overlooking the main entrance to see who was there."

Reese nodded. That did make sense.

"What if she was downstairs?"

"The door is made of glass. She would have looked to see who was there."

Now Reese understood Sophie's concern, and her mouth went so dry she could hardly say the words. "And she wouldn't have opened it unless she knew the person standing on the other side. Oh, God, Mrs. Gates, I think you're right. Steph knew her killer."

CHAPTER 9: BACKYARD BARBECUE

It was Friday afternoon, and Ella was relaxing in the hammock hung from Pip's porch when a voice disturbed her quiet reflections.

"Do you have dinner plans? We're having a cookout, nothing fancy, but it would be nice if you could join us."

Ella turned to see Sharon Ryan leaning against the fence.

"Hi, neighbor."

"How's it going? Would you like to join us for dinner?"

Ella had purchased burgers and hot dogs at the market the day before, with just such a thought in mind. The weather was perfect for it, only she hadn't planned on company. But her neighbor's company would be nice. Sharon was funny, her husband Chris sharp, and Cass was a gem. Would Reese be there? She didn't live with her parents, but Ella noticed her car there nearly every day, so she knew it was possible she might join them. Did it matter? She'd enjoyed her company the week before and even thought about her bright blue eyes a few times. Yes, Reese was definitely attractive, but that didn't mean Ella was interested in her. But why shouldn't she be? Unless Reese was straight. That was a possibility.

Why didn't lesbians come with name tags? Something simple, like "Hello, my name is Reese and I'm a lesbian."

She'd thought about Reese the night in the park, long after returning home after their walk. "Good to know," she'd said after Ella came out to her. What did that mean? Was knowing a lesbian like knowing a doctor, who could give free medical advice, or an auto mechanic, who could fix that annoying knock your car made when it hit seventy on the highway? What was so good about knowing a lesbian, unless you were one, which was also quite possible. Reese was her age, in her early forties, and had never been married. Cass had spilled that unsolicited information on one of their walks. As far as she could tell, there was no boyfriend. Did that mean there was a girlfriend? Or the possibility of a girlfriend?

Telling herself it didn't matter, she answered Sharon. "No plans. I'd love to join you. What can I bring?" She deliberately didn't ask if Reese would be there.

"How about dessert?"

Ella wasted no time in heading to the kitchen, where she mixed all the ingredients for a chocolate cake and put it in the oven. She showered quickly, changed for the cookout, and emerged in the kitchen just in time to remove two round cake pans from the oven. After setting them out to cool, she went about drying her hair and applying her makeup.

Her hair needed cutting, and she'd made an appointment with Pip's stylist at Lox Unlimited in Dunmore. The spelling intrigued her, and she liked Pip's hair, so she figured she'd give it a try. She'd been highlighting it for years, loved the golden hues brought out by her hairdresser so much better than the brown shades nature provided. Her eyes were dark, and she highlighted them with a pencil before applying shimmering shadow. A few wrinkles were starting to appear around the corners, but she wasn't worried about them. Not yet, anyway.

Smiling at herself, she felt attractive. She knew she was. Many women, and some unwelcome men, had told her so. Yet she took extra care, knowing she wanted to look good when, and if, she met Reese at the cookout.

When the cake was complete and the clock indicated it was time, Ella carried the heavy glass cake plate and marched across the backyard. What was proper etiquette for entering a neighbor's yard? Should she knock on the fence, or give a cheerful yell, or just barge on up to the deck and have a seat?

Her angst was quieted when Reese appeared out of nowhere and opened the gate for her. "Can I take that? It looks heavy."

"Hi," Ella said as she passed the plate. "Thanks. It is. Very."

"Hmm. Is it a *pound* cake?"

She shook her head and tsked. "Lame, Reese. Extraordinarily ordinary."

Reese took the zing in stride. "Where's the little fur ball?"

Ella felt her eyes rise in surprise. "Should I bring him? I mean, I'm not sure of neighborly etiquette at all. If you hadn't opened the gate, I would have just stood there knocking. And bringing your dog along to a cookout? That seems a little too fresh."

"Not if Cass is around."

"Should I go get him?"

"I would. Or she'll just pester you until you do."

Bijou seemed to know the plan and scrambled out the door toward the gate before Ella had a chance to leash him. When she finally caught him and attached the lead to his collar, Cass was standing at the door waiting.

"Hi, Bijou and Ella. Do you want a hamburger or a hot dog? I have to count them."

"A burger, please," Ella said as she made her way toward an old-fashioned picnic table made of wooden slats. It was piled high with plates and cups, bottles of soft drinks, and plastic containers of food. Her cake, on its glass plate, sat in the center.

"Have a seat," Reese said. "What can I get you to drink? Beer, some sort of cheap, probably deadly white wine, soda, water. You name it."

"The wine sounds interesting."

"My mom usually buys whatever's on sale. Brand and variety matter not. If it's less than seven bucks, she brings it home."

"I see. And what would you prefer? The most expensive bottle?"

Reese shook her head. "Nope. I prefer vodka."

A smile spread across her face. "I didn't realize that was a choice."

Reese winked. "Coming right up. How would you like it?"

Ella couldn't resist a little tease. "Neat."

Reese's eyes flew open wide. "I'm running with the big dogs now."

Ella laughed. "I'm kidding. Tonic and lime, please."

"Whew. That's a relief. I would've worried about you making it across the yard later on."

"While you take care of the mixology, is there anything I can do?"

"When the time comes, you can cut the pound cake, but until then, just relax and enjoy. How are you settling in?"

"It's been a smooth transition, both at work and home." Ella pursed her lips. "Home. It's funny to think of Pip's place as home, but I guess it is, for now."

"Hold that thought," Reese said, and she ran into the house. Dressed in faded blue jeans and black, tapered T-shirt, she looked great. And the view of her ass she ran into the house was fabulous as well.

Ella turned her attention to Cass, who was throwing a ball to Bijou. The dog hopped and ran in circles before dropping it at her feet, starting the cycle all over again. The joy on Cass's face filled Ella with happiness, and she was startled when Reese reappeared with their drinks.

"Thanks," Ella said.

Raising her glass toward Ella's, Reese nodded. "To new beginnings."

"Yes." Ella sipped the drink and found it to be perfect, then told Reese so.

"I have some experience with mixing drinks. If the ER gig doesn't work out, I may open a bar. But you were saying this is home *for now*. Don't you plan on staying in the mountains? Is this just a step on your career ladder?"

Ella didn't hesitate. She'd been thinking about that question for weeks, and after just a short time, she knew the answer. "No, the temporary part is about Pip's place, not the job. I love it here, and unless something horrific happens, I think I'll spend the rest of my career here. I can visit friends in Philly if I want, see my parents a few times a year in Florida, but I'd like to come home at night to this," Ella said, waving her free hand around the yard. "To have a little space and a little place that's calm and peaceful."

"Hello, Ella," Sharon said as she made her way across the yard carrying a plate of raw burgers and dogs. Reese jumped up and took the plate from her. "Do you mind cooking, Reese? If we wait for your father, we might be here all night."

"On it," she said.

Ella watched as Reese bent to light the grill, inspected her spatula and fork, and then finally the grill itself. When everything seemed to be to her liking, she checked the temperature gauge and joined Ella and her mother at the table, where she took a sip of her drink. Ella watched as she closed her eyes and seemed to savor it for a moment.

When she opened them and caught Ella staring, she smiled. "You're right. That is perfect." Turning to her mom, Reese said, "Ella thinks she'd like to stay in the mountains, Mom."

"Well, that's wonderful. I think a house is coming up for sale in the next block." She continued in a near whisper. "Mr. Flowers passed away."

"He didn't die in the house, did he?" Ella asked. "That would freak me out."

Sharon laughed. "Okay, then. Cross that one off the list. Maybe you should wait a while anyway, Ella. What if you don't like the job?

What if you don't like it here? It snows a lot, you know. Maybe you should wait until the winter's over before you decide."

"Lately, I think we've had more snow in Philly than you've had here."

"We still get our share, don't worry," Reese said before turning back to the grill. After checking the temperature once again, she carefully pulled the plastic wrap from the food and rolled it into a little ball. She made a show of throwing it into the trash. Then she meticulously arranged the burgers in a neat line across the front of the grill before returning to the conversation. Ella appreciated how Reese handled the food and thought Reese must be a great doctor. Attention to detail in medicine was obviously important.

Turning her thoughts back to the conversation, she drank her vodka and tonic. "I've spent a lot of time here, mostly in the summer, though."

"Really?" Reese asked. She didn't seem surprised. "Doing what?"

She told them about her summers at the lake. As she spoke, she noticed Reese looking away, as if something was drawing her attention. Or as if Ella didn't have the ability to capture it.

"Reese spent some summers at the lake, too. In high school. She had a dear, dear friend, Stephanie Gates, who lived there."

At the mention of Steph's name, Reese turned to Ella and flashed a guilty grin. "Mrs. Gates told me your grandparents lived at the lake. What a small world."

Ella was speechless. She supposed it shouldn't have surprised her—after all, they were the same age, but still, what where the chances that she would meet people who'd known Steph? Who still knew her mom?

"Steph was my best friend at the lake. I stopped by to see her mom when I heard what had happened to her."

Reese surveyed her for a moment before speaking. "I'm sure it made her happy to see you."

Ella nodded. "I think it did. I wasn't sure how it would go. I thought it might upset her to see me, you know—all those memories—but she was fine. We're going to see each other again."

"Did she serve you lunch?" Reese asked softly.

"Cookies," Ella said with a nod.

"She still entertains, and I don't know how she does it. I don't think I could live in that house, knowing someone murdered my daughter there," Sharon said.

Ella had been thinking the same thing and told them so.

Reese took a gulp of her drink. "Where else would she go? All she had of Steph, all her memories are in that house. Why give up seventeen years of good memories because of one bad one?"

"I'll say it's a bad one," Sharon said. "Couldn't get any worse."

Reese stood and went to check on the grill, and once again, Ella studied her. Instead of the relaxed posture she'd shown earlier, she now seemed tense, holding herself erect. Talking about Steph hadn't been good for Reese. It probably hadn't been good for her, either.

"Well, it is a small world," Ella said, "even if that is a cliché."

"It certainly is," Sharon said, and then she ordered Cass into the house to announce dinner to her father.

Ella had met Chris Ryan on a few occasions since moving into the house beside his, and each time he found a new way to charm her. He talked sports, politics, money, food, and every other topic Ella could ever wish to discuss. He didn't dominate the conversation, though, just added insightful comments and seemed to direct the exchange among everyone else.

"Perfect timing," he said. "The Phillies game will be on in half an hour."

And then, just as he had on the other occasions she'd been with him, he engaged them all in a discussion of baseball. Reese served the burgers and dogs, Bijou rested in the shade of the tree, and the humans dug into their food as they debated Pete Rose's chances of getting reinstated to major-league baseball. Like everyone else, Reese took part in the conversation, but she seemed distracted. The light mood they'd shared at the beginning of the evening had changed, and Ella wanted more than anything to get it back.

In spite of his earlier claims about watching the game, after their food, Sharon and Chris followed Cass and Bijou to the park, leaving Ella and Reese to clean up. They sat for a moment, looking at each other. "Are you okay?" Ella asked. The sadness in Reese's eyes was unmistakable.

Ella watched as Reese took a deep breath and slowly exhaled. "Just tired. I had a busy day at work."

Holding her with her eyes, Ella nodded. She was sure Reese was lying, or at least smudging the truth, but she wouldn't push. What right did she have? She'd only just met Reese, and if she didn't want to talk about Steph, Ella wouldn't push. "I can understand that."

Working together, they had the picnic cleaned up in just a few minutes. Reese found dessert plates and a large cake knife and carried them outside.

"Do you want to join them at the park?" Reese asked.

Even if Reese was lying, Ella really was tired. She'd put in sixty hours at the office that week, and the vodka wasn't helping her energy level. "I'd be happy to sit and talk."

They traded the picnic table for padded deck chairs, and Reese poured them both another drink before she settled in. "Have you heard from Pip?" she asked.

"Actually, I have, and she doesn't seem happy. She says Miles Jones is kind of strange. She's staying in his guest house, and they're both working all the time, so she doesn't see him much, but when she does, he creeps her out."

Shaking her head, she remembered the young man who'd grown up in Scranton and ran away to Hollywood, never to return. "He was always a strange dude," Reese said and sipped her drink.

"You know him, too?" When Reese nodded, Ella shook her head. "Is there anyone in town you don't know?"

"Probably a few people, but not many. Don't forget, I've lived here all my life, and went to college here, too."

"Did you go to school with Miles?"

"Yeah." Reese was used to questions about Miles. He'd been very successful in Hollywood, first as an actor, and then as a producer. At interviews, he often mentioned his "humble" beginning. As if being the heir to a mining fortune was humble! But she knew his success was due more to his good looks and hard work than his family money.

"What's he like?"

Laughing, Reese shook her head. "I haven't seen him in twenty years. As far as I know, he doesn't come back here. His parents are dead, and I don't think he has much family."

"What was he like then?"

Ella's reaction to the inside information on a huge Hollywood start was pretty typical. She sat forward a little, listening to every word. Sometimes it bothered her that people probed the way they did into Miles's private life—there was even a Miles Jones tour in the visitor guide. You could visit the home where he was raised, the open-air theatre in the park he'd donated to the city, the graves of his ancestors. Reese thought it absurd, yet the business seemed to flourish. And while other people's questions might have annoyed her, Ella's didn't. She enjoyed talking to Ella. It was becoming clear that her mom and Cass had been right. Ella was someone special.

Clearing her throat, she answered the question. "Unique. He wore clothes that would make your head spin—period clothes, punk, leather, tuxedos, short-shorts. His hair was many colors, different lengths. Sometimes he wore wigs or long beards. His parents were members of the country club, and he was a great golfer, but he was always getting tossed off the course for improper clothing. He was always trying to turn heads. His family was loaded, and he never let anyone forget it. He lavished people with gifts—I mean out of nowhere, unexpected things. One day in college he rented a bus and took everyone who could fit in to New York, bought everyone tickets to see a Broadway show, and then bought everyone dinner. I don't know about you, but in college I didn't have much money to throw around. Miles rained money. He threw catered parties, always with some theme or another, put together spectacular theatrical productions, ran charity concerts to raise money. Yet he always seemed lonely, like he didn't let anyone really close. He was surrounded by people, but he didn't fit in with them. Even the theater crowd, who he worked with every day."

"His movies are different, that's for sure."

"He's like a blond Johnny Depp. At least his movies are similar."

"Maybe I'm just not smart enough to understand his message."

Reese chortled. "I can sum it up for you. It's okay to be different. Very different."

After a pleasant pause, Reese broke the silence. "So tell me about you, Ella. Other than the obvious."

"What's obvious?"

"You live over there," she said, nodding toward Pip's house. "And you work at PMU."

"I drive a convertible."

"Obviously."

"Is that too obvious?"

Reese squinted. "Obviously."

Ella smiled at the pleasant banter they were enjoying, and was happy in the reality that she'd made a friend. "I like to bake."

Reese nodded toward the cake. "I'm going to have to give you another drink so you'll loosen up."

"Trust me. If you give me another drink, I'll be unconscious."

"But will you talk?"

"You think I'll talk in my sleep?"

"I think I'd like to find out."

Ella felt her mouth open as she watched Reese blush. "I didn't mean that. I'm so sorry."

Realizing she could have a lot of fun teasing Reese and find out exactly what she wanted to know, Ella didn't let her off the hook. "Do you make a habit of spying on women while they sleep?"

Shifting in her chair, Reese studied her glass for a moment, as if the answer was hidden in the melting cubes of ice. She seemed to wrestle with a smile before managing to keep her expression neutral. "Well, I'd rather watch women than men, but sadly, I don't have the chance to do it often."

Bingo! Ella thought as she fought the desire to raise her arms in triumph.

"That's hard to imagine," Ella said after a moment. She might have been flirting, but in reality, she was only stating the obvious. Reese was a successful, attractive woman, with a wonderful sense of humor. She was kind. She was sweet. What more could anyone want?

"Thanks."

It was time to change the subject. "Golf."

"What?"

"I like to play golf. I've been hitting balls, getting ready for the PMU tournament next week."

Once again, Ella surprised her, and Reese didn't know why. The golf tournament was a fund-raiser; of course Ella would be there. Why hadn't she thought of that? "What a coincidence. I'm on the tournament committee."

"Get out! It'll be a blast! I've never played the course, though. I hear it's a beast."

"Not if you hit the ball perfectly straight and can land your irons on the green with enough backspin that they don't end up in a trap."

"Yeah. Not me."

"Me neither, but that's why we play captain and crew."

"Who's on your team?"

"Colleagues from the hospital. How about yours?"

"Development people."

Reese would have loved to ask more, but Bijou's bark signaled her family's return. She fought her disappointment. It would have been nice to talk to Ella all night. Her dad demanded cake, though, and Ella served it as Cass complained about the brevity of their walk. The sky was already turning the colors of sunset, though, and it would be dark soon. "You don't want to get lost in the dark, do you?" she asked.

Waving her hand dismissively, Cass quieted Reese. "Bijou can find his way home in the dark. And that's why I have a flashlight."

Laughter erupted from the table. "It's hard to argue with that logic," Reese said.

Ella smiled at her, floated in the pools of her eyes, warmed by the obvious love she saw there. Reese held her gaze for a moment before turning her head, and Ella couldn't help but feel a little lost when Reese looked away.

CHAPTER 10: SUSPICIOUS MINDS

He turned the postcard over and over in his hand, studying it. It had arrived in the mail the day before, and he'd been playing with it since, wondering what to do next. Did he have to do anything? The announcement of his reunion at Pocono Mountains University should have brought him some happiness, but it only reminded him of the trouble all around him. Everyone he talked to these days spoke of one thing and one thing only—the Stephanie Gates case.

A reliable source told him the authorities had no new evidence to implicate her killer, but they did have a new lead. With a little push from Steph's mom, the investigators had changed their focus and were now strongly considering the possibility that a random burglar hadn't killed Steph, but someone she knew. Back then, everyone was questioned, but it was just a formality. From the outset they'd fallen for the drama he'd staged, convinced a burglar had done the deed. The police had gone through the motions, asking friends about enemies, talking to teachers and teammates, quizzing every romantic interest she'd ever had—including him.

In the end, their questions had led nowhere, because they really had no proof of anything. No one knew anything, no one saw anything, no one found anything. No one even suspected anything. The theory about the burglar won out, because it seemed more probable than one of Steph's classmates turning on her in a rabid moment.

Now that they were reconsidering their stance, the police would come calling again. As one of her classmates, he'd surely be interviewed. And of course, he knew what he'd say. The same thing he'd said then. Practically nothing. He'd dated Steph off and on but knew her mainly because of their common academic and extracurricular pursuits at PMP.

He didn't know anyone who'd want to hurt her. He couldn't imagine a motive for killing her. He had an alibi.

He was safe, right? The police hadn't given him a second thought then, had only questioned him because they'd questioned everyone who might know something—and with the paucity of information, that meant everyone. They had absolutely no reason to suspect him now.

So why did he feel this anxiety, this irritating inability to focus on anything but the most basic task? Why did he feel vulnerable?

The obvious answer was, of course, that he'd killed her. He was the only one on the planet with a reason to feel nervous, because he was guilty.

Or did someone else have a reason for concern as well?

In the years after the murder, time and again he'd asked himself the same question. Why? Why had Steph done that to him? Before he killed her, she'd said she'd explain it one day. Why couldn't she explain it then? What was so difficult that she couldn't talk about it?

It made no sense, no matter how he tried to understand it, until one year at Christmas, when Reese had gathered them all at her house for a little party. The attendees were mostly from Prep, with a few other friends she'd met at PMU. She was on break from med school, and the rest of them still lived in the area or were home for the holidays as well.

Reese, always somewhat reserved, was obviously very nervous. He knew something was going on but had no idea what until she brought them all together in the living room at her parents' house and told them all she was gay.

Some of their friends said they'd always known it, some suspected it, and some—like him—were flabbergasted. He supposed he'd just never thought about Reese's sexuality, but when he did, all the clues were there. Reese never dated. She had many friends who were boys, but no boyfriends. And in their senior year at Prep, when his relationship with Steph was crumbling, it seemed that Reese and Steph grew closer and closer.

Ignoring the crowd at Reese's house that night, he drifted back to high school. All the nights Reese had slept over at Steph's house. Even when she had a ride back from the lake, Reese would find an excuse to spend the night. He'd always thought they were just good friends. The student council trip to Washington, when they could have switched rooms without the chaperones knowing, Steph had elected to stay put, holed up in the hotel room alone with Reese. She'd told him she didn't want to get into any trouble, but he knew now it was more than that. Steph wanted to be with Reese. And on their senior trip to Florida, it was the same situation. Many of the kids had elected to bunk four to a room, to save money. He'd only booked one roommate, because he knew Steph and Reese were staying together. Instead of the romantic time he'd envisioned when they switched rooms, he'd spent most of the trip looking for Steph because she kept disappearing with Reese.

Until Reese came out to him, he'd thought of her as a good friend to both him and Steph. At that moment he realized she wasn't a friend at all. She'd been Steph's lover. She was the reason Steph hurt him.

In the years that had passed since then, he'd never said a word to Reese about what he knew. What would have been the point? It would certainly have strained their relationship, and it might have even made him look suspicious in Reese's eyes, because why would he really care about Steph's sexuality? But now that the police were looking into the murder again, he might say something to them about Reese and Steph. Wasn't the significant other always the first suspect?

He needed to consider something else, too. The loose end. What exactly did Cass Ryan remember about that night? He'd always played it cool around her, just in case she understood that the night he showed up at Nay Aug Park and borrowed two bucks was the same night Steph had been murdered. They'd never talked about it, so he didn't know for sure what she knew. Maybe it was time to find out.

CHAPTER 11: THE SCHOLARSHIP

There's a Sophie Gates on the line for you."

Reflexively, Ella looked at the intercom through which her assistant's voice had just projected and smiled. "Thanks, Carm," she said as she picked up the line. "Hello, Mrs. Gates."

"Hello to you. How are you settling in? How's the new job?"

"It's all good."

"Would you happen to be free for dinner tonight? I have to run into Scranton to meet with my attorney this afternoon, and I thought it would be nice to go out."

Ella had no plans for the night. It had been raining all afternoon and the forecast was the same for the evening, so golf was out of the question. After she walked Bijou—probably a short walk because of the weather—she'd settle in with some work or perhaps watch television. Nothing that couldn't be put off in favor of a better offer. And having dinner with Sophie was definitely a better offer. Although their last meeting had been emotional, she had no doubt she wanted to see her again. It was the least she could do to honor the memory of her old friend and of her grandmother, who'd been a friend to Sophie. "I'd love to."

They set the time, and Ella settled back into her desk chair and then finally decided to call it a day. It was early, but that was okay. If she punched a clock, she'd have overtime on the books every week.

Bijou was thrilled to see her, and Ella made sure the gates were locked before she headed into the house to change. There was a temporary break in the storm, and the sun peeked through the clouds a few minutes later when she came back outside to find him chasing a frog through the garden. She hesitated only a moment before opening the gate to the Ryans' yard in search of Cass. She didn't have much time before her dinner with Mrs. Gates, but knowing how much Cass loved walking the dog, it was an easy decision.

Cass was excited to see them both, and after asking her mom's permission, she joined Ella and Bijou. Ella was relieved that Sharon didn't come along. She wanted to know more about Reese, and Cass was the perfect one to tell her.

"How was your day?" she asked Cass.

"Boring."

Ella laughed. "Why was it boring?"

"Nothing happened."

"I guess that's how it is sometimes on rainy days." She paused for a minute. "How's Reese?"

"Good."

Okay. That was easy. "Where does Reese live?"

"In her house."

Ella laughed, but she realized Cass was serious. "What's her house like?"

"I like it because she has stools to sit on. And she lets me eat by the TV. And sometimes deer come in her yard and I can see them."

Ella gathered from the information that Reese didn't live in the city, but considering the mountains surrounding them on all sides, Cass's description didn't narrow the location down. "Does she live in Scranton?"

Cass pursed her lips in thought, and then suddenly her face lit up. "She lives by Lake Scranton. But you still have to drive in the car if you want to go to her house."

Ella bit her lip. What had she expected? Perhaps she should treasure her career in development, because her chances as a detective weren't looking good.

The rest of their walk was uneventful, and after returning home, she gave Bijou his dinner and hurried up the stairs to change. Mrs. Gates had told her the State Street Grill in Clarks Summit was casual, so she pulled on a lightweight sweater, jeans, and loafers, then covered her shoulders with a blazer before heading out. It was an easy, fifteen-minute drive, and she found her date waiting at their table.

After hugging Mrs. Gates, Ella threw her blazer over the back of an empty chair and sat beside her. Looking around, she decided she liked the place. The bar at one end of the room seemed well stocked, and cocktail tables all around were filled. Mrs. Gates had claimed a cozy table for two in the corner, and from there Ella saw all varieties of people coming and going. There were no kids, but the age of the patrons ranged from twenty-something to seventy-something. A glance at the eclectic menu told Ella her first impression was spot-on, and if the food was any good, she knew she'd be visiting the restaurant again.

"So, what's new? How's the investigation going?"

Sophie's eyes brightened. "Finally, they're listening to me. After Bucky brought Steph back into the limelight, some detectives came and talked to me again about that night. I told them my theory, explained how Steph would never have let a stranger in, and they thought it made sense. They're questioning everyone again. Her classmates, her teammates, people from the print shop. Everyone."

"Did Steph have a boyfriend?" If Ella had to guess, she would have thought Steph was gay. Not that she'd known about such matters at the age of twelve, but when she looked back on it all later, she understood that Steph was her first crush. And it seemed to be a mutual feeling, although who really knew? They never had the chance to explore it.

"She dated a dozen boys, but no one serious. It seems like she enjoyed dating until her senior year. Then she started to focus more on school and her friends, as if she knew she was going away and didn't want to get involved."

"So there really is no one who looks guilty, is there?"

"I'm afraid not. But maybe someone will finally come forward with information. Someone out there has to know something."

Ella squeezed Sophie's hand. "I really hope it works out and they find the killer."

"Me, too."

The waitress interrupted with a query about drinks.

"I'm so happy you called me," Ella said after perusing the menu for a few moments.

"I've been thinking about you since you visited me, Ella. Something you said really resonated with me, and the more I debate it, the more convinced I am that it's the right thing to do."

Confused, Ella shook her head. "I'm sorry. I think I missed something. What are you talking about?"

"A scholarship, Ella. I want to start a scholarship at PMU, in memory of my daughter."

Ella turned and sat back in her chair. This wasn't the first time someone had said those words to her, but this was different. She'd never been involved in a scholarship memorializing someone she actually knew. Furthermore, she wasn't sure Mrs. Gates understood exactly what a scholarship involved.

"Thanks," she said as the waitress placed a vodka and tonic in front of her and then took their dinner orders. After she'd left, Ella took a sip before responding to Mrs. Gates. "Wow, a scholarship. That's wonderful."

A huge smile spread across Sophie's face. "Yes, it is. I've been thinking about the word you used. Legacy. Stephanie was my legacy, and now she's gone. When I'm dead, a few friends will still remember her, but once they're gone, she'll be forgotten. But if I give a scholarship in her name, a part of her will live forever. Or at least as long as PMU is around, which I think should be for a considerable amount of time."

"What a lovely idea," Ella said as she squeezed Sophie's hand again. "What sort of scholarship do you have in mind, Mrs. Gates?"

Looking confused, she squinted at Ella. "How many kinds are there?"

Ella tried not to sound too official. This was, after all, a dinner date. "It can be full or partial, or even something as basic as paying for a student's textbooks."

Sophie nodded. "I love this idea, Ella. I love the idea of celebrating my daughter like this. Could I choose who gets the scholarship?"

"Not per se. You can't give it to your neighbor's cousin, for instance. But you can establish criteria, such as the gender of the recipient, the religion, the ethnicity. It could be for people from your grandmother's hometown in Bolivia. You can designate it for pre-vet students, since Steph wanted to be a vet. You can give it to children of servicemen and women killed in action. It's your money, so you can set the parameters. You can make it as vague or specific as you'd like."

"*Specifically*, how much would this cost me?"

Ella laughed. "Again, it's up to you. You can give five hundred dollars or five million. You can pay for books, a portion of tuition, a meal plan, or all of the above."

"How much would the 'all of the above' option be?"

Ella studied her for a moment, looking for some clue to her frame of mind. There was no joking smile. She was serious.

"Whew. Full tuition, room and board, with books, for one student— for example, one student gets the scholarship for four years, and then when they graduate, another student gets the scholarship, as opposed to a new student every year, meaning four students going to school at any one time, which is what you sometimes see with corporate gifts—one student every four years would cost about a million dollars."

"I didn't realize PMU was so costly," she said and sipped her drink.

Her response didn't surprise or disappoint Ella. Many people inquired about creating scholarships, but most didn't follow through. Fortunately, she hadn't come to dinner with Sophie to solicit money but simply to enjoy her company.

"It's not, really. Our tuition is reasonable for a private school of our size. But that money—the million dollars, for example—is invested. Only the dividends are actually spent on things like housing and meals. The cost of the tuition is theoretical, since the university doesn't have to pay itself. But in this kind of financial market, the interest on a million dollars isn't very much money."

"Don't I know it? But I think I understand what you're saying. If I want to give a scholarship to one student every four years, it would cost a million. If I want to give a four-year scholarship every year, it would cost four million. Is that correct?"

Ella sipped her drink and nodded. "You got it. It's a lot of money."

"What else am I going to spend it on? Let's go with the four million."

CHAPTER 12: THE LOOSE END

Ella didn't often have difficulty sleeping because of work, but last night had been one of those times. Her head was spinning so off center she was surprised she made it home in one piece. Even a relaxing bath in Pip's Jacuzzi tub didn't quiet her mind.

Out of nowhere, and totally unsolicited, Sophie Gates was donating four million dollars to PMU. The paint was barely dry on Ella's door, and she'd landed her first multimillion-dollar gift. Sleep was the last thing on her mind. Since she'd left the restaurant she'd been thinking of the scholarship. How they'd announce it. The story they'd tell about Steph. The first student who'd be chosen to memorialize her old friend. She had so much to think about, so much to plan, and since she'd known Steph—although briefly—she was even more excited to be a part of the scholarship.

Ella had stayed late with Sophie at the restaurant, just talking. She really was an amazing woman, and Ella suspected she had a great deal to do with accumulating the fortune she wanted to give to PMU. Although she suspected Steve Gates had gotten much of the credit for the success of their printing company, Sophie seemed to know the business inside and out and had a keen mind as well.

As Ella lay there, still thinking about the Stephanie Gates scholarship, she was grateful she didn't have to get up and go to work on the little sleep she'd had. The PMU golf tournament was today, and since she'd be there late, she'd scheduled the morning off.

She whacked the snooze button when the alarm sounded for the second time and rolled onto her side, her mind racing. Setting up a scholarship involved a number of steps, and normally, she would have started the process immediately. But this time, she was holding back. Four million dollars was a huge gift, and while Sophie Gates could apparently afford it, Ella wanted to give her the chance to reconsider without any pressure from the university. She'd seemed shocked at the cost of the full package and might decide on another way to spend her money if she had a few days to think it through. On Tuesday, if Ella hadn't received a call canceling the plan, she'd move ahead with it. For now, she'd have to concentrate on not bouncing around like she'd just won the lottery, because, in the development world, she had. It wasn't a super, mega jackpot, but it was a big one.

The alarm sounded for the third time, and Ella pulled the mask from her eyes and immediately closed them. If the sun peeking around the blinds was any clue, the rain had cleared. Pulling herself out of bed, she opened the door to the balcony facing the park and stepped outside.

It was indeed clear, with few clouds marring a bright sky. It was cool, but Ella had read the forecast and knew by the time she teed off, the temperature would be in the high seventies. Perfect golf weather.

Glancing down, Ella noticed a man on the sidewalk in front of the Ryans' house. He wore sunglasses and a navy-blue ball cap, with a green Phillies *P*. She'd never seen an Irish Phillies cap before, but she supposed that's what it was. She was surprised when the man turned and walked up the sidewalk and rang the Ryans' doorbell.

She hadn't been their neighbor for very long, but Ella knew enough about the Ryan family to be concerned about the stranger. Unfortunately, she couldn't see their front door from her angle, but she stared in that direction anyway, contemplating what to do. She could go over there and make sure everything was okay, or she could simply call Sharon. She'd decided on the latter course of action when the man reappeared on the sidewalk, talking with both Cass and Sharon. Good! Whoever he was, he obviously knew the Ryans quite well. Ella watched as Sharon retrieved the newspaper from the box, and the stranger and Cass disappeared across the street and into the park.

Exhaling loudly, Ella shook her head. You have to stop watching *CSI*, she told herself and turned to get ready.

❖

He'd parked in the same place he had all those years ago, because the spot afforded some anonymity. He looked just like any other visitor to the park, rather than a guest of the Ryans. The last thing he wanted was for anyone to know he'd been there.

Mrs. Ryan answered the door and invited him in while she called Cass.

"I was wondering if you'd like to have a doughnut with me." He held up a bag from Krispy Kreme and waved it at Cass.

The smile on her face nearly melted him. Nearly. This was no longer a world where they could both exist, and he'd come to understand that. And if only one of them could live, he thought he had more to offer than she did. She had to be sacrificed.

Across the street in the park they found an empty bench, and they sat, facing each other.

"What are you up to?" he asked. "Is the baseball season over?"

"Pretty soon," she said, more interested in the food than the conversation.

Reaching into his pocket, he pulled two dollar bills out and placed them on the table. He'd often given her two dollars when he'd seen her. It was sort of his way of hiding in plain sight, making light of what was one of the most important events of his life.

She was interested in the money, and it disappeared into her pocket in a flash.

"How long have I been giving you two dollars?" he asked, beginning the script he'd written and practiced in his mind a dozen times.

Licking her fingers, she shrugged. "A long time."

"It has been. I think it's been since I was in college."

"I don't remember," she said.

Sighing with relief, he bit his doughnut, and then did something he rarely did—talked with food in his mouth. "Really? I thought you remember everything. Reese says you never forget a thing." If she really didn't remember, maybe he wouldn't have to kill her.

"Well, I don't remember exactly, but I know it was the time when Steph died."

Nearly choking, he swallowed hard. "What makes you say that?"

Looking at him as if he were the one with the intellectual disability, she answered. "First, I had eight dollars. When I gave you two dollars, I only had six. Then I gave one dollar to Reese to buy flowers for Steph, because she died, and I only had five left. Then you gave me two dollars back at graduation, and I had seven, and I was very happy."

If he wasn't so sad, he would have laughed. There was no question now. He was going to have to kill Cass.

CHAPTER 13: TEE TIME

Reese pulled up to the bag-drop kiosk in front of Pocono Farms Country Club and popped the hatch of her Jeep.

"Can I have your name, please?" the attendant asked as he appeared at her window.

"Reese Ryan," she said.

After he scanned the computer sheet, without finding her name, she spoke up. "I believe I'm in group 10A."

He eyed her suspiciously. "Are you psychic?"

"Yes. And I'm also on the tournament committee."

"Ah, well, that explains it. Welcome to the Farms," he said, and directed her toward the parking lot.

Only a few cars had pulled in ahead of her, and Reese wasn't surprised. It was still two hours until the twelve o'clock shotgun start for PMU's annual alumni golf tournament, and she knew most of the people who'd want to hit balls before playing would arrive an hour or so ahead of time. Since she'd helped organize the event, she was expected to be here before those early birds arrived, to make sure everyone who signed up got here, and to figure out what to do with the people who didn't register but showed up anyway.

The club was taking care of placing sponsors' signs on tee boxes and greens, as well as the lunch buffet, and the alumni director had the welcome bags, so all Reese had to do was welcome people, sign them in, and thank them for their support. When the horn blew, she'd tee off with three of her colleagues from the hospital, all PMU grads and great golfers. Not only did her group sponsor a hole for the event, but they usually took home the first-place trophy.

Only one obligation prevented her from heading directly to the driving range—she needed to purchase gift certificates. As a thank-you to the club for all their work toward making the golf tournament a success, she always bought them at the club's pro shop. They typically offered a variety of men's and women's clothing, as well as a large selection of equipment. With a check in hand, she headed for the shop.

It was a magnificent late-summer day, the Friday before Labor Day, and Reese wore black shorts and a white golf shirt. Boring, she knew, but she liked her outfit anyway. Fashion awards were never her goal, and she thought she looked fine while still feeling comfortable in her clothing. If she was fortunate enough to win a prize this year, she planned to use it on a new pair of golf shoes. Black ones.

Stopping just a step inside the pro-shop door, Reese looked around in disbelief. The shop was nearly empty. A clearance rack held a few shirts, most of them hanging between the XL and XXL men's placards, but the walls and shelves were bare.

"What the fuck?" she asked under her breath as she approached the counter.

A cheerful young man greeted her enthusiastically.

"Where's all your merchandise?" she asked.

"Oh, we're doing a big remodeling job over the winter, so we've had everything on clearance since the end of July. Then we don't have to store it."

Trying to hide her irritation, Reese bit her lip. "Where's Tom?" she asked.

"I can get him, but I'm sure I can help you."

"What's your name?"

"Jonah."

"Okay, Jonah, here's the problem. Every year I buy gift certificates to use as prizes for the golf tournament. Fifteen *hundred* dollars' worth of gift certificates. I don't think you have fifteen *dollars'* worth of merchandise for the winners to buy. So what do I do now?"

Reese had a check, payable to the golf course, just for the prizes. And the players loved this type of award. Rather than getting a putter they didn't want, or balls they'd never use, they could buy exactly what they wanted with their prize money. But not this year. Since many of them were from out of town, they weren't likely to come back just to spend a hundred dollars at the shop.

Jonah nodded solemnly. "I'll get Tom."

A minute later, the pro was standing in front of her, apologizing for his error.

"Okay, well, I've registered my displeasure, but what do I do now? Is there a sporting goods store nearby? Maybe I can get some gift cards there."

"Reese, I don't want you to do that. How about this? What if I double the value of the gift certificates, at no additional charge to you? Maybe people won't mind driving back if they have a little extra money to spend."

Reese didn't even have to think about it. Offering her hand, she smiled. "Deal." She handed him the check and turned at the sound of a voice.

"I hope you bought some extra golf balls, Reese. I hear the rough is knee-high."

Reese turned and stepped into Senator Josh Nathan's open arms. "Hi, buddy. How are you?"

"Super. How about you?"

Reese squeezed him tight before stepping back to look at him. "Perfect. How's your mom?"

"Doing great. They switched the medication and no more stomach bleeding. Thanks for taking such good care of her."

"It was my pleasure. How long are you in town? Did you bring your trophy wife and perfect children?"

"As a matter of fact, I did. We're going to look at some lakefront property to build a house. Something with an in-law suite for my mom. This little bleeding episode was a real wake-up call for me. I don't know how much time she has, and I want the kids to be able to spend some time with her."

"It would be nice if you move home."

He shook his head. "I think so, too. Wanna hit some balls?" he asked.

Reese linked her arm in his, and they headed to the range.

She needed to hit some balls. To practice, yes. But to knock down her anxiety as well. Organizing the golf tournament this year had been especially stressful, with all the talk about Steph's murder. No one knew that they'd been lovers. In the early nineties, kids didn't come out in high school. Now that she was out, and Steph's murder was being investigated, Reese thought it a logical question.

How would she answer it? Convinced that Sophie didn't know, Reese had never bared her soul about her feelings for Steph. When Steph died, she had lost not only her best friend, but her lover as well. She'd been forced to mourn the woman she loved in silence, because to do otherwise would have been to out herself and her dead girlfriend.

She'd seen no point in doing that. Steph had died in the closet, and Reese didn't want to posthumously drag her out.

Could she lie to the police to protect Steph? Should she? At the back of her mind was the fear that she'd be the number-one suspect. And even though she was home that night, in bed with a terrible migraine, the only one who could testify to that was her sister, the one with a faulty memory and a vivid imagination.

If she ever became a suspect in Steph's murder, she was really screwed. Shaking the thought from her mind, she walked toward the driving range.

❖

"I'm so happy the weather turned out nice," Ella said. "It'll give me a chance to circulate and meet some of our alums." She was also happy for the chance to wear a new golf skirt she'd picked up at the end of the season. It was red and white with a bold floral print, and the white shirt with pearly red buttons matched perfectly. And though she was still flabbergasted by Sophie Gates's four-million-dollar gift, the reality seemed to buoy her just a bit. Less than a month on the job, and she'd landed one of the biggest gifts PMU had ever received.

"There's usually a great turnout, no matter what the weather. But at least people will be in a good mood," Mary Ann Bingham said.

"I'm going to get something to eat and circulate," Ella said. "I'll catch up with you after the golf." A few steps from the dining room, Ella saw the registration line, already three deep.

"Can I help you, ma'am?"

Looking up to the voice she already recognized, Ella met Reese's gaze. Her heart thudded as the blue eyes twinkled at her. "I was looking for a friendly face. I guess I got lucky."

Reese's blush rose from beneath the white collar of her shirt and bloomed over her face. Ella was beginning to enjoy seeing Reese blush, and it seemed she had a knack for making it happen. "Friendly. And helpful. That's me."

Reaching into a box, she pulled out an envelope inscribed with Ella's name and handed her a gift bag from a large bin. "It looks like Team Development has already picked up mulligans and raffle tickets, so you're all set. It should be a great day out there."

Ella lowered her voice and glanced around before looking Reese's way again. "It beats the office any day."

"I'll say."

"I thought I'd get here early so I can mingle and meet people, but it doesn't look like I'm early at all."

"I think the noon start time and the good weather are excuses to be early. You're fine. But you're planning on mingling, huh? Is there anyone special you'd like to meet? I know most of the people here."

Ella wanted to meet everyone, at least to introduce herself, but Jeremy Nathan was the one she really wanted to talk to.

"Can you point out Jeremy Nathan?"

Reese nodded. "Better yet, follow me. You can meet his brother, too. You may have heard of him. He's our senator."

"That sounds vaguely familiar."

Ella felt a bounce in her step as she climbed the stairs to the dining room behind Reese. Once again, she had the opportunity to enjoy the view of Reese's butt, and she did, failing to notice the final step. Before she realized she was falling, she was in Reese's arms.

"I'm so sorry," she said, pushing herself away before anyone noticed the scene she'd created. She'd noticed, though. Reese's fresh, citrus scent. Her hard body. Her gentle hands.

"If you wanted to get close to me..." Reese said as a smile spread across her face.

Closing her eyes, Ella found her strength. "Thank you," she said, stepping farther away from Reese and testing her legs. They seemed to be functional, and as she glanced around, she was relieved to find no one staring.

"No problem. Let's find the Nathans."

By the size of the crowd gathered around one table, Ella might have guessed the senator's location. Having a personal escort made the crowd seem less formidable, and she was grateful again for Reese's presence.

"What's going on here?" she asked. "Is there free food or something?"

"Something better. Free drinks." The crowd parted, and Ella recognized the jokester. He'd been in the news often in recent years, thanks to the gun debate, and she'd seen his picture at PMU as well.

"No drinking with a golf club in your hand, Josh. I don't want to have to stitch you up again."

"Or me." The voice came from someone sitting at the table, a man of forty whose dark features and resemblance to the senator suggested they were somehow related.

"Hi, Jeremy. You're actually the one I'm looking for. I want to introduce you to Ella—Elizabeth Townes, from the development office."

Jeremy's face lit up and he stood, quickly wiped his mouth and hands on the linen napkin, and then extended his right in greeting. "I've been looking forward to meeting you," he said, a huge smile on his face.

"And I have as well," Josh said, extending his hand as he playfully wedged himself between his brother and Ella.

She couldn't help laughing at their childish antics. "I have enough time for both of you. There's no need to fight."

"My brother simply can't stand it that all the beautiful women approach me first," Jeremy said.

"That's not true, because this is the first time it's ever happened," Josh countered. Nodding at his brother, the senator said, "He has an inferiority complex. He's half an inch shorter."

"Not where..." Jeremy stopped. "Anyway, it's nice to meet you. Why you wish to honor this guy is beyond me, but I'll be happy to help in any way I can."

"And I will as well," Josh said.

"How about you, Reese? Are you going to help get this reunion together? It is our twentieth, after all."

"Ah, well, I think you guys have all the help you need."

Once again the desire to tease Reese overcame Ella. "Actually, we don't. It would be wonderful if you can join us. Why didn't I think of it?"

Reese rolled her eyes.

"Oh, come on, Reese. What could be more important than honoring me?" Josh asked.

"Your ego seems to be growing with your resume, Senator. I'll tell you what. If your team beats mine, I'll be on the committee. If not...I get something. I'm not sure what I want yet, but I'll get something from you."

Josh squinted and held out his hand, which Reese took and kissed playfully. "Deal," he said.

"Don't you even care what I want?"

"Nah. 'Cuz we're going to win this year."

Reese shook her head and was about to excuse herself when Josh spoke again. "Reese, we were just talking about Stephanie Gates. A couple of guys from our class were called to go over their statements. They're sh—crapping their pants."

Expecting a phone call herself, Reese had tried to remember every detail she could from the night Steph died.

They'd planned to get together that night, and Reese had her bag packed for a sleepover when she left for school in the morning. After school, she did her normal three-to-five shift at the pediatrics office, thinking she'd leave from there to go to the lake. Halfway through work, she'd developed all the telltale signs of an impending migraine, and even though she took her medication immediately, within half an hour, her head was throbbing. She'd called Steph from work and changed their plans. Even though she could have napped at Steph's, with Steph in the same house she wouldn't have rested. Ever since they'd started sleeping together in the fall of their senior year, they couldn't keep their hands off each other.

Instead of the lake, she'd gone home, hoping a nap would help ease her pain. Her parents took advantage of her presence and went to dinner and a movie, and she'd stayed home with Cass. A few hours later, when they arrived home, she'd tried calling Steph to tell her she was on her way, but had no answer. Unsure what to do, she'd kept calling, until an hour later when a policeman answered the phone and refused to let her talk to any members of the Gates family. Frantic, she'd climbed into her dad's car and raced to the lake, only to be greeted by the flashing lights of the police cruisers lining the road.

The coroner's car was in the driveway.

Reese's heart pounded with fear. Was it Steph's mom or dad? The loss of either would have been devastating. As an only child, Steph was the center of her parents' universe, and she treasured them both. Together, the three of them made a wonderful family— traveling together, volunteering together, even working together. Just as she spent her afternoons at the doctor's office, Steph worked at the print shop her parents owned, and that shared time made them even closer.

Forcing her way through the gawkers, she'd pushed past the police officer on the porch and run into the house. When she saw the people gathered there, Reese's stomach dropped. In the living room adjacent to the main hallway, a police officer was seated, an open notebook in his lap as he interviewed Steve and Sophie Gates. They looked up at the intrusion, seeming surprised, but then that look faded as Sophie began sobbing.

"Where's Steph?" she'd asked, but she knew the words were incomprehensible through the choking sobs.

The policeman she'd hurdled on the way through the door grabbed her from behind, tried ushering her out.

"It's okay," Steve said. "She's family."

He rose and walked toward her, each step pounding her like a punch to the gut, until he was standing before her. She noticed Sophie attempt to join him before collapsing on the couch. As the police officer rushed to her side, Steve opened his arms to Reese and pulled her in. "Steph's dead, Reesie. Someone murdered her."

Clearing her throat of the tears that still came all these years later, she nodded. "Let's just hope they find the guy who killed her. It's been long enough." Reese excused herself to go back to the check-in table.

"It looks like I picked a crazy time to come to Scranton," Ella said, trying to lighten the mood.

"It is pretty crazy," Josh said.

"Did you know her? Steph, I mean?"

"Oh, of course. All my life. Sometimes it's still hard to believe she's dead. She was a very feisty young lady." It might have been a criticism, but Ella saw the smile in his eyes.

"I actually knew her," Ella said, and told him about the summers of her youth.

"Reese is right," he said wistfully. "It's time to catch the guy who did this."

"Hey, with DNA now, who knows?" Jeremy added. "They'll probably have him tried before Christmas."

"Let's hope so," someone else added. The conversation turned to golf, and the group wagered as to who'd finish on top. Ella couldn't help smiling at their easy banter. It seemed they were more like a family than classmates, and she silently applauded PMU and her decision to make the career move. It felt good to be there, to be among them. She didn't even feel like an outsider.

After making a luncheon date with Jeremy to plan Josh's award ceremony, Ella excused herself. She made her way to the buffet and packed a plate with food. Spotting a small group standing alone, Ella approached and introduced herself. They welcomed her to PMU and gave her some tips on navigating the course, which she'd never played.

After committing their names to memory, she wished them well and moved on to another small group. By the time the ranger announced they had fifteen minutes until start time, Ella had met more than twenty alums.

Happy at the success of her morning, Ella wished the last group well and turned toward the garbage. At the same time, a man walking backward as he yelled across the room swung his arm into Ella's, knocking her plate into her chest. Fortunately, it was almost empty, but the marinara and olive oil leftover rendered her shirt a disaster. As someone rushed to pick up the mess from the floor, Ella stared in disbelief at the mess. The man who'd caused it all apologized profusely and seemed genuinely remorseful, but it took all of her will to hold her tongue and reply graciously, "No worries. It's only a shirt."

As quickly as she could, Ella excused herself and hurried toward the restroom, already aware she could do nothing to save her shirt, or her pride.

❖

Reese headed into the dining room to make sure everyone made it to their carts in time for the announcements. Just as she opened the door, she saw one of her classmates, Jim Lucci, slam into Ella. Before she could reach them, Ella had bolted toward the ladies' room.

"I see you're still smooth with the ladies, Lucky," Reese said as she rushed by.

"I'll never be as smooth as you!" he retorted.

Pushing open the door, Reese was startled to find Ella standing before the sink, wearing just her sports bra. Her shirt was in her hands as she rubbed hand soap into the stains in what was surely a futile effort to save it.

"What can I do to help?" Reese asked.

"I was just thinking I have to put this back on and head to the pro shop. It's never going to come clean, and now it's wet, too. Can you just pick me out a white golf shirt? Medium?"

Reese sighed. "I wish I could, Ella, but the pro shop is empty. They're remodeling and had a clearance sale."

"Well, that's bad luck," she said as she stared at her shirt. "Oh, well. It'll be fine. I've worn dirty shirts before. Never in front of a hundred and twenty alums, but there's a first time for everything."

"Maybe I can help," Reese said.

"How?"

Reese tried not to stare as Ella turned, revealing her picture-perfect cleavage. Forcing her eyes to Ella's, she swallowed and found her voice. "I have a shirt in my car. It's black, but it's clean. And it's a size medium."

Ella didn't notice her attempt at humor and instead seemed to weigh her decision, pursing her lips for a moment before nodding.

With only a few minutes until the shotgun start, Reese sprinted to her car and pulled a clean shirt from the bag in her trunk. A minute later she was back in the restroom watching Ella slip it over her head.

"What do you think?" Ella asked, laughter in her voice. "Black and red look good together, right? I'm trying for the biker vibe."

Reese chuckled. Ella was obviously worried about making a good impression at her first official event at PMU, and thanks to Lucky Lucci, it wasn't going well. Hesitating for only a moment, she pulled her shirt from her shorts and raised it over her head.

"What are you doing?" Ella asked, and Reese caught her surveying her chest.

"You can wear this one. It'll look perfect."

"I can't take your shirt."

"Why not? You were planning to wear the black one, so why not this one?"

Ella tilted her head and frowned. "Well, this is literally the shirt off your back. That's a lot to ask of anyone."

"I'm not just anyone," Reese said, her voice a husky murmur just above a whisper.

Caught in her gaze, Ella nodded. "No. I suspect you're not."

❖

Shaking his head at Lucky, he tried not to watch Reese as she hurried into the women's restroom behind Ella Townes. What was that about? He didn't notice anything odd about their interaction; in fact, Ella appeared to be the consummate professional. She'd treated Reese cordially but wasn't overly friendly. He knew too well, though, that appearances aren't everything.

Steph had appeared to the entire world as the All-American girl. Attractive, athletic, intelligent, civic-minded, and sweet, she was the fantasy of most of the boys in high school. Yet she'd fooled them all. Even while she'd dated him and a half dozen other boys during their four years at Prep, she was a closeted lesbian. She'd been in the closet with Reese, and that's why she'd done what she did to him.

Was Reese pursing Ella? It was an interesting thought. He'd watch them later and find out what he could. With the investigation into Steph's death gaining steam and his plans to once again move the focus away from him, he'd need to monitor the situation carefully. It wouldn't do for Reese to get all chummy now, when he needed her to keep to her routine. Forcing his eyes from the bathroom door, he made his way to the exit.

CHAPTER 14: DIRTY LAUNDRY

It was Saturday, also known as laundry day, and the job had taken more of Ella's concentration than it ever had before.

Sitting on her bed, she was totally engrossed by the golf shirt spread out a few feet away. It was an ordinary shirt, but she had received it under such extraordinary circumstances that she couldn't stop thinking about it, or the woman who'd given it to her. Reese's kindness to offer her shirt. How she'd looked when she took it off and showed that tantalizing cleavage. How to return it. It would be easy enough to place it in a bag and give it to Sharon, but then Ella wouldn't have the chance to see Reese, to thank her. She could have written a note, but somehow that didn't seem adequate. If she waited until she saw Reese's red Jeep in the driveway of her parents' house, she could return it in person, but that wouldn't be very personal, with all of the Ryans looking on as Ella bumbled through the speech she'd written in her head.

None of those options seemed fitting, when what she really wanted to do was ask Reese to join her for dinner. Not a backyard cookout, or even something at her house, with her parents next door wondering what was going on. No. She wanted something special, something for just the two of them. She'd found Reese attractive from the first, and after Reese had ogled her breasts in the bathroom the day before, Ella suspected the attraction she felt was mutual. If she was wrong, all she had to lose was her pride. And after the incident with her shirt, that was long gone anyway.

Picking up the phone, Ella dialed the number for the ER. Her sleuthing skills had helped her not only find the hospital where Reese worked, but also her schedule. Thank the gods for Cass. "Can I speak with Dr. Ryan, please?" she asked the pleasant woman who answered the phone.

The woman's tone quickly turned icy. "May I tell her who's calling?"

Ella gave her name and waited for a moment, leaning back with her eyes closed as she took a few deep breaths. What am I doing? she asked herself. I'm not looking to date anyone. Or am I? Didn't I move to Scranton and take the job at PMU so I could focus on my career? She didn't have much time for a girlfriend, so why was she going out of her way to reach out to Reese, hoping to get together with her? It didn't make any sense, this phone call. But neither did her thoughts of Reese. She only knew they made her smile. Reese made her smile. It felt good.

"Ella?" Reese asked, jolting her back to reality.

"Hi," she said, suddenly at a loss for words. Where was the soliloquy she'd practiced? Where was her normally sharp tongue? Where was the voice of the woman who felt comfortable asking donors for millions of dollars? Why could she feel at ease in the company of company presidents and bankers and judges and yet suddenly feel so inadequate around a simple woman?

She supposed it was because, as Reese pointed out, she wasn't just anyone. Reese was someone special.

"How are you? Is everything okay?" she asked, and Ella forced herself to focus, as if waking from sleep. She blinked her eyes and shook her head and felt a little better.

"Yes. Everything's fine. I'm great. Very well dressed. I have this beautiful golf shirt on my bed, and I was hoping we could get together so I can give it back to you. I even washed it. And ironed it."

"Is it on a hanger and wrapped in plastic?"

"I can arrange that, if you'd like."

"You're sweet."

Ella sucked in a breath and let it out slowly, then found her voice. It was low and gravelly, and packed with emotion. "No, Reese. You are."

Silence fell between them as Ella let her observation hang, and Reese seemed to weigh its relevance. It was a game changer, or at least it had the potential to be. They'd been acquaintances, nothing more, but Ella was letting Reese know it didn't have to be that way.

"You can leave it with my mom. If you want."

Fuck! Ella thought. She'd opened the door, and Reese had slammed it in her face. Either Reese was playing hard to get, or she wasn't interested in Ella. Either way, it wasn't the response Ella had hoped for.

She'd give it one more shot before she crawled under a rock and never came back out. "I was hoping we could get together. Just the two of us. Maybe I could buy you dinner, to thank you for your kindness."

Reese didn't hesitate. "I'm having a cookout tomorrow. Around five. Just my family and a few friends. Why don't you join us?"

Ella was a bit disappointed. She'd hoped for the opportunity to spend time with Reese one-on-one, not in a group setting. Hell, she still didn't even know if Reese was attracted to her. Maybe this invitation was just her way of being friendly.

"I would love to, but..." Ella was about to speak her mind but then held back. If the cookout went well, she could always ask Reese out again. "Never mind. Yes, I'd love to come."

Reese felt giddy as she recited the directions to her house and suggested that Ella bring her bathing suit. The image of Ella in practically nothing flashed through her mind, and Reese felt herself blushing. The tantalizing cleavage she'd seen at the golf course was Victoria's Secret–model quality, and it would be so very nice to see it again. Ella volunteered to bring a cake for dessert, promised to see her at five o'clock, and suddenly, Reese's small party took on a huge significance.

Ella was gay. Ella was hot. And Ella was coming to her party!

The party and seeing Ella were a good distraction. At the golf tournament the day before, they'd mentioned the investigation into Steph's murder. When she'd gotten home that night, she'd called Karen, under the pretense of discussing her Labor Day party, and casually mentioned what she'd heard.

Karen had confirmed that everyone who the police had questioned twenty years ago would be interviewed again. That certainly included her. She'd worried about it for an hour after hanging up the phone and then cleaned her appliances to a sparkling shine to work out her frustrations. In the end, she'd told herself she'd done nothing wrong and had no reason for concern. Still, it had been a restless night, and she'd had a headache when the alarm rang at five thirty. Two cups of coffee later, she'd begun to feel human, and not until Ella agreed to come to her party had she felt like the day was salvageable.

"What's up with you?" one of the nurses asked as Reese reviewed labs on a patient who'd presented with chest pain.

"Hmm?" she asked.

"The ER is a like a battlefield today and you've seemed miserable since you walked through the door, but suddenly you're smiling like you just got laid."

Reese chuckled. She hadn't, not in quite a while. Her last relationship had disintegrated more than a year ago, and she was feeling too old for casual sex. But if things turned out with Ella, maybe she'd change her mind.

❖

Reese was on her deck, rearranging furniture, when she heard Karen's voice. "Looks like all the work is done. As usual, my timing is perfect."

Reese paused, grabbed a handful of ice and water from the tub beside her, and hurled it in Karen's direction. "It's a felony to assault an officer of the court, you know."

"In that case, I apologize. I'm already under investigation by your office for one crime, so I should probably keep a low profile."

The comment was made jokingly, but Reese hoped Karen would water the seed she'd planted. She still needed to know more about the Steph's case.

Sure enough, Karen came through. "You're not under investigation, Reese. Unless you consider the entire class of 1993 suspect."

"Well, with this new perspective, isn't that true?"

Karen shrugged. "There isn't one bit of evidence in this case. It's all posturing on my boss's part, trying to infuse some energy into Bucky's campaign. And let's face it—Bucky needs the support."

Reese had to agree. Bucky was smart but a total nerd. He'd lost his hair and found some weight, and some allergy or another prevented him from wearing contact lenses, so he really looked the part with his Coke-bottle glasses. If he was going to win the election, he'd have to overcome his appearance. The sitting DA's plan to bring attention to Bucky was just the kind of spark his campaign needed. "You're right. I just can't imagine it was someone Steph knew. Everyone loved her. Why would anyone want to hurt her? Her letting a stranger into the house that night may not make much sense, but it's certainly easier to swallow, you know?"

Reese grabbed two bottles of beer and handed one to Karen, then pulled out a chair. Her guests wouldn't arrive for another half hour, and thanks to her preparation the night before, she had little left to do.

Reese watched Karen as she opened the beer and sipped it somewhat conservatively for a hot day. She was being cautious, and Reese wondered why, but she didn't ask. With Karen leading the investigation, allowing her to give up what she wanted was the only way to maintain their friendship through this ordeal.

"It could have been someone she knew casually, like the older brother of one of her friends, home from college and hoping to get lucky. Or the janitor at her parents' shop. Or the mechanic she took her car to. It really makes sense that she would only open the door for someone she knew, but I can understand that it's hard to accept that possibility."

"I keep thinking of all my friends. All of *Steph's* friends. The way they acted before the murder, and the way they acted afterward. Nothing was out of the ordinary. We were all excited about graduation, and then we were all devastated by her death. Everyone behaved typically, at least what I think was typical for that situation. And more importantly, everyone I know who was ever questioned in the murder had an alibi. It couldn't have been one of us."

"You're probably right, Reese. As I said, it could have been someone she knew less intimately, but well enough that she'd open the door for them."

"Maybe. I just can't believe they didn't think of this sooner," Reese said between swallows.

"They did, but there was really no motive. She didn't have any enemies, she didn't have a jealous boyfriend—there was nothing. And motive is a big clue to finding suspects. If you know why they wanted her dead, then you know who benefitted from the death. In Steph's case, no one benefitted. She had no financial assets, and again, she was well liked. Under the circumstances, I think the robbery fit, and Mr. and Mrs. Gates were too shocked to think straight. By the time they questioned it, the police had already settled into the robber theory."

"So what happens next?"

"We'll just keep questioning her acquaintances, comparing their responses to the responses from the first investigation, seeing if we can find any inconsistencies."

"It really is a needle in a haystack, huh?"

"It's worse. At least you know the needle's in the haystack *somewhere*. In this case, there may not be any needle at all."

They were quiet for a minute before Reese spoke again. "It would be nice to know the truth. Sort of a closure for all of us, especially Steph's mom."

"It would be. Anyway, in case you're watching your phone, you should be getting a call this week."

"Already?"

"They'll just be calling to schedule your interview. You might not actually come in for questioning for six weeks."

"Thanks for the warning," Reese said, raising her beer bottle toward Karen.

"Any time, my friend," Karen said.

"I thought there was a party here! Why's it so quiet?"

Reese turned toward the sound of her father's voice, and as she did, her mom and sister rounded the corner of the house. When Cass saw Reese and Karen on the deck, she began waving.

Reese stood and hugged her parents, then high-fived her sister. As they sat, Reese went into the house and returned a minute later carrying bowls of snacks. She was greeted by a few more friends who'd arrived and forced herself to appear interested in them, rather than the sidewalk that might lead Ella to the deck. She'd said she'd come, and something told Reese that Ella would never be so rude as to stand someone up. Until she arrived, though, she'd keep Reese wondering.

She didn't have a moment more to consider the idea before Ella appeared around the corner, wearing a sundress and huge sunglasses, and carrying the same glass cake plate she'd brought to Reese's parents' house for their cookout. Ella caught her looking, and a smile spread across her face. Launching herself from the deck, Reese met Ella in the yard and took the cake from her.

"Hi," she said. "I was beginning to worry you weren't coming."

"I got lost."

"It is sort of remote," Reese said. "Not many street signs and landmarks to guide you. 'Turn left at the big tree' isn't very helpful out here."

"No worries. I found you."

Reese felt herself melting at the words. Not "I found it" or "I found the house," but "I found *you*." It didn't matter where this was heading with Ella. Reese was enjoying the journey, and every moment they spent together seemed to be good.

"Let me introduce you to everyone," Reese said, and, nodding in the direction of the deck, she headed that way.

Ella had been impressed by the house as she drove up the long gravel drive. It was a combination of stone and timber with a tall, sloped roof, chalet style. Shrubs and flowers lined the yard and walkways, and the entire dwelling was surrounded by trees. The backyard had been taken over by a pool, and at one end, a pergola was covered in vines. Hanging baskets of flowers dangled from the corners. Either Reese was a gardener, or she hired a good one, because the place looked fantastic.

Ten people were gathered at two tables on the deck, and other than Chris Ryan, they were all female. Friends, Ella assumed, because Reese offered no titles along with the introductions. After offering her a vodka and tonic, which she accepted, Reese disappeared into the house to pour it, and Ella took a seat at the end of the larger table, where the Ryans sat.

"You could have come in our car," Cass said.

"I thought you had a ball game today?"

Cass slapped herself in the forehead. "I did!"

Everyone at both tables laughed. They were subtly checking her out, Ella noticed, and the woman named Mac took advantage of the opening and began the interrogation Ella was sure would come from a group of friends.

"Reese says you're living next to her parents. In Pip's house."

It wasn't a question, and Ella might have waited for one before responding, but she understood the dynamics of the situation. Since she was the newcomer, everyone was curious about her, and she wanted to make a good impression on Reese's crowd. Why? she wondered, but didn't debate the reason for long.

"Yes, I'm house- and dog-sitting while Pip is in film school."

"Watch out for the neighbors," a woman named Kerry said.

"Thanks for the warning."

"You work at PMU?" Jessica asked. When Ella nodded, she smiled. "Most of us are alums. It's a great school. Congratulations on the new job."

"What do you do?" Mindy asked.

"I'm in development."

"Is that the people who call and ask for money all the time?"

Reese stepped onto the deck and was about to redirect the conversation, but she noticed that the question didn't seem to faze Ella. Besides, she hadn't talked in depth about her job, and she was really curious about what Ella did. Other than attend golf tournaments, of course.

After thanking Reese and taking a sip of the proffered drink, Ella answered the question. "Directing the phoneathon is part of our student-based fund-raising, but it's run by someone else in the department, so I'll never call you and ask you for money."

"Whew," someone said, and the rest of the group laughed.

"What exactly do you do to raise money?"

"I meet with people like you, alums who are established, and inform them of opportunities to give back to the school. For instance, we have an upcoming project in the computer science department, so I'll talk to people in that field, get ideas from them about what they think would be helpful to the students, and then explain how they can help fund a lab or a lecture hall, or perhaps a wing."

"So, you ask them for money," Mac said.

Reese held her breath. Mac was a detective and could be somewhat…aggressive at times, but the tone didn't seem to bother Ella. She shrugged. "Yes, but I'm not going to ask *you guys* for money, so you can all relax."

They laughed, and a woman named Rae spoke next. "What's the biggest donation you've ever gotten?"

Ella immediately thought of Sophie Gates. Would she go through with the scholarship, or would she change her mind? The four million dollars she'd promised would be the third largest gift Ella had orchestrated in nearly twenty years on the job.

"Ten million dollars."

"Holy shit," the woman beside Rae replied. She introduced herself as Nicole and then asked her own question. "What does someone do that they can afford such a gift?"

"That particular bequest was from an eye surgeon. He was one of the first to use a laser for cataract extraction, and he opened a few clinics in the Philly area. He hired young docs and trained them on the laser and did very well. The ten million was for a science lab at his collegiate alma mater. He gave a larger gift to his medical school."

"I guess I chose the wrong specialty," Nicole said with a laugh.

"Are you a physician?" Ella asked.

"Yes, and one of the few at the table who didn't go to PMU."

"Where did you go?"

"Scranton."

"You can't beat that," Ella said. "What's your specialty?"

"Emergency medicine."

Reese watched Ella's face brighten. "Oh, like Reese," she said.

Feeling comfortable that Ella could handle herself with her group of friends, Reese turned, walked to her grill, and turned on the gas. She'd cleaned it the night before, and it lit on the first try.

"She seems nice."

Reese looked from Karen to Ella and nodded. Her only experiences with Ella were at her parents' house and at the golf tournament, but it did seem Ella went out of her way to engage others. Her manners were impeccable, which Reese figured was essential to her job. It could have all been an act, but the way Ella behaved around Cass told Reese that she was genuinely a nice person. "Yeah, I think so, too."

"Sooo?"

Reese could only hope. Winking at Karen, she headed toward the kitchen. "Leave the detecting to Mac. When there's something to tell, you'll be the first to know. Come help me with food."

Ella watched Reese out of the corner of her eye but then focused on the conversation at the table. It turned out that Rae, a lawyer, was Nicole's partner. Jess, another ER doctor, was dating Mac. Mindy, Kerry, and another woman named Mary were all single. They all seemed like nice women and were clearly fond of Reese.

"I'm going in the pool," Cass said, distracting her. "Are you guys coming in or what?"

To her surprise, all of the women nodded. "How long until food?" Mac asked as she poked her head through the sliding glass door to the kitchen.

Ella recognized Reese's voice. "Twenty minutes."

"Perfect time for a dip."

It seemed everyone had a suit on under their clothes, and Ella followed Reese's friends with her eyes from the deck to the pool. Cass was the first to jump in. She emerged from beneath the water with a smile on her face that warmed Ella's heart.

"She really loves the water," Reese said.

"It appears so."

"It was one of the reasons I bought the house. For the pool. Aren't you going in?"

"Actually, it looks like your sister has enough sitters. I was going to check with you to see if you need help with anything."

Reese smiled. "That's very sweet, and as much as I would love your company, I think I have it all under control."

Ella looked at the cart Reese had wheeled onto the deck. It was made of wicker and was probably meant for bar use, but Reese had it piled with food and grill utensils, paper plates, and napkins. "So it seems. I could just talk to you, though. Find out about the single women at the party."

The deck was in the shade, and Reese's sunglasses were pushed up on her head, allowing Ella to see her eyes. Their color deepened, and she squinted slightly as she answered. "There is only one single woman at the party who you should think about."

Ella suspected she knew the answer; she hoped Reese was going to say what she wanted to hear. It was with a suddenly dry mouth that she asked the question. "Who's that?"

Reese placed her hand over her heart and rewarded Ella with a hint of a smile. "Why, me, of course."

Ella felt herself blushing, a rare thing. Seldom did she meet an unattached woman as attractive and intelligent and successful as Reese. But Reese had set the tone of this conversation, and it was light and playful, so Ella relaxed and followed her lead. "I did notice that the women I was talking with were not quite as amazing as you."

"I knew you were smart," Reese said with a wink.

She turned and pulled a plate of burgers from her cart. "So, where's my golf shirt?"

Ella bit her lip. She'd contemplated bringing the shirt but in the end decided against it. She wanted to see Reese again, and returning her shirt was a good excuse.

"It's on my dresser."

Reese's eyebrows shot up, and she turned her eyes from the grill to face Ella. "I thought that's why you were coming over today. To return it."

Ella swallowed. "Actually, I was just making an excuse to see you."

Reese's eyes darkened and she nodded. "I wanted to see you, too."

Karen interrupted them, and then the food was ready, and with everyone gathered, Ella had no chance to sit beside Reese. Instead, her sister entertained Ella as she ate.

"So how come you came to Reese's house? Is she your friend?"

Ella nodded. "I suppose she is, but the real reason I came was to return something I borrowed from her."

"What did you borrow?" Cass asked, and Ella heard the conversations at the table turn to murmurs as everyone seemed to listen for her answer.

"Did Reese tell you about the accident with my shirt?"

"No. What happened to your shirt?"

"Some rude man ran into me and spilled food all over me. I was such a mess, and I was upset, so Reese gave me her shirt to wear."

"What did Reese wear?"

"She had another one."

"She has a lot of shirts. And pants. She brings them to my house sometimes to wash them."

"Doesn't she have a washing machine?" Ella asked, her hands in the air in an expression of disbelief that made everyone at the table, except Cass, roar with laughter.

"Yes. My mom says she's just lazy. When she brings them to my house, my mom washes them."

Again, everyone laughed, and Cass looked at them all. Clearly, she didn't understand the impact her information had on everyone else.

"Be quiet, Cassidy," Reese said playfully.

Ella came to her rescue. "It sounds pretty smart, if you ask me. I wish my mom lived close by so she could do my wash."

Cass laughed. "It's fair that Mom washes Reese's clothes, because she washes my clothes, too. If you ask her, I think she'll wash yours."

Mindy spoke up. "Will you wash mine, too, Mrs. Ryan?"

"I'll even iron them," Sharon said.

"Count me in," Rae said.

"Me, too," Mac added.

"Oh, no, Cass. Look what you've done? Mom's going to be so busy washing clothes, she won't have time to cook dinner and clean the house," Reese said, shaking her head.

Cass smiled. "That's okay. I'll cook, because I'm a great chef. And you can clean the bathroom."

Once again, Cass brought the house down.

CHAPTER 15: THE SCHOLARSHIP COMMITTEE

Having a long weekend agreed with Ella, and she was full of energy as she sat at her desk on the Tuesday after Labor Day. She'd wanted to linger and talk to Reese at her party on Sunday, but it seemed that none of the crowd had to work on Monday, and they were all intent on making a night of it at Reese's. Ella had excused herself well after eleven o'clock, and the only people who'd left before her were the Ryans.

She'd spent her Monday morning relaxing and catching up on email, until a knock on her door and an invitation by Cass forced her to dress and face the world. To her delight, Reese joined them on their walk, and she'd spent the rest of the day with the Ryans. They ate, tossed a Frisbee around the yard, and then watched a movie on the television on their screened porch. Only the thought of her busy Tuesday convinced Ella to break up the party, and she'd made it an early night.

She was ready to face the fall semester full steam. The students had reported to school on Friday, and one of the reasons PMU had their golf tournament at Labor Day was as a sort of homecoming, when alums could meet the new students. After a wild weekend of orientation, they were ready for their first day of classes, and Ella was ready to roll up her sleeves and get to work.

Her first order of business was a call to Sophie to confirm the scholarship. She answered on the first ring.

"Good morning, Ella. Is the scholarship all ready to go?"

Ella leaned back in her chair and looked out at the campus, just coming to life at eight o'clock. "No, not quite."

"Then I'd imagine you're calling to make sure I didn't change my mind."

Ella laughed. There was no sense pretending; Sophie saw right through her. "That's exactly what I'm doing. I think you were a bit shocked by the cost of the whole thing, so I wanted to give you the weekend to think about it. If you're still committed today, I'll get moving. If not, we'll work out another plan."

"Thank you, dear. It's very kind of you to be so concerned, but I'm comfortable with my decision. You can move ahead with it as we discussed."

"For four million?"

"I believe that's the number we spoke of."

"I just wanted to be double sure, Mrs. Gates."

"Four million. Now you're triple sure."

"In that case, I'd better get to work. But truly, your timing couldn't be more perfect. I have a scholarship committee meeting at lunch today, and with your permission, I'll announce—to the committee only—the Stephanie Gates Scholarship."

"Oh, that sounds so wonderful, doesn't it?"

"It sure does. Have you decided on any criteria? You don't have to, but it will help narrow down the field of candidates."

Sophie rattled off a short list, and Ella jotted the items on her blotter.

"And would you consider having each candidate write an essay to help the committee decide? Something like *How I'll Use the Stephanie Gates Scholarship to Improve the Lives of Stray Cats.*"

Sophie chuckled. "That sounds like an essay my daughter would have written! How about something simpler? *How I'll Make the World a Better Place.*"

Ella smiled. "Generic, but perfect for an eighteen-year-old ready to conquer the world. Now I'm going to get to work, conquering these forms, and I'll talk to you soon. We'll want to hold a press conference to announce the scholarship before we mail out the scholarship applications. We're reviewing them today, so that gives us about a month if we want them to be in the packet for all incoming freshmen."

"Good, good."

They said their good-byes, and two hours later, Ella had talked to the university's in-house counsel and had reviewed the paperwork for the scholarship template. Since this was her first such donation at PMU, she wanted to become familiar with the legalities. Filling in as much as she could without Mrs. Gates, she made progress, and by the time she walked into her lunch meeting, the foundation for the scholarship had been set.

She was excited to attend the first scholarship meeting at the school. It consisted of a group of people that included the university president, members of the faculty, admissions, financial aid, and institutional advancement—the official title of Ella's office. As she walked into the boardroom, she scanned the faces and was delighted to find most of them familiar. Remembering the names that matched the faces would be a challenge, but the agenda she grabbed on the way to her seat would help.

The luncheon was a simple affair of salad and sandwiches, and after depositing her briefcase on an open seat, she proceeded to collect her food. Mary Ann Bingham was all business as she began the meeting on time, and the tactic worked, as some committee members who were still queuing for their food grew silent and then scurried to their seats.

A total of 135 scholarships were to be awarded, and the committee's job on this day was to review the criteria for each scholarship so the applications could be mailed to students who were accepted into the next freshman class. Most of this work was already done, because the committee simply reviewed the prior year's checklist and duplicated it. In rare instances a scholarship changed, but it was Ella's job as the one whose department had secured the funds to make sure they were distributed appropriately. In the next weeks, she or one of her associates would personally reach out to every contact person on that list of 135, thank them for their support, review the requirements, and make any necessary changes.

Before they even started, though, there was a change. Pocono Mountains University no longer offered 135 scholarships. Thanks to Sophie Gates, they had added another.

"For anyone who is new to this committee, let me explain the process. Today we review the scholarships. Ella Townes," Mary Ann nodded in Ella's direction, "and her staff will contact all the individuals and corporations and foundations who've established them and review the criteria as well as the gifts themselves. At our next meeting, which will take place on the first Tuesday in October, we'll review the scholarship application that will be sent to all admitted students. By November, we should have some back, and the selection committee— that's the people from admissions and financial aid, and with some exceptions development and department chairs—will begin ranking the applicants. In May, we'll have the list whittled down to two or three choices for each scholarship. We will confirm their intentions to attend PMU and announce the recipients at the scholarship luncheon on Memorial Day Weekend."

When Mary Ann paused for a breath, Ella asked, "Is this the appropriate time to announce a new scholarship?"

Ella's eyes were on the university president, who arched her eyebrows in surprise, but she sensed that everyone else was looking at her. It was a good feeling.

"Ms. Townes, you haven't even been here a month, and already you've gotten us a scholarship? That's rather impressive."

"Thank you."

"Well, then, yes. This would be the perfect time to tell us about a new scholarship."

"Sophie Gates, the former owner of GateWay Printing, has decided to make a gift to PMU. She's funding four endowed scholarships in memory of her daughter Stephanie."

"Four?" someone asked, and Ella nodded.

"For how much?" someone else asked.

"Full tuition, room, board, books, and a stipend."

"That's four million dollars," someone else said.

"Yes, it is."

Mary Ann Bingham smiled at Ella and asked her to share the details. Ten minutes later, she knew she'd earned the respect of everyone in the room. Her career at PMU was off to a great start.

When the meeting concluded, Mary Ann called out to Ella, and Ella waited to speak with her. Before she had a chance, the director of admissions, Dick Price, grabbed her arm.

"Congratulations, Ella. What a wonderful way to begin your career at PMU."

Ella tried to control her smile. "Thank you. This'll be hard to top."

He laughed. "Stephanie Gates was a lovely young woman. I'm happy her mother is able to do this for her memory."

"Oh, did you know her?"

He waved his hand dismissively. "Of course, of course. She was valedictorian of her class. She would have gotten the Cognitio if she'd come here. I met with her several times to show her what we had to offer."

"I'm surprised to hear that. I thought she was heading to Cornell and vet school."

"It would amaze you to learn how many times an eighteen-year-old can change their mind. Even the smart ones don't know for sure what they want. So I meet with all the valedictorians I can and hope the seed I plant takes root."

Ella nodded. It had been much the same for her. She'd wanted to go away for college, but she didn't want to be away from her friends. She'd wanted to be far enough away that she could gain her independence, but not so far that she couldn't drive home for the holidays. She'd wanted to be in a city, but not too big a city. Making a choice had been a little overwhelming, and she could appreciate that others felt the same way.

"Have you set the wheels in motion yet?" Mary Ann asked as she joined them, and Dick excused himself.

"Yes. Just this morning."

"I'd like to meet with her, of course, to thank her. And we'll do something wonderful to announce the scholarship."

"I think she'd like that. It's important to her to create a legacy so her daughter will be remembered. The more attention, the better."

"Why PMU?" she asked.

Of all the things she and Sophie had talked about, that question hadn't come up. Ella had been so thrilled about the scholarship, and moved by the memories of her friend, that she hadn't thought to ask. She shrugged.

"Well, I won't question it, then."

Ella nodded in agreement, knowing she'd ask Sophie the first chance she had.

❖

One of the most difficult aspects of Reese's job was the constant switch from day shifts to evenings to overnights. Her Labor Day weekend schedule had consisted of three consecutive day shifts, followed by a day off, and now she'd transition into a string of evenings. If she truly left the ER at eleven o'clock, when she was supposed to, she wouldn't have minded it so much. In reality, the hours between six and midnight were killers. It was a rare night that she was home before the clock struck twelve. More typically, she'd walk through her door at one in the morning, and by the time she showered and her mind stopped racing, it would be closer to two. In preparation for the night, she'd stayed up well after midnight and slept until nearly ten. As a result, she'd missed the phone call from the DA's office when she was showering at eleven.

They'd been courteous enough to respect her schedule constraints and offered several options for her to come in and "talk" about the Stephanie Gates homicide investigation. After checking her calendar, she realized the option for the following Tuesday was the best bet for her. Besides, it was the first date they'd suggested, and as far as she was concerned, the sooner she talked to them, the better. Thinking about the case was totally nerve-racking, and she just wanted it over.

Trying not to think about it, Reese instead thought of Ella. She'd hung out with Reese's friends for hours, and they'd all had a great time on the deck, talking and joking. Mindy brought her guitar and played for them, and they'd eventually lit a fire in the pit to chase the chill and the bugs away. Reese was disappointed when Ella decided to leave, but an hour later, when everyone else had departed as well, she'd sent her a text, thanking her for coming. To Reese's surprise and delight, Ella replied with a winking smiley face and a four-word message.

The pleasure was mine.

They'd talked on Monday and taken a walk through the gorge with Cass and had another informal cookout at her parents' house. Reese smiled. Even with the investigation hovering over her head, thinking of Ella made her happy.

He wasn't sure how he'd set the wheels in motion, but the DA's office helped him make up his mind when they called and asked him to come in and answer questions about Stephanie Gates. He managed to get an appointment for the same day, and that was perfect. The sooner they began looking at Reese as a suspect, the better. Of course he knew that no physical evidence linked him to the crime, but if Cass ever told anyone what she'd told him, he'd have no alibi for the murder. In the past, an alibi was the only thing that had kept him from coming under scrutiny in Steph's murder investigation. He needed to keep it that way.

But as much as he despised Reese for turning Steph on him, he didn't actually want her to go to jail. And he knew she wouldn't. They had no evidence to convict anyone of this crime. Throwing her out there as a suspect would just confuse things, and if he ever came under scrutiny, the same clouds of uncertainty would protect him.

Even so, it would be nice to watch Reese squirm. Always so confident and cocky, she'd paled at the golf tournament when the investigation was mentioned. She wasn't stupid; she knew that, as Steph's lover, she'd be the number-one suspect in her murder. He could imagine her dilemma as she debated how she'd answer the question if it was asked. *Were you and Stephanie lovers?*

He could imagine her weighing the odds, wondering if anyone suspected anything. What were the chances the police might divine the true nature of her relationship with Steph? Probably pretty slim, because he'd never once heard even a murmur about it, even after Reese came out of the closet.

It was his job to change the odds.

Two hours later, he met with one of the assistant district attorneys and went through many of the same questions he'd answered in the days and weeks after Steph's accident. How did he know Steph? What had their relationship been? Where was he at the time of her murder? Could he think of any reason why someone would want to harm her? Did she have any enemies? They asked about classmates and events going on around the time of the murders, such as the prom and sporting events at school. He honestly couldn't answer some details, and others he'd rehashed so many times he felt like the memories were real rather than fabricated. When he was done, the woman thanked him for his time and told him she would be in touch if she had any further questions.

He thanked her for her efforts to find the killer, not with an obnoxious amount of enthusiasm, but with the concern of an old friend. Before leaving the building, he sought another attorney in the office.

"May I tell him what this is about?" the secretary asked.

"Bucky Draper," he said, knowing the upcoming campaign for district attorney was a hot topic around town. She nodded, smiled, and walked through a set of double doors while he waited patiently for her return.

"The district attorney can give you five minutes of his time," she said with a smile, and she ushered him through the same doors. "Second office on the left. His door is open."

He walked in and closed the door behind him. The DA rose from his chair and shook his hand without emerging from behind a desk covered with papers. "So what's going on with Bucky?" he asked as he returned to his seat.

He shook his head. "I'm sorry. I didn't want to tell your secretary why I'm really here," he said, and he watched the DA's posture change. He sat taller, leaned a little forward in his chair. The cobra ready to strike.

Before the DA could go on attack, he continued. "I'm here about Stephanie Gates. I didn't want to say what I have to say to the assistant who questioned me, because the information I'm going to share with you is somewhat sensitive, and I definitely don't want anyone to know where this came from."

The DA studied him for a moment, then leaned back in his chair. "Go on."

"I didn't tell this to the police back then. I simply didn't know what was happening," he said. "I was asked if Stephanie had a boyfriend and told the detective no, and I still believe that to be true. But I think she may have had a girlfriend."

The DA's head popped up so quickly his neck might have snapped, and his expression was one of sheer disbelief.

"What? Are you saying Stephanie was a lesbian?"

He nodded. "That's exactly what I'm saying."

"What proof do you have?"

He shook his head and frowned. "None. But five years after Steph died, Christine Ryan came out of the closet. She's had one girlfriend after another since then. And she and Steph were like this," he said, holding up his hand and crossing his middle finger over his second.

"A high-school friendship with a woman who later turns out to be homosexual doesn't prove much."

"I know it doesn't. But when Steph died, the detectives asked me if she was dating, and when they asked me again today, I figured it must be important. Honestly, when Christine told me she was a lesbian twenty years ago, the first thing—the very first thing that came to mind was Stephanie Gates. Our senior year, those two were inseparable. That's the time when a girl like Steph should have been dating and hanging out with guys, but the only one she was interested in was Reese. And vice versa."

He told the DA about their class trip to Disney and his hopes of hooking up with Steph.

"Are you sure this isn't just sour grapes because Steph wasn't interested in you?"

"If it was, I would have mentioned it back then. Truthfully, Steph was such a feminine girl, it never occurred to me that she could be gay until Reese came out. Don't forget, that was 1993. No one was openly gay back then. My perception of a lesbian was a woman with short hair wearing work pants and boots with a ring of keys on her hip."

The DA swallowed a smile and covered his mouth as he cleared his throat. "Even if this theory is true, what reason would Christine Ryan have for murdering Steph?"

He shrugged. "I have no idea. But you're the one who wants to know who she was dating. That question must have some significance."

The DA nodded. "We're working on another lead at the moment, but when Christine Ryan comes in, we'll definitely have a few new questions for her."

CHAPTER 16: DINNER DATE

You're very happy at one in the morning."

Reese looked up from her computer screen and smiled at Scoop Timlin, a colleague and friend she'd known since high school. Scoop had followed her from high school to college to medical school, and even did his residency in the same hospital, although he'd gone into the business of delivering babies. He was the biggest flirt she'd ever known, and if the rumors were true, he did more than flirt on some occasions, even now that he was married with children. They'd always been friends, though, and she was the one woman he didn't have to impress.

"Do I look happy?"

"You're humming. What's her name?"

"If I told you, you'd probably be at her door five minutes before I get there, trying to poach her."

"Good point. Do I at least know her?"

"I hope not." Reese leaned back in her chair and watched as he tilted his head and let out a belly laugh. Scoop was as good-looking as a man could be, with chiseled features, olive skin, and black hair that had just a hint of body. He wore it to his shoulders, much in the same style she did, and she had to admit the style looked better on him. At least she looked like a doctor, though. With his tailored suits, he looked more like a model or a businessman than an obstetrician.

"What brings you to the cellar?" she asked.

"Consult. Wasn't it from you?"

"Nope. Must have been the PA."

"Oh, Christ. I hate PAs! I hope I'm not missing sleep because of some nonsense."

"I guess it depends on how important you consider an abruption."

Reese's eyes flew open wide at the word, but the PA who'd uttered them remained calm as she handed a clipboard to Scoop. "Marley Lynott. She says you know her."

Suddenly Scoop was all business. "Ultrasound?"

The PA nodded toward the chart. "The report's there. I ordered the cross match for blood, and according to her chart, she's Rh negative. Thanks for coming by," she said as she casually walked away, leaving Scoop with an absolute disaster in the middle of the night. If he was lucky, he'd make it home in the morning in time to shower before office hours.

"Shit fuck," he said, and Reese bit her lip to suppress her smile. Thoughts of Scoop quickly faded from her mind as she finished the charts she needed to complete before heading home. Home to shower and sleep before waking up to spend her Friday thinking about her evening out with Ella.

She refused to consider it a date, even though they were going out together, alone, to eat. That was often how a date was described, but Ella hadn't said that word. Instead, she'd offered to buy her dinner to thank her for saving her pride at the golf tournament, and she'd promised to bring the shirt this time. So, it was dinner, and apparently, thoughts of dinner were enough to make her hum.

Why? What was so special about Ella? She was attractive, certainly. Anyone with eyes could see that. And intelligent. All you had to do was talk to her for thirty seconds to realize it. And kind. The way she acted with Bijou and Cass was enough to make the Grinch's heart grow three sizes. But Reese was also an attractive, intelligent woman, and she dated mostly attractive, intelligent women. Nothing ever came of dating, though, and she tended to keep it all in perspective. She'd go out, share something nice. Dinner, conversation, a movie. Perhaps sex. Perhaps they'd do it repeatedly, which would constitute dating, but none of it ever made her hum. So why was she humming now?

After finishing her work, Reese hopped into her Jeep and headed home to Moscow. The drive helped quiet her mind, for the darkness was nearly complete as she left the city. Her house really was in the country, where there was no crime, no taxes, and no neighbors visible in any direction. Her house was a divorce special, built with love by newlyweds and sold at a loss when they couldn't sever the ties that bound them quickly enough. It was at the end of a long drive, in a clearing that allowed enough sunlight to nourish a small yard of grass and some flowers, and Reese pulled around them and into her garage fifteen minutes after leaving the hospital.

Her shower was a quick one, and to her surprise, she slept well and awoke without the alarm the next day. It was nearly ten, which gave her only eight hours to decide on her wardrobe for her non-date.

Since Ella had given her full rein in planning the evening, Reese had decided to bring Ella in her direction, closer to the Pocono Mountains, rather than the foothills where Ella lived. There was a French restaurant Reese loved, and Ella had told her she was up for anything where food was concerned, so she'd booked a table for two. She'd asked the owner for a special table, and she hoped they'd get one near the expansive stone fireplace in the main dining room. Once she'd taken care of that, her thoughts had turned to her wardrobe, or lack thereof.

Reese wasn't much into fashion, usually choosing jeans for any occasion that didn't require something formal. For work, she wore scrubs. Yet she wanted to look good for Ella, and so she'd fretted for days about what to wear. In the end, a trip to the mall had provided the solution. She walked out with new black jeans and a lightweight black sweater, and ankle-high black boots. It was nearly fall, so the evenings were growing colder as the sun set earlier, and she thought the boots were very stylish. Even if they weren't, they were comfortable, and she liked them. She hoped Ella would, too.

After showering the germs from her body, she dried her hair and changed into her new outfit, and she was sitting in her living room waiting for Ella when she arrived.

"I really love your house," Ella said by way of greeting.

It was almost seven, and nearly dark, but the landscaping lights set strategically around the property still allowed a good view of the trees and flowers, as well as the chalet-style house. "Thanks," Reese said as she pulled back the door. "Come in."

"This is for you. Washed and ironed," Ella said, as she handed Reese her golf shirt, tied up with a ribbon. Dangling from the bow was a candy from the local confectioner.

"Oh, wow! A chocolate-covered pretzel! My favorite. And the shirt has never been ironed before, so thanks for that, too."

"Cass may have let it slip that you like chocolate."

"She can't keep a secret."

"Yeah. You probably shouldn't tell her anything confidential."

"Oh, no. What else did she say?" Reese demanded, a stern look on her face.

"Unlike Cass, I can keep a secret, so I'm not saying a word. I will say it was useful information, though."

"Oh, boy. I think I'm in trouble."

"Nothing you can't get yourself out of. But how about showing me this beautiful house? I didn't see much the other day."

The living room ran from the front of the house to the back, and Reese guided her toward the rear, where her couch and chairs flanked the fireplace. "This is my living room," she said. "Obviously."

Remembering their conversation during their first cookout, Ella laughed, then surveyed her surroundings. "What a great room." Looking from the high tongue-and-groove ceiling to the wall of stone flanking the fireplace, Ella marveled at the craftsmanship. It had been almost a month since she'd moved to the mountains, and she was settling in at her job, making friends, and learning her way around, enough to know she wanted to stay. Pip would be home from California for Christmas, and Ella had to start thinking about a house of her own. For the first time, the prospect excited her. She would love something lakefront, where she could sit on her deck and look out over the water, watch the sunrise over the mountains, or perhaps the sunset, depending on her vista. Either way, it wasn't in her budget, but something like this, like Reese's place, would be just as perfect. It would be a lovely place to come home to after a day at the office or a week away on business.

"Thanks," Reese said. "Would you like to see the rest?"

"Absolutely, if there's time."

"Sure. We can make it quick."

"I think it's time for me to start looking to buy a house," Ella said.

"So you like it here, huh?"

Ella nodded. "Very much."

"That's great. I can hook you up with my friend Doug. He's a realtor. He found this place for me."

"Is he an alum?" she asked.

Reese looked at her, curiosity in her eyes. "Does it matter?"

"Of course it does! As an employee of the university, I feel a responsibility to support the businesses of our graduates. The more successful they are, the more successful we are."

Reese couldn't help smile. "And maybe they'll make a little donation, right?"

Ella wasn't offended. "Maybe they will."

Now Reese laughed. "I guess that makes sense. But to answer your question, yes. He was in my class, both in high school and college. He married one of our college classmates, so you get double credit by supporting his real-estate business."

The thought delighted Ella. "Absolutely perfect!"

The house was, too. The kitchen, which she'd seen on Labor Day, was contiguous with the living room, and on the other side of the house, two other, large rooms served as a study and guest bedroom. "My room's upstairs," Reese said. "Would you like to see it?"

It felt like a loaded question, but Ella didn't hesitate. "Of course."

Following Reese up the stairs, she got another glimpse of her curvy shape, but remembering her trip up the steps at the golf course, Ella quickly turned her gaze to the stairs. They opened to a small sitting area, where a reading chair and lamp were set up atop a thick, white area rug. Beyond, in Reese's bedroom, a large sleigh bed stood in the center of the room, on a similar rug, facing a wall of glass. The room wasn't huge, but the furniture was spread across three walls, and nothing else crowded the space, so it seemed perfect.

"Closet," Reese said, pointing to a door. "And bathroom," she said, pointing to another.

Always a sucker for a bubble bath, Ella poked her head through the bathroom door and was impressed with what she saw. A huge tub was the main feature of the room, with the shower tucked into the corner. "Ah, heaven," Ella said. "I love baths."

Staring at the tub, and then at Ella, Reese imagined Ella soaking, bubbles up to her ears and wearing a contented expression, brown eyes looking at her through half-closed lids. Ella returned her stare, and Reese's heartbeat skipped. She licked her bottom lip, imagined pressing both of them gently to Ella's, and found Ella's gaze directed at her mouth. Ella was thinking the same thing, and knowing that filled Reese with courage. Tilting her head, she smiled seductively, then reached out a finger to brush the hair back from Ella's face.

Reese watched as Ella closed her eyes and moved into her hand, turning the innocent touch into a tantalizing caress. And then, Ella stepped back.

Clearing her throat, she broke the spell. "Don't we have a dinner reservation?" she asked, her voice husky with desire.

Reese pulled back as well. "Yes. We should get going."

"Would you mind if I drive?" Ella asked as they descended the stairs. "I'd like to learn my way around, and driving's the best way to do it."

"Do I need a crash helmet?"

"If you're scared, I'll go slowly."

Reese grabbed a jacket, and they made their way out of the house and into the driveway, where Ella's SUV was parked.

"I was hoping for a ride in the convertible," Reese said as she noticed the car.

"Can I give you a rain check?" Ella asked. She stopped to look at Reese, whose pulse quickened once again. When she'd accepted Ella's invitation to dinner, she'd hoped to get to know her better, to explore the attraction she felt and see where it might lead. Of course, she hoped it would lead to something, and all the indications were there that her wish might come true. It was an intoxicating thought, and Reese felt like a young girl, awkward and shy, fumbling for words.

"Um, yeah, sure."

After buckling up, Reese pointed Ella in the right direction and sat back to enjoy the view of Ella in the driver's seat. In spite of their heated encounter in her bathroom, the conversation was still easy. Ella talked about houses and how much more affordable they were in the mountains than in Philadelphia.

"I kind of like this area," Ella said.

"It's certainly private."

"You don't sound enthusiastic."

"No. That's not it. I love it here. I would never want to live in the city, or even one of the more crowded suburbs. I like the solitude out here. And I'm only fifteen minutes from town, twenty from the mall."

"We're east of Scranton, right?"

"Yes. West of PMU. I'm about in the middle of the two places."

"So your house would be an ideal place for me to live."

"Um, yeah."

"I mean out here, not your house specifically."

"Yep. Perfect," Reese said, feeling herself blush.

"What's north? And south? And west?"

Reese told Ella where to turn and then gave her a local geography lesson, including the best places to eat, play, and dine. Even though it was a thirty-minute drive to the restaurant, they hadn't finished talking about Ella's housing options when they pulled into the parking lot of the Chalet.

"That was easy," Ella said. It was easy being with Reese. The conversation flowed, with give-and-take, point and counterpoint balanced with a barb or a bit of humor. The silence was comfortable, too, though, and Ella liked that almost as much as she liked talking to Reese.

They entered through a stone archway into what had probably once been a grand hallway. At some point it had been partitioned, and in the area nearest the front door, a cheese shop had opened. Two large cases held a variety of cheeses, most of them French. Fake grapes and empty bottles of wine were scattered about the cases, and the image nearly made Ella's mouth water. Cheese (and wine) were both at the top of her favorites list, and she'd take a better look at the selection before they left. If she shopped on an empty stomach, she'd spend a fortune.

A little way down the hallway, past a large, ornate decorative screen, a podium stood in the middle of the hallway. A young man in a form-fitting sport coat and tie greeted them.

"Reservation for Ryan."

"Last name?" he asked.

"Yes."

He looked up, confused. "Can I have the last name?"

"Ryan."

Ella bit her tongue as she watched Reese having fun with the young man. Obviously, she was used to this sort of confusion. The hazard of having a first name for a last name, she supposed.

"Oh, yes. I see it. Right this way, please," he said, and took them a few feet to a coat closet, then into a twenty-by-forty-foot room with paneled walls and ceilings. The room was arranged as Ella would have expected a Parisian salon would have been a hundred years earlier. It had art on the walls, books on shelves, a woven rug on the floor, and club chairs arranged in groupings all around the room. Most of the chairs surrounded small tables, and she imagined it would be difficult to gather a group for dinner, but it was perfect for a party of two. A dozen parties of two were already seated as their host escorted them to a table near a large fireplace.

Before he could offer, Reese pulled out a chair for Ella and then pushed it toward the table. "I'm good," she said to him, and he politely retreated.

"Thank you," Ella said as Reese pulled her own chair out and sat.

"This is a cool place," Ella observed.

"During the week, they serve only breakfast and lunch. Friday and Saturday nights they add dinner. People come during the day to talk and read, and drink coffee and eat cheese. You might find some PMU students here during the day. It's a good place to go when you skip class."

"I'll avoid it, then."

Reese chuckled. "Not that I'd know."

"I'd imagine it's unwise to skip class when you're trying to get into medical school."

"Everyone needs a break once in a while."

Ella looked at Reese as she relaxed in the oversized chair. Her dark hair was perfectly straight, parted in the middle, and pushed back behind her ears. A black sweater contrasted with her bright eyes, and Ella sensed she was quite relaxed. That wasn't always the case, she knew. Her job had to be crazy, and she seemed to make a second career out of worrying about her parents and her sister. "What do you do now when you need a break?"

"What makes you think I need a break?"

"Everyone needs a break once in a while."

"Touché!"

Their server appeared, then took their drink orders and poured water, leaving menus in her wake. Ella studied hers for a minute before looking up at Reese.

"You obviously know this place well. What do you recommend?"

"Do you like cheese?"

Ella moaned.

"Then we should have cheese. Baked brie in a pastry, with fruit. Apples, I'd guess, since it's fall. Or a plate of assorted cheeses with a baguette. The entries are Americanized French but still superb. And save room for dessert."

"I'd like to try the brie." Ella leaned forward conspiratorially. "But I'll take home one of those cheese plates from the lobby."

This time Reese moaned. "I'm coming to visit. I'll bring the bread."

"Don't forget the wine."

"Speaking of wine," Reese said as the waiter appeared with a tray and set glasses before each of them.

"To new friends," Reese said, raising her glass.

"Indeed," Ella said as their glasses clinked.

Ella sat back and took a sip of the wine, closing her eyes as it warmed her mouth and then her throat. She savored the smell and the taste, and sighed before opening her eyes to find Reese staring at her.

"That was erotic," Reese said.

Fortunately, Ella didn't have any wine in her mouth, because if she had, she would have spit it out as she laughed. "I just like wine. What can I say?"

"Obviously."

"What is also obvious is that you're very good at deflecting questions."

"Me? I think you're the queen of deflecting. Obviously."

"I guess we're both a bit private, then."

Reese sipped her wine, studying Ella with a friendly gaze. "So, relaxing, you asked. Hmm. I read, or watch movies. Go out for dinner." She spread her hand before her.

"The company of friends is always nice," Ella said, as she realized how much she missed a simple pleasure like this one.

"Something tells me you don't do it often enough."

"Guilty. I tend to work a lot."

"It's paid off, though. Right? You have a great job, and you're very successful, I'd imagine, if they made you VP."

"I am successful, yes. And I tell myself it's important, but sitting here with you, next to this warm fire, with this magnificent wine…it suddenly seems quite unimportant."

"And you haven't even tasted the brie yet."

Ella laughed. "What do you like to read?"

"Everything."

"I like her, too. Her last novel was spectacular."

Reese ignored the tease, but the corners of her mouth turned up in a smile. "Mystery, suspense. That sort of thing. I try to figure out the plots to prove how smart I am."

"No predictable romance novels for you, huh?"

Reese shook her head.

"And is that what you like to watch, too?"

"I'll tolerate anything for five minutes. I can usually tell by then if I'll like a movie. I make sure to see everything that's up for an award, and I follow some actors and actresses. Whenever they release something new, I'll see that at the movies. And then, I'll go back in time and watch something ancient in black and white."

"Who are these must-see actors?" Ella asked just as the waiter returned to take their order.

"Oh, I'm sorry. We haven't even looked at the menu. But let's start with the brie," she said, looking to Reese for approval.

"Sounds perfect."

"Maybe we should study our menus instead of gabbing."

"Good idea."

Ella looked over the selections and decided on tuna, to balance all the fat and calories in the cheese. Reese didn't seem to be counting, as she ordered Beef Wellington.

They settled back in with the wine and talked about their favorite actors and actresses, then dove into the cheese when it came. It was mild and creamy, and with the baked apple atop, it was heavenly.

"So, I think it's time I got to the real purpose of our dinner," Ella said.

Reese licked cheese off her finger in a most seductive manner and then sat back, swirling her wineglass as she looked at Ella.

"So, it's not just the pleasure of my company that brought you out tonight?"

Ella shook her head.

"And not just my shirt, either, huh?"

"I'm afraid not. You made a wager at the golf tournament, and you lost. It's time to pay up."

"I was hoping you'd forgotten," Reese said as she hid behind her glass.

"No such luck. I met with Jeremy yesterday, and we made tremendous progress. He gave me a list of speakers who he thought would be appropriate to honor the senator, so that's a big first step. There's a lot to do, though, Ms. Committee Member."

"Who's going to speak?"

"He wants his old priest, his high school debate-team moderator, his college advisor, the governor, and you."

"Me?"

"It's typical to include a classmate, especially one like you, who's stayed in touch."

Reese cleared her throat. "As you know, I've never been to one of these things before. How does it work?"

"PMU always announces its scholarships and awards on the day before graduation, at the end of May. Memorial Day Weekend. It's a huge event. Everyone who gives a scholarship is there, as are all the current recipients—the incoming freshmen and the graduating seniors, and everyone in between. It's called the Cognitio Brunch. We gather in the great hall to recognize the donors, the benefactors, and then the winner of the alumni award."

"That's when I come in?"

"Exactly. So the program will start with me welcoming everyone, and I'll introduce you. You'll give your speech, then introduce the next speaker, and so on. We try to encourage everyone to focus on something different, so you don't have five people up there saying the same thing. From a friend perspective, you can add something special. Something no one else can, really. The university president will wrap it up and introduce the senator."

"Can I mention the time I knocked his front teeth out?"

"Absolutely. And how it helped build his character. Then you'll say something like there are a few people here who'd like to say nice things about him, so let's get this show on the road."

"Sounds easy. Why are you so worried?"

"We have to decide on the menu, the décor, the theme. Send invitational letters and confirmational letters. This is only eight months away. People book their schedules years in advance, Reese."

"True. I have plans well into the next decade. It was fortunate I could squeeze you in tonight for dinner."

Ella gave her a chastising look. "Anyway. We have to order flowers, linens, pick songs for the orchestra."

"Orchestra?"

"Well, you didn't think we'd have a DJ over brunch, did you?"

Reese sipped her wine and used a piece of bread to scoop up the last bit of cheese. She offered it to Ella.

"No, thanks."

"I guess a DJ wouldn't be quite right." Reese looked at Ella and saw a fire in her eyes. "You love this, don't you? All the planning and organizing."

"Oh, yes. I get to throw huge parties on the university's dime."

"Is this on the university's dime, too? I mean, since this is a business meeting and all." She waved her glass of wine again, and Ella sucked in a breath as she wondered just how good Dr. Ryan was with her hands.

She cleared her throat. "Of course."

"Damn. If I'd had known, I would have ordered the lobster pot pie instead of the beef."

"You can have an extra glass of wine to make up for it. I'm driving, after all."

Reese seemed to have a full glass of wine, even though she kept taking sips. Ella wondered how she did that. Her glass, on the other hand, was nearly empty. And she was the driver.

"I think I will, thanks. Just so you know, I'll pay my debt. I'll help out with Josh's celebration."

"I had no doubt."

The waiter arrived with their food, and Ella dug into the perfectly seasoned fish over a bed of greens. It was so good she didn't even envy Reese's red meat. Not until Reese started moaning.

"This is incredible," she said, then offered a forkful to Ella. "Would you like to try it?"

Instead of taking the fork, Ella leaned forward and allowed Reese to feed her. "Mmm. You're right. That's good."

Looking pleased, Reese leaned back and took another sip of her bottomless glass of wine. "My mom tells me you're leaving town."

"Yes, for a few days. Eight, to be exact."

"Where are you heading?"

"Connecticut, Rhode Island, and Massachusetts."

"What will you do?"

"Visit with alumni, attend a few parties, meet with current donors and potential new ones. I'll basically have meetings for breakfast, lunch, and dinner, every day."

"How much weight will you gain?"

Ella half-smiled. "It's really tricky to pretend to eat while you push things around your plate. But I couldn't possibly eat all those meals without putting on weight. Even if I run on the treadmill in the gym between meetings, I'd still get fat."

"Do you like to run?"

"No. I detest it. But it does burn calories."

"That it does. In the interest of weight-watching, shall we skip dessert?"

"Are you out of your mind?"

"Oh, thank God! I was worried I was going to have to take something home and devour it on the floor inside the front door."

"No worries. I'll probably eat something here and get something to go, too."

Reese winked. "You're my kind of girl."

Ella met her gaze, and a smile formed slowly, ending in a seductive half grin.

When the waiter returned with the dessert menu, Ella sighed. "This is so unfair, making me choose."

"Let's each choose one, and we'll share."

"Can I choose both?"

They decided on honey crepes and chocolate mousse to enjoy with coffee, and Napoleons and chouquettes to go.

"I think I know what I'll say," Reese said after a moment of silence.

"Hmm?" Ella asked, looking confused.

"About Josh. Senator Nathan."

"Oh. What will you say?"

"That he helped me through the worst time of my life—when Stephanie Gates died. She was my best friend. And probably just as close to Josh. We were all on student council together, for four years. We became very close. Just before she died, we traveled to Washington together, had an absolutely great time. It was us and five other boys. A great group. Doug—the realtor. Bucky, who's running for DA. Scoop Timlin, who's a gynecologist. Paul Pearl, who's a businessman downtown. And Rudy Simmons, who's a computer guy. That trip sort of cemented us. You know what I mean? We've all been friends ever since. Being away from home, meeting politicians, representing our school...we were growing up, and it was great."

"That's a nice story."

"That's not the story."

"Oh. What's the story?"

While Reese was nervous about the investigation and didn't typically like to talk about Steph, with Ella it was different. Ella made it seem safe, and in a way, Reese felt like she was finally going to put Steph to rest.

"Josh's mom had cancer, and he went with her to Philly for a bone-marrow transplant. He was the donor. He was there when Steph died, and his mom was so sick he couldn't leave, but he called me every day, like ten times a day, in the days when long distance wasn't free—and the Nathans didn't have much money. The truth is, I think he was grieving more than I was. I always suspected he had a secret crush on Steph, but she...I don't think she ever saw him as any more than a friend."

"Tough situation."

"Well, if it bothered him, he never let on. When she died, he reminded me about Washington, how we'd all talked about our future. He didn't say we'd finished a chapter. He said we'd finished a book and were about to start a new one. He said his was dedicated to Steph, and whenever he achieved something in his life, he would think of her and how much she'd helped him become the person he was. And he said the same thing about me. She's always with me. The people we love never really leave us."

Ella wiped a tear from her eye. "I didn't even know the woman she became, but I feel the same way. I'd always felt I'd find her again, and we'd be instant friends, just like when we were kids."

"Knowing her, you probably would have been."

"Well, it's a good story. He sounds like a good person."

Reese nodded. "For a lawyer."

Ella laughed and tilted the conversation back to Steph. She knew what Sophie had told her, but there was often a huge gap between the truth and what a teenage girl confided in her mother. "So, Steph wasn't dating anyone when she died, huh?"

Reese seemed to pale at the question, and Ella wondered why. Quickly recovering, she answered in much the same fashion as Sophie. "She dated every guy on the student council and half the swim team, but she never got serious with anyone."

"Why is that?"

"She was driven. She had goals, and nothing was going to stop her."

Ella thought about the irony of Reese's words but didn't comment. Someone had permanently stopped Steph. Was Sophie right? Was the murderer someone Steph knew, possibly from the student council? The thought was sobering as she sipped her wine. She didn't yet know Doug, the realtor, or two of the others, but she'd met Josh Nathan, and she'd been acquainted with Bucky and Scoop from childhood. None of them seemed capable of murder. But if Sophie was right, one of them, or someone just like them, had murdered Steph.

Ella decided a change of topic was in order. "So, this place has been around since you were a student, huh?"

Reese began to tell stories from her days at PMU, and Ella shared as well. The mood quickly became light, and Ella was grateful. They were still laughing about their collegiate antics when their plates arrived. "It looks almost too good to eat. Almost."

The childish delight on Ella's face warmed Reese. If only everyone was as happy with a bit of sugar and whipped cream. When the last bite was gone, they leaned back in their seats. Reese had never seen a woman as lovely as Ella looked at that moment, with her hair loose across her shoulders, flowing honey, and her brown eyes puddles of melted chocolate.

"Can you walk, or should I call an ambulance?" Reese asked.

"I can walk. Maybe."

As promised, Ella charged the dinner to her corporate card.

"Thanks for that. I didn't expect you to pay."

"Don't mention it. You really are a business associate."

Ella retrieved her coat and handed Reese hers as well, but she was too busy sliding into it to notice how much her comment stung Reese. Was that how Ella regarded this? Was all the flirting and friendly chatter just business to Ella? Because if it was, Reese would have a hard time adjusting to that. Not when she'd been humming at the thought of spending time together.

Reese was quiet on the way to the car, distracted by Ella's words and her own confused emotions. Not the kind to worry needlessly, or brood, she grabbed Ella's arm as they reached the car, stopping her progress.

Shaking her head, she searched Ella's eyes, lit only by the scarce dregs seeping through the windows. "I don't want to be a business associate, Ella."

Ella stood still and returned the stare, then quietly stepped closer, invading Reese's space. The air had chilled, but Reese could feel the warmth of Ella's body from a foot away, and she was absolutely sizzling by the time Ella touched her, bringing her fingers to Reese's lips before sliding them along her jaw, and her throat, before replacing them with her lips.

It was a soft kiss, a gentle touch of their lips meant to say more than any words ever could. It lasted only a second but gave a hint of something more to come, something Reese sensed could last for a lifetime.

How had this happened? She'd never really been against relationships. They just never seemed to work for her. Her job and her family took up too much of her time, so much so that she never seemed to have enough for anyone else. But she'd never met anyone who made her want to change that situation. In Ella, she sensed she'd found someone who wouldn't ask her to change. Ella fit into her world perfectly. She also had a demanding career, one she'd sacrificed for and had succeeded in, so she could understand Reese's dedication to her job. And she fit into her family. Reese had never met anyone—well, except for Steph—who adored Cass and could be a part of her family, instead of a separate piece of it.

With Ella, new, strange things seemed to be possible. As Reese opened the door for Ella and walked back to her own side, she began to hum.

CHAPTER 17: A SUSPECT

As she began the short drive home from Reese's house, her skin still tingling where Reese had kissed her neck and her lips, Ella was happy she lived so close by. She was too agitated to concentrate on the drive.

Part of her wanted Reese to ask her in, and part of her wanted to invite herself in, but an even bigger part of her was enjoying this little dance of seduction they'd started. It was fun, the flirting. And the more time she spent with Reese, the more she liked her. It was no longer a question of *if* they were going to end up in bed, but *when*. And three days before she had to leave for a long trip didn't seem like the ideal *when*. So, she'd dropped Reese off, and before she could ask, Ella had told her she'd call her the next day. The car was too dark for her to tell if Reese looked disappointed, but she suspected Reese was enjoying this buildup as much as she was, and so she kissed her softly on the lips and climbed out of the car without another word.

It was after eleven o'clock and dark when she pulled into the driveway at Pip's, and she stopped the car as soon as she realized every light in the houses was on. She was sure she'd turned them off before she left. And wouldn't Sharon have called her if she hadn't? Sharon had a key, but why would she be at Pip's place now, so late at night? And if she did decide to pay Ella a visit, why all the lights? Something was going on, and whatever it was couldn't be good.

Not bothering to pull into the garage, Ella found her house key and hurried to the back door. It had grown cold as well as dark, and she shivered. Her reaction was due just as much to nerves as the temperature.

Before she could put her key in the lock, the door opened, and waiting there to greet her she found a smiling Pip, holding a squirming Bijou in her arms.

"Hi!" she said.

Ella was stunned. "Pip, hi. What's going on? Is everything okay? Why are you home so soon?"

"Oh, everything's fine. I was just homesick, and it wasn't working out in California, so I decided to come home."

"For good?"

Ella had thought about house hunting, and she wanted to meet Reese's friend Doug but hadn't set that up yet. If Pip was home and Ella had to move now...she couldn't even think about it.

Pip nodded, and then, sensing Ella's angst for seemingly the first time, she quickly shook her head as she wrestled to control the dog. "Don't worry. You don't have to leave. The house is plenty big enough for both of us."

Relieved, Ella nodded and reached out to pet Bijou. "Hi, buddy, I'm back. It's so good to see you." She looked at Pip.

"You're sweet. And I mean it. You're not going anywhere."

"That's good. Because right now, I'm too tired to walk up the steps, let alone to a hotel."

Pip laughed. "Well, come in, and we'll have some tea and talk."

"I was startled by the lights, so I parked in the driveway. I'll pull the car into the garage. Then we can catch up."

Pip smiled. "I'll put the kettle on."

"Be back in a minute," Ella said before returning to the car. This was certainly a wrench in the works. It wasn't that she didn't like Pip, but she was used to living alone, and no matter how big the house, it was still Pip's, and she was the guest. She didn't want to be anyone's guest for more than a few hours at a time.

"Just let me change my clothes, Pip, and I'll be down soon," she said when she came back. She'd worn a casual skirt with a cardigan duo and swapped them for a baggy T-shirt and sweats. As she pulled her phone out of her bag to plug it into the charger, she saw a text from Sharon.

I just want to give you a heads-up. Pip's home. She didn't say why, but she popped over a little while ago to let me know she's back, and she picked up the dog. See you soon.

The text had come in an hour before, so Pip hadn't arrived much before Ella. Hmm. It was so strange, this sudden homecoming. Fortunately, she'd be leaving in a few days for a week-long business trip, so she would have a little time to think about her next move. At the moment, her mind was still spinning from Reese, and it was difficult to concentrate on the fact that she might soon be homeless.

She found Pip in the den, sitting on the couch before a fire and sipping from her mug. Bijou was curled up next to her, and he barely looked in her direction as he basked in the warmth of his mom. Ella took a seat on the other end of the couch and reached for the mug Pip had set on the coffee table.

"Thanks for the tea," she said.

"I didn't know what you like, so I just made plain decaf tea with honey."

"Perfect," Ella said, and as she took a sip, she realized that it was. "Mmm."

"You were out to dinner? With whom? Where'd you go?"

Ella wasn't sure how much she wanted to disclose, but she wasn't up for keeping secrets. "I was out with Reese Ryan."

Pip's eyebrow shot up. "Good choice."

Ella choked on her tea. She would have defended herself, told her they were just friends, but she would have been lying. They'd barely kissed, but much more was going on than friendship.

"Did you bring me anything?"

"I have dessert. If I'd known you were coming, I would have brought you a feast."

Pip looked down into her mug and shook her head. "It was a sort of sudden decision."

"I know you weren't fond of Miles, but the last time I talked to you, you said you loved your class. What happened?"

"I did love it. I do. I love filmmaking. It wasn't that. It was Miles. At first, I thought he was just a little hyper. You know—high energy. Then I started to suspect he was using drugs. Now I don't know what to think. He's one very strange guy, I'll say that, and I knew I couldn't stay there anymore. I thought of renting a place, but the more I thought about it, the more I wanted to get as far away from him as I could."

The look on Pip's face was blank, and Ella was concerned. "Pip, what happened? Did he do something to you? Did he hurt you?"

"Not me…but I'm wondering."

"Wondering what?"

Pip sat up, startling Bijou. She leaned forward and rested her arms on her elbows. "He told me I could have the run of the house, whatever I needed, what was his was mine. It was much as I said to you, so I felt his offer was genuine. Of course, I didn't take advantage of him. I was in the guest house, so I wasn't underfoot. I bought my own food and cleaned up the place. He's a slob, by the way. I cooked a little, too. You know, I was trying to show my appreciation for his hospitality. I treated him to dinner a few times, even met some of his friends. He took me on the set with him, and I got to meet a ton of people. It was all going well, until last week."

"What happened last week?"

"Well, as I said, he's strange. He gets right in your face when he talks to you. He has no appreciation for personal space. Ditto for the guest house. His house has twenty rooms, and he was always walking in unannounced. Like we were bosom buddies. And he'd walk around naked. Now *that* was a scary sight. The man is in the wrong kind of movies—could be a porn star. And he plays this strange, strange music. Movie themes. It's like you're on the set of *Star Wars*, or *Schindler's List*. Wacky. Just crazy."

Ella nodded. Reese had told her Miles was a little different, but what Pip was describing sounded worse. She was no psychiatrist, but Miles sounded crazy.

"That's not the worst of it. You should see the scrapbooks."

"The scrapbooks?"

Pip nodded. "I had a project for class. We had to set a series of pictures to music, for dramatic effect. Wouldn't you know I bought a new camera card before I left? I didn't want to risk losing my pictures, so I had none to draw from. I figured everyone would be using the California coastline, so I wanted something different. Miles told me to help myself to any pictures I found. I started looking around his scrapbook room. Can you believe it? Famous movie star and film producer, and his favorite hobby is scrapbooking?"

Ella shrugged. It was something she'd never gotten into, but she understood it was quite popular.

"He doesn't document normal things, Ella. Not parties and vacations. He preserves death. Plane crashes. Fires. Earthquakes. Murdered women. And the strangest one of all—he has a scrapbook, an entire, huge book about Stephanie Gates."

Ella felt as if she'd been slapped. "What?"

"It's so weird. I hadn't even thought of Stephanie for years until you asked about her that day. Then I fly across the country to find this amazing chronicle of her life and death. He has photos of her, hundreds of them. Her high school yearbooks. Newspaper articles from swim meets and school activities. And, of course, the murder. He has every article about her murder, with words highlighted and underlined. And the worst part, Ella, made me want to throw up. He has a mutilated picture of her, with blood dripping from her head. It's the centerfold of the book."

Ella was speechless, felt her head spinning and her mouth go dry. No wonder Pip had left. She would have wanted to get as far away from Miles Jones as she could, too.

"Holy shit, Pip. He sounds scary. It's good that you left."

Pip shook her head. "I know, Ella. I had to get out of there. I've never been so petrified."

"Do you think he's dangerous?"

Pip nodded. "I do, Ella. More than that, though—I think he murdered Stephanie."

CHAPTER 18: BUSINESS AND PLEASURE

With an adrenaline rush born of facing a new challenge, Ella hopped out of bed on Monday morning, showered, dressed, and walked out the door by eight o'clock. The first leg of her trip was a short one—across the yard, to say good-bye to the Ryans.

Cass answered the door with an enthusiasm that suggested she'd been up for hours, her mother close behind and not looking nearly as alert.

"How's the new roommate?" Sharon asked.

Ella felt her eyes fly open wide. She'd still not absorbed the information Pip had told her, and she wasn't sure what to do with it. She'd suggested Pip call Reese's friend Karen in the DA's office, and Pip had agreed to do that this morning. As far as having a roommate, though—that had been pretty benign. Pip had slept through most of Saturday and had spent Sunday visiting relatives she hadn't seen in a month. Ella had hardly seen her for five minutes since she'd been back and told Sharon so.

"I wouldn't be in a hurry to find a place," Sharon said. "Pip's likely to be on a plane to Europe next week."

Ella shrugged. She simply couldn't worry about it now.

"So, you're all set for the trip?" Sharon asked.

Ella nodded. "My first road trip for PMU. How do I look?" She'd worn a simple brown cardigan over a bold-pattern dress, with flecks of orange and green. It had seemed strong and sophisticated in the dressing room at Boscov's, but now she wondered if it was the right look.

Sharon's smile told her that first instinct was right. "I'd write you a check. How much do you want?"

"Thanks," she said, stepping around Cass to give Sharon a hug. "I'm a little nervous."

"It sounds like you won't have time for nerves," she said.

"True." Over Sunday dinner, Ella had shared her itinerary with the Ryans. They'd become like family to her, and she felt comfortable spending time with them, even giving details about her job.

She'd grown fond of them, all of them, but especially Reese. When she'd received the invitation to dinner on Sunday, Reese had called this time, instead of Sharon or Cass. And though the question was asked and answered in thirty seconds, they'd lingered on the phone for thirty minutes, talking about their dinner the night before, and the dog, and the weather, and a bunch of other things. It was only her sense of decorum that forced her to end the conversation. If she didn't care that Reese knew she was sitting home on a Saturday night with nothing to do, she would have talked to her for hours.

"I think Reese will miss you," Sharon said. Her eyes bored into Ella's in a manner that suggested she knew how'd they'd spent Friday evening, even though neither of them had told her. They'd agreed not to talk about it with Sharon and Cass until they figured out what *IT* was. Yet here she was, on the spot, searching for a rejoinder that wouldn't be telling or deceitful.

"I'll miss her, too. I'll miss all of you. You've been so kind to me—I could never have imagined meeting such wonderful neighbors."

"I guess my job will be easy, now that Pip's back. I'll call you if she leaves again."

"I'm thinking she'll stay put for a while," Ella said and nearly shuddered as she thought of Miles Jones and his macabre scrapbook of Steph.

Sharon laughed. "Maybe I'll call just to chat."

"I'd like that," Ella said, and hugged her again.

A minute later, she was in her SUV, heading north into New England. She'd had a light breakfast, since she was meeting a potential donor for lunch, and another for dinner, and if she wasn't careful, the schedule of meetings over food would soon make her obese. She hadn't sacrificed her coffee, though, and an hour into the trip, she made her first stop, to use the restroom. Two hours later, she arrived at the restaurant where she was meeting a retired anesthesiologist, and even though it was early, she found a table and pulled out her iPad while she waited. Though she'd reviewed the doctor's file the night before, she pulled it up again to refresh her memory.

He was seventy-nine years old, had majored in chemistry at PMU, and went to medical school after serving in the army. He'd used his background to help develop new drugs for a pharmaceutical company and had made a fortune. He'd already donated money to PMU, and Ella wasn't looking for anything further than to meet him, thank him, and find out what they could do for each other. She often worried about older donors, who, like this gentleman, were giving their money to worthy causes because they had no children who would benefit from the inheritance. Who took care of them, helped with shopping and household chores that had become too difficult to manage? She'd helped many of her donors over the years in handling similar issues, and it gave her as much satisfaction as the million-dollar gifts. More, perhaps.

Loud voices interrupted her studies, and she looked up to see the waiter who'd seated her earlier escorting an elderly gentleman toward her table. By the looks of things, she didn't have to worry about the doctor. On his arm, wearing a much-too-tight sweater, was a buxom redhead half his age.

Ella stood as they approached. "Dr. Adler?" she asked, as she reached for his hand. "I'm Elizabeth Townes."

"A pleasure, Miss Townes. Call me Dr. Joe. Everybody does. And this is my wife, Candy."

She sure is, Ella thought as she tried hard not to stare at the huge breasts threatening the fabric that contained them.

"What brings you to Stamford?" he asked as he settled back in the cozy club chair.

"You do, Dr. Joe. You're a major benefactor for the university, and as the new vice president of development, I wanted to reach out to you and show you our appreciation, let you know what your money's doing for the school, and see if we can do anything for you."

"What you can do for me? What could the school possibly do for me?"

Ella sat back as the waiter appeared to take their drink orders. She opted for coffee, while the Adlers chose something a little stronger.

"Well, that depends. As you know, our alumni base stretches well into New England, so there are always people around to help each other. I'm sure you don't have to worry about medical care, since you know a ton of doctors, but for some people that's an issue. We can help connect you with lawyers, accountants, other alumni for social gatherings. That sort of thing."

He suddenly sat forward and pointed a finger at her. "Do you know what I need?" he asked.

"What?" Ella asked, as she thought *a penile implant.*

"A new set of dentures. Do we have anyone who does that?"

Ella swallowed her smile as she reached for her tablet. "Let me check." She punched in her codes and accessed the alumni database. "In New Haven, we have a husband and wife team of prosthodontists. I can connect you with them, if you'd like."

"Swell. It's very nice of you to think of me."

"Tell me your story, Dr. Joe. How'd you go from PMU to the military to Yale and beyond? You've had quite a journey."

Dr. Joe began talking, and Ella wasn't surprised when she couldn't get him to stop. She'd allowed two hours on her schedule for lunch, figuring she could check into her hotel and relax for a few hours before dinner with another alum. It was nearly three o'clock, though, by the time she got back to her car, and she wasn't surprised when Dr. Joe wrapped his arms around her and gave her a big hug. Ella liked him, and she even liked Candy, who seemed genuinely sweet and attentive to Dr. Joe. And although she hadn't solicited a penny, by the time they'd finished their fourth and final cocktail of the afternoon, Dr. Joe had suggested he might reconsider the multimillion-dollar gift he'd given the university, in favor of something even more generous.

Ella didn't kick off her pumps and rest her feet on the bed in her hotel room until after four. She'd had only two hours to rest and regroup before her six o'clock dinner, and the stuffy accountant and his wife she met at the posh Italian restaurant had nearly bored her into unconsciousness. She was grateful to be back in her room by eight.

Reflecting on the day as she showered, Ella thought it had gone well. She wasn't counting on another gift from Dr. Joe—people often reconsidered such spontaneous offers. Yet she liked him, and she'd make a call to the prosthodontist in the morning. The accountant had been giving small annual gifts to the university, and after meeting him, Ella had no doubt it was simply a deduction for him, rather than a gift of gratitude or affection. That was okay, though. All donations were welcome.

Her soft, cotton pajamas felt wonderful after a day in a dress and pantyhose, and Ella pulled her iPad, her Kindle, and her phone into bed with her when she crashed a few minutes later. It was early, yet she was tired, and as she closed her eyes, she found her thoughts drifting. Not to work, or donors, but to Reese Ryan and her smile. Her easy laugh.

Their evening together had been one of the nicest nights Ella had ever spent, and Sunday dinner had been fun, too. They'd all worn

Philadelphia Eagles jerseys to the dinner table, and the food was timed
to end before kickoff. To Ella's delight, they'd abandoned the mess in
the kitchen and dining room until halftime, when she and Reese took
charge of cleanup. After the game, they took Bijou for a walk, and
when Ella could avoid it no longer, she hugged them all good night.
All of them except Reese, who insisted on walking her across the yard.

On her back porch, as Bijou wound his way between their feet,
they'd talked for another ten minutes before Ella finally forced herself
through the door. She had to pack for an eight-day trip, and she hadn't
even started.

Ella stared at her phone. Reese was working the overnight shift in
the ER. Would she be sleeping now, in preparation for a long night? Or
would she already be up and about, getting ready for work? Would she
welcome a call from Ella, or would it be a distraction? Ella hoped it was
the former as she shot off a text.

Greetings from Connecticut. You awake?

Nope. Sound asleep. How about you?

Sleeping, too, but having a very nice dream.

Am I in it?

Ella paused for a moment, wondering just how flirtatious she
should be. But she was two hundred miles away; how dangerous could
a little flirting be?

As a matter of fact, you are.

Ella stared at the phone in her hand, awaiting a reply. She was
startled when it rang, but not surprised it was Reese calling.

"Hi."

"I'm tired of typing."

"Already? We've only just begun to text."

"We've already surpassed the total number of texts I've ever sent
to any other human being."

"I thought you had tons of friends."

"I do, but I don't text them."

"How do you communicate?"

"We converse."

"How novel."

"Would you like to try it? I mean, it worked the other night."

"Surprisingly well."

"Surprising that you could talk on the phone...or that you could talk to me?"

Instead of a quick retort, Ella took a breath and paused. It was time to tell Reese what was going on, because she was feeling things she hadn't in ages. Daydreaming, singing in the shower, imagining all kinds of Reese-related things. "I...this is kind of strange for me, Reese. I left Philly thinking I would never meet another interesting woman, especially in the mountains. And I was really fine with that. I have a wonderful career, right? Who needs a girlfriend? And then I met you, and ever since, I can't stop thinking about you and wanting to see you again. And when I do see you, it's even more amazing to be with you than I thought it would be. I don't want to go when it's time to go, and I don't want to hang up the phone when I should. I just want to keep on talking...to you."

Her confession was met with silence.

"Reese? Are you there?"

"I'm here."

"Are you blushing?"

"Big-time."

Ella laughed. "So I like you. Do you want to go on a real date with me when I get back?"

"I would love to."

"When?"

"What time will you be home on Monday?"

Ella laughed. "Probably too late for a proper date, I'm afraid."

"How about after Cass's party? You'll have the week to recover from your trip, and on Saturday, we can spend the evening together. The party will be over at four. Would you like to do something afterward?"

"It's a date."

"A date. Yes."

"You're blushing again, aren't you?"

Reese felt herself nodding and realized she had to speak. Ella couldn't see her through the phone. Then she thought of something. "Why don't we FaceTime? Then you can see for yourself."

Reese didn't expect the silence that followed her question. "Ella? Are you blushing?"

"No, but I'm in my PJs, and I have wet hair."

"Better I see this now, rather than later. This way, if I want to cancel the plans for next Saturday, I have ample time."

"That's very practical. Please let me know as soon as you've made your decision."

"Is that a yes?"

Reese held her breath while Ella debated. Why did she care so much?

"Yes."

A few seconds later, Ella's face appeared on her iPad, and Reese was struck once again. Even with wet hair and no makeup, she was beautiful. "Hi."

"You're blushing," Ella said.

"Obviously. And you're beautiful. I've made my decision. The date is on."

Ella smiled as she ran her hand through her hair. "Whatever will I wear? I mean, how can I possibly top this?" she asked, pointing to her pink pajama top.

"I bet you'll think of something."

"Tell me about the party. What *should* I wear to the pumpkin patch?"

"I just checked the forecast, and it's going to be fifty-five and sunny, but there's rain for the next few days, so it'll be muddy. Wear old shoes, or boots, and something you can wash, because your clothes will smell like smoke from all the campfires."

"Can you believe I've never been to a pumpkin patch before?"

"You haven't lived."

"I think you're right. Who's going to be there?"

"It's a pretty fun group of people. Old school friends, mostly—people who've known Cass her whole life. The girls from the Labor Day cookout. And some of her friends, too, and some people from work. I called the RailRiders, and they're going to send Champ and Quill."

"Who are Champ and Quill?"

"The team mascots. They love Cass."

Ella's smile warmed Reese's heart. "That's so sweet."

"I think she'll have a great day."

"You're a good sister, Reese."

Reese wished she could accept the compliment, but she couldn't. Not when the Fates had dealt her such a great hand and had cheated

Cass. What she did for her sister wasn't nearly enough. It could never be.

When Ella yawned again, Reese decided she'd better say good night. Ella had an early meeting. "Can we do this again tomorrow?" she asked.

"Same time?"

"Perfect," Reese said as she hung up her phone.

It amazed her how she and Ella had connected. Who would have thought she could find such an amazing woman dog-sitting for her parents' neighbor?

Reese brushed her teeth, turned out the light, and relaxed on her bed for a half hour of meditation before she left for work. As much as Ella had distracted her, she couldn't help thinking about her plans for the next day. It was the day of her interview with the district attorney's office. Because of her friendship with Karen, someone else would be conducting her interview, but that didn't matter. Reese would have been equally nervous answering questions from anyone in that office.

Pulling the pillow over her head, she sighed. Her life was going so well right now. She hoped she could finally put Steph to rest and relax a little.

CHAPTER 19: THE GIRLFRIEND DID IT

Seven days later, Reese was curled up on her couch staring at the iPad, willing it to ring. She'd spent every evening FaceTiming with Ella and had looked so forward to it that she'd actually changed her schedule, switching a string of three evenings for overnight shifts, just so she'd be free when Ella was. That was crazy! Who did extra night shifts? Apparently, women who hummed did, and Reese found herself humming often.

They'd spent the week getting to know each other better, and she looked forward to hearing about Ella's days, her donors, and her journey through New England. Reese loved to look at her when she talked, seeing the passion in her eyes when she was excited, and her job clearly had that effect on her. They talked about the mundane, too, and their conversations were so easy Reese felt like they were an old married couple.

Tonight, though, she had a big reason to talk to Ella. She had news about Steph's murder. She'd been scheduled to go in to the DA's office a week earlier, but before she could leave the ER that morning, she'd had a message telling her the interview had been canceled. Reese had called Karen but hadn't been able to find out why. Karen's only response was that the office was devoting all its resources to a lead that had developed and was suspending all interviews.

"Ring," she instructed the iPad for the tenth time, but it didn't listen. When it finally did ring, she quickly answered and noticed that Ella was once again wearing her jammies and sporting the wet look, as she often had during their week apart.

"How was your day?" she asked.

Ella spent a few minutes filling her in, and Reese listened attentively. It was sort of mundane, the details of a job few would have been interested in, but to Reese, it was as fascinating as surgery. It amazed her, that with all her education, she knew so very little about fund-raising.

"How was your day? Or should I ask how was your sleep? Or your last night?"

"Everything's good. But I have big news. I found out what's going on with Stephanie's murder investigation."

Ella was eager to hear more. When Reese told her that her interview had been canceled, she thought it might have something to do with Miles Jones and the information Pip had given the police, but she didn't want to gossip without knowing any facts. Reese might just know more than she did at this point.

"My friend Karen and another woman from her office left for California on Thursday to interview a key witness. You'll never guess who."

California? It couldn't be a coincidence. "Miles Jones?"

"What? How did you guess that?" she asked, sounding incredulous.

Ella laughed and told her about Pip's experience in California and her suggestion that she talk to the DA's office. "So how did it go? Are they going to arrest him?"

"I don't know what's going on. My friend Bucky, who's running for DA, filled me in. Karen has been very quiet about this."

"As she should be, I would say. I'm sorry I didn't say anything to you about Miles. I should have realized how anxious you are to get this all over with. But I didn't want to gossip about him. First of all, he's your friend. And second of all, being creepy does not equate to being guilty. For all we know, he could have been in jail at the time of the murder and his scrapbook isn't a souvenir at all, just some warped tribute to Steph."

When Reese was silent, Ella spoke again. "Reese? Are you still there?"

Ella heard her sigh. "I'm here. I was just thinking that you're right. You did the right thing. And as much as I'd like for them to find Steph's murderer, I don't want it to be Miles."

"When will we know?"

"They probably talked to him on Friday. For all I know, they could be home by now. Or maybe they waited to get some court order to bring him back to Pennsylvania. Who knows? I don't want to take advantage of my friendship with Karen by asking her what's going on."

"It sounds like she wouldn't tell you anyway."

Reese laughed and decided to change the subject. "So, when will you be home?"

"By lunchtime, I hope. I have a breakfast meeting, and then I'm on my way."

"You'll drive right past my house, but I'll be sleeping."

"And you need your sleep. Lives depend on you."

"I'll try to keep that in mind."

Reese's call-waiting beeped and she looked at the phone. The interloper was Karen. "Ella, Karen is calling. Let me take this and get back to you."

"Hi, pal. What's up?"

Karen's voice sounded strained. "Reese, I just got back from California, and I have to tell you, something strange is going on here."

"With Miles Jones?"

"No. Miles was in Australia when Steph was murdered. He just has some odd fantasy about dead girls. Really weird. What's odd is I've been taken off the Stephanie Gates murder investigation. Wanna know why?"

Reese had a sinking feeling, and she grasped the phone tighter in her hand as she waited for Karen to answer.

"Because of my relationship with you."

"What does this have to do with me?"

"I was hoping you could tell me."

Reese didn't know what to say. Which hat was Karen wearing at the moment, friend or prosecutor? She decided to ask.

"I wouldn't be calling if I wasn't your friend. I want you to have a heads-up. Someone from the DA's office will be at the hospital in the morning to talk to you. They're going to wait until the end of your shift, when you're tired, so you'll be more likely to say something stupid."

"Should I get a lawyer?"

"It's never a bad idea."

"Thank you for telling me, Karen. I owe you one."

Reese hung up the phone and pursed her lips in thought. Rather than the terror she suspected she should feel, she was curious. What was this about? Why her? Why now? They had to know she and Steph had been lovers. But how? They'd been deep in the closet then, hadn't even known anyone else who was gay. She'd never told a soul, and she was certain Steph hadn't either. Steph had dozens of friends, but no one she was close enough to that she'd share that sort of confidence with. And back then, this was top-secret information.

No. No one could know the truth.

Why take Karen off the case, then? What else would make the DA's office suspicious of her? She had an alibi, even if a woman with an intellectual disability provided it, and absolutely no motive. The only reason anyone would ever think she'd harm Steph was if they were involved in a lovers' quarrel.

If they asked her that question, what would she say? Should she be honest, tell the DA the truth, out Steph to her mom, and put herself under further scrutiny? Or should she lie? How would they ever know, either way? The only witness, the only one who could verify her statement to the DA, was dead.

Her phone beeped with a text. It was from Ella.

What's up? Are they going to arrest Miles?

No. He was out of the country when Steph was killed. I'm going in tomorrow to give my statement. Have a safe drive, and I'll talk to you tomorrow night.

K. Night.

It was the longest night shift she'd ever spent, and she tried to act surprised when the investigator from the DA's office showed up in the ER fifteen minutes before the end of her shift.

"Is everything okay?" she asked.

"Yes. Just some routine questions. The DA would like you come down to the courthouse so he can talk to you."

Reese eyed him suspiciously. He was freshly shaved, his short hair was slicked back, and he was dressed impeccably, with a tailored suit and shiny loafers. He didn't look like he worked in public service.

"Now? I've been up all night, and I have to work again tonight. I need to sleep." She knew this was inevitable, but she knew she'd betray Karen if she didn't act somewhat surprised at the invitation. Or was it a command?

"This won't take long."

"Okay," she said. "I need to finish up here."

Reese purposefully delayed her departure, completing all her charts and making the smug-looking man in the suit wait. In the staff lounge, she brushed her teeth and her hair and washed her face before changing into jeans and a sweater. Only then, forty-five minutes after her shift ended, she followed him out of the parking lot and to the courthouse, where he ushered her through a back door and down a few corridors and into the office of the district attorney. Before the investigator left her, Ella pointed to her watch. "I have a busy night shift ahead of me. Please remind the DA of your promise not to keep me here long."

He nodded, and within five minutes, Ella was ushered into a conference room. The Lackawanna County District Attorney, Andrew Miller, was waiting for her.

He didn't stand to greet her but told her to have a seat. "I understand you're in a hurry, Dr. Ryan. Thanks for coming down today. As you know, my office is investigating the homicide of Stephanie Gates. We are interviewing every single person we talked to in 1993 and trying to follow whatever leads develop as a result of those interviews."

Reese looked him in the eye but didn't speak. She wondered if he could see the pulse pounding in her throat. It should be visible from New Jersey.

"I have here the statement you made back then. I'm going to ask you the very same questions, and I'd like you to answer them as honestly as possible. If you don't remember or don't know how to answer, please state that, rather than guessing."

"Okay."

"How did you know Stephanie Gates?"

"We went to the same high school."

"What school was that?"

"Pocono Mountains Prep."

"You'd never met her before then?"

"No."

"And when did you meet her? For example, your freshman year."

"Yes. It was freshman year."

"And under what circumstances did you meet? Were you in the same homeroom?"

"No. We met on student council. We were both elected to the council, and I met her at the first meeting."

"So, at the time of her death, you'd known her for approximately four years?"

"Yes."

"Did you see each other outside of school?"

Reese tried not to let her mind wander to all the things she and Steph had done outside the boundaries of the high school.

"Yes."

"What sort of things did you do outside of school?"

Reese tried to think, not of what she and Steph had done—that was easy. Had they asked her these questions after Steph died? She didn't think so. The question that stood out was "Did Steph have any enemies?" The answer hadn't changed in all these years. No. Everyone loved her, including Reese.

"Dr. Ryan? Do you need a moment?"

Reese cleared her throat. "We went shopping at the Viewmont Mall, went to movies, swam at the lake, studied, rode bikes. Everything. We did everything together. We were best friends."

"You did everything together? Did you have sex?"

Reese had expected the question, but not like that. She didn't have to feign her surprise. "What?"

"Were you and Ms. Gates lovers?"

Reese had debated the answer to the question for weeks, since she'd learned the DA was reopening the investigation. It was her biggest fear, this question, and she still didn't know how to answer it.

"Am I under arrest, Mr. Miller? Because if I'm not, I think I'd like to leave now."

He eyed her with a sleazy smile. "No, you aren't under arrest, so you can leave at any time. But I don't see why you'd want to. Don't you want to help us find Steph's killer?"

Reese was tempted to speak from the heart, but she suspected anything she might say would only get her into trouble. Instead, she stood, and without saying a word, she walked out of the room.

The walls really did feel as if they were closing in on her, and she identified the sensation as vertigo. She should probably sit down, but instead she kept walking. When she reached the sidewalk, the sun had warmed the day a few degrees, but not enough to chase her chill. Instead of heading to her car, she walked across the street and into the office building there. After studying the marquis for a moment, she found the name she was looking for and pressed the appropriate button on the elevator.

"Good morning," she said to the casually dressed woman in the lobby of the Draper Law Firm. "Reese Ryan for Bucky Draper."

He appeared at the doorway so quickly, she suspected he must have known she was coming. He looked like he'd lost weight, but his suit still bunched in all the wrong places, and his forehead was shiny, as if he was sweating. "I can't help you, Reese."

"What? Why?"

"Reese, if you're arrested for Steph's murder, I could be the one prosecuting you. I can't talk to you about this."

"Buck, you don't actually think I did this, do you?"

"I...I don't know, Reese. I...no, I don't. But I'm still running for DA, and you're still a suspect in a murder investigation."

"But why? Why would they think I did this?"

He sighed and walked across the room to his secretary's desk. The woman, Reese noticed, was listening to every word, as if she might have to testify to what she'd heard. Perhaps she would, Reese thought.

Bucky wrote something on a piece of paper and handed it to her. "Go see Gina Leone. She's not running for office. She'll advise you."

The vertigo threatened to return as she turned, and she had to sit down for a moment. "I can't believe this is happening, Buck."

He patted her shoulder. "Go see Gina. Now. I'll tell her you're coming."

Reese glanced at the paper.

Gina Leone. Suite 302.

Two floors down, Reese found Gina Leone waiting in the lobby. Her name sounded Italian, and she looked the part, too, with long, curling brown hair, dark eyes and skin. Reese guessed she was in her mid-fifties.

"Gina," she said as she gripped Reese's hand in the tightest handshake of her life.

"Reese Ryan."

"I figured. Bucky told me this is an emergency, but that's all he said. What kind of trouble are you in?"

"Do we have to talk in the lobby?" Reese asked. Even though it was early, and the place was empty, that could change at any minute.

"Of course not. Follow me."

Reese did, to a conference room overlooking the courthouse square. They were just a hundred yards away from the office where Andrew Miller was plotting her demise.

"Coffee?" she asked.

Reese debated the offer. If she loaded up on caffeine, it would certainly help her get through the next few hours of questioning, but it wouldn't help her sleep later. "No, thanks. I'm going to try to get some sleep when I go home."

"Wait. Did you just work all night?"

Reese nodded. "The investigator showed up in the ER at quarter to seven this morning and told me the DA wanted to go over my statement from 1993."

"And you went with him," she stated.

Again Reese nodded.

"And now, you need a lawyer. Okay." She sat and pulled out a pad and a pen from the credenza at the front of the room. "What exactly did he ask you, and what exactly did you say?"

Reese thought back and tried to remember all the questions Andrew Miller had asked before he reached the one that had been his sole reason for interrogating her personally. She went through them all, and her answers, as Gina took notes.

"Sounds pretty routine," she said.

"It's getting more interesting, believe me," Reese deadpanned.

"Okay. Go on."

"He asked if Steph and I were lovers."

Gina stopped writing and leaned back in her chair, studying Reese. "How did you answer?"

"I didn't. I asked him if I was under arrest, and he said no, so I just walked out without saying another word."

"Good girl! Okay. So Stephanie—Steph—was your best friend. You've come out as a lesbian, and now someone they've interviewed has suggested you and Steph were perhaps *more than friends*. They've had no motive in this killing since day one, so they finally have something, and they're going to wring everything they can out of it. At least until after Bucky gets elected."

"Great," Reese said, shaking her head.

"Is there any proof that you and Steph were lovers?"

Reese shook her head. Shouldn't Gina ask her if they were? "Don't you want to know if we were lovers?"

Gina smiled. "I'll assume you were. Otherwise, you wouldn't be here."

"So by refusing to answer the DA's question, I answered his question."

"Not necessarily. Sometimes when an interrogation takes an unfriendly turn, people stop talking. But they don't necessarily end up in my office five minutes later."

Reese nodded and looked out the window. She'd never told anyone, but she supposed Steph would understand why she had to.

Someone had given her up to the DA. He or she was apparently trying to implicate Reese in the murder. Steph had loved her, and even if they weren't ready to come out of the closet back then, she was pretty sure she would have by now.

"We were. Lovers. But anything anyone says is pure speculation. No one knows. We were very deeply tucked in the closet."

"You've never told anyone?"

Shaking her head, Reese answered. "No. You're the first one. Ever."

"And Steph? Would she have told anyone?"

Again, Reese shook her head. "Steph's parents *adored* her, and she lived to please them. She definitely didn't want them to know. No way would she ever have told anyone. Maybe later, when the questions about a husband started, but not then. Not in high school."

"How about cards, letters? Did you put anything in writing?"

Reese shrugged. "We sent each other a lot of notes during school, but other than the sheer excess, there was nothing suggestive about them. Again, we were very careful."

"No one ever saw you kissing in the stairwell, for instance?"

Reese laughed, shifted in her chair. "No such drama. We were paranoid about getting caught. We never did anything in public, not even secret little touches when we thought no one was looking. It was a different time, you know? No one was out, and we didn't intend to lead the charge."

Gina stared at the wall, tapping her pen on the tablet, then quickly stared back at her. "How about cell phones? Did you have phones then?"

"Some people did—those box phones—but not us."

"So, in your opinion, there is absolutely no proof that you and Steph were lovers."

Reese nodded. "Correct. There's no proof."

"Okay, so there's no proof of a motive, and no proof to link you to the crime, because if they didn't have any evidence in 1993, they don't have any now. How about an alibi?"

Reese told her about the events of the day.

"So, your sister is your alibi for the time of the crime, and your parents came home shortly after that. They can't back up your alibi, and I'm going to guess the coroner can't give an exact time of death, so they're no help. How about a car? Did you have a way to get to the lake that night?"

"My mom left her car at the house when they went out, so I could have taken hers."

Gina nodded, processing the information. "Okay, you said you called Steph. I have no idea about phone records from back then, but if they exist, the calls could place you at your house. When you called, did you leave a message?"

"I don't know. But probably not. I talked to her late in the afternoon, and then I went to bed. When I called later and she didn't answer, I think I just hung up. I was always worried about leaving messages because the answering machine was in the kitchen, and her mother usually checked it. Steph was concerned about her mother figuring things out, so we tried to alternate calls. I'd call her, and then she'd call me, you know?"

Gina twirled the pencil in her fingers as she stared at the wall.

"Okay, Reese, here's what I think. The DA has nothing. He had to bring you in after someone suggested this connection with Steph, right? I mean, that's a no-brainer. Maybe he'd get lucky and you'd confess. You didn't, so what now? Even if he could prove you and Steph were lovers—which he can't—he still has no evidence to link you to the crime, and you have an alibi. Ergo, he has nothing."

"What should I do?"

"Nothing. Don't talk to anyone about the case, and if he calls you in again—which could happen—I want you to phone me immediately. Morning, noon, or night, okay?"

Handing Reese her business card, she stood, and Reese did the same.

"Okay. This is all going to be fine," she said as she ushered her to the door.

Reese sure didn't feel that way.

The elevator arrived promptly, and Reese took it to the ground floor, then crossed the street to the courthouse square. Her car was still there, and she sat in it for a few minutes, wondering what she should do. Gina had told her not to discuss the case with anyone, but her heart was telling her something else.

Putting the Jeep into gear, she turned out of the parking lot and maneuvered through town, heading west, not toward home but toward Lake Winola. A glance at the clock told her it was a silly move; it was already close to nine o'clock, and the drive to the lake and back would eat up more than an hour of her sleep time, if she didn't drive into a tree when she fell asleep at the wheel. When the adrenaline wore off, a mental crash was almost guaranteed. Hopefully, she'd make it home in one piece.

The winding roads heightened her awareness, and she rehearsed her speech over and over in her mind as she guided the Jeep toward Sophie's house. It was probably foolish to do this, and she knew it, but she also knew that she didn't want Steph's mother learning about them from the DA or, worse, from the TV news.

The driveway was empty, and belatedly Reese wished she'd called. With the kind of day she was having, it wouldn't surprise her if Sophie wasn't at home. But she answered the door shortly after Reese rang the bell and pulled her into a deep hug before seeming to sense something was wrong.

"What is it?" she said, clutching her heart with both hands.

"Can we talk?" Reese asked.

"Of course. Come in. Can I get you a cup of coffee? And I baked blueberry muffins yesterday. They're still fresh."

"Maybe some juice. And a muffin," she said, surprised she could even think about eating.

When Reese's breakfast was on the table, Sophie sat and stared at her. After a bite of muffin and a drink of juice, Reese met her gaze.

"I was called into the DA's office this morning. About Steph."

Sophie nodded. "Yes, of course. They're calling everyone in."

"I know. But it's more than that. It seems that someone…suggested to the DA…that…because I'm gay…and Steph and I were so close…"

Reese didn't want to finish the sentence, and she let it hang there. What more should she say? Should she out Steph to her mom? Surely, Sophie knew she would never have hurt her, but would the knowledge of their love affair skew her thinking?

"They think Steph was a lesbian, too," Sophie said, as her gaze locked on Reese.

"Yes."

"And that you and she were lovers."

Sighing, Reese nodded. "Yes."

Sophie looked past her, off to the side and out at the lake. Reese's appetite had vanished, and she just sat, eventually looking out at the view as well.

"It would explain a lot," Sophie said, finally looking back at her.

She didn't respond. What more could she say, unless Sophie asked her a direct question?

"You look exhausted, Reese. They must have really grilled you."

"It's not that. I worked last night. The investigator showed up at the ER early this morning. I went straight from the hospital to the courthouse, and then here." She didn't mention the fact that she'd lawyered up in between stops.

"My word. You have a right to be exhausted, then. Why don't you take a nap before you go? I'd never forgive myself if you crashed on the way home."

As many times as Reese had visited over the years, she knew she couldn't sleep there. It just didn't seem right. "I'll be okay," she said, thinking of Gina's promise.

They both stood, and Sophie walked her to the door. "Thank you for preparing me, Reese. I'm sure this won't be the last I hear of this."

Then Sophie opened her arms, and Reese stepped into them, and Sophie held her as she sobbed.

"This doesn't change anything, Reese," Sophie said.

Reese hoped she meant it.

CHAPTER 20: CONFESSIONS

Miraculously, Reese had managed to sleep. A vodka and tonic for breakfast helped, and when she awakened it was dark outside. After a quick shower, she was ready for work, three hours ahead of schedule. Picking up her phone, she dialed Ella's number.

"Hi. No FaceTime tonight?" she asked.

In spite of her anxiety, Reese laughed. "I thought I might stop by on my way to work for live, up-close-and-personal face time. How late will you be up?"

"Well, you know me. It's eight o'clock, and I'm already in my jammies."

"I can come by now," she said.

"I'll be waiting," Ella said.

Reese stuffed the duffel she always took to work with the essential items: emergency power bars, an apple, a banana, a bottle of water, a bottle of Coke (in case of a migraine at work, which was a good possibility on this night), Motrin, and a few other items. Zipping it closed, she picked it up and headed out the door.

She had to talk to Ella. Soon, it would be all over Scranton that she and Steph were lovers and that she was currently number one on the short list of suspects in Steph's murder. Who knew how long this nonsense would go on? It might be over in a matter of weeks, but it could take until the election almost three months away before the new DA dropped her from the list. Bucky knew her; he'd admitted to her he didn't think she'd done it. Surely, he'd knock the task force in line and get them looking for the real killer, instead of focusing on the inconsequential detail that she and Steph had been more than friends.

What if it didn't work out that way, though? What if the public was crying for blood, and Bucky—or whoever won the election—

decided to keep investigating her? How long would she be subjected to impromptu visits to the ER? Would she go to jail because they thought she was a flight risk? Would she be suspended from her job because she'd lost the public's trust?

There were too many uncertainties, and with all the questions spinning through her mind, Reese couldn't add the distraction of her attraction to Ella. Whatever was going on with them—and Reese sincerely hoped it was leading toward something wonderful—would have to wait. She couldn't pull Ella into a police investigation. She didn't know how she'd stand up to the pressure, how she'd hold up if reporters started showing up at her house and colleagues started whispering when she passed in the hallways. And based on her knowledge of such matters, it wouldn't be long until everyone in Northeastern Pennsylvania learned she was a suspect in Steph's murder.

No, the only way to spare Ella the grief that surely awaited her, and the only chance she had to ever have something with Ella, was to end it now. When this was all over, perhaps—if Ella could forgive her for lying about Steph—then they could pick up where they'd left off.

Reese hoped they could. Ella was the most amazing woman she'd ever met. She was beautiful. She was intelligent. She had a sense of humor. And she didn't have to sell Cass to Ella. If anything, Cass had sold Reese.

If they'd just met a few months earlier and had a chance to get to know each other better before all of this started, their relationship would have stood a chance. Once Ella knew her, she'd have no doubt about Reese's innocence. Reese would have been able to call her and talk about this, lean on her when she felt like collapsing. Like now.

If they'd met a few months later, all of this would have been behind her, and she'd have a funny tale to tell about the time she'd gotten mixed up in a murder investigation.

But they didn't meet then, and they didn't meet when. They'd met now, and Reese had to do one of the hardest things she'd ever done: say good-bye to someone special, again.

The light was on at Ella and Pip's, and Reese parked in front, instead of in her parents' driveway where she usually did. If her parents—or more likely, her sister—saw her, they'd wonder why she was visiting the neighbors. The thought made her happy she hadn't shared any details about her evening with Ella. Since she hadn't really told anyone they'd gone out, there was no one to tell when they stopped seeing each other.

Ella met her at the door, wearing the same pajamas she'd seen all week when they'd talked on the computer. "I know what you're thinking," Ella said. "But they're clean. I washed them as soon as I got home this afternoon."

The teasing banter made Reese want to cry, because it just reinforced Reese's decision. She couldn't be casual with Ella. She couldn't "just be friends" because Ella constantly made her laugh, touched her in a way few others had the ability to do.

"It's a good thing," Reese said. "I was a little nervous when I saw you."

Ella grabbed her hand, pulled her inside, and closed the door behind her. "We're letting in the cold."

Reese tried to summon her courage. The best way to do this was quickly, but somehow, she couldn't. Her feelings for Ella were too significant to blow her off in the hallway by the front door. Hell, it would have been better to send her a text.

"Can we talk?" Reese asked.

Ella looked at her, concern on her face. "Of course. Is everything all right?"

"It's going to be okay," she said, remembering what her lawyer had said earlier that day. Was it just this morning she'd run from the DA's office to Bucky's, only to be kicked out the door and into Gina Leone's? It seemed like a lifetime ago.

Ella ushered her into the living room, where the couch was positioned in front of the large stone fireplace. It had been outfitted with a gas insert, and a fire danced across the faux logs behind the glass screen.

"Sit, here. Can I get you a drink?"

Reese meant to say no, to do this quickly, but she couldn't. She just didn't want to say good-bye to Ella, knowing how much she'd miss her when she did. They'd known each other for less than a month, but in that short time Ella had risen to an important place in the small circle of friends in her life. "Yes, sure. That'd be great."

"What would you like? Water? Or how about coffee? It'll keep you awake for your shift."

Reese nodded. "Perfect."

"Cream? Sugar?"

"Both, please."

"I'll be back in a snap," she said, and when she left, Reese closed her eyes and leaned back into the buttery soft leather of the couch.

This is so fucking hard, Reese thought, and she fought tears of self-pity while she mentally rehearsed this speech once again.

"Here you go," Ella said, handing her a large PMU mug. "You really look tired, Reese. Are you getting sick?"

"No, I'm not sick," she said as she sipped the coffee. "This is perfect, Ella. Thank you." Reese turned her head and looked at her. Her tan had faded a little, even as her blond hair had darkened, but the brown eyes staring back at her were the same shade of chocolate that always pulled her in. The connection made Reese even more nervous, made her hate herself for what she was doing, not just to herself, but to Ella as well.

"What is it, Reese? You're making me nervous."

"I'm sorry. I just…I have to cancel our date. We're supposed to go out on Saturday after Cass's party, but I can't do it. I can't date you. I can't date anyone, really, not just you." Reese looked at Ella and saw a jumble of expressions. Fear, confusion, sadness.

"What? Why?"

Reese struggled to remember what she was supposed to say now. Had Ella asked questions when she rehearsed this in her mind?

"I'm sorry, Ella. You are the sweetest, funniest woman I've ever met. I would love more than anything to follow this attraction I have for you…because I think you're feeling the connection, too. It's just not a good time for me."

Ella shook her head. "What does that mean? Last night seemed like a fine time. What changed in twenty-four hours?"

How could Reese explain what was going on without betraying Steph? Was it possible? If she told Ella about the investigation, surely her first question would be the one she couldn't answer. Had Reese and Steph been lovers? It was the question everyone would soon be asking, and Reese still wasn't sure how she would answer. If Sophie had asked when Reese was there earlier, she would have told her the truth. Everyone else, she'd ignore, just as her lawyer had suggested. When she was under oath…Reese still wasn't sure how she'd handle that. She just wasn't ready to out Steph, and the only way to keep her safely in the closet was to avoid the question. She could do that with everyone on the planet except Ella.

"I just realized that with everything going on in my life, it would be a bad time to start a new relationship."

"What's going on in your life? What aren't you telling me? Are you getting sued for malpractice? Is someone in your family sick? What's wrong, Reese?"

Reese swallowed her coffee and put her mug on the coffee table, and then she stood. Swallowing her sadness was much harder. She couldn't do this. She couldn't stay here and listen to Ella without crumbling. "I have to go."

Rushing to the door, Reese didn't give Ella a chance to come after her. To her credit, Ella was still sitting on the couch when Reese closed the door behind her.

CHAPTER 21: THE END OF THE LOOSE END

It had been a long week. After Reese walked out, Ella had sat in front of the fire for hours, too numb to even think. Sure, they'd been friends for only a few weeks and hadn't even really been on a date, but it was sure heading in that direction. They actually had a date scheduled, for after Cass's party. They'd kissed, sort of. They'd talked and texted and FaceTimed. Reese had seen her with wet hair and no makeup! This was as serious as Ella had been in a long, long time.

That was precisely why she was married to her job. In development, the team set goals and worked toward them. If her individual goal was to raise a million dollars, and the team goal five million, she knew she had to call on a hundred donors to reach the mark. She needed to travel, host parties, eat way too many high-calorie dinners. But it was all pretty cut-and-dried in the end. People were either philanthropic, or they weren't. They gave or they didn't call her back. She understood that. It was the way it worked.

Women, though, were too difficult to figure out. It had been going great with Reese. For the first time in ages she'd looked forward to talking to someone. She saw a future. Reese's job was so demanding that she understood Ella's crazy hours and need to travel. They were both Phillies fans, which was huge. In 2009, she'd been dating a Yankees fan, and when their respective teams faced each other in the World Series, that had been the end of them. Reese seemed so easy-going and pleasant all the time, she was smart and funny, and Ella couldn't help but thinking of what might happen with them.

And then boom. The "I don't want to see you anymore" came out of nowhere. At least it wasn't an "I just want to be friends," because Ella wouldn't have been able to handle that. How could she, when she spent every moment she was with Reese thinking about kissing her, wondering how soft her skin was, longing to hold her close and smell her scent. And every moment they weren't together was filled with thoughts of Reese. Ella had fallen hard and fast, and she felt bruised and battered.

At least the sun was shining, she thought as she put the top down on her convertible. On the way home, she took the scenic route and stopped at Riccardo's Market in Dunmore, picking up a few things for the weekend. Her instinct was to skip Cass's party, to take off for Philly and spend a couple of nights with friends and forget about Reese. But Cass wasn't aware of the rift between Ella and Reese, still came over twice a day, and all she talked about was her party. Every time she saw Ella, she reminded Ella to bring a jacket, because it's windy at Roba's, and to wear old shoes, in case of mud.

The rain had held off, but not the gloom. If only Ella could convince herself that Reese was a jerk and just forget about her, it would be easier. Maybe after the party. She had to see her there, but after that, they might never meet again. She'd called Doug, the realtor, and was going to talk to him at the party as well, in the hopes that she might find something soon so she could finally get settled. Moving away from Reese's family surely had to be a good thing. Although she'd miss Sharon and Cass, at least they wouldn't constantly remind her of what might have been with Reese.

Turning right out of the parking lot, Ella soon found herself on the crowded streets of the hill section, heading toward Nay Aug Park and home. When she reached the stop sign, she looked both ways, startled when she recognized the man walking briskly toward the park. Not that he didn't have the right to be there; it was a public park, after all. But his head was down, and he hurried as if avoiding people. If it wasn't for the blue hat with the green Phillies *P*, she wouldn't have realized she was seeing the same man who'd recently visited the Ryans.

He crossed before her, and she traveled through the intersection and then turned left and right and into the driveway. After parking in the garage, she carried her bag inside. Pip's car was gone, and Ella wondered if Pip was avoiding her, so as to not make Ella feel uncomfortable about her sudden return to town. In her bedroom, she kicked off her shoes and opened the balcony door and walked out. Maybe a walk in the park would help her relax. Or better yet, she'd take a blanket and sit under a tree and read. It was nearly seventy degrees outside, and in the middle of September, a day like this was a blessing. She turned to go back inside when she saw him again, entering the park near the pool.

If she saw him on her trek through Nay Aug, she'd say hello. He was one of the many alums she'd met at the golf tournament, and she wasn't sure if he'd remember her, but that didn't matter. It was her job to know him, not vice versa.

After pulling on a pair of denim capri pants and T-shirt, then her sneakers, she grabbed her blanket and her book and set off for the gorge.

❖

On television, arranging a murder looks so easy. He hadn't found that to be the case in real life. Making discreet inquiries about who might be able to do such a job hadn't been a simple matter, and after a dozen phone calls and ten thousand dollars, he'd finally found someone willing to kill Cass Ryan before she could blow his alibi.

Doing it himself wasn't an option. First of all, there would be witnesses. Cass didn't leave the house unattended except to go to the park, and even when the park wasn't busy, people were coming and going from the hospital, the nursery, or the Everhart Museum. He couldn't take that chance. And he had to think about his conscience as well. After more than twenty years, Steph's murder still haunted him, and that had been an accident. How would he feel about Cass? He was sure it would be just as bad, although in this case, it was either her or him. That made it a little easier to handle.

He sat on a bench just inside the park, pretending to read his phone but really watching the entrance. They'd planned for the man to lure Cass to the park and then push her into the gorge, where she'd be pulled under the waters of Roaring Brook and drown. Even strong swimmers couldn't handle the powerful current in the gorge; Cass had no hope.

He'd read that drowning was a horrible way to die, that people were very afraid as they clawed their way helplessly toward the surface of the lake or stream, desperate for a breath of life-saving air. It was sad to think of Cass suffering like that, but it was really the best way. It would look like an accident, and no one would ask questions. Besides, with Cass's disabilities, she might not even understand what was happening. It might not be so bad.

He was sitting, waiting and watching, when he saw her. Not Cass, running frantically toward the park in search of the neighbor's little poodle. It was Ella Townes, the woman from PMU. He'd met her at the golf tournament and was sure she'd recognize him if she saw him. She was on her phone and hadn't yet noticed him, so he stood and rushed deeper into the park, hopefully away from the direction she was taking. If only he knew which way that was.

A minute later, he saw Ella disappear around the corner near the old coal mine, by the museum. Good, he thought. She wouldn't be anywhere near the gorge.

❖

Ella closed her phone as she rounded the corner by the museum and then began power-walking. The talk with her mom, who was too busy playing golf to give her any sound advice, was exactly what she needed. Proof that she could rely on no one and had to look out for herself. It was just as she'd always known, but she had to admit that it still stung. Reese had gotten to her, made her care. It would take a little time to undo that mistake, but she would, and in the end, everything would be fine. She'd be fine.

Remembering her thought that she'd never meet any interesting women in the mountains, Ella laughed. If she'd met one, chances were she'd meet another. And if not—well, she always had work.

She caught the walking path on the edge of the park, near the greenhouse, and in ten minutes she'd made her way to a secluded section of cliff overlooking the gorge. It was loud, and Ella wondered if it was the right spot to be in. Something a little quieter might be better, but then she shook her head, tossed her blanket over the rocks, and leaned up against the wall of rock behind her. After opening her book she began to read, and before long, the roar of Roaring Brook was just background noise.

A few minutes later, a group of Scouts walked by. "Nice day to be out," one of the adult leaders, an attractive woman dressed in scouting T-shirt and shorts, said with a smile. A rather flirty smile, Ella thought. See, there are lots of other women in the mountains, she said to herself before answering.

"It sure is. Out for a hike?"

"Yes. The boys have hiking requirements to advance in rank, and this is a beautiful spot."

"One of my favorites."

She had stopped to talk, but the rest of her troop marched on, and she looked at their backs and waved. "I'd better catch up," she said with a smile.

Definitely flirting, Ella thought as she watched a perfectly shaped body walk down toward the stream.

"All right!" she said and fist-pumped the air. She'd never been much of a scout kind of girl—camping, for instance, sounded totally like torture—but she did love the outdoors. A relationship with a scouty kind of woman could bring all kinds of new adventures with it.

With a contented sigh, she turned back to her book.

❖

It was a bad idea to come here, he thought as he glanced at his watch. It was after four o'clock, he'd been gone from his office for more than an hour, and eventually someone would wonder where he was. He wanted to be here, though, to make sure the job got done right, and at this point, it was too late to back out. He supposed he could just climb into his car and go home, but then what? More hours of waiting to find out what happened. This way, he'd know right away.

He'd repositioned himself far enough away from the Arthur Avenue entrance that he could make his way to the gorge to watch, but close enough that he could still see her when she entered the park. If she came at all. Knowing Cass, she might be asking his guy for an ID or checking with her mother before she came to rescue the dog. In that case, the guy was instructed to abort the mission while he figured out plan B.

Just when he thought of going home, he saw her, running with that awkward waddle of hers. A car almost did him a favor by hitting her but braked in time as Cass edged by and into the park. Turning toward the gorge, he began striding along, checking over his shoulder to see if Cass was being followed. Sure enough, his guy was a few yards behind her. More importantly, no one else was on their tail. Making his way to the tree house, he walked on the circuitous gangway and out onto the overlook, where he could see the water below.

❖

Ella paused from her book to take a sip from the water bottle in her bag. To her surprise, she'd been able to forget about Reese for a little while as she got lost in her novel, a work of fiction by a new lesbian author. The story was about a woman who bought a condo in an all-lesbian community in Staten Island, and Ella found herself wondering if she should buy property there, instead of in Scranton. There must be a college in Staten Island, right? She could always find a new job, right? Look how easy it had been at PMU.

Falling rocks bouncing off the façade of the cliff above the water caused Ella to look up. At times, the path was very close to the edge, and it wasn't paved, so it wasn't unusual to see someone slip and send loose gravel skidding. She was startled not to see just anyone, but Cass, leaning far over the railing on the level above. Before she could warn her to be careful, a stocky man wearing a dark baseball cap and jersey shoved Cass forward.

Ella screamed in horror as Cass, already positioned precariously on the top rail, went tumbling over and down into the ravine.

Jumping up, Ella ran down the path toward the stream, mindful of the loose rock and steep pitch of the trail. When she rounded a bend, ahead on the other side, she spotted the Scouts she'd seen earlier. She looked up the cliff face to where Cass had been standing; there was no place she could have landed except the water. Scanning the stream as she ran, she looked for some sign of her, and then, after a few seconds, she saw a head and arms appear above the white water, only to disappear again a split second later.

She could never reach her on time! Ella was fifty yards behind where she'd seen Cass, and the current was so swift it would carry her away too quickly for Ella to catch up.

The Scouts might be able to reach her, though!

"Help!" Ella screamed as she ran, waving her arms. "Help!" How could anyone hear over the roar of Roaring Brook?

To her amazement, a young boy looked up at her and touched the arm of another Scout beside him. Ella pointed with both arms at Roaring Brook, and as if carried on the wings of angels, at that moment, Cass's head and arms appeared again above the surface.

All at once, the entire troop burst into action, rushing a few steps ahead, locking arms and racing into the choppy water. Two, then three, then six of them made it in, spanning nearly half the width of the stream. The boy farthest out was a head taller than the smallest one, and the water was nearly up to his head. Cass, who was barely five feet tall, was surely buried under the water.

Then Cass came up again, pushed by the current or the angels, to within a few feet of the last Scout. Ella saw him reaching as the others stretched to lengthen their human chain, and then he turned, as if he felt something, and she cried with joy as he pulled Cass toward him. The others gathered around him, helping him bring her ashore.

Ella hurried back upstream to a trail of rocks that crossed the water, looking over her shoulder to see the rescue efforts. The Scouts had pulled Cass up onto the rocks beside the water. She didn't appear to be moving.

Fighting for footing against the raging current, Ella crossed the rocks as quickly as she could, and when she reached the other side, she sprinted in wet sneakers to the circle of humans that had formed downstream. "Is she okay?" she shouted when she was closer, and they turned.

Through a break in the circle she could see the female Scout leader doing CPR, and Ella began sobbing as she ran. "No! Cass, no!"

Pushing through the perimeter, she knelt beside Cass just as her rescuer pulled up from delivering a breath. Then, as if hearing her cries, Cass began coughing.

"She's alive!" Ella shouted, and she began to shake her. "Cass, open your eyes! It's Ella, Cass. Talk to me."

Cass tried to murmur something that came out as a cough.

"She's alive! Did anyone call 9-1-1?" she asked.

"Yes. They're on their way."

"Good! Cass, open your eyes. You're going to be okay."

On command, Cass opened her eyes, and Ella leaned close and hugged her again. "You're okay, too," she said.

"Yes, yes, I'm doing much better now that I know you're okay."

"The baseball player said you fell in the gorge. I went to save you."

"The baseball player? What baseball player?"

Cass coughed again.

"Cass, what baseball player?" Ella asked. In her fervor to rescue Cass, she'd forgotten about the man who caused this near catastrophe. He'd been wearing a cap and jersey, and suddenly Ella was filled with dread as she waited for Cass's answer.

"The baseball player. He knows me from the RailRiders, but I didn't know him. He said you fell and hurt your leg, and I had to help you right away. There wasn't even time to tell Mom."

Ella heard a siren drawing closer and breathed a sigh of relief.

Even though Cass seemed to be okay, Ella wanted her checked out by the professionals. She had nothing against the Scouts but thought it prudent that Cass go to the hospital.

As if defending herself against Ella's unspoken vote of no confidence, the female Scout leader spoke. "Cass, my name is Jody. I know first aid, and I just want to make sure you're not hurt, okay?" The woman looked at Cass and then to Ella for approval.

Raising both hands, Ella nodded. "By all means," she said.

"Does anything hurt you?" she asked.

"No. Not any more. Last week I had an earache, though. My mom took me to the doctor, and it's all better now."

Ella wanted to hug her for her sweet innocence and was immediately reminded that someone had tried to kill her. The baseball player had lied to her and lured her to the gorge, then pushed her over the rail. Why? Why would anyone want to hurt Cass? It didn't make sense. Everyone loved her.

"Are you breathing okay?" Jody asked.

"Yes, really okay."

"You really shouldn't swim in the gorge, Cass," one of the Scouts said. "It's very dangerous."

Ella wanted to tell them she hadn't been swimming, that she was pushed, but she didn't think it was right to scare them unnecessarily. She'd tell the police and let them decide what to do. Truthfully, it wasn't likely that any of them had seen a thing from their angle downstream, but maybe they'd seen the man earlier. Thinking the police might want to talk to the Scouts, Ella asked for Jody's contact information. "Would you mind giving me your name and number, Jody? I'm sure Cass's family will want to thank you and your troop."

"Sure. Do you have something to write on? Or your phone?"

"It's up there. Would you mind walking up with me?" she said, and as she looked, she saw the ambulance crew picking their way down the steep slope. Apparently that was the easiest way out. "We can walk up when they take Cass."

"Sure, of course," Jody said.

In another minute, the first medic reached Cass, and in addition to asking the same questions Jody had, she checked Cass out, squeezing her neck and her stomach, listening to her lungs. Two more medics followed with the stretcher, and they placed an oxygen mask over Cass's face before lifting her onto the mattress. A moment later, an entire squadron of rescue personnel and two police officers arrived on the scene. Six of them flanked the stretcher and carried it over the rough terrain back toward the crossing.

"It's too tight," Cass complained of the mask.

"I'll fix it," the medic said with a smile, and their progress halted for a moment while she fulfilled the promise.

"It looks like you knew just what to do," Ella said to Jody as they began moving again. "Thank you," she said as she squeezed her arm.

"I'm a merit-badge counselor for first aid. It's good to put it into action. It shows the boys how important the things they learn are in real life, not just in scouting."

"That's for sure. I wish I knew a little first aid. If it was up to me...I hate to even think of what would have happened."

"I suppose we were in the right place at the right time," Jody said.

Ella didn't share her philosophy that much of the very good in life involved being in the right place at the right time, because, at the moment, she didn't have the energy for a mental debate. She wasn't even sure if her legs could carry her across the stream and up the hill. But they had to, because with the baseball player on the loose, she wasn't about to leave Cass's side.

After waiting for the medics to navigate the stream with Cass's stretcher, she crossed and began the trek up the cliff. Stopping briefly, she gathered her things—which, thankfully, were just where she'd left them, then quickly typed in Jody's contact information. It took only a few seconds to catch up to Cass again. Even with six rescuers carrying her, the climb was a slow one.

At the top, they maneuvered her stretcher toward the ambulance, and Ella rushed to one of the two officers. The other had stayed behind to talk to the Scouts. "Hi, Officer. My name is Elizabeth Townes. Cass—the victim—she's my neighbor. I saw the whole thing."

He shook his head. "What was she doing there by herself?"

Ella glanced in Cass's direction. They'd almost reached the ambulance. "Officer, I really need to talk to you, but I can't leave her. She'll be scared. Can you come to the hospital?"

"Yes, of course," he said. Then, "Guys, this woman is going to accompany your patient, got it?"

With that instruction, the medics parted and ushered Ella into the back of the ambulance, where they helped her into a seat complete with seat belts. "Hi, Ella. I never rode in an ambulance before," Cass said.

"First time for me, too," she said.

"I have something special for you, then," the medic, whose name was Tiffany, said to Cass. Reaching into a cabinet behind her, she pulled out a plastic fire hat. "This is for you. It makes you an official volunteer member of the rescue team."

She playfully rubbed Cass's still-wet hair before crowning her with the hat, and when everyone was buckled up, the ambulance took off. "It'll be just a few seconds to the hospital. Okay, Cass?"

"Wait," Ella interjected. "Do you have to take her to this hospital? I mean, I have nothing personally against this one, but her sister works at the other one. Dr. Ryan. She's an ER doctor."

"Reese?" the medic asked, surprise on her face.

"Yes, Reese Ryan. This is Cass, her sister."

The medic turned and shouted to the driver. "Change of plans, Todd. We're going down the hill."

"I should call Reese," Ella said. "And your mother."

"Good idea," the medic said. "They'll need some information at the hospital, so it'll be good if a family member's there."

Ella met her gaze and mouthed her question. "She's okay, right?"

"She's fine."

Ella wasn't religious, but she said a three-word prayer of gratitude and then pulled her phone out to call Reese.

CHAPTER 22: EXPOSURE

As the phone rang, Ella told herself she was calling Reese because she was a doctor and this was a medical emergency, but she knew it was more than that. She wanted to talk to Reese, to be the one to tell her that Cass was okay, to be the one to comfort her. Since Reese had been the one to end their...relationship, Ella wondered if she'd answer the phone. Obviously, Reese didn't want to talk to her.

It surprised her, then, when Reese's breathless "hello" interrupted her thoughts.

Ella wasted no time. "Reese, it's Ella. There's been a small accident. Everything is fine, but Cass fell in the gorge, and we're taking her to your ER as a precaution."

"Is she awake and talking?" Reese asked.

"Yes. The medic thinks she's fine."

"Who's the medic?"

"Her name is Tiffany."

"Tiffany White?"

Ella confirmed the medic's identity and relayed the information to Reese.

"I'm already in the car. I'll be there in fifteen."

The phone clicked in Ella's ears, but it stung her heart. Obviously, Reese really didn't want anything to do with her. Swallowing her emotions, she turned to Cass, pushed the hat up on her head, and pulled down the mask.

"I wanted to make sure it was you. I can't see your beautiful face with all that stuff on."

"Can I take off this mask now?" she asked.

Ella looked at Tiffany for the answer. "You know what? Why

don't I check you without it. Then I'll be able to give the doctor a better report."

Moving carefully, she removed the mask and immediately turned her eyes to the monitor sitting on the stretcher between Cass's legs. "See that white number?" she said as she pointed it out. "Right now, it's 100. That's perfect."

"Like a test," Cass said.

"Exactly. It's testing your lungs to see if you need this oxygen mask. Let's see if you can stay at 100, or even 99 or 98, without the mask. If you do, then it's bye-bye mask," she said, bending her fingers frantically in a comical wave.

The ambulance came to a stop, and then Ella heard obnoxious beeping as it began moving backward, and she realized they'd reached the hospital. Glancing at the white number, she was relieved to see it hadn't changed.

The rear door opened, and the medics went to work again, pulling the stretcher out and popping down the legs. Ella hopped out and went to Cass's side, wanting her to know she was still there.

"Hey," she said gleefully. "This is my sister's hospital!"

Ella breathed a sigh of relief that, rather than fear, Cass seemed to feel excited to have just finished her first ambulance ride, only to end up at *Reese's* hospital. It had been an instantaneous decision, but she was glad she'd redirected the medics here instead of letting them take Cass to the closer hospital.

A cruiser pulled in behind the ambulance, and Ella was relieved when the same officer she'd spoken with at the park stepped out of the vehicle. Since Cass seemed so comfortable, Ella would have a chance to step out of the room and tell him exactly what she'd seen, and what Cass had told her about the baseball player.

Motioning with her hands, Ella let the officer know she was going inside, and he nodded. Obviously, taking care of Cass was his priority, too.

They wheeled Cass directly to a large room sporting fancy equipment on every wall. It even had a light hanging from the ceiling. A hospital-style chandelier, she supposed. After Cass scooted from their stretcher to the hospital's, Tiffany transferred the wires and hooked up the monitor on the wall. Ella looked for the white number, relieved to see it had dropped only a point. Maybe a drop wasn't good though. She asked Tiffany. "You said ninety-nine is good, right?"

"Yes. She's been off the oxygen for a few minutes. If it was going to drop, it would have done it by now."

Ella smiled at her and then at Cass. "Do you know what that means?"

Cass mimicked the medic's earlier motion by waving her hand. "Bye-bye, mask."

They both laughed, and Tiffany repositioned Cass's helmet. "Listen, Cass. I have to go take care of the sick people, but I'm leaving you in good hands. All the people who work here know Reese, and they'll take excellent care of you. Thanks for being such a great patient."

Cass nodded soberly. "You're welcome."

"The nursing staff will be in momentarily, or sooner when they realize they have a VIP in here."

"Thank you so, so much."

"My pleasure."

Ella barely had the chance to adjust the blanket over Cass's wet clothes, when Tiffany's prediction proved accurate. Three women entered the room. One introduced herself as Dr. Light and told Cass she knew her sister.

"She knows everybody, I think."

As she began to ask Cass questions, the policeman appeared at the door, and Ella slipped to his side. "My name is Elizabeth Townes. I'm her neighbor. I saw the whole incident."

"Where are her parents?"

"Gosh, I'm not sure. I should call them. With all the excitement, I forgot. I did call her sister, though. She's a doctor here. She's on her way."

"Good, good. So how did she fall in?"

"That's why I didn't want to leave her, Officer. She didn't fall. Someone pushed her. From the path just above where they pulled her out of the water."

Leaning back, the officer studied Ella as if she had three eyes. "Wait a minute. Someone *pushed* her? Like clowning around, and she slipped and fell, or *pushed her*, like on purpose."

"Definitely on purpose." Ella told him everything she saw.

"Wait a minute, wait a minute," he said as he waved his pen. "Wasn't she at the park with you?"

"No, and that's another thing. The man who pushed her was wearing a dark cap and baseball jersey. Cass told me a baseball player told her I fell in the gorge and needed her help. When I saw her, she was standing on the top railing, leaning over toward the water, apparently looking for me. That's when he pushed her."

Ella stood behind him and demonstrated by placing her hands on his mid-back and shoving him.

He turned, and once again he studied her. "You're telling me someone dressed like a RailRider lured her into the park and then practically threw her into the gorge?"

Ella nodded. "If you don't believe me, ask her."

"Oh, I will," he said, and turned toward the doctor. "Doc, would it be okay if I ask the patient a few questions?"

Nodding, she agreed. "They're coming to shoot a chest X-ray, so you'll have to step out of the room then. But otherwise, I think she's fine to talk to you."

"Hi, Cass," he said and then introduced himself. "I have to ask you some questions. Now I don't want you to worry, because you're not in any trouble, okay? I just want to know what happened, so we can make the park safe. I don't want anyone else to fall in and hurt themselves. Okay?"

Cass nodded, and Ella sensed that the police officer, by his title alone, made her nervous. Moving a step closer, she grabbed Cass's hand in both of hers and began stroking it.

"How'd you fall in?" he asked.

She told him she was looking for Ella in the gorge, but she couldn't see her. The baseball player told her she would see better if she stood on the fence, and so she did.

"Did you lose your balance?" he asked.

Nodding her head, she made a lopsided frown. "I'm very clumsy."

The officer tried not to smile. "Do you think the baseball player might have...bumped you when you were on the railing? Did you feel anything like that?"

She shook her head.

"How did you meet the baseball player?"

"I was at my house, in my yard, and I saw him. He plays on the RailRiders."

"Do you know his name?"

"No."

"Did you ever see him before?"

"No."

"How do you know he plays on the RailRiders?"

"Duh! He told me. And he had a *real* uniform."

"What happened after you met him?"

"He told me Ella was in the park and she fell into the gorge and hurt her leg. He said I had to help her right away. He said it was safe for me to go with him, since he plays for the RailRiders."

"So you went to the gorge?"

"Yes. I ran as fast as I could."

"Do you remember anything else, Cass? Can you tell me what he looked like?"

"He looked like a baseball player," she said, and although she omitted the "duh" this time, it was implied.

Knowing Cass, Ella thought she understood what she was trying to say. "Cass, I don't think he understands. Do you mean he was tall?"

"Yes. Very tall."

"And did he have big muscles?"

Cass nodded.

"Okay, what else? Did he have a beard?"

"Yes, and cool sunglasses."

Ella pulled up a picture of sporty sunglasses on her phone. "This kind?" she asked.

"Yep. That kind."

"What color was his beard?" the officer asked.

"Black, but with a little white, too."

After a few more questions, he patted Cass on the arm. "You're the best witness I've had all day, Cass.

"I'll be back when the parents get here," he said as he left.

"I'll call right now," Ella said, as she reached into her purse for her phone. She didn't even have time to dial before Sharon and Chris came running through the door.

"Hi, Mommy. Hi, Daddy," she said. "I got to ride in the ambulance."

As they rushed to her side, Reese ran through the door, too. Wearing a T-shirt, golf shorts, and slides, Ella thought she'd never seen her look so sexy. For a moment, she forgot where she was, and why she was there, and the fact that Reese had broken their date.

Although concern masked her beautiful features, she smiled for her sister. "Nice hat, Cass."

"I fell in the gorge," she said.

Sharon's hand flew to her mouth as she tried to hold back her emotions. Ella could imagine what she was thinking—how hard they worked with Cass to teach her right from wrong, and stranger danger, and to stay away from the gorge—and yet here she was, on a stretcher in the ER, lucky to be alive.

Ella was amazed by Sharon's calm demeanor. "Honey, you know the gorge is dangerous. Why did you go there by yourself?"

This is where it gets tricky, Ella thought. She had to tell the Ryans what had happened; someone had purposefully tried to harm Cass, and they might just try again. Yet she didn't want to say anything in front of Cass and frighten her. Even though she remembered the baseball player taking her into the park, she had no idea he'd pushed her over the railing and into the raging waters below. As far as Ella was concerned, it should stay that way, but the ultimate decision was the Ryans'.

"X-ray," a woman said as she poked her head through the door. Then, "Oh, hi, Dr. Ryan. Is this Cassidy Ryan related to you?"

Reese smiled for the first time since she'd come into the room. "She sure is. This is my sister, so take good care of her."

"I sure will. Cass, sweetie, can you walk to the wheelchair? We're going to the X-ray department to take a picture of your lungs."

The nurses had changed her out of the wet clothing, and now she wore only the standard hospital gown, but she had no difficulty walking in her hospital socks and plopped down into the chair. "This is my first time in a wheelchair," she said excitedly. "Don't go too fast."

When they'd left, Ella scanned all three of their faces. "You guys should sit. I have to tell you something."

"What is it?" Sharon asked, even as Reese pushed the chair under her mother and then nudged her into it.

"This is what I know. I was down in the gorge, reading a book, when some pebbles fell. I looked up to see what was happening, and I saw Cass, standing on the railing at the scenic-overlook part of the path. She was looking down into the gorge. A man was behind her, and he pushed her over the railing. It wasn't an accident. He deliberately took both hands and shoved her. She doesn't remember it—I think it just didn't register that he pushed her. I ran down into the gorge and saw some Scouts downstream and was able to get their attention. They went in and pulled her out of the water."

Reese's head dropped a few degrees, but her eyes remained level as she stared at Reese. "You're telling me someone tried to murder Cass?"

"I think so."

"That's ridiculous."

"Why would anyone want to hurt her?" Sharon asked.

Chris shook his head. "There's all kinds of nut-jobs in the world, Sharon. Nothing surprises me. He probably saw her and thought he could pick on her because she's an easy target."

"It wasn't that, Chris," Ella said. She told them how the man had lured Cass from the yard and into the gorge by telling her she'd fallen, and how he'd gained her trust by telling her he played for the RailRiders.

"So this guy deliberately targeted her. He knew who she was, wore the uniform—knew who you are—" he said, looking at Ella. "That's a lot of personal information about Cass."

"It doesn't make any sense," Sharon said. "Cass can be a handful at times, but she's harmless. Why would anyone want to hurt her?"

"That's a really good question."

Reese looked up to see a Scranton police officer and another man, one she recognized. He was the man who'd shown up at this very ER a few days earlier and escorted her to the DA's office.

After introducing himself to the group, he spoke. "I have a theory." He paused for dramatic effect, for they were already looking at him.

"As you know, the DA's office has reopened the Stephanie Gates murder investigation. A few days ago, the DA himself spoke with Dr. Ryan about the case." He studied their faces, as if to see if any of them was shocked by the news. They weren't, and he continued. "It might surprise you to learn that Dr. Ryan is a person of interest in the Gates case."

"What?" her father said, standing to face the investigator. "That's ridiculous!"

"Is it? Did you know that your daughter and Stephanie Gates were lovers?"

Reese looked around and now saw the shock he'd been aiming for. At once, all three of them looked at her. She did her best to keep her face a blank mask. Remembering Gina Leone's advice, she said nothing.

"You're not going to deny it, Dr. Ryan? You and Stephanie were lovers, weren't you? And you had a fight that night, and you killed her. Then you went home, and you asked your sister to cover for you. For twenty years, she's been protecting you, and now, just when this investigation is getting interesting, someone tries to murder her. Imagine that? The one person who could prove you were lying about that night…"

"Get out of here, right now!" Chris shouted. "And don't come back unless you have some proof, or a warrant, or something more than meritless theories."

"Don't worry. I'll be back," he said.

The Scranton cop remained. "Sorry about that. I have nothing to do with that other matter, but I am looking into the attempt on your daughter's life."

"How did he know about Cass?" Reese asked. She'd been notified only twenty minutes earlier. The DA must really be keeping a close eye on her if they'd already sent their investigator to the hospital.

"I have no idea," the officer said.

"I need to ask you all some questions," he said, and then he did. He asked the Ryans about the neighborhood, whether they'd seen anyone suspicious hanging around, if Cass had mentioned anyone befriending her at work or in the park. No one could think of anything out of the ordinary. As far as their day went, Chris had been playing golf when the incident happened, and Sharon had been shampooing her rugs. She'd never even known Cass was missing.

"How about you, Dr. Ryan? Have you noticed anything different lately, anyone hanging out around your parents' house or following you in the park?"

Reese shook her head. This was so bizarre. People loved Cass. No one would ever want to hurt her.

"And where were you when this happened?" he asked.

"I was home."

"What were you doing?" he asked, and Reese tried not to let the questions alarm her. It was all routine, she assured herself. He was just doing his job. She took a fortifying breath before answering.

"I worked last night, so I slept till about two. When I got up I ate a sandwich, worked out for about an hour, and then got a shower. I'd just finished dressing when Ella called me."

"Any company? Anyone to verify your whereabouts?"

"Uh, no," Reese said, suddenly wondering if she should call her lawyer.

Then he turned his attention to Ella and asked her many of the same questions, and the relief Reese felt nearly caused her knees to buckle.

"Have you told anyone else what you saw? Anyone except the family and the police?"

Ella shook her head.

"Good. Don't. I don't want to start a panic. We're going to look at the security tapes from the park and around the hospital and see if we can find this baseball player." He passed out his calling cards, in case they thought of anything else to share, and turned and left the room.

Before they could talk, Cass returned, sporting a sticker of a skeleton on her shirt. She pointed at it. "I got my X-ray," she said.

"And I'm going to go look at it. First, I want to check you."

Ella watched absentmindedly as Reese examined Cass. The detective said Reese and Steph had been lovers. The thought had never occurred to Ella, but it certainly made sense. She'd first began experimenting with girls at that age, so why not them, too? And somehow, someone had figured that out, and now Reese was a suspect in the murder. That, too, made sense, although the idea of Reese killing Steph was as ridiculous as the idea of Reese trying to kill her sister. Reese was wonderful and kind and adored Cass. She was protective of her. Even if she had killed Steph, which Ella certainly did not believe, she would never do anything to harm her sister. Ella believed, when it came right down to it, Reese would die rather than let anything happen to Cass.

Even if it made no sense, this new development possibly explained something else: Reese's sudden decision to end their relationship. The man had mentioned that the DA had questioned Reese and considered her a suspect in Steph's murder. It was that same night, after she met with the DA, that she'd called things off. The timing made sense. Who can concentrate on wooing a girl when you're worried about going to jail for the rest of your life?

Poor Reese! Ella could only imagine what she was feeling right now. Watching Reese tickle her sister's stomach, and seeing Cass giggle and squirm in response, she saw the vulnerability Reese so carefully hid from everyone. It was really only exposed at times like this, when she was not just with Cass but responsible for her. Now, she was the doctor examining Cass, and the weight of that responsibility seemed to pull Reese's shoulders down.

"I'm going to check the X-ray," Reese said.

"I'm number ninety-nine," Cass said.

"Huh?" Reese asked.

"Her oxygen," Ella said, nodding toward the screen.

Reese rewarded her with a smile. "Ninety-nine is good."

Ella watched as Reese left and made up her mind that she was not going to allow Reese to shoulder this burden alone. Reese was hurting, Ella knew it, and although she'd tried to push her away, now that Ella knew why, she refused to allow it. And Reese could resist all she wanted. The effort would be futile, because Ella knew the key to Reese's heart was sitting right there on the stretcher, playing with her fireman's hat. And since Cass had won Ella's heart, too, she knew it would all work out, with time.

"Perfect X-ray," Reese said as she came back into the room, followed by Dr. Light.

"Normally, I'd like to keep her for a while to observe her, but I think she really did dodge a bullet here."

Cass shook her head. "It wasn't a bullet. I fell in the gorge."

They all laughed.

"It's a good thing I can swim," Cass said proudly.

Ella saw them all smile, and she remembered Reese telling her Cass's love of swimming was one of the reasons she'd bought the house with the pool.

"I'll stay at my parents' tonight. I have a fingertip O2 sat monitor, so I can keep an eye on her."

"I have to be better by tomorrow," Cass said. "It's my birthday party."

"I think you're already better," Reese said.

"I'll do the discharge instructions."

Sharon walked over and hugged Ella. "I can't thank you enough, Ella. You saved her."

Ella echoed the Scout leader's words. "I was in the right place at the right time."

"Mommy, can we get pizza tonight? It's Friday."

"Well, I'm not in the mood to cook, so pizza sounds good to me."

"And I want Ella and Reese to come, too."

"Of course." Sharon looked at Ella. "If you're not busy, would you like to join us for dinner?"

Ella looked at Reese before answering, holding her breath, wishing for Reese to reconsider her harsh decision to end things between them. Reese seemed to debate for a second, before nodding almost imperceptibly, filling Ella with hope.

"I would. But only if you can give me a ride home. I came in the ambulance with Cass, so I'm stranded. And right about now, it's looking like a long walk back to Nay Aug."

"I'll give you a ride," Reese said.

They waited until Cass's paperwork arrived, and even though she was quite capable of walking, she insisted on a ride to the door in the wheelchair. Reese pushed her and even did a wheelie in front of the nurses' station. At the front door, the group split, and Ella followed Reese a few feet to her car in the doctors' lot.

"Tiffany told me it was your idea to bring Cass here," she said. Turning in her seat, she offered Ella a hesitant smile. "That was good thinking."

"I thought you would feel more comfortable here, but once we got here, I realized it was a good move for Cass, too. She felt right at home."

"She's been here with me several times," Reese said as she pulled onto the street.

They were quiet for a few minutes, and Ella contemplated what to say next. The conversation with the investigator from the DA's office was like the elephant between them in the car, and she decided the sooner they discussed it, the better.

"We should talk about it, Reese."

"Why?"

"Because I suspect you canceled our date tomorrow because of the investigation. Because it's on your mind and it's difficult for you to relax and think about anything else."

"Yes, yes, and yes."

"I do not believe for one second that you had anything to do with Steph's murder. And if it's too much for you to date me right now, because you're nervous or depressed, or whatever—I understand. But I care about you, and I'm not going to let you push me away while you deal with this all by yourself."

"You can't help, Ella."

"How do you know? Maybe it would be helpful just to have someone to talk to. Or someone to be with who you don't have to explain it to. Maybe what you need is great sex to take your mind off your troubles."

They were at a stop sign and Reese turned to her, laughing. "Was that a pickup line?"

"Maybe."

"It's the best one I've ever heard."

Ella winked, and Reese grabbed her hand. After squeezing it, Reese didn't let go.

Leaning back into her seat, Ella was quiet, happy the tension between them was broken. When Reese pulled into her parents' driveway, Ella turned to her. "My sneakers are wet, and I need a shower. Will you call me when the pizza arrives?"

"Certainly."

"Can I bring anything?"

"I don't suppose you have time to bake a cake, do you?"

"I'll bring the vodka. I think we both could use a drink."

"See you in a bit."

CHAPTER 23: OVERNIGHT SHIFT

In the kitchen, Ella washed her hands, then pulled out her baking supplies. Ten minutes later, a cake was in the oven. It was from a box, but she found that to be acceptable in a pinch.

With the timer set, she took off her grimy sneakers and set them on the porch to dry, then headed upstairs for a shower. After dressing in comfortable jeans and a lightweight sweater, she dried her hair and made it downstairs with three minutes left on the oven timer. She was mixing the icing when the cake finished, and she moved it to the counter to cool.

After washing her hands again, she picked up her phone and dialed the Ryans. Cass answered.

"Do I smell pizza?" she asked.

"It's not here yet."

"Can you come over and help me carry the cake? I'll let you put the frosting on it."

"I have to ask Mom," she said, and Ella suspected Cass wouldn't be leaving the house without her mother's permission for a very long time.

A minute later she heard a knock on the door, and Ella handed Cass a box containing the ingredients for decorating. She followed her out the door with the cake on a glass plate.

Reese laughed when she saw the cake.

"I aim to please," Ella said, and Reese closed her eyes as a blush spread across her face. When she opened them again, Ella was still staring at her. "I'm not flirting with you, Reese. I just want you to know I'm here. And I'm interested. And I'm not going to let this nonsense scare me away."

Reese nodded in understanding, and the doorbell saved them from further discussion. "You answer it, Reese," Cass said, and Ella worried again that Cass would suffer the repercussions of her ordeal for a long time.

It was after seven o'clock when they finished the pizza, and by then the cake was cool, so Cass frosted it and decorated it with thirty different toppings, which blended together amazingly well.

"How about that drink?" Reese asked as they began cleaning up. She'd dismissed her parents and Cass to the living room, and after the day they'd both had, she thought the vodka and tonics were in order.

"Sounds heavenly," Ella said.

"Okay. Would you like to sit out on the patio? It's a little cool, but if I light the fire, it should be fine."

"I'll go grab a jacket," Ella said, and when she returned, the fire was blazing and Reese was sitting on a glider, her feet tucked under her, a blanket over her lap, and a drink in each hand. Ella laughed at the sight. "Don't you look cozy?" she asked.

Reese patted the spot next to her, and Ella lifted the blanket and sat beside her. She sipped her drink and felt the heat singe her throat as if she'd swallowed the fire in the pit. It felt wonderful, and she sighed contentedly.

"That bad, huh?"

"It's been a rotten week."

"I'm sorry about that."

"When did you find out you're a suspect?"

"Tuesday."

Just as Ella suspected. "I guess that explains everything, then."

Reese didn't answer, and Ella took another sip of her drink. This one went down easier. Too easy, she thought, and made a promise to nurse the rest of it.

"So, you and Steph were an item, huh?"

Ella could hear Reese sigh in the darkness. "That's the rumor."

"It rings true."

"Does it?"

Ella didn't know how to explain it, but once the investigator had said it, Reese and Steph made sense to Ella. There was nothing obvious, no tell, just a reverence Reese had for Steph that went beyond friendship. She told her so.

Reese was silent as she thought about Ella's words. Was it so obvious? How come no one else had ever sensed it? Did Ella have some special perception that others lacked? Or was it just that Ella had known both of them and could see her and Steph together in her mind's eye? But, then again, she hadn't suspected anything until the DA's investigator had voiced his suspicions to her in the ER.

She thought of Steph and what they'd shared. Theirs had been a passionate affair, fueled by teenage hormones, and over the years Reese had often wondered where their relationship would have gone. Few teen romances survive, and theirs likely wouldn't have been any different. But that didn't lessen her feelings or detract from the precious times they shared. *It's time to talk about it, Steph. I'm sorry for outing you, but I trust Ella. I really do.*

"I suppose it rings true because it was."

Turning slightly, Ella looked at Reese and spoke softly. "I'm happy to know that, Reese. Steph missed out on so much because she died so young. It's good to know that she didn't miss out on love."

Reese reached across the space between them and gently squeezed Ella's thigh. "Thank you for believing in me."

Ella placed her hand on Reese's and laced their fingers together. "I have an ulterior motive," she said.

Reese nudged closer and whispered. "Oh, yeah? What's that?"

"I want that date with you."

"I'm still free tomorrow night, although by then, I'll probably be too tired to stand."

"It would be okay with me if we sit."

"I have a fire pit just like this at my house, but there's no one in the living room to spy on us."

"It sounds perfect." Ella leaned, and turned her head, and found herself a mere inch away from Reese. Reese turned, too, and suddenly they both gave in to the growing attraction. Their lips met just as before—softly, sweetly. Then Ella felt her hunger growing and she deepened the kiss, seeking Reese's tongue, probing her gently. Reese answered in kind and then pulled away and trailed kisses along Ella's jaw and neck that left her shuddering.

Ella moaned, acknowledging the sensations that flooded her— desire, of course, and excitement, but also a unity born in the bonds they'd forged during the hours since Cass's dip in Roaring Brook.

Ella closed her eyes and arched her neck, giving herself to Reese, and she felt Reese shifting, the glider moving, and Reese eased her onto her lap. Beneath the blanket, Reese pulled her closer, moved her hands under Ella's shirt, teased the skin of her back with feathery touches.

Ella thought she might come just from Reese kissing her and touching her that way, and the thought was sobering.

Arching back, she placed her fingers on Reese's lips. "What are your plans for the evening, Doctor? Because if you're going to stay at your parents' and watch out for your sister, you have to stop turning me on like this."

"Is Pip home?" she asked between kisses.

"No."

"Are you allowed guests?"

Reese rubbed her palm across Ella's nipple, and suddenly it didn't matter if they made love in her car, as long as they did it soon. All the flirting on the phone the week before, and then the emotion of the past few days, had her spinning.

Ella laughed. "What's she going to do? Ground me? Let's go."

Reese stood and killed the gas feeding the fire, then reached for Ella's hand.

They kissed their way across the yard and through the house, up the stairs, and into Ella's room. With the door closed and locked behind them, Ella pulled Reese's sweatshirt up over her head. No bra kept her lips from Reese's breasts, and she leaned forward and sucked one into her mouth, while she caressed the other. She felt Reese moving back toward the bed, and she followed, joined to her by mouth and breast.

Reese pulled her down, on top of her, and positioned her legs between Ella's. Ella ground her pelvis down as Reese slid her hands up, pulling the layers of clothing with her. With one hand, she unhooked Ella's bra while she clutched her ass with the other, urging their centers together.

Ella shimmied out of her bra, rolling far enough over to slip her hand into the waistband of Reese's jeans. Reese moaned at the contact, and Ella quieted her with her mouth, this kiss hungrier than the others, deeper and more demanding. Reese answered the call with her hands, opening Ella's jeans, sliding them down her hips and over her ass.

"Let me get these off," Ella said as she rolled a little and kicked them aside. Watching Reese do the same, Ella grew hotter and wetter as she throbbed with need. When they were naked beside each other, they buried fingers in each other, opened to each other, found each other's flesh with lips and tongues.

Ella felt the force of the tide sucking her out to sea as she ground against Reese's hand, and then she went under as she sucked in a huge breath and exploded. She sought Reese's mouth, kissed her as she rode out her orgasm.

"Holy fuck," she gasped a minute later as she regained the ability to form intelligible words.

Reese had stilled beneath her, both her own hips and the hand that had given Ella so much pleasure.

"Have you lost interest in me already?" Ella asked playfully.

"Not a chance."

"Good. Because I'm not done with you."

"Really?"

"Really," Ella said as she eased her way down Reese's body, kissing a path from her ear to her neck, then finally her breast. As she sucked a nipple into her mouth, Reese moaned, and Ella slipped one finger, then a second into her wet folds. Reese clenched around her, paralyzing Ella's fingers, and Ella stilled until she felt her begin to relax.

"Please, Ella, I need to come," Reese pleaded, and Ella slid between Reese's legs. Covering Reese's clit with her mouth, she licked softly as Reese arched into her. She moved her fingers slowly, allowing Reese to drive into her mouth and her fingers by turns, and when Reese buried her hands in Ella's hair to hold her in place, Ella let Reese take over. In seconds, Ella felt the trembling begin, and Reese groaned in ecstasy.

CHAPTER 24: THE PUMPKIN PATCH

Ella's bed felt empty when she awakened, but she only had to roll over and hug the pillow to imagine Reese beside her. It had been very late, or perhaps very early by the time Reese went back to her parents', and as much as Ella would have liked her to stay, she knew it was best that she check on Cass and not raise her parents' suspicions too high.

Besides, they had a date planned for tonight, and this time, no way was she going to let Reese out of bed before morning.

Her first order of business was to check on Cass, but as she dialed the number for the Ryans' house, she found herself hoping Reese would answer. When Sharon assured her that Cass was up, showered, dressed, and staring at the clock, Ella laughed. Apparently, she suffered no after-effects from her dunk in the gorge.

After showering and dressing appropriately for the pumpkin patch, Ella hopped into her car. Her first stop was at the bakery, and it was an easy trip to the lake. She'd agreed to drive Sophie, since parking was an issue at the pumpkin patch. It was a sunny day, and overhead a clear, cloudless sky hinted it would be a nice one for Cass's party. They encountered surprisingly little traffic, and Ella found herself in Sophie's driveway twenty minutes later.

"Welcome back," Sophie said by way of greeting. "I'm so happy you had such a productive trip."

It seemed like so long ago that Ella had been away that she needed to press the rewind button in her mind.

They'd talked twice while she was gone, mostly because Ella had begun to worry about Sophie, and she wanted to make sure she was okay. Even though she didn't look it, Sophie was nearly eighty years old, and she lived alone, practically in the middle of nowhere. Since she didn't have any family to look after her, Ella felt someone needed to do it, and she liked Sophie, so it didn't seem like a chore.

"It's good to be back."

Ella followed her into the sunroom, where Sophie had all the essentials for a wonderful lox sandwich prepared. "Oh, boy. I'm going to put on weight if I keep hanging around you."

"Nonsense. Salmon is low-fat. The cream cheese is low-fat. The onion and capers are low-fat. It practically takes more calories to digest this food than you get from eating it."

"It's a good thing I stopped at the bakery, then. I don't want us starving."

Sophie's smile lit up her face. "You are precious, Ella."

Ella felt herself blushing and thought of Reese. If the light had been on last night, would she have seen Reese blushing?

"What's that smile about?" Sophie asked as she poured coffee.

Ella hesitated. Even though she'd first come here as a friend, their relationship had changed when Sophie started the scholarship for Steph at PMU. At this point, Ella felt it best to maintain some boundaries, and sharing the detail of her night in bed with Reese would definitely cross them.

"Nothing. I'm just happy, I guess. Excited about the party this afternoon."

"Really? Any particular reason why?"

Sophie studied her over her coffee cup, and Ella felt totally naked. It wasn't possible that Sophie could know—certainly Reese wouldn't have shared that with her—yet she seemed to sense something.

Ella wasn't showing her cards just yet. "Lots of potential donors will be there," she said with a wink.

"No wonder they made you a VP. Is Cass excited? I haven't seen the dear girl since Reese put the boat away."

Ella immediately realized that Sophie didn't know about Cass's adventure in the gorge, and she wasn't sure how much of that tale she should tell her, either. But how would she explain Cass ending up in the water without explaining about the baseball player who'd pushed her? She couldn't, but she could leave out the detail about the police questioning Reese.

When Ella told Sophie about the events of the day before, she visibly paled. "Why would anyone try to hurt that dear girl?"

Since Ella didn't believe Reese had anything to do with it, she shook her head and offered her honest opinion. "I have no idea. It's really bizarre."

"I would imagine the Ryans are a little spooked."

Ella sat back and nodded, but it was the first time she'd thought about it. While she'd been molesting their daughter the night before, the Ryans were probably worried sick about why someone had tried to harm Cass and whether they'd try again. And who would know that anguish better than Sophie? Steph had been assaulted, too, only no Scouts were there to save her. Ella was sure Sophie was thinking the same thing, and rather than skirt the issue, she addressed it.

"If only some Scouts had been here that night," she said softly.

"Or some parents."

Ella sat up in surprise. Did Sophie blame herself for Steph's death? "Oh, Mrs. Gates, you can't say that! Don't think that! Steph was a teenager—certainly old enough to be alone in the house. It wasn't your fault."

"Those philosophers who offer comfort after a tragedy say 'God called her home.' Or 'It was her time.' It makes me wonder, Ella. If I had been home, would something else have happened? Would she have gone over to Reese's to study and been hit by a drunk driver?"

"My gram said the same thing. 'Our days are numbered.'"

"I remember her saying that whenever someone young died."

Ella nodded and then was quiet for a moment. "How's the investigation going?" she asked.

"I don't hear much, truthfully." She looked out the window and studied a view she surely knew by heart. "There is a new angle, though."

Ella suspected she knew what Sophie was about to say. "What's that?"

"They're investigating Reese. Apparently, they believe that she and Steph were...more than friends, and that might be the motive for the murder."

Ella didn't want to be deceitful, so she told Sophie what she'd heard at the hospital. She omitted so many other details that she couldn't face Sophie. Instead, she followed her gaze out the window.

"What do you think about that?" Ella's voice was soft as she asked. How much did she really want to talk about this with Sophie? She hadn't even come out to her.

"The notion that Reese might have murdered Steph is preposterous. As for the other matter, I don't know, and I'm not sure I want to."

Ella gently rubbed Sophie's arm in response, and it seemed to awaken her inner tiger.

"Enough of that nonsense. It's supposed to be a happy day. Am I dressed okay?"

Ella looked down to the sweater and jeans she had on, and then at the pantsuit Sophie was wearing. "Do you own jeans? Or sneakers?"

"Of course I have sneakers! And a jogging suit," she said hopefully. "Will that do?"

"It'll be perfect."

Sophie sat up a little taller, as if she was proud of herself for owning the proper attire for the pumpkin patch, and they sat quietly for a while, eating their brunch.

"And how's the situation at home now that Pip's back?"

"She's been scarce since I got back from my trip. I think she's trying not to crowd me, but I'm going to start house hunting. As a matter of fact, I'm supposed to talk to a realtor today at the party."

"Who's that? Doug?"

"You don't miss a trick, do you?"

"Not often," she said with a grin. "He's a good realtor, but he has a little bit of a temper. I've known him since he was a boy, and…well, let's just say, I've seen the good, the bad, and the ugly."

Ella frowned, and Sophie patted her arm this time. "Don't worry. He's harmless, and very good at his job. I'm thinking of having him list this place."

Ella was shocked, and she knew her surprise showed on her face. "What? Why? You've lived here forever."

"I know, but truthfully, what do I need this big house for?"

Ella watched Sophie turn and look back through the window toward the lake. The trees framing the view were covered in leaves starting to change color, and if Ella snapped a picture, it could have been printed as a postcard.

"For the view," she said softly. "For the neighbors who you've known forever. For the memories of your husband and your daughter."

Sophie sighed and ignored her remarks. "What brought Pip home so soon? Is she staying or going back?"

Ella wasn't about to tell Sophie what Pip had discovered in Miles Jones's scrapbook. "Yes. She's home for good. She wasn't happy in California, so she decided to quit film school and come back."

"How soon will you move?"

Ella blew out a breath. "It'll be fine for a little while, until I can find my own place. I work 'til six most nights, and I travel at least one week out of the month for work. If I can get out of town for the other weekends, it might not be so bad. Maybe I'll go to Philly to see friends or catch a flight to Florida to visit my parents. We'll see."

"And you sure you want to stay here? Buying is a commitment."

"I know! But yes, I want to stay in the mountains. The question is where. I was hoping for a few more months to look around before I have to make a decision. Hopefully, Pip and I won't drive each other crazy while I'm searching."

"It's hard to find the right home when you're under pressure. It's so much easier when you have time on your side."

"I agree."

"What are you thinking about? Will you stay in Scranton?"

Ella sat back and looked out the windows to the lake beyond. What was it about water that filled her with such peace? "I'd love to live here. Is there anything for sale?" Ella knew she couldn't afford a lake house, but…it never hurt to dream.

"I don't think so, but I'll keep my eyes and ears open."

"I'd appreciate that."

"How's the scholarship coming along?"

"Everything is with the lawyers—Bucky has the documents. Then we'll just need your input about the recipient, and we'll be set. The sooner, the better. The incoming freshman class will want to know about this opportunity as soon as possible, and it looks like we'll be able to send out the criteria for Steph's scholarship next month when we mail out the application packets. The award won't be officially announced until May, but we have a lot to do before then."

"That seems ridiculous, doesn't it? Why wait so long, when these kids are deciding on their futures?"

Ella shrugged. She agreed. By delaying the announcement about scholarship winners until May, a lot of kids were on edge, waiting to hear if they'd received full rides or just partial packages. It seemed cruel, but this was how it was done. Everyone had time to change their minds before the decisions were made, and hopefully, not afterward. That way, the young men and women who were announced at the Cognitio luncheon in May were the ones on campus in September.

Ella explained the reasoning. "There's no reason you can't select your candidate sooner, though, and tell them your decision. It just won't be announced until the luncheon."

"When do you need the check? I've liquidated some assets, so I can give it to you at any time."

"How about next week? Dr. Bingham, the president, would like to meet with you. We can have lunch or dinner."

"Will I get all this attention after I give you the check?"

Ella laughed and squeezed Sophie's hand. "I can't promise anything for Dr. Bingham, but I'll still be here."

Sophie looked at her intently, and Ella saw her eyes begin to swim as a tear formed. "You will, won't you?"

Not wanting either of them to cry, Ella winked.

"Your grandmother would be so proud of you. I wish she were still here. There have been nice people in the house, but they're all too young for me. No one plays cards anymore—unless it's poker. Argh! And you can't share recipes or borrow a cup of sugar like in the old days. No one cooks!"

Ella swallowed and considered Sophie's words. "People are hard to replace. What we like, or love about someone is an individual trait. No one else will ever be them or make us feel the way we did when we were with them."

They'd finished their lox, and regrettably, Ella had no room left for the pastries she'd picked up at the bakery. But since she'd be giving Sophie a lift home later, she'd have an opportunity then.

Ella cleaned up while Sophie changed into her jogging suit, and then she helped her into the car for their trip to Roba's Farm.

The party was scheduled from noon to four, and Ella thought they were early when she pulled into the lane fifteen minutes ahead of schedule. She was dismayed to see dozens of cars in front of her and a field filled with others already parked. After displaying Sophie's handicap-parking placard, she was allowed to park on the top of the hill, and Ella easily found a place beside the main entrance.

Ella purchased tickets for them, and they caught the tractor to the center of the pumpkin patch, where dozens of campfire sites were scattered among attractions like a bouncing pillow, children's slides, and a gigantic fort made out of hay bales.

Everything was clearly marked, and it took only a few minutes to find the Ryans' campfire site. As they approached, she spotted Reese. Reese caught her eye, and Ella couldn't contain the smile that erupted on her face. She hadn't had much time to think about what had happened the night before, but it had been a wonderful couple of hours, with fantastic sex and warm conversation. It was just what she'd been fantasizing about, but now that it had happened—what next? Was Reese as happy about their plans for the night as she was?

Maybe she should have called and asked, to save them both some embarrassment if Reese had changed her mind.

Then Reese smiled, a lopsided grin that spread slowly across her face, and Ella had the sudden feeling that she wouldn't get much sleep tonight.

❖

Reese had a crazy-busy morning, between picking up Cass's cake and packing her car to take all the food to the party. Once at the pumpkin patch, she'd found a large garden wagon and loaded it high, and she still had to make two trips up the hill to their campfire site to haul everything she'd brought. At one point, she'd wished she'd accepted someone's offer of help, but in the end, when it was all set up just as she'd imagined, she was glad she'd done it alone. The site was perfect, with a tent to cover the food and a circle of wooden benches surrounding a fire pit. Her parents had brought balloons, and they flanked the tent, giving it an even more festive look.

She'd gotten there early, and Doug, the realtor, and his three kids had already stopped by, grabbed snacks, dropped off a gift bag, and run off to play. A dozen other people had been by as well, some to grab food, but most to just leave presents and jackets behind. Even though she'd encouraged Cass to stay and meet her guests, she'd refused. She was across the pond on a jumping pillow shaped and colored like a gigantic pumpkin. Now Reese was hanging out, alone, awaiting her guests. With Cass's friends and coworkers, a few family members, and Reese's friends, not to mention everyone's children, she expected about fifty people.

All of the activity had kept her so busy she hardly had a chance to think about what had happened with Ella. Ella—the sweet, funny, smokin' hot woman of her most recent fantasies—had seduced her. And seduced her very well, and thoroughly. Fantastically, in fact. And they had plans to see each other again after Cass's party.

Although she hadn't thought too much about it, she'd checked her phone a few times, hoping for a call from Ella, a little message about the night before. At the same time, she was relieved that no call came through, because part of her was petrified that Ella would cancel. And while it wouldn't have been the worst disappointment of her love life— no, it would have. After the evening they'd had, Reese would have been crushed if Ella had reconsidered.

Resting her back against the edge of her chair, she looked up and was delighted to see Ella approaching. Ella's smile was as bright as the magnificent fall day, and Reese took that to be a good sign. She smiled in return and stood to help Ella guide Sophie down the small hill toward their site.

"I don't suppose you have cocktails, do you?" Sophie asked.

"The pumpkin patch does not allow alcohol. But I can give you some of my special punch, if you'd like." Reese winked and Sophie laughed.

"That sounds like my cup of tea."

"And for you, Ella?" Reese asked, her lips pursed.

"Oh, let's make it tea for two, shall we?"

"No. I'd say three."

"Let me help you," Ella said, and she walked with Reese into the tent. "Shall I stand guard?" she asked when they were inside.

"Yes. I'd hate to get thrown out before we sing 'Happy Birthday.'"

Taking the cup, Ella touched it to Reese's. "I'll drink to that."

Ella took a sip and immediately started coughing. "Whoa. What did you do? Put pink food coloring in vodka to make this punch?"

"Who told you my secret recipe?"

Ella coughed again for show, then looked around. "Do you have anything to mix with this?"

"How about some lemonade?"

"Perfect," she said a minute later when Reese had diluted her drink enough to satisfy Ella's taste buds.

Reese nodded and then watered down Sophie's as well. "Now that I'm getting a better look at you, I think I recognize you from last night."

Ella smiled around her glass. "That was me all right."

"Any regrets?" Reese couldn't believe she'd asked the question. But she had to know. Although she was very attracted to Ella, they barely knew each other. They hadn't even been on an official date, yet they'd torn each other's clothes off and shared multiple orgasms after they'd both basically collapsed from the stress of a tough day. It was entirely possible Ella was hoping Reese had forgotten about their night together.

"Only that you left."

Reese had to swallow a tear that appeared out of nowhere. "Wow. You're perfect. Do you know that?"

"Is that the famous Ryan Knockout Punch?" someone asked, interrupting them.

Ella looked up to see a tall, well-built man with dark, model good looks. Instead of a day at the pumpkin patch, he was dressed to shoot a cover for a fashion magazine, with a striped shirt and a coordinating kelly-green sweater draped across his shoulders. He wore tight-fitting jeans and green sneaker-shoes, and if it wasn't for the way he was checking her out, she would have sworn he was gay. No heterosexual man she'd ever known would have worn that outfit.

Ella recognized him, but before she could say anything, he spoke.

"Scoop Timlin," he said as he extended his hand.

"Ella Townes." She grasped his hand firmly, to let him know she wasn't weakened by his amazing show of manliness, and to his credit, when she pulled back, he made a show of rubbing his hand.

"That's a killer grip you have there, Ella Townes."

"I met her at my kickboxing class," Reese said and gave Scoop a kiss on the cheek. "Ella, don't mind Dr. Timlin. I'm sure his wife and children will be along shortly to put him in his place."

Scoop smiled. "She's so hard on me."

Ella smirked. "Something tells me you deserve it."

He laughed as Reese handed him a drink.

"We've actually met before, Scoop. Do you remember the little blond girl with skinned knees who lived next to Stephanie Gates during the summers?"

Scoop studied her, and slowly the light of recognition filled his eyes, and he put down his drink to hug her. "Wow! Of course I do. It's so nice to see you!"

"And you as well. I looked for you at the golf tournament, so I could say hi."

"Wait. You're beautiful, and you play golf...talk about a fantasy woman."

Ella rolled her eyes in response and changed the subject. "So, you're a doctor, too?" she asked, even though she already knew the answer.

"Gynecology," he said, the smile returning to his face. "Let me get you my business card. In case you need my services."

Reese punched him in the arm. "Stop hitting on my date."

Scoop's face fell. "No! Say it ain't so."

"I'm afraid it is."

"Is it possibly a case of where you just haven't met the right man yet, or do you think it's irreversible?"

"I'm pretty set in my ways."

He snapped his fingers. "Well, as I'm sure you already realize, Reese is quite a catch. I've known her since high school, and if you need any references or that sort of thing, I can supply them."

Reese held up her cup to toast him. "Thanks, Scoop. You're not so bad yourself."

"High school, huh? That's a long time."

"Not only high school, but college and medical school, too. He followed me around for years."

"And now we work at the same hospital."

The word "college" got Ella's attention. "Speaking of college, I recently started at PMU," she said, and told him about her new position. "Maybe I will take that card. We can have lunch while I describe all the wonderful things your alma mater is doing."

"If you're looking for a donation, you should save your breath. Wife number one has most of my money, and wife number two is doing a good job at spending the remains. At the rate I'm going, I'll be lucky to put my kids through college."

Ella had to laugh. "We can still have lunch, even without your checkbook. You can give in other ways."

"Maybe you can help out with the blood drive," Reese suggested.

"When is that? Soon, right?"

"Yes, the first week in October. I'll text you."

"I haven't heard about the blood drive," Ella said. "What's that about?"

"Every year I give a lecture to the pre-med students about blood, and we talk about all kinds of things. Typing, blood-borne diseases, the structure of hemoglobin. Whatever. Then they all help. We try to make it fun, with a vampire theme for Halloween. It's good experience for them, and it's good for the school and for humankind as well. Everybody wins."

"It sounds wonderful. Why don't I know about it?"

Reese shrugged. "It's not that big a deal, just the pre-med club. It's not a big alumni event or anything like that. We just give blood, not money," she added with a wink.

Ella sipped her drink to hide her laugh, while Scoop moved in and put his arm around Reese's shoulders. "Don't let her modesty fool you. It is a big deal, for the students who help organize it and for the community."

Ella could sense Reese's discomfort at the attention, so she changed the subject. "There's someone here you might know."

Reese jumped in. "Mrs. Gates is here. Come say hi."

Scoop's cheerful expression turned instantly. "She hates me."

"She does not."

"She thinks I was trying to bed her daughter."

"You *were* trying to bed her daughter."

Scoop grinned sheepishly.

"Sounds complicated," Ella said as she shook her head.

Scoop and Reese exchanged a glance before Scoop shook his head and turned. "I'd better get this over with," he said, before handing Reese a large gift bag. "It's not for you," he deadpanned.

"Here, give her some punch," Reese said and handed him the extra glass.

Ella watched him, giving Reese time to elaborate about Scoop. Instead, she greeted the next party guest. "Hi, Lucky. Be careful, Ella. I don't have a spare shirt for you today."

Ella turned to the startled face of the man who'd so rudely spoiled her shirt at the golf tournament. He'd never even sought her out to apologize, and she hadn't been able to get the stains out of her shirt. If he wasn't an alum, she would have sent him the bill for replacing it.

"Hi, Ms. Townes," he said. "I have something for you." Reaching for his wallet, he pulled out the folded piece of paper that served as the Pocono Farms Pro Shop gift certificate. "I want you to have this, so you can buy a new shirt. And this is for Cass," he said as he handed a card to Reese.

Glancing at the paper, Ella felt embarrassed by the thoughts she'd been entertaining, and she shook her head. "I can't accept this. It wasn't a two-hundred-dollar shirt."

"It doesn't matter. What matters is I did something stupid, and you handled it so well. If I was you, I would have let a few f-bombs drop."

"Well..." Ella said, and both he and Reese laughed.

"It's a nice gesture, really, but I couldn't."

"I'm going to insist, so you should take it. Besides, it's not my money. I won it."

Reluctantly, Ella took the paper. "Thank you very much, Mr. Lucci."

"I think you're going to win this election, Lucky. You've become a real politician."

Ella saw his cheeks color, but then he smiled. "Do you think so?"

Seeing Ella's confusion, Reese explained. "Lucky is running for county commissioner in the November election."

Ella held up her glass. "He certainly has my vote."

They laughed, and Reese pointed him toward Sophie Gates. Lucky bit his lip. "I wasn't going to say anything…but how's the investigation going?"

Apparently, he hadn't heard the rumors, and Reese chose not to enlighten him. "No news, I think. How's the family?" she asked, quickly changing the subject.

"They're wandering around somewhere. Carrying campaign posters! I'll catch you later," he said and wandered off toward the fire, where Sophie was chatting with Scoop Timlin.

"Oh, here comes Doug," Reese said.

Ella looked up to see a sandy-haired man pulling a little girl on each arm. "If you don't wise up, we're going home, right now. I don't care if we get any cake or not. Now stop whining."

The venom in his words nearly knocked Ella over, and she saw Reese's eyes fly open wide. "Hey, guys, what's going on? Are you having a good time?"

One of the girls shook her head. "Daddy says we can't do the pumpkin cannon because it costs too much money."

Ella watched his face grow red, and she hoped he didn't take his anger out on the children.

Reese came to the rescue. "Well, it's a good thing I have these free coupons for the pumpkin cannon."

Both girls' faces brightened, and their father's crimson glow faded. "Wow! Thanks, Dr. Reese," one said as she reached for a ticket.

"You're welcome. Would you like to do it one time or two?" she asked.

"Two!" they screamed, and Reese handed over the four tickets. "How about your dad? Should I give him a ticket, or was he a bad boy?"

"Well, he is a little cranky today," the taller girl said. Reese and Ella both chuckled, and to her relief, Doug did as well.

"Go get something to eat," Doug ordered them, and they looked up sheepishly before heading deeper into the tent.

"I'll help them," Reese said. "Doug, I'd like you to talk to Ella. She's looking for a house."

At the mention of potential business, Doug's demeanor changed completely. A suave salesman replaced the impatient father.

"Doug Dewar," he said as he held out his hand, and Ella reluctantly shook his, unsure of him. But he was Reese's friend, and Sophie was considering using him, so she figured she'd give him the benefit of the doubt.

"Have you been working with anyone?" he asked.

"No," she said, and then to her delightful surprise, he rattled off a stream of facts and questions that indicated he was quite knowledgeable about his profession. In the five minutes it took Reese to feed the girls, he'd given her a ton of information about the local real-estate market, where the good deals could be found, and which neighborhoods to avoid. As his daughters reattached themselves to him, one on each leg, he seemed much less stressed than he had been earlier. With a smile on his face, he handed her a business card. "I'll be happy to help you find your dream house, Ella. Just call me."

"What time's the cake?" he asked Reese.

"Around three."

"See you then," he said.

"Let's check on Mrs. Gates," Ella said after Doug and his family left. Chris Ryan and some others had taken seats by the fire, and a few kids were weaving through the trees in a game of tag. After greeting the newcomers and introducing Ella, they flanked Sophie on the bench in front of the fire. "What can I get you?" Reese asked.

Laying a hand on Reese's thigh, Sophie shook her head. "Nothing. I'm really fine. It's a beautiful day, and I'm out in the sunshine, enjoying the fresh air and company."

Reese settled in, happy that Ella had brought Sophie. It was truly good to see that she and Ella had reconnected after so many years. Each slender connection to Steph was precious to Sophie, and she knew Ella and the scholarship had brought a little light back to Sophie's eyes. She'd tried, over the years, and she knew that Sophie loved her and Cass, but it wasn't until Ella showed up that she saw this change.

"Did you bake the cake, Reese?" Sophie asked.

Reese shook her head and frowned. Mrs. Gates had been a career woman, helping run the family business, but she always made time for Steph and her friends. When Reese visited, there was always something to eat, and the house had the perpetual smell of a bakery. Although she'd tried to teach her skills to Reese, it hadn't worked. Everything fell flat or burned, and the truth was, Reese just didn't like the kitchen.

Steph was another story, though. She'd inherited her mother's love of baking and made everything from cupcakes for friends' birthdays to dog treats as gifts for her friends' pets.

Reese decided to share that memory with Sophie. "She never cleaned up, though. She'd make a batch of dog biscuits, and I'd find dough on the refrigerator door, on the stove, on the floor. She was a disaster."

"I suppose she needed a better assistant," Reese said, remembering the times she'd helped with the baking.

"I think she needed a full-time assistant. She was brilliant but not very organized."

They enjoyed the sunshine in silence until the kids started squealing with delight. The RailRiders mascots, Champ and Quill, had arrived, surrounded by a dozen little fans.

"I have to find Cass," Reese said as she stood.

"No," Ella said. "You stay. I'll go find her."

"She's probably still on the pumpkin pillow," Chris said.

"Got it," Ella said as she trotted off in that direction, weaving through the congestion. The number of people at the pumpkin patch was staggering, and she couldn't believe all the activities they had for the children to enjoy. When she was a child, she'd gone on a hayride and picked out a pumpkin. Here, that was just a small part of the adventure. After crossing a bridge over the duck pond and navigating the food court, Ella found Sharon Ryan plopped on a post beside the jumping pillow.

"How's it going?" Ella asked as she hugged her.

"This is about the fifteenth consecutive time she's been on the pillow. She refuses to come off when her turn is over, and the attendant just lets her stay on. But who am I to argue? She's having a ball."

"The mascots from the RailRiders are here. Reese thinks she should come back to the camp."

"Why don't you tell her?" Sharon suggested.

"Sure," Ella said.

She cut into the line and explained the situation to the attendant, then removed her shoes and went through the fence to the pillow. Cass was bouncing up and down, a smile on her face as her hair flew around like a halo.

Ella climbed up and bounced with her. "High five," Cass said, as she lifted her palm toward Ella.

Ella raised her hand to meet Cass's. "This is great," Ella said, feeling like a six-year-old.

"If you stay with me, you don't have to get off when the time's up. It's my birthday, so the lady lets me stay on."

"Will you stay on forever?"

Cass seemed to ponder the question. "Only till I get hungry."

"Will you get off to see Champ and Quill?"

Cass's face lit up. "Are they here?"

"They're over by the fire, talking to Reese and your dad. If you don't go over and say hello to them, they might feel sad and leave."

"We better go right now," she said and, as quickly as she could, descended to solid ground.

Ella helped her with her sneakers and then picked Sharon up near the gate. They followed Cass, who was still bouncing, as she guided them on the circuitous route back to the campfire site. As soon she spotted the mascots, Cass took off in a run and tackled Quill. He turned and rubbed her head, and then both of the big, furry creatures surrounded Cass and did a little dance with her.

"These are my friends," she said excitedly, to everyone around.

It was quite a crowd, too. In her absence, twenty new faces had arrived, some young, some old. There were four adults with Down syndrome, and they seemed to enjoy the mascots as much as Cass did. Children from other parties came over to meet them, and everyone wanted a photo.

Ella grabbed two bottles of water and walked back to the fire and sat beside Sophie.

"Thank you, dear," she said when Ella handed her the water. "This is some party," she said after taking a sip.

Joy was on everyone's face, from the small children to the eighty-year-old woman sitting beside her. Not a cloud marred the perfect blue sky, and the fire warmed them. She had to agree. It was quite a party.

"Oh, dear," Sophie said a moment later. "I didn't think he'd show up today."

"Who?" Ella asked as she scanned the crowd. The dozens of faces, most of them strangers, all seemed to be smiling, like they belonged.

"Did Reese tell you about her meeting with Bucky the other day?"

And then Ella spotted him, standing off to the side, talking with Senator Nathan.

"No. Why?"

"Perhaps it's not my tale to tell…but I see the way you and Reese are together. She trusts you."

After the night before, Ella sure hoped so. She avoided looking at Sophie, knowing how intuitive she was. She'd know, and Ella wasn't quite ready to share the news just yet. Instead, she stared at the senator and the prospective DA. "What happened with Bucky?"

"After the DA questioned her, she went to Bucky's office for advice. I guess he's her lawyer, but more importantly, they've been friends since high school. He basically threw her out of the office. He said it was a conflict of interest."

"Because he's running for DA?"

Sophie nodded, and Ella looked for Reese in the crowd, wondering if she'd seen Bucky yet and how she'd feel when she did. It had been a tough week for her, and she was finally relaxing a little bit, enjoying herself. Ella was sure a confrontation with him right now would bring her down.

Just as she spotted Reese, Reese spotted Bucky, and Ella rose to follow her as she began walking in his direction. Ella wasn't sure what the reaction would be when the two came together, but she wanted to be there for Reese. "Excuse me, please."

Ella arrived at Bucky's side at the same time as Reese, who said, "Nice of you to stop by, Bucky. It's not too much of an ethical dilemma, I hope?"

Bucky shrugged. "Hey, Ella. How's it going?" he said and hugged her. He clearly remembered her from the lake, and the call she'd made to say hello had lasted thirty minutes. They had a lunch meeting planned for after the election, and Ella was looking forward to it. Bucky seemed as genuine as he had as a boy—a nice man, totally unaffected by his family's wealth and political influence. Whatever happened with Reese had to be a more complicated matter than Sophie had described.

"Reese, I'm sorry. I didn't handle that day well."

Reese opened her mouth in mock surprise. "Ya think?"

"Look, I know you didn't hurt Steph. I can't prove it, but I know it. And I know you'd never hurt Cass. I told Andrew that, and I think he believes it. But he also had to question you, you know? I mean, we don't have any leads in Steph's case. None. And then you have a VIP come in and offer him not only a potential motive, but a suspect as well—what's he supposed to do? Even if it was preposterous, he had to question you."

Reese looked at him, unable to process everything he'd said. Was he saying she'd been ruled out as a suspect or just that they couldn't prove she'd done anything? And who was this VIP?

"Buck, what are you talking about? Who told the DA about me and Steph?"

Reese realized she'd just admitted their relationship, or at least suggested it, but it didn't matter. Bucky knew who'd been talking about her, and she wanted to know, too. Suddenly, he looked uncomfortable.

"I...I probably shouldn't say, Reese. It's sort of confidential."

"Listen, Buck. Someone is telling tales about me—dragging me into a murder investigation, trying to ruin my life. Don't you think I deserve to know who it is?"

Bucky visibly paled. "Reese, I think he was just trying to clear his conscience, you know? When they asked him if Steph was dating anyone...he wondered. It was a logical question, right? You're gay, you and Steph were close, right? So maybe..."

"Who was it, Bucky?" Reese asked again, standing taller and folding her arms across her chest.

Bucky looked around nervously. "Promise me you won't say anything, Reese. Andrew told me in confidence, and I need his support to win this election."

"Who was it?" Reese asked, looking around herself. Ella suspected she was trying to act casual, and as if on cue, Reese laughed. "He's watching us, right? That's okay. I'll never mention it. Just tell me, Bucky," she said as a huge smile appeared suddenly on her face.

"It was Josh."

The smile didn't fade, but Reese shook her head. "No, Buck. I don't believe it."

He shrugged.

"What? Who are you talking about?" Ella asked.

Bucky looked at Reese, then Ella. "Josh. Senator Nathan. He told the DA that Reese and Steph were lovers."

No, it couldn't be, Reese thought. He knew Reese as well as anyone. He *had* to know she could never hurt another human being. She was a doctor! She healed people, had cared for his mother a dozen times in the ER. What had she ever done to make him think otherwise? And she'd come out fifteen years ago, so why step forward with these suspicions now? It just didn't make sense. She'd thought they were friends, but was there a side to Josh she didn't know?

No. She didn't believe it. Josh was her friend. He, more than anyone, had helped her heal after Steph died. They'd talked about her and kept her memory alive, even all these years later, but not because he'd had some sort of creepy love for a dead girl. He'd liked Steph, but Reese didn't believe he'd ever loved her, except as a friend. Reese had always thought Josh was sort of lucky that Steph broke up with him, because he'd dated a dozen other girls after Steph. He'd married right after law school and had five children. Even if Steph broke his heart in eleventh grade, by the next month, he'd moved on. And always, over all these years, they'd been friends.

Reese shook her head again, denying his words. Bucky was wrong. No way had Josh Nathan been responsible for this rumor.

❖

He needed another glass of punch. Nothing was going right. In spite of a brilliant plan, Cass hadn't died, and he'd still had to pay a small fortune to the man who'd tried to kill her. At least he didn't have a murder on his conscience, but for how long? Because truthfully, nothing had changed, and he still needed to worry about Cass. He'd thought for sure Reese would come under suspicion in the attack on her, but no one seemed to believe her capable of hurting her sister, even to save her own hide. He'd handed the DA the suspect, and the motive for not one, but two crimes, but nothing seemed to be happening. They'd interrogated Reese and let her go, and that was that. The DA's office was still questioning old witnesses as if they had no suspect, and he wasn't in a position to challenge the DA's strategy without drawing attention to himself.

He made his way to the food tent as he watched Reese and Bucky laughing about something with Ella Townes. What could they possibly be laughing about? As the probable next DA, Bucky would be prosecuting the crimes Reese was being investigated for. He should be keeping his distance, not kissing Reese's ass. But that was Reese, right? She'd wormed her way into Steph's heart, making Steph turn on him. It wouldn't surprise him if Bucky dropped the investigation into Reese once he was in office. He liked her too much.

Josh poured the vodka into his paper cup and thought how juvenile this was. Here he was, a United States senator, one of the most powerful men in the country, sneaking alcohol at the pumpkin patch. The thought made him laugh.

"What's so funny?" Reese asked.

He told her, and she laughed, too. "I think it tastes better when it's forbidden," Reese said. "How are you, Josh? Is everything okay with you?"

Suddenly he felt naked, as if his crimes were tattooed like a scarlet letter, visible to Reese's prying eyes.

"Yes, of course. I'm great. Busy, juggling a million things, but good. And how's Cass? She must be really freaked out by what happened."

Reese shrugged. "She's okay. She thinks she fell, and we haven't corrected her misconception. Why worry her?"

"That's a smart idea," he said with a pat on her back.

"So hey, I want to ask a favor of you."

"Anything," he said, and Reese knew Bucky was wrong. Josh was her friend. "The Scouts who rescued Cass. Can you give them some sort of senatorial merit badge or something, to recognize their heroism?"

"Oh, yes! What a great idea."

"I'll text you the information with the name of their troop leader, okay?"

"Perfect. I'll be back in town for the blood drive in a couple of weeks. Maybe we can do some sort of presentation then—you know, with Cass, and the mayor, and all the people involved."

"You're the best," she said, but the look she was giving him made him uncomfortable, and fortunately, his escape presented itself.

"Perfect. Now, there's my wife. I'll see you later," he said, and with a quick hug, he headed out of the tent.

"Don't forget to be back at three for the cake," Reese called after him.

If he could leave Roba's and the entire Commonwealth of Pennsylvania, and go somewhere, anywhere else, he would. Instead, he plastered on a smile. "I wouldn't miss it."

CHAPTER 25: BEYOND SUSPICION

Ella dropped a tired Sophie off at the lake before heading back to Scranton. Once at Pip's, she showered and packed an overnight bag, and at six o'clock, she was knocking on Reese's door.

Not surprisingly, Reese looked exhausted, and Ella shocked herself by mentally adjusting her expectations of the night. Reese had only piqued her interest; they had much more to explore. Yet, even though she'd thought about a naked Reese all day long, sex suddenly seemed very unimportant.

Reese's mood seemed to mirror her own. She pulled Ella into a tight hug and then kissed her tenderly on the lips. It was a sweet, gentle kiss and held none of the passion Ella remembered from the night before.

Ella pulled a bottle of cab from her bag. "Would you like some wine?"

Reese nodded. "Best idea I've heard all day."

As Reese poured the wine, Ella got cozy on the couch, and a moment later, Reese joined her. "To a great day," Ella said.

"I was kind of hoping for a great night," Reese said.

Ella tilted her head and studied Reese. "You look exhausted. I'm thinking early night."

Leaning back into the cushions, Reese sipped her wine and then closed her eyes, allowing the taste to soak into her tongue. Ella was right. She was exhausted. It had been three o'clock by the time she'd gotten back to her parents, and she'd been up by seven to prepare things for Cass's party. And between hauling the supplies in and Cass's birthday loot out, and serving as hostess for the duration of the four-hour party, Reese felt like she'd worked hard.

"Maybe you're right."

Ella reached across and gently touched Reese's cheek. "It's okay. I'm pretty tired, too."

Reese leaned sideways for another kiss, this one as tender and soft as the first but lasting much longer. "On second thought…"

Ella playfully pushed her away. "I don't have any place to be in the morning. No rush."

"We haven't even been lovers for twenty-four hours, and we sound like an old married couple."

"Hardly. It's been a tough spell."

"It has. I didn't really stop to think about everything, because so much was going on, but on the way home, I just started thinking and, you know—it's all unbelievable."

"It is."

"Why would someone want to hurt Cass?"

"It doesn't make sense, Reese. Just some predator, I guess."

"But it wasn't random—that's the thing. He knew her story, wore the baseball uniform. She was deliberately targeted."

Ella nodded. Reese was right.

"And this whole thing with Josh turning me in to the DA. I don't believe it. Why would he do that? I think the DA is lying about this to cover for someone else."

The mention of Josh's name reminded Ella she'd seen him in the park. And it made no sense, but…hey, nothing did right now. But Josh had apparently tried to implicate Reese in Steph's murder. And then, someone had tried to murder Reese's alibi. And Josh Nathan just happened to be in the park at the time Cass was attacked.

"What? Josh was at the park? Why?"

"I don't know, Reese. I didn't talk to him. I saw him when I was driving home, and again from my balcony, but once I got to the park, he was gone."

"And you're sure it was Josh?"

"Yes. I recognized his hat."

"Huh?" Reese looked confused, and Ella explained how she'd seen him at her parents' house the week earlier wearing the same funky Phillies cap.

Suddenly Reese grew cold with fear, and she sat up on the couch as she turned to face Ella. "Did you talk to him? Tell him about the baseball player?"

Ella shook her head. "No. As I said, I didn't see him at the park, and then the police officer said we should keep this to ourselves."

"Yes, they did. So how'd he know Cass was pushed?"

"What?" Ella asked, turning her body and her head toward Reese, as if that would help clarify her confusion.

"He asked how Cass was, said she must be freaked out. He might have meant about nearly drowning, but I assumed he was talking about her being pushed. I told him we were keeping the news from her, and he agreed. But he wasn't surprised to know she'd been pushed. He *already knew*."

"You're sure?"

Reese replayed their conversation in her mind, and she was convinced. Suddenly, adrenaline chased the fatigue she'd been feeling, and she stood.

"Ella, listen to me. I mean, this is absurd, but you're a reasonable person, so just listen before you tell me I'm nuts. First, Josh tells the DA that Steph and I were lovers, giving me a motive for murdering her. Then he shows up at the park when someone tries to murder the only person who can prove my innocence. My *alibi*. Then he has knowledge about the attack that he shouldn't have." Reese shrugged. "Do I sound crazy to you, Ella? Because I sound crazy to me."

Ella scrunched her face as if the words had formed an unpleasant taste in her mouth. She adjusted again and felt a sudden chill. "If you're asking if all this is a coincidence…maybe. But if you're asking if Josh Nathan looks suspicious, I'd say you're not crazy at all."

"Why in the world would Josh want to hurt Cass, Ella? He loves her. They get along great. As a matter of fact, he even takes her to lunch a few times a year."

"Yes, I know. That's when I saw him the first time. He had the Phillies hat on, and he looked like a criminal. I was actually nervous when I saw him walking toward your parents' front door."

"He probably didn't want anyone to recognize him."

Ella shrugged. "Well, it worked. I had to ask your mom about him. But why hide? Because he's famous and doesn't want to be bothered? Or because he was up to no good? Why don't we talk to Cass? She's pretty smart. Maybe she knows what's going on."

Reese glanced toward the fireplace, where a clock sat on the mantle. "Are you up for a trip? Because we can't do this on the phone."

Fifteen minutes later, Reese startled her mother when she knocked on the back door before using her key to get in. "I'm concerned about Josh Nathan, Mom. Ella saw him in the park yesterday just before Cass was attacked, and he's the one who told the DA about me and Steph."

"You think Josh pushed her?" Sharon asked, not sounding surprised, but she brought a hand to her mouth to hold in any further reply.

Ella shook her head emphatically. "It definitely wasn't him. But he was there."

"Mom, the police are questioning everyone, and he didn't admit he was there. Why? What was he up to? And how did he find out Cass was pushed? The police told us to keep that part quiet, but when I talked to him at Roba's, he seemed to know."

"He's a very important man, Reese. Don't you think someone may have shared that information with him?"

Suddenly, Reese felt foolish. Her mom was right. What was she thinking? Just because Josh might have turned on her, did that mean he was suddenly some sort of homicidal maniac? It was ludicrous. But still…

"Why don't we just talk to Cass? I mean, we're here." Ella's voice of reason calmed Reese a little.

"Where is she?"

Mrs. Ryan called Cass, eight times, before she finally appeared in the kitchen for questioning. Reese started the probe. "Cass, when you and Josh go out for lunch, what do you talk about?"

Cass shrugged. "I can't remember."

Sharon shook her head and smirked. "Do you ever talk about Reese?"

Cass nodded enthusiastically. "Sometimes he tells me stories about when Reese was bad in school."

Reese was shocked. "Like what?"

"Like when you didn't go to class in college because you didn't like to get up early."

Shaking her head, Reese laughed. "Well, that's true. What else?"

"He said you were a good president, and he wants to be president one day."

Reese smiled. She, Steph, Josh, and Bucky had all worked together so well as student council leaders that they had rotated positions. All four of them had held major offices at one time or another, but Josh and Bucky were the only ones who went into politics.

Reese was baffled, but her sister was on a roll now. "He likes to know about baseball. He likes the RailRiders. He always asks if I can get him a ball. And yesterday, I let him meet Champ and Quill."

"It sounds like you and Josh are good friends, Cass," Ella said. Suddenly, she had an idea. "Friends always do fun things together, like having lunch or baking cakes. Sometimes, they have secrets. Do you and Josh have any secrets?"

Cass grew still, and Ella caught Reese's eye, then Sharon's. She might have hit on something here.

"Cass, I know Josh is your friend, but can you tell us your secret? Please?"

Cass frowned. "It's a secret, Reese. I can't tell."

Sharon patted Cass's hand. "Sometimes it's okay. You should never have secrets from your mom."

"Okay," Cass said. "Josh borrowed my two dollars, and he told me not to tell Reese because he borrowed money from a girl."

Talk about a disappointing reveal, Ella thought. Two bucks was hardly worth murdering someone.

Reese took the lead, though, and kept probing. "Did he pay you back?"

Cass smiled. "Yes. He gives me two dollars every time I see him."

"Did he give you two dollars yesterday?"

Cass looked impatient. "Yes. Every time."

Ella had another idea. "Cass, do you know why Josh borrowed the two dollars?"

Nodding, she was silent.

"Why?" Reese asked.

"For car gas."

"Car gas?"

"Yes. Not grill gas."

"He needed gas in his car?" Reese asked.

Now they had it. Cass nodded happily. "Yes. Gas for his car, so he could go see his mom in the hospital."

Reese's heart thumped, and she leaned forward. Josh's mom had been in the hospital many times since her cancer was discovered years ago. The time that stood out in Reese's mind was when she was first diagnosed, back when they were in high school. Josh's mom was in the hospital in Philly when Steph was murdered. Reese knew that with certainty because it was Josh's alibi for Steph's murder. While everyone else was considered a suspect, Josh never was, because on the day of the murder, he had given his bone marrow to his mom and had ended up fainting or something, and he'd been admitted to the hospital right along with her.

Reese had a bad feeling, though, with all that was going on. "When, Cass? When did you give him the money?"

"When you were sick with a migraine and Steph died."

Cass told them the story of how she'd been bored. Her parents were out and Reese was sleeping, so she was sitting in the window watching for her parents to come home, and she saw Josh. She went outside to talk to him.

"Cass, are you sure? Are you sure it was that night?" Josh and his mom had told the story about the bone-marrow transplant so many times over the years, it was like gospel. But had it ever been proved? It must have been, right? The police would have checked out the story.

"Yes. Because then I didn't have enough money to give for Steph's flowers." As they listened patiently, Cass did her math equation and explained how Josh hadn't returned the money until the night of their graduation.

Reese hugged her sister and sent her back to bed, but not before Sharon and Ella hugged her, too.

Reese sighed. "Mom, I need a drink."

"I think we all do," Sharon said, and she retrieved three short glasses and the ingredients to fill them.

"So, Josh was in Scranton on the night Steph was murdered. And he's been lying about it ever since. And Cass knows it. And now the investigation has been opened again, and suddenly someone tries to kill Cass. Does this sound crazy to anyone but me?" Reese asked.

"It sounds crazy," Sharon said as she put the vodka tonics on the table. "But crazier things have been true."

Ella squeezed the lime into her drink. "So, Cass can blow his alibi for the night of Steph's murder. But does it really matter? I mean, if he didn't murder her, it's irrelevant. So the next, biggest question is—did Josh murder Steph?"

Reese shook her head. "That's the craziest part of all. They were friends. Good friends. There is absolutely no reason I can think of—and I've had twenty years to think about it—for anyone—including Josh—to murder Steph."

"Yes, I understand that. But even with no motive, Steph is dead. And at the moment, Josh looks like a suspect to me. Let's disregard the motive for a moment and talk about the alibi. If he was lying about being in Philly, can we prove it? A credit card? Or phone records? Do they still exist? They can track cell phones, but did we even have them back then?"

Reese nodded. "Steph's dad had a bag phone. Remember those? But Josh certainly didn't have one. They were kind of poor after his father died."

"Hmm. How about the hospital records? Would they go back that far? Could that prove Josh is lying about giving the bone marrow?"

Reese sat upright and pointed her finger at Ella. "Bingo. Millie Nathan has a stack of charts two feet high, and they reach back all the way to her cancer treatment in Philly. Also, I happen to have access to them. We might find something in them to indicate who her bone-marrow donor was."

Ella downed the last of her drink and stood. "Let's get to work."

CHAPTER 26: PROVE IT

Reese parked in a spot near the ER designated for doctors and used her ID badge to gain access to the building. Once inside, she picked up a phone and dialed medical records. "This is Dr. Ryan," she said into the phone. "I need Millie Nathan's chart. The whole thing, with the old records in it. Can you bring it to the ER doctors' lounge, please?

"Easy enough," Reese said as she disconnected the phone.

A moment later, Reese used her access card again and opened the door to a small lounge. A couch sat in front of an old-model television. A battered desk, covered with papers, napkins, and condiment packets, sat beside it.

"This is the life of an ER doctor," Reese deadpanned as she waved her arm across the room.

"Is there cable?" Ella asked.

"I don't know. I don't usually have time to watch television at work."

"What's the plan?"

"I'm not sure." Reese grinned. "Just kidding. There has to be some sort of record of the bone-marrow donor, especially after the reaction he supposedly had during the procedure."

"And if his alibi doesn't pan out, we can turn the DA on him, right?"

Reese shrugged. It was going to take something significant in the medical records to convince anyone that Josh Nathan had done anything wrong. He was a local hero and one of the most powerful men in Washington. No one would dare point a finger at him unless they were certain he was guilty.

A knock on the door caused them both to flinch, and they both laughed. "We're a little jumpy, aren't we?" Reese asked as she opened to door and accepted a cart loaded with medical charts.

"Here you are, Dr. Ryan," the clerk said, and Reese thanked her before dragging it into the room.

"I'm walking the ethical fence with these charts, Ella. I don't think you can read them. It would be a total HIPAA violation."

Ella nodded. "I understand. Maybe I can just organize them, help you find the right time frame?"

"Sounds good. Look old and battered first. Millie Nathan was in perfect health until her cancer, and she's been sick since, so the relevant charts will be the oldest ones."

Ella scanned the piles and reached for one that looked kind of ragged. Opening up the manila folder, she found the papers inside bound with a large clip at the top. Scanning the top lines, she found the date. "This is from 2005." She zipped through to the last page, and just as she suspected, the documents were in chronological order.

"Do you think I can write on this?" she asked.

"I'm surprised no one's done it already," Reese answered.

Reaching into her purse, Ella retrieved a pen and wrote the date on the edge of the file, then opened another. "We're getting closer. 1998."

After a few more tries, Reese found the one she was looking for. "Here it is. 1993."

Ella stopped her own efforts and slid closer to Reese. "What does it say?"

Reese flipped through several pages. "This is her initial consultation, where they recommend the high-dose chemo followed by a bone-marrow transplant. It states she has two sons who are potential donors."

"Good, good."

Reese continued to page through the chart. "Okay, here it is. This might be what we're looking for. It says both sons could give the bone marrow, but Jeremy is the closer match."

"Jeremy! They've been lying all this time?"

Reese gave Ella a scolding look. "Easy, girl. We're not done yet."

"It's hard to sit here while you have all the fun."

"Oh, this is a real party I'm having. I wish you could join me."

Ella punched her playfully.

"Okay, here it is. Bone-marrow-harvest consent form. Date, name, date of birth, description of procedure…"

"Wait. What's a harvest? Is that the same as the transplant?"

"No. The harvest is the collection of bone marrow from a donor. The transplant is the 'planting' of the collection into the recipient."

"Okay. What's it say? Who gave the bone marrow?"

Reese couldn't hide her disappointment. If the document said Jeremy, she would have had the evidence she was looking for. Not that Josh had committed any crime but that he'd been lying all these years about giving his bone marrow to save his mother's life. And if he was lying about that, and in Scranton on the night Steph was murdered... well, it still meant absolutely nothing. But it was something.

Yet it was nothing. The consent form was for Joshua L. Nathan, and it was signed the day Steph had died.

Reese sighed in frustration. Could Cass's memory be faulty? Was Josh really in Scranton that night? What if it was the night before, or the night after Steph's murder? Yet Cass seemed so clear about it— remembering how Reese had been suffering from a headache and how her parents had gone to the movies. How the money she'd leant Josh left her short for her flower donation.

"Josh. The consent is from Josh."

"So, he gave the bone marrow after all."

"It looks like it."

Ella sighed in frustration. What were they even doing here, in the doctors' lounge at the ER at nine o'clock at night, when they could have been relaxing at Reese's house, getting to know each other better? Yet, how could they relax, with everything going on? Reese had been practically accused of a murder Ella knew she didn't commit, and an attempt had been made on Cass's life. And the one who'd turned Reese in was not only a trusted friend, but perhaps a liar with secrets of his own.

Feeling the defeat, she rubbed Reese's shoulders. "Let's call it..."

Her words and her thoughts were halted when the room went black. The hum of the small refrigerator stopped, and the digital readout on the clock radio faded. Since the room was in the interior of the hospital, with no ambient light, the darkness was complete, and shards of fear shot through Ella. Josh Nathan knew they were investigating him, and now he was back, not for Cass this time, but for her and Reese.

"Oh, God," she said, just as the power came back on.

"Emergency generator," Reese said.

The lights didn't assuage her fears. "Let's get out of here. I'm spooked."

Even with the power outage, Reese hadn't closed the chart in front of her, but she had flipped the page. "Holy shit! Would you look at this?"

"What is it?"

"Another consent form. This one's for Jeremy."

"So they both consented to give their bone marrow?"

"Yes. That's correct."

"Why? Would they need both?"

Reese pondered the question. "They wouldn't, but I guess the doctors were covering their bases."

"So, it could have been either one of them, huh?"

"Yes."

"And we've learned absolutely nothing."

Reese sighed. "That is also correct."

CHAPTER 27: THE MOTIVE

Never in her life had Ella felt so emotionally drained. The high of Reese was not just tempered, but truly negated by all that had happened. It was rare for her to second-guess herself, but she almost wished she and Reese hadn't slept together. While the sex had been delightful, Reese wasn't in a good place at the moment, and Ella hoped the fragile bud of their relationship could withstand all that Reese was going through.

It hadn't been easy on her, either. First Reese had pushed her away, and then she'd witnessed firsthand the attack on Cass. Those moments between when the baseball player pushed Cass and the Scouts pulled her from the water were some of the longest of her life. Not to mention the most stressful.

Even though she'd had the night with Reese she'd hoped for, it had been a quiet one, and they'd both slept in late on Sunday. And although Reese made breakfast for her, she felt as if Reese was going through the motions and was almost relieved when Ella told her she needed to get home.

It was a total lie. She didn't need to get back on a Sunday afternoon, but she'd gone anyway and felt a twinge of sadness when she saw Reese's car in the Ryans' driveway later that day. It was the first time since she'd arrived in Scranton more than a month earlier that she hadn't been invited to Sunday dinner.

Reese had knocked on her door later, and they'd sat and talked for a while, which gave Ella hope that they'd be able to work through the stressful time, but she was still sad. Sad that it wasn't the way it could be with Reese and sad for all the reasons why it wasn't.

It was almost a relief when her alarm rang on Monday morning. Work would distract her and give her a new reason to focus, and she was grateful for both. At her office, she answered a few calls and emails before turning to the pile of snail-mail in her box.

After scanning the envelopes, her heart beat a little faster when she saw a large one from the university's in-house attorney. Tearing it open, she was delighted to see it was paperwork for the Stephanie Gates Scholarship. Bucky had finished it and returned it, and now all Ella needed was a check to make it complete.

Ella quickly read through the document, and finding it to be accurate, she set it on her desk and dialed Sophie's number. It took a few rings, and Ella found herself impatient as she waited for an answer. She was too excited to postpone this announcement.

"Hello, Ella," she heard when Sophie finally answered.

"It's ready!"

"Wonderful! What do we do now?"

"You sign the scholarship agreement and make it official."

"How about dinner Wednesday?"

"Absolutely."

They finalized their plan, and then Ella dialed Bucky's number to thank him for his efforts.

"Glad to help," he said, and they chatted for a few minutes about the party and the attack on Cass.

"You don't think Reese will be in any trouble, do you, Buck? I think she's worried."

"It's like the threat of malpractice, I would imagine. You try your best and someone dies, and not only do you have to live with that, but you have to worry about getting sued. She's worried about this. Even though she did nothing wrong, it could still cause her a lot of grief."

"Maybe you should call her again. Just to reassure her."

"I don't think she wants to talk to me, but I will."

An hour later, a beeping phone drew Ella from the plans for a fund-raising conference she was considering. She had a text from Reese, who was working a day shift in the ER. Her dour mood lifted before she even read Reese's words.

1. *Are you free for dinner?*
2. *If so, would you like to have dinner with me?*
3. *I'm sorry about the way you left on Sunday—I think I was just a little stressed.*
4. *If you give me another chance, I'll make it up to you.*

In spite of her earlier misgivings, Ella didn't hesitate to reply.

1. *Yes.*
2. *Yes.*
3. *Understandable.*
4. *I'm counting on it.*

They agreed on the time, and suddenly Ella felt excited again. She and Reese had a sure attraction, on a multitude of levels. If they could get through these hard times, they had a chance to have something really good.

It took several wardrobe and hairstyle changes to get ready for dinner, but when she was ready, she thought the effort worth it. Pulling her hair off her face made her feel elegant, even sexy, and she wore a scooped-neck sweater to show off earrings and a necklace she'd picked up in the islands. She refreshed her makeup and added a dab of perfume before sitting on the couch to stare at the door fifteen minutes early.

Reese didn't make her wait long. Arriving ten minutes early, and bearing a bouquet of fresh-cut flowers, she looked quite amazing in a tailored, button-down shirt under a blazer, and jeans.

A kiss on the cheek to thank Reese for the flowers turned into a hug, and the hug, at first comforting, turned into something more, until they pulled away and searched each other's eyes. "This has been a tough week," Reese said. "But I'm really happy you're helping me through it."

Ella nodded. "Glad to be here."

Once the flowers were taken care of, she and Reese walked hand in hand to Vito's restaurant overlooking the park. Ella had wanted to check it out since she'd met Vito, but she hadn't had a chance. Now she would. They talked about food as they walked—Reese wanted to make sure Ella was up for the menu—and they were still discussing their favorite dishes when Vito himself came to the table to offer them both hugs and a fresh salad of tomatoes and mozzarella drizzled with balsamic vinegar and olive oil. "I infused the oil with basil from the garden—it's scrumptious!"

"Everything is scrumptious," Reese told him, and he beamed.

"Don't forget, it's not too late to sign up for my cooking cruise. We sail in less than a month, and you know your sister would love it."

Reese nodded. "One day, Vito," she said, and he left them to their food. It was as good as he'd promised, and soon the waitress took their orders, and before she knew it, their dinner arrived. Ella could have lingered for hours, enjoying the conversation and the company.

Instead of dessert they decided on the cookies Ella had made the day before. It wasn't until they were seated on Pip's couch, with coffee and cookies in hand, that Reese mentioned a call from Bucky.

"He said what we already know—there's no evidence of anything, and I shouldn't be worried."

"It's good to hear it, isn't it?"

"It sure is."

"Any word on the baseball player?"

"My mom talked to the police today. They have footage from the Everhart Museum's cameras and also from the hospital's, but they don't see him. He must have come into the park from the other side. There are no businesses there. Therefore, no cameras."

"And no witnesses?"

"No one so far."

"It's frustrating. And scary. I mean…what if he's out to get her?"

"Oh, I know. My parents are on guard, and the police have increased patrols around the park and our house."

"Good, good," Ella said as she bit a chewy chocolate-chip cookie and moaned.

Reese laughed. "It's nice to hear you moan."

Suddenly Ella felt the enormity of the situation, and she wanted Reese to know she shared her troubles. Putting down the cookie and the coffee, she scooted over on the couch and sat beside her, resting her head on Reese's shoulder. "It's going to be okay, Reese."

Feeling the rise and fall of Reese's chest, Ella knew how worried Reese was, despite her earlier disclaimers. She took Reese's cup and placed it on the table, then sat in Reese's lap, her head resting on Reese's shoulder. Immediately, Reese encircled her and pulled her close, and Ella felt better than she had in days. She'd crawled into Reese's lap to comfort her, but it seemed she was getting as much comfort as she was giving. Suddenly she knew her earlier proclamation was true. Somehow, some way, it would all be okay.

The warmth and comfort she felt began to stir other feelings, and Ella gently nibbled on Reese's neck. "Do you think we're moving too fast?" she asked a moment later.

"It's a little late to ask that question."

Ella tickled her. "I mean…should we maybe take a time-out?"

Reese pulled back and searched her eyes. "Is that what you want?"

Ella had always been a woman of conviction. A child of conviction, too. When she made up her mind, no one could make her change it. When she set her mind to a goal or set her hand to a task, she usually didn't stop until she got what she wanted.

Her attraction to Reese was still as strong as it had been before all this nonsense started. Stronger, perhaps, because they'd shouldered some of the burdens together. "Absolutely not," she said after a moment.

Reese responded with a smile and then a kiss.

❖

Before leaving on Monday night, Reese had agreed to accompany Ella to Sophie's house for dinner on Wednesday. It would make Reese happy to see Sophie and would make the evening drive to the lake much more pleasant for Ella.

Reese showered at her parents' house after work, and by four thirty, they were on their way to the lake. Of course, the recent events came up as soon as they got into the car.

"I still don't know what to think about all of this. Assuming Cass isn't confused, why would Josh lie about being in Scranton the night Steph died?"

Ella shrugged and then reached across the console to grab Reese's hand. "Who knows? He was a young kid, hardly experienced in police investigations. He probably panicked. When the police asked him for an alibi, he got nervous, and he lied."

"But Ella," Reese said. "That's just it. Why lie? What was he doing in Nay Aug Park, in Scranton, when his mother was near death in Philadelphia? What was so important that he came home that night, and then why couldn't he tell anyone about it?"

"I don't know, Reese. I just don't know."

Speculation about Josh Nathan consumed their conversation, and Ella paused to look at Reese when she parked the car in Sophie's driveway. "Do we say anything to her?"

"What do you think?"

"I don't know. I'm not sure what the senator has to do with Steph's murder—but I suspect he knows something. Too many links are pointing to him. But what can we prove? Nothing. Unless she's in danger, why upset her?"

Reese nodded and frowned. "You're right. We can speculate all we want, but we can't prove anything. And without a motive, I'm not even sure I believe Josh did anything wrong. Maybe he really had some reason to be in Scranton and lied because he was scared, and all of this is just a coincidence."

Ella leaned over and squeezed Reese's hand. "Maybe. Now let's go in. And then, if I can take care of business in an expeditious fashion, I can sneak you up to my room later."

"I don't have work tomorrow…"

"Then it's settled. Do you think you're up for climbing the trellis to my balcony, so Pip won't know?"

Reese paled, and Ella reached for her. "What?"

"Oh, God. I don't know…this summer when Sophie and I were talking about the investigation, she told me it always bothered her that there was no forced entry. Steph wouldn't have opened the door for a stranger. That's why she always suspected Steph knew her murderer."

"Yes, so?"

"What if the murderer came up the trellis onto her balcony? Steph might have heard him and opened her sliding door to investigate."

"Well, that sort of gives credit to the burglar theory again, huh?"

"Except for one thing. When Steph was dating Josh, they were together the summer between junior and senior year. He would drive out to the lake after work to see Steph. He'd park on the road and climb the trellis up to her balcony."

Ella sucked in a deep breath. "Would she have let him in?"

"Of course. They were friends."

"Steph wouldn't have been uncomfortable having her ex show up on her balcony when she was home all alone and expecting you at any moment? Wasn't she trying to keep your relationship a secret?"

Reese sighed. What would Steph have done? She and Josh were friends. Great friends. They'd never been lovers, though. Josh had pressured her to sleep with him, and the understanding that she had no desire for him had helped clarify the feelings she had for Reese. As they approached the last year of high school, instead of all the joy she'd anticipated, Steph told Reese she'd felt sad, because she didn't want to be away from her. She thought of her all the time. And when Josh kissed her, she couldn't help wishing it was Reese's arms around her and Reese's lips caressing hers.

Steph's confession had come on the night of the first football game that fall, and after Reese confessed a similar crush, their relationship had exploded.

But Josh had always been a gentleman, and Steph wouldn't have feared him. In fact, because of his dad's death that fall and his mom's illness a few months later, Steph would have gladly opened the door for Josh, even if he showed up unexpectedly on a dark, rainy night.

Sharing her thoughts, Reese sighed. "See? This case just goes in circles."

"Then let's take a break from it. We'll eat, and go back to my house—no trellis involved—and we'll talk about something other than this for a little while."

A smiling Sophie and the delectable aroma of pot roast greeted them at the door.

"It smells divine," Ella said.

"It's been cooking all day, and it's starting to get to me. I can't wait a moment longer. You two come in and I'll put the biscuits in the oven and we'll eat."

The table was set, and Ella sat as Reese poured water and wine in elegant cut-crystal glasses. "The table looks so beautiful, Mrs. Gates."

"Thank you," she said. "It's a special night, and I wanted it to look good. The food's pretty basic, but I can still present it properly."

"Well, you get five stars for the presentation. And if the smell is any indicator, I think I'll be recommending this place to everyone."

Sophie pointed a spatula at her. "Don't you dare tell a soul I fed you pot roast. I used to serve five-course meals—my reputation will be in tatters."

"The secret is ours."

"It is a big night, though," Reese said as she took the old cast-iron roaster and placed it on the pad in the center of the table. "Congratulations."

"Thank you. I'm pleased."

"Ella didn't give me any details, so I'm looking forward to hearing them from you while we eat."

Sophie sat and raised her glass to the others. "To Steph. May her memory live on in all those young women who make the world a better place, thanks to the opportunities this scholarship gives them."

"To Steph," Reese and Ella said, and they touched glasses at the center of the table.

"So, you've decided on a girl for the scholarship?" Reese asked.

"Yes. A girl who shows financial need." She paused. "I've been mulling it all over—all the many options—and I think this is what Steph would have wanted."

Reese and Ella sipped their drinks and nodded. "Even though she was deserving of the scholarship at PMU, she worried about taking it from Josh. We could afford the tuition, you see, and the Nathans were struggling after Mr. Nathan died."

Ella felt the sudden rush of the wine as Sophie's words hit her, and she was sure she'd misheard, so looked at Reese to see her expression. She looked as shocked as Ella felt.

"What?" Reese asked. "Steph had a scholarship at PMU?"

Sipping her wine, she looked at Reese in puzzlement. "Well, of course she did. She was valedictorian. The Prep valedictorian always gets a scholarship to PMU."

Reese nodded, and Ella could see her measuring her words. "Yes, I understand that. I guess what I mean to say is that Steph was heading to Cornell. She'd turned down the PMU scholarship."

"No, Reese. She'd changed her mind."

Taking a big gulp of her wine, Reese sat back, and Ella could see the wheels of her mind turning. Surely, Reese's thoughts were the same as her own. Surprise at the news, and surprise that Sophie didn't understand its significance. Suddenly, Josh Nathan had a motive to murder Steph, and it was one of the classics: money.

"I didn't know that," Reese said as she studied Sophie. "Wasn't it too late?"

Sophie shook her head. "You would think so, but apparently not."

"What happened? Why?" Reese's senses were all off-kilter, and she put down the wine, exchanging the glass in her hand for water. While this news was a surprise, it really wasn't. Steph had been questioning her college choice for months before she died, and the night she died, she told Reese she had a surprise for her. Could that have been it? They'd often talked about going away to school together, sharing an apartment, having the freedom to do as they pleased. Yet Steph knew that an apartment wasn't an option for Reese; unlike Steph's parents, the Ryans were a middle-class family and were sacrificing just to pay Reese's tuition. She would never have asked them to splurge on an apartment, too, when she lived so close to campus.

The timer on the stove beeped, and before Sophie could move, Ella jumped up to check the biscuits. "I'll get them." They were just browning on the edges, so Ella pulled on an oven mitt and removed the tray from the oven, then plated them on the dish Sophie had set out.

After carrying them to the table, she sat, but in spite of the fact that Sophie started serving the pot roast, neither Reese nor Ella was interested.

"So," Reese asked again, fidgeting with her food and trying to appear casual. "Why'd she change her mind about the ivy?"

Sophie chewed, sipped her wine, and wiped her mouth with a crisp linen napkin before answering. "Josh. First his dad died, and then his mom got sick. As you know, Steve and I weren't young when Steph was born, and she said she realized we weren't going to be around forever. She said she wanted to go to college here, so she could spend four more years with us."

Reese nodded, still avoiding the food as she focused on Sophie. "But when Steph took the scholarship, Josh lost it. Did she realize what that meant to him?" Reese's mouth was so dry she could hardly speak. Didn't Sophie realize what she was saying? Josh was the only one in the world with a motive to kill her daughter, and she'd kept this news quiet for nearly twenty-five years!

"Of course, and she felt just awful. It was why she debated so long and waited until the last minute, because she wanted to be sure of her decision. And then, after she discussed it with me and Steve, she went to the university and talked to the scholarship people. It was only after they assured her that Josh would still get a scholarship too that she made her final decision to go to PMU and accept the award—what's it called, Ella? The Cognitio?"

Ella nodded, and Reese looked past her as she added it all up. So, they had another scholarship for Josh. That made sense. He was second in the class, and his father was dead, so Reese was sure that was worth a fortune in scholarship money. And it blew a big fat hole in her motive. Why did she care? Josh was her friend, so why was she so anxious to prove he had something to do with Steph's death? Was she the one now seeking revenge, since he'd sicced the DA on her?

"When was that? When did she meet with PMU?" Reese was trying to understand it all, everything she knew about Steph and what she'd recently learned about Josh's movements on the night of her murder.

"She actually met with him the day she died. She signed her acceptance letter that day."

Reese sipped her water and thought about the logistics. Steph decided during the weeks leading up to her death and made it official on the day she died. The remaining question might never be answered—did Steph tell Josh? She asked Sophie.

"I'm not really sure. She wanted to wait to tell him, until she knew whether the university had a scholarship for him. And since she only found out that day, and he was in Philly with his mom, I don't think he ever knew."

Reese was willing to bet he did. "So did he go to the ceremony and get the award?"

Sophie shrugged. "Reese—I have no idea. After Steph died, none of it really mattered anymore."

Ella had heard enough. They knew Josh was in Scranton the night Steph died, but they hadn't been able to convince themselves he'd held any malice toward Steph. Not until now. No matter what kind of scholarship Josh had received from PMU, it wouldn't have been the one he was expecting—full tuition, room, and board. Although the Stephanie Gates Scholarship was similar, few others were of that caliber at the university, and Ella doubted Josh would have been able to secure one at the eleventh hour.

"Mrs. Gates, I want to ask you a serious question." Ella paused to make sure Sophie was listening. "Did you ever tell anyone about this? About Steph changing her plans?"

Once again Sophie chewed before swallowing. The stew had smelled delicious, and Sophie looked like she was enjoying it, but Ella's taste buds—like everything else—were numb.

"I don't know, Ella. Why?"

Ella's voice was thick with emotion—fear, anxiety, sadness. "Because I think we've just discovered a motive for Steph's murder."

CHAPTER 28: REASONABLE DOUBT

Sophie had a hard time believing Josh could have killed her daughter, but when Ella and Reese detailed all the facts that were coming together, she had to admit they cast Josh in an unfavorable light.

"Did you have any idea?" Ella asked on the way to the car a little while later.

The temperature had dropped, and she rubbed her arms through the light jacked she wore, but she wasn't convinced the weather was the cause of her shivering.

"None. But I think she was going to tell me that night." Reese told Ella about the surprise Steph had planned.

Ella started the car, and they looked at each other as the engine warmed up. "What was he doing at your house that night, Reese?"

"Cass said he needed to borrow money."

Ella thought about it for a moment when an idea struck her. Pulling out her phone, she checked the price of gas in 1993. "Okay, Reese. A gallon of regular unleaded gasoline cost $1.16 at the time Steph died. Where was he going on two bucks' worth of gas?"

"Not far."

"So, let's assume he was lying about the gas. He was there for another reason. Do you think he was there before he murdered Steph, to talk to you? Maybe see if you could get her to change her mind?"

Reese shuddered too, as a deeper cold set in. "That's the first time we've stated it, rather than questioned it, but that's what this is all about, right? Josh killed Steph and then tried to kill Cass to cover it up. We really think that, don't we?"

The words seemed so strange to Reese, the thought so foreign. Her friend, the United States senator, a killer. Even worse, her friend from student council, the lifeguard, the member of the honor society and the swim team. An eighteen-year-old boy, a murderer. It was hard to fathom, and she had to admit she liked it much better when the theory involved a stranger killing Steph.

"We should talk to Bucky."

"Have you two made up?"

"I don't know what was going on with him, but I know he has my back now."

"Should we call him?"

"Better yet, let's take a drive around the lake. He still lives in the same house he grew up in."

A minute later, Ella stood nervously beside Reese as they awaited Bucky at his front door.

"This can't be good," he said, and Ella laughed in spite of herself.

"Boy, Buckaroo, do we have a theory to plant on you," Reese said.

He offered them drinks, which they declined, and then they sat in the richly paneled den they'd never been allowed to enter as children. "It seems strange to be in this room," Ella said.

He smiled. "Right? Sometimes I stay in here just because I can. Anyway, what's on your collective mind?"

Without hesitation, Reese began telling him her theory. He listened attentively, but his face remained passive, as if he was weighing all the facts before forming his opinion. "I have to admit, everything you say makes our senator look a little suspicious. But there's nothing solid here, just a whole lot of coincidence. We don't even know that Josh knew about Steph's decision."

"I know they talked almost every day. The long-distance fees in those days were steep, and Steph insisted he call her collect so she could check on him. Remember how she'd update everyone about Mrs. Nathan's condition?"

Bucky nodded. "How long were they out of town?"

Reese shrugged as she thought about it. At the time, it had seemed like forever, but it was probably only a few weeks. Josh and Jeremy had essentially stayed at their mother's side for the duration of her treatment.

"I have an idea," Ella said. Reaching into her purse, she retrieved her phone and dialed the university switchboard. "It's Elizabeth Townes. Can you give me Dick Price's phone number?"

A moment later, Ella dialed the phone. "Hi, Dick," Ella said, realizing she hadn't really thought about what she'd say. Scrambling,

Ella came up with a plausible explanation. "You know I'm working with Mrs. Gates on a scholarship." Ella went on to ask if Stephanie had in fact accepted the scholarship to PMU.

"Yes," he answered. "I wasn't sure she'd told her parents, so I never mentioned it, but she was in my office the day she died."

"What scholarship would Senator Nathan have received?" Ella asked him.

"Oh, he would have been fine! I told Steph not to worry about Josh because he had good grades. And when Josh called, I told him the same thing."

The phone was on speaker, and Ella, Reese, and Bucky all looked at each other. Josh had called the university about another scholarship. He knew! Steph had told him her decision.

"So Josh would have gotten a full scholarship?" Ella asked, not sure what was happening to her theory as Dick seemed to tear it apart.

He laughed. "Oh, no. Everything had been decided by then, but with his financial situation, he would have gotten aid. Plenty of aid. I told him to take care of his mother and to come in and see me when he got back from Philly."

Ella's eyes met Reese's as she nodded. "Thanks, Dick," she said before disconnecting.

"We have a motive, Bucky," Reese said. "Josh knew."

Leaning back in his chair, he shook his head. "Maybe Josh killed Steph. Maybe he didn't. But either way, we don't have any proof he's done something wrong. You can't even prove that he lied about the bone marrow, because the medical records are long gone by this time. So are the phone records. There was no E-ZPass then to track the movements of his car, and if he used a credit card to buy something in Scranton that night, the records of that would be next to impossible to trace. So, we've got a motive, but other than that, we've got nothing."

"Buck..." Reese whined.

Holding up his hand, he stopped her. "Reese, this isn't some bum from the park you're talking about. It's Josh Nathan. If we were going to arrest him, we'd need a smoking gun and a video of him committing the crime, plus a busload of nuns who witnessed it."

"I know he did this, Buck."

Bucky shook his head. "It all looks kind of suspicious, but you're forgetting one thing—he has an alibi. The guy was in the ICU at the time of Steph's murder. He practically died from that shot of Novocain they gave him for the bone-marrow thing."

Bucky was right—if that had really happened. "Did anyone ever check that story out?"

Bucky nodded. "The police called down there, Reese. Josh was in the ICU when Steph died. There's no way he could have done it. And just to be sure, I called myself to check."

Reese was surprised. "You did?"

Bucky shrugged. "I thought it was a little strange that he threw you under the bus. I asked myself why he'd do it…and, well, I just wanted to be sure."

Reese felt a huge relief. Bucky cared about her enough to try to clear her. She'd lost one friend, for sure. Even if they couldn't prove Josh's link to Steph's murder, Reese could never trust him again. First, he'd tossed her to the wolves, and now he looked like a suspect. No way could Reese even look at him again without wanting to poke him in the eyes with needles.

For Bucky's friendship, though, she was very grateful. "Thank you," she said to him, and he simply nodded and opened his arms for a hug.

CHAPTER 29: DRACULA'S SECRET

H ey, Dr. Ryan. Do you need some help?"
Reese looked up to see a young pre-med student hurrying toward her. "You can help carry doughnuts."

"Yeah, take these," Cass said and handed the girl a plastic bag containing a few boxes of Krispy Kreme donuts that the local store had donated.

"Take them yourself, Cass," Reese said as she nodded toward her car. "There's more in the Jeep."

Cass grunted and continued her walk to the student center, where the pre-med club was holding their annual Vampire's Kiss blood drive. Reese had initiated the event years ago as a student and had taken over mentoring the pre-med crowd when the previous doctor retired. Cass served as her assistant, helping to register people for the event and checking in those who'd pre-registered.

A large table was set up at the entrance to the student center, and strategically placed wall units provided privacy and directed people to where they needed to go. Behind those walls were the stretchers, supplies, and staff from the Red Cross who actually collected the blood. As they were setting up, two dozen students, all in vampire garb, arranged chairs in the waiting area and snacks in the refreshment zone.

Reese was happy for the blood drive to occupy her mind. She still hadn't recovered from the whole ordeal of being questioned as a murder suspect, and even though Bucky reassured her that she was safe, when she thought about it, Reese still worried. And she might never get over the shock about Josh. Meeting with the students, reviewing the leaflets and posters, and getting ready for the day had been a welcome distraction from the daily routine that the realities of life had tarnished.

Glancing around, Reese hoped to find Ella. She'd been away for a few days, and their conflicting schedules hadn't allowed them to see each other since her return. Reese was off for two days after the blood drive, though, and they'd made plans to drive along the Susquehanna River and view the foliage, then launch their kayaks and picnic on an island in the middle of the river. Afterward…the possibilities gave Reese butterflies.

"Cass, why don't you hunt for Ella?" she asked, knowing her sister would much rather wander around than do any real work.

"Okay," she said as she scurried off, leaving Reese alone to set up the registration table.

She pulled clipboards from a bin and placed a dozen pens in a cup on the table, then piled the forms between the two. Behind her, she hung the registration sign, and after putting away the packaging materials, she went off to check out everyone's progress.

She found Ella mingling with some of the Red Cross volunteers, to whom she'd proudly distributed PMU mugs, pens, and hats. Warmth flushed through her as she watched Ella talk to the men and women, thanking them for their efforts on behalf of their fellow man. It was hard for her to believe that only two months had passed since Ella had appeared in her parents' backyard. So much had happened since then, but in the end, the most important thing was the beautiful woman who floated so effortlessly through the crowd, making them all feel important and appreciated.

For a few moments she just watched, and then Ella caught her eye, and she melted. As a smile spread across the breadth of Ella's face, Reese winked and walked in her direction.

"Good morning," Ella said as she pulled Reese into a chaste hug.

"Hi," Reese said as she reluctantly released her grip on Ella's arms.

"Nice job," Ella said, and Reese felt a telltale blush spread across her, its heat so familiar in Ella's presence. How could one woman have such an effect on her?

"Thanks, but it wasn't me. Two dozen students organized this."

Ella nodded. "Of course they did. And their message is so powerful that I've decided to donate blood for the first time."

Reese feigned surprise. "You're a virgin?"

Ella made an exaggerated frown. "The forty-year-old. Don't you think it's time?"

Reese nodded. "I do. And what a great way for you to lose your innocence. It's a great experience for future donors."

Ella shifted her weight and spread her hands in question. "Well, where do I sign up? I'd like to be the first one to give blood today, unless someone else has claimed that honor."

"No. In fact, we've never had a 'first donor.' Maybe it's a tradition we should start."

"I have a reporter and photographer from the *PMU Times* to do a story." It was Ella's turn to blush, and Reese didn't have to wonder why for very long. "They want to interview you, and I think it's great. You deserve some credit for getting this together."

"Oooookaaaay," Reese said, and Ella led her though the crowd to where a young man and woman were interviewing one of the volunteers.

When they were done, Ella approached them and introduced Reese. They began asking questions, and Ella suggested she go get her paperwork so they could start the process. She playfully patted Reese on the butt and headed in the other direction. Cass was sitting at the registration table, eating a doughnut. Much of it was on her face, and she looked adorable.

Grabbing a bottle of water from the snack area, Ella spilled some on a napkin and handed it to Cass. "Wipe," she commanded, and Cass did a passable job of cleaning up. "Mind if I help?" she asked, and before Cass could answer, she'd removed the dried sugar from Cass's face.

"I need a registration form," she announced.

Cass beamed. "Should I help you fill it out?"

They had a few minutes, so Ella agreed, and she wiped down the table as Cass pulled a paper from the pile and placed it before her.

"What's your name?" Cass asked.

"Elizabeth Townes," she answered, and then she spelled it.

"What is your D.O.B.?"

Ella smiled and revealed her birth date.

"Have you ever given blood before?"

"No."

"Do you take any medicine?"

"No."

"Do you have annamea?"

"Anemia?"

"Yes. Do you have that?"

"No."

"Do you have any allergies?"

"Penicillin."

"Hey, I have that, too," Cass said as she smiled in solidarity.

"I think it's very common," Ella said.

"Do you have any community diseases?"

"None."

"Ella, you're perfect for donating blood."

"Why, thank you, Cass."

"You have to write your name here," she said and pointed to the place on the permission slip. "In cursive."

Ella signed her name, and Cass handed her an envelope that she carried toward the back, where she found a nurse and explained what she needed. The woman agreed to be photographed, and together they approached Reese and the newspaper crew. A moment later, Ella reclined on a stretcher, and while Reese held her hand, the woman punctured her vein and began collecting her blood. Reese stayed beside her for the fifteen minutes it took to complete the process, and when they were done, Reese escorted her to the refreshment area for a doughnut.

"So, congrats!" she said. "You just saved someone's life."

Ella waved her off. "It was nothin'!"

"Well, good, because in about ten minutes, we're going to open those doors, and it might get a little crazy."

Sure enough, Reese's prediction came true. At precisely eight o'clock, the doors were opened and students, faculty, and members of the public marched through them, eager to do their part to save their fellow man.

Ella helped with the registration, directing people to pick up their packets and then directing them toward the chairs to complete their paperwork. When they returned, either she, Cass, or Reese scanned the form to assure completion, and then students guided them to the donation stations in the back.

They were an hour into the busy morning when a murmur drew their attention to the front doors. Josh Nathan waved to some well-wishers before walking toward the registration table with a smile and a wave. "Hi, Cass. Where's your sister today?"

Reese, who was sitting beside Cass, rolled her eyes as Cass eyed him suspiciously and pointed. "You should get glasses, Josh. She's right there."

"Oh, hi!" he said, and Reese took a deep breath, practicing the cordial greeting she'd promised herself she'd offer Josh. There was no proof, she reminded herself, and even if she knew he wasn't the man he pretended to be, she'd pretend he was.

Reese stood and accepted his hug, and when she stepped out of his arms, his brother, Jeremy, stepped in to hug both her and Cass.

"You have to sit down over there," Cass said as she handed them paperwork. "Answer all the questions, or you can't donate your blood."

"Yes, ma'am," Jeremy said, and he and Josh walked to the bank of chairs arranged for them to complete their paperwork.

Ella watched their exchange closely, knowing how difficult the charade was for Reese. Yet she agreed it was best. They still had no proof of Josh's guilt, and Reese had no reason to be angry at him unless she betrayed Bucky's confidence. If she did that, it might cost him the election. So, they'd both pretend and hope they didn't have to face the senator until the election was over.

As other donors walked through the door, Ella decided to ease the tension she knew Reese was feeling. "Hey, Reese," she said.

"Hmm?" Reese asked.

"I just thought of something else we have in common." When Reese looked at her, she smirked. "We're both looking for donors."

Reese sniggered but then turned serious as she sought Ella's eyes. "As a matter of fact, I think we have a few other things in common, too."

Before Ella could respond, the Nathan brothers returned to the table. "I'll take it, Jeremy," Cass said, and he handed her the clipboard.

"Okay. It looks perfect. Oh, you are allergic to penicillin. I have that too, and so does Ella."

"I've been allergic to penicillin since I was a little boy. I was so sick, I had to get my tonsils out."

Reese, who was scanning Josh's paperwork to ensure completion, had just reached the allergy section. She read it once, and then again, and looked from Jeremy to Josh.

"It says you're allergic to lidocaine, Josh."

"Yes, that's right."

Reese looked at Josh, watched as his face fell for a moment, and then the mask returned to its place. It all made sense now. Two consent forms. Josh had consented to give the bone marrow, but his allergy to lidocaine prevented it. Jeremy had given his mother the bone marrow, and his penicillin allergy, and his brother had taken the credit, using his experience as the alibi he needed to cover him for the time Steph was murdered.

"Jeremy is allergic to penicillin. He gave your mom that bone marrow. But you somehow falsified the medical record so you had an alibi. The police thought you were in the hospital that night, but you were really here. You killed Steph."

She could see him swallow, then look around to ensure no bystanders overheard their conversation. "Reese, don't be crazy,"

"I'm not crazy, Josh. Just stupid. I trusted you. I thought you were my friend, Steph's friend."

"I am. I was. This is ridiculous!" Again he looked around as he laughed nervously.

"No. I don't think so. Steph told you she was going to PMU and taking the scholarship. Dick Price told you you'd still get financial aid, but it wouldn't be a free ride. You were desperate, and you didn't have money for a phone call to talk to her. You came home and murdered Steph so you could keep the scholarship. Then you came to the park—who knows why?" Something suddenly occurred to her. It had been a brutal attack, one that surely soiled the murderer with blood. "Perhaps to get rid of some bloody clothes in the trash. And since you were a lifeguard at Nay Aug, you knew the park well. You slipped in in the dark, but Cass saw you and ruined your alibi. So you came up with the story about the gas money and paid her to keep quiet."

"Reese, this is insane."

"You're insane, Josh. You killed Steph, and then you tried to kill Cass so she couldn't tell anyone you were in Scranton that night."

He laughed. "Even if this is all true, you can't prove anything," he said. "There's no evidence."

Reese stepped out from behind the table. "My sister has given a statement to the DA. It's videotaped. You don't have any reason to hurt her, Josh. Do you understand?"

Josh paled again and stepped back. Reese saw him swallow. "I...I understand."

"Now get the fuck out of here before I break your face."

CHAPTER 30: CELEBRITY CRUISE

"Let's go back to the cabin," Ella suggested. "I don't want to watch it in the bar. What if it's noisy and we can't hear?"

"True," Reese said, "but if we're in the bar, we can see how people react."

Ella pondered Reese's point before nodding. "Well, I do like being out with you when you look so spiffy." It was the second evening of their cruise, and Ella and her traveling companions had been invited to sit at the captain's table, along with Chef Vito, and Reese had dressed in a smartly tailored tux for the event. She wore a white shell under the champagne jacket, and with the tan she'd perfected at the booth, she looked radiant.

Reese smirked as she checked her watch. "If Cass asked me why I was dressed like a man one more time…"

"You do *not* look anything like a man. In fact, I might ask you to conceal that cleavage, or I won't be able to keep my hands off you in the bar."

"You won't have to suffer long. It's a quarter to nine. The show's starting in fifteen minutes. Let's go find a seat."

The lounge area was crowded, and since it was a Sunday night during football season, every screen showed the games. There was a long bar and twenty tables for two and four, all of them with a view of one of the many televisions. "Maybe not such a good idea, huh?" Ella asked.

"No. I think we'll just have to wait until one of the games is over. Look." Reese pointed. "Fourth quarter."

They ordered drinks and were seated at a table near a television broadcasting the appropriate channel.

"I can't believe this is happening," Ella said.

Reese nodded. "Me either. It's been an unbelievable few months."

Ella gently touched Reese's fingers. "It has been, and it was a good idea to get away, especially with the election coming up." Reese had decided to take Cass on the cooking cruise she'd been saving for, but instead of Cass using her own money, Reese had splurged and treated her entire family. Sophie had joined them on the cruise as well but, like Reese's parents, had retired to her room for the evening.

"I don't think I've ever seen Cass so happy," Reese said, smiling around her drink.

"Can you believe Chef Vito made her the sous celebrity chef today?"

"It doesn't surprise me. He's a good guy, and he really likes her."

"And I think everyone on the ship knows her name now."

Reese laughed. "Does that surprise you?"

Ella looked around at the richly paneled room, filled with fifty or so travelers. Many were from Scranton, here to eat wonderful food and drink good wine, all while learning a few tricks from Chef Vito. Others were strangers, here for the same reason, and some, she suspected, were interested only in eating the food, not preparing it. All of them, though, were friendly to Cass and encouraged her in her unofficial role as Vito's assistant, making suggestions about the menu and even sharing cooking tips.

Cass had been looking forward to this trip for years, and after only a day, Ella knew Cass was making memories she'd talk about for the rest of her life. "You're a good sister," Ella said as she playfully tapped Reese's nose.

Reese wasn't feeling playful though.

Staring into her drink, Reese's face betrayed the emotions Ella knew she was trying to hide. She squeezed the fingers. "This is a good thing, Reese."

"Hmm," she said. "I wish I could feel good about it."

"Nothing about this can possibly feel good."

"It's right, though, even if it feels bad. If he can't be tried in the court, at least he can be tried by the people. Everyone will know about who they've elected to the Senate."

One of the football games ended, and suddenly, several of the televisions in the room showed a very familiar scene, with the word *PROBE*. The word faded, and a picture of Cass filled the screen for a second, followed by pictures of Steph and then Josh. As the clip faded to a commercial, several people around the bar pointed at the television screens and commented.

Ella could barely hear them above the football games, but she heard enough to realize they recognized Cass.

"Whew," Reese said. "This is really happening."

Ella remained silent as they sipped their drinks, their eyes glued to the television. After several ads for must-have items, the *PROBE* logo reappeared on the screen, and Ella's heart pounded in time to the deep base of the television show's soundtrack.

The camera zoomed around the park and then focused on a familiar face.

"I'm Pip Pearl, and this is Nay Aug Park, in Scranton, Pennsylvania, the scene of a recent brutal attack on a local handicapped woman, Cassidy Ryan. What makes the crime so intriguing is its connection to a twenty-four-year-old murder of a high school student. Local police say Miss Ryan may be the key to solving the mystery of Stephanie Gates's death at nearby Lake Winola on the night of May twenty-first, 1993."

The camera panned out to show more of the park, and Miles Jones stepped into the picture beside Pip.

"Even more peculiar—the key person of interest in both cases is a United States senator."

"Turn it up!" someone yelled as the scene shifted, showing Cass and Pip walking with Bijou near the gorge.

"It's Cass! The little chef!" someone yelled, and Ella watched, amazed, as eyes shifted from the screens of football to the investigative piece put together by Pip and Miles. Within a minute, every television in the bar had been tuned to the show.

"They're watching," Reese said as she scanned the room, amazed.

"Yes. And with Miles at the head of this investigation, so is the rest of America. Josh Nathan may have gotten away with murder and assault, but his career is going to be over, Reese. He's done."

"I hope so."

They watched the entire thirty-minute piece, saw the crimes unfold on screen and how seamlessly Miles and Pip filled in the circumstantial evidence that pointed to Josh Nathan. Steph's decision to attend PMU, taking the scholarship away from Josh, giving him motive. The lie about donating bone marrow to his dying mother, destroying his alibi. His appearance in Scranton on the night of the murder, giving him opportunity, and his bribery of Cass to keep quiet about his presence at Nay Aug Park that night. His attempts to turn the DA's attention toward Reese. His presence at Nay Aug on the day Cass was attacked.

When it was over, the people watching shook their heads in wonder, making comments about justice and injustice and expressing their hope that the DA would shift the focus in both investigations toward the senator.

"It doesn't matter if they convict him. I just hope all the publicity convinces him he shouldn't try to hurt Cass again."

Ella nodded in agreement.

Reese's worry was unfounded. The following morning, the news show was featured on *Good Morning America.* And that night, the eve of the election, it replayed on every major news station and show in the country.

"I'm glad we got out of Dodge," Reese said as they watched the news from their bed that night.

Television vans lined Arthur Avenue, and reporters interviewed neighbors and joggers while they waited for a glimpse of Cass. Meanwhile, she charmed the guests on the ship and was invited to be the *permanent* sous chef on all of Chef Vito's cruises.

After watching another segment on the investigation, Reese looked at Ella. "Had enough?" she asked.

Ella took the remote from Reese's hand. "Of that," she said, nodding toward the television. "Yes. Of you—not quite yet."

They helped each other out of their sleepwear and then spent the next hours exploring each other. Each time they made love, Ella was delighted to know how smooth their coupling was, how easily they blended spirits and hearts and bodies. Reese was a perfect fit for her, but not only that. Ella fit perfectly with Reese, and her family, and the community she called home. Ella had given up on love when she took the job at PMU. Who would have thought she could find such a wonderful woman in a small town like Scranton? Yet she had, and Ella was grateful for the new journey she'd started with Reese and the Ryans.

"I love you," she said as she nestled into Reese's arms after her first orgasm of Tuesday. She felt Reese still beside her and wondered what it meant. Fear? Relief? A little of both? The answer came quickly, carried on small kisses dropped along the trail from Ella's forehead to her mouth.

"I. Love. You. Too."

Ella smiled into Reese's kiss, pulled her in, and consumed her mouth as her hands sought to know every inch of Reese's flesh.

When morning came, they were both exhausted, but they forced themselves out of bed and socialized with the people who hadn't spent the entire night having sex, and they tried hard not to follow the election news on their phones and iPads.

Shortly after the polls closed, all the major news outlets broadcast live from Senator Josh Nathan's headquarters in Scranton, and it didn't take them long to declare him the loser in the race for his seat in the Senate. All the reporters talked about Josh and Steph, and how Josh had lied about his alibi. How he'd gotten Steph's scholarship when she died. How Cass had seen him in the park on the night of the murder, and how Josh was seen in the park on the day someone attempted to kill Cass. It seemed that none of the other elections were as important as the one for Josh's seat in the Senate. His opponent, who'd been virtually unknown prior to the *PROBE* investigation, was suddenly hurdled into the spotlight. The race, like so many, became more about the scandal than the issues. But, of course, that was exactly why Ella had suggested the feature piece to Pip. America can't get enough of a good scandal, and the whole drama in Scranton was as juicy as it gets.

Deep down, Ella knew Josh would never stand trial for Steph's murder. The evidence was all circumstantial, and it would be difficult to convince Bucky or any prosecutor to move ahead with it. But he would also never run for president of the United States. He'd stolen a life, deprived the world of the opportunity to benefit from all the goodness Steph would have brought to it, and in return, he'd lose the thing most precious to him—his career.

Instead of a night of passion, Ella and Reese had a quiet one, holding each other and talking. When the sun began peeking in around the curtains, Ella slipped out from under Reese's arm, dressed, and made her way to the promenade deck. A dozen other passengers were there as well, awaiting the full glory of the sunrise over the Atlantic. Ella recognized one of them and took her place beside Sophie.

"The greatest peace I've ever felt is watching the sunrise. You would think it would be opposite—the day's just beginning, the world is awakening. I should feel all excited. I don't, though. I feel calm and confident. Strengthened, like it's charging me." Sophie didn't take her eyes from the amber orb floating on the edge of the earth.

"I don't know what it is about the water," Ella said, "but it is magical."

"I would imagine you heard the election results," Sophie said a moment later.

Ella moved closer, put an arm around her.

"It will never make any sense to me that such a smart young man, such a good boy, could do something so horrific."

Ella agreed. What more could she say?

"I feel blessed again, though. For so many years, I've just wanted an answer. Now I have one. I knew it would never be a good answer, so this is no worse than any other. But at least I know what happened. Thank you for helping to put the puzzle pieces together. And for Pip. Josh will never hold an office again, and there's some comfort to be had in knowing that."

"This will follow him forever, Sophie."

"Yes. Do you know what I'm most grateful for now?"

"What?"

"I see you and Reese together, and it reminds me of Steph. I know that Reese loved her. And I know Steph loved Reese. She was much too young to die, and she missed out on so many things. I'm grateful that she didn't miss out on love."

Ella was speechless. How could she say a word without betraying Reese's confidence?

She was startled to hear the voice behind her saving her from a decision.

"You're right, Sophie."

Ella turned to find Reese, her bed-head flipping in the breeze and a sad smile on her face. She slipped into the space between them and slid her arms around them both. "I loved her very much."

"It was obvious to see, if only I'd been looking."

"Steph wasn't ready for you to see."

Sophie, who was never anything but solid and strong, began to cry. Reese folded her into her arms, and Sophie pulled Ella in, too.

"Thank you both. For finding her killer. For making this scholarship that will keep her memory alive. For being her friend."

Ella wiped away a tear. "She was a good friend."

Reese nodded.

Sophie pulled back and steadied herself against the rail. "I'm not getting any younger," she said, completely off topic. "And I don't want to burden anyone. But I'm wondering if you would like to live in your grandparents' house again. Then I can see more of you." Sophie winked. "And Reese can visit."

Ella was confused. "What do you mean? People live there."

"I know. I found out a few weeks ago that the husband is being transferred. I'll need a new tenant."

It would be perfect for Ella. She could live at the lake without having to come up with half a million bucks for a house. Provided she could afford the rent.

"How much will you charge?" she asked.

Sophie gave her a scolding look. "Don't be ridiculous. You're like another daughter to me. If you want to stay there, it's yours. For free. It's a little far from Reese, but closer to your work, I think."

"Oh, no. I couldn't take it for free."

Sophie sighed and shook her head. "Oh, fine. How's a thousand dollars a month?"

The price was affordable. And Ella had actually driven to the lake after work on a few occasions, so she knew Sophie was right. "It *is* closer. It would be perfect. When is it available?"

"They'll be gone when I get back."

"It isn't that far from work," Reese said, tilting her head and pointing her finger for emphasis.

Ella tried to calculate the pros and cons. She'd wanted to buy, because it was a good investment, and she wasn't sure she wanted to spend all that money that she'd never recover, even if it gave her a chance to live in her grandparents' house.

"I was considering buying," Ella said, and looked out over the water, hoping to find the answer in the rising sun. "Let me think."

"Oh, don't be difficult. How about rent to own? The property's a good investment for my estate, and when I kick the bucket, you can settle it with Bucky."

Ella didn't have to debate for long. The lake was exactly where she'd always wanted to be, and now she had the chance. It was an expense, but really—what else was she doing with her money, anyway? Why not invest it in a place she'd love to come home to after those long business trips?

Nodding, she hugged Sophie. "It's a deal," she said.

She met Reese's eyes over Sophie's shoulder, and Reese winked at her. Then they both turned to face the rising sun and all the promise of a new day and the future they would share.

About the Author

Jaime Maddox grew up on the banks of the Susquehanna River in northeastern Pennsylvania. As the baby in a family of many children, she was part adored and part ignored, forcing her to find creative ways to fill her time. Her childhood was idyllic, spent hiking, rafting, biking, climbing, and otherwise skinning knees and knuckles. Reading and writing became passions. Although she left home for a brief stint in the big cities of Philadelphia, PA, and Newark, NJ, as soon as she acquired the required paperwork—a medical degree and residency certificate—she came running back. She fills her hours with a bustling medical practice, two precocious sons, a disobedient dog, and an extraordinary woman who helps her to keep it all together. In her abundant spare time, she reads, writes, twists her body into punishing yoga poses, and whacks golf balls deep into forests. She detests airplanes, snakes, and people who aren't nice. Her loves are the foods of the world, Broadway musicals, traveling, sandy beaches, massages and pedicures, and the Philadelphia Phillies. On the bucket list: publishing a children's book, recording a song, creating a board game, obtaining a patent, exploring Alaska.

Books Available From Bold Strokes Books

A Lamentation of Swans by Valerie Bronwen. Ariel Montgomery returns to Sea Oats to try to save her broken marriage but soon finds herself also fighting to save her own life and catch a murderer. (978-1-62639-828-3)

Freedom to Love by Ronica Black. What happens when the woman who spent her life worrying about caring for her family finally finds the freedom to love without borders? (978-1-63555-001-6)

House of Fate by Barbara Ann Wright. Two women must throw off the lives they've known as a guardian and an assassin and save two rival houses before their secrets tear the galaxy apart. (978-1-62639-780-4)

Planning for Love by Erin Dutton. Could true love be the one thing that wedding coordinator Faith McKenna didn't plan for? (978-1-62639-954-9)

Sidebar by Carsen Taite. Judge Camille Avery and her clerk, attorney West Fallon, agree on little except their mutual attraction, but can their relationship and their careers survive a headline-grabbing case? (978-1-62639-752-1)

Sweet Boy and Wild One by T. L. Hayes. When Rachel Cole meets soulful singer Bobby Layton at an open mic, she is immediately in thrall. What she soon discovers will rock her world in ways she never imagined. (978-1-62639-963-1)

To Be Determined by Mardi Alexander and Laurie Eichler. Charlie Dickerson escapes her life in the US to rescue Australian wildlife with Pip Atkins, but can they save each other? (978-1-62639-946-4)

True Colors by Yolanda Wallace. Blogger Robby Rawlins plans to use First Daughter Taylor Crenshaw to get ahead, but she never planned on falling in love with her in the process. (978-1-62639-927-3)

Heart Stop by Radclyffe. Two women, one with a damaged body, the other a damaged spirit, challenge each other to dare to live again. (978-1-62639-899-3)

Undercover Affairs by Julie Blair. Searching for stolen documents crucial to U.S. security, CIA agent Rett Spenser confronts lies, deceit, and unexpected romance as she investigates art gallery owner Shannon Kent. (978-1-62639-905-1)

Unexpected by Jenny Frame. When Dale McGuire falls for Rebecca Harper, the mother of the son she never knew she had, will Rebecca's troubled past stop them from making the family they both truly crave? (978-1-62639-942-6)

Canvas for Love by Charlotte Greene. When ghosts from Amelia's past threaten to undermine their relationship, Chloé must navigate the greatest romance of her life without losing sight of who she is. (978-1-62639-944-0)

Repercussions by Jessica L. Webb. Someone planted information in Edie Black's brain and now they want it back, but with the protection of shy former soldier Skye Kenny, Edie has a chance at life and love. (978-1-62639-925-9)

Spark by Catherine Friend. Jamie's life is turned upside down when her consciousness travels back to 1560 and lands in the body of one of Queen Elizabeth I's ladies-in-waiting...or has she totally lost her grip on reality? (978-1-62639-930-3)

Taking Sides by Kathleen Knowles. When passion and politics collide, can love survive? (978-1-62639-876-4)

Thorns of the Past by Gun Brooke. Former cop Darcy Flynn's heart broke when her career on the force ended in disgrace, but perhaps saving Sabrina Hawk's life will mend it in more ways than one. (978-1-62639-857-3)

You Make Me Tremble by Karis Walsh. Seismologist Casey Radnor comes to the San Juan Islands to study an earthquake but finds her heart shaken by passion when she meets animal rescuer Iris Mallery. (978-1-62639-901-3)

Complications by MJ Williamz. Two women battle for the heart of one. (978-1-62639-769-9)

boldstrokesbooks.com

Bold Strokes Books

Quality and Diversity in LGBTQ Literature

victory
EDITIONS

Drama

MATINEE BOOKS

E-BOOKS

SCI-FI

MYSTERY

BSB
SOLILOQUY

HE
erotica

EROTICA

YOUNG ADULT

BS
BOLD
STROKES
BOOKS

LIBERTY
EDITION

Romance

W·E·B·S·T·O·R·E

PRINT AND EBOOKS